Praise for *A Wild Ride Up the Cupboards*

"A precisely observed first novel. . . . Bauer draws the reader into her world."

—*Newsday*

"In writing about the passions and sacrifices of motherhood, Ann Bauer has given us a novel that goes deeply and bravely into the heart of one family, showing outsiders what it's like on the inside. *A Wild Ride Up the Cupboards* is original and astonishing."

—Meg Wolitzer, author of *The Position*

"A sensitive debut . . . [about a] family in peril, portrayed by Bauer with unflinching honesty."

—*Booklist*

"Ann Bauer has written a novel of seasons and cycles. They take place within the body of a woman, inside the mind of her child, and during the life of a marriage. The core of the story is a little boy at risk who is composed without a single sentimental note. Ms. Bauer writes him, and her other memorable characters, with courageous precision."

—Frederick Busch, author of *Girls* and *The Night Inspector*

"A harrowing story, and an intriguing, disturbing, and moving portrait of a family set loose into wide open and unknown territory."

—Eliza Minot, author of *The Tiny One*

A WILD RIDE UP THE CUPBOARDS

a novel

Ann Bauer

SCRIBNER

New York London Toronto Sydney

SCRIBNER
1230 Avenue of the Americas
New York, NY 10020

First Scribner trade paperback edition 2006

SCRIBNER and design are trademarks of
Macmillan Library Reference USA, Inc., used under license
by Simon & Schuster, the publisher of this work.

For information about special discounts for bulk purchases,
please contact Simon & Schuster Special Sales:
1-800-456-6798 or business@simonandschuster.com

Designed by Kyoko Watanabe
Text set in Minion

Manufactured in the United States of America

1 3 5 7 9 10 8 6 4 2

Library of Congress Control Number: 2004065392

ISBN-13: 978-0-7432-6949-0
ISBN-10: 0-7432-6949-7
ISBN-13: 978-0-7432-6950-6 (Pbk)
ISBN-10: 0-7432-6950-0 (Pbk)

AUTHOR'S NOTE

This book is a work of fiction and while certain aspects of it were inspired by my life, its characters, dialogue, and plot are purely imaginary. I owe an enormous debt to my children—Andrew, Maxwell, and Elena—for teaching me exactly how relentless and fierce a mother's love can be. They provided material for the bravest moments in my story and tolerated my moods and periodic absences during the writing. For these and so many other reasons, *A Wild Ride Up the Cupboards* is dedicated to them. Also to Jim Bauer, a man who read every word and supported me no matter where he had wandered and what our state of matrimony. Thank you.

THE NOWHERE PLACE

THERE IS A STRETCH of Highway 63, about two hundred yards long, that runs from the massive Minnesota-shaped sign inscribed THANK YOU FOR VISITING THE LAND OF TEN THOUSAND LAKES to a simple white plaque that bears a timid WELCOME TO IOWA. In the only full sentence he uttered during the summer he was six, Edward named the space between the Nowhere Place.

Still fields filled with prairie grass and wildflowers lined the road. There were no houses there, and no people. No movement. Each time we passed through I would look for deer or squirrels or even a stray cow from a neighboring farm; but there was none. There were insects here. I knew because I could hear the ceaseless, metallic hum of the cicadas. But this did not comfort me. Insects can survive atomic explosions, poisons, and plague. It made sense they would exist to defy nothingness.

"We're nowhere now," Edward would announce gravely as we entered. "We aren't anywhere in the world." He came to this concept early.

Still mostly silent then, he sat behind me, staring out the window. It was I who pointed to the signs and read their messages aloud as we hurtled past. I was marking our progress, proving my competence as a driver. You see, I have gotten us out of Minnesota. And forty seconds later: Look now, I've managed to reach Iowa. Matthew, asleep in his booster seat with his heavy melon head lolling to one shoulder, did not hear me. He was happy, rocked by our movement, tucked away in warm, storybook dreams.

But Edward, ever watchful, never sleepy, took the simple, square facts

I gave him—we have left one state . . . we are entering another—and deconstructed them. In the elaborate folds of his brain, these truths fractured until their crystals of reality came apart and floated free. He worked them, like one of his thousand-piece jigsaw puzzles, and discovered they fit together to make a completely unexpected shape: We were, briefly, lost to the world. We were nowhere.

For a long time, Edward was fascinated with the Nowhere Place. Later, when he spoke regularly but in a halting way, he would ask if anyone lived there, if we could move there. Occasionally, he would tell other people about his desire to live in Nowhere—his grandparents and random children he met in the park who would look at him quizzically and then run away. Edward seemed to take comfort from the fact that there could be an actual lack of place. A tiny country stranded in the Midwest that he might call his own.

Because even then Edward knew, as I did, that a human being can be knocked off the continuum of this ordinary, sweaty, oxygen-filled existence and into the locked stillness of nowhere. It can happen in a second, simply because molecules, dust funnels, or ideas configure in a certain way. I shared my son's obsession with the Nowhere Place, feeling daring each time I drove the distance and successfully reclaimed solid ground. I came to believe it was our momentum, traveling sixty or even sixty-five miles an hour, that anchored us and kept us safe. And that if we were to stop between the signs, all three of us might just tumble out of the car and out of our lives, into a nameless expanse of space.

1

DURING THE WINTER of Edward's first-grade year, I would often dream that he was dead. These were long, complicated nightmares from which I would awaken—gasping, wild with grief, my heart pounding—into total darkness.

It was early January, a night so cold I had piled four blankets on the bed before getting in just hours before. I opened my eyes and lay still for a long time, letting my dream fade and listening to the ticking of snow crystals against the windowpane. Gradually, the rapid drumbeat in my chest died down. My eyes focused and shapes emerged: fuzzy gray outlines against black air. For weeks I had awakened every morning around three-thirty, but I had never once succeeded in falling back to sleep.

Jack turned and sighed, a gust of warm air against my neck. My husband could sleep through anything, including my thrashing and the stiff terror that followed. Edward could sleep through nothing, not even perfect silence. Now, I could feel him in the next room, alert and anxious, twitchy, concentrating hard on trying not to move. I imagined his thoughts streaming through the wall between us, spangling like stars.

A ghost of vapor hung over the radiator and the window above us was covered with rime. For a moment I burrowed backward into Jack, who radiated heat like a furnace. Still sleeping, he slipped his arms around me and I stayed inside them, contented, for a few minutes. But when my back began to perspire against his bare chest, I knew it was time to get up.

My body was so large at this point, my stomach so distended, I had to set myself up in order to vault out of bed. I twisted to the side of the mattress and flattened a palm squarely against Jack's top shoulder, then shoved hard against his immovable bulk and made it over the edge on the first try. I stood, panting, and reached out to the wall to steady myself.

The wooden floor was hard and cold and my feet immediately started to ache. I needed socks, which presented a problem. Finding the socks wasn't difficult. We'd given the larger bedroom, the "master," to the boys, and set up a nursery in the smaller bedroom across the hall. Jack and I slept in an alcove meant for storage, or a tiny office. It was L-shaped, roughly the size of a Ping-Pong table with a little air pocket attached to the top. I could stretch out one arm and retrieve a pair of socks from the dresser. But putting them on was a different story.

During the day, Jack helped dress me: I would stand in line along with the boys as he moved from one of us to the next, folding white socks neatly over our ankles and tying bows on our shoes. Rather than wake him now, which he had told me to do, I decided to apply the socks myself. I took a deep breath and held it, bending over and reaching for one foot, terrified that I was squeezing the baby to death. After slipping the first one on, I rested for a few seconds before repeating the maneuver on the other side.

I knew I should let Edward alone but it was as if there were an invisible cord strung between us, pulling me toward him. I shuffled softly down the carpeted hall and pushed open the door. Jack had hung special room-darkening shades in the boys' room so the blackness was even thicker than in ours. Stepping inside was like moving through cloth and it took a full minute for me to see the outline of Matt sleeping under his covers, his breath sounds smoothly puttering, his humped-up body a miniature version of his father's.

Edward didn't raise his head from the pillow but the air was full of him, tight and crackling with his energy. Every night he waged the same battle with sleep: mind racing, eyes blinking. For twelve straight nights now he'd lost.

"Sweetheart, try to relax." I knew this was pointless but found myself saying it every time I stared down at him. What I wanted was to walk over and smooth back his hair, or lie down on the bed and pull him in, cradling him as I did when he was a baby, when he would relax against me and let his eyelids sag until he fell asleep. But now his pale eyes were wrinkled and wary and I was afraid if I touched him he'd flinch and retract, like those tiny worms that coil into tight springs when you poke them with your finger.

"Close your eyes and think about Lake Superior." I tried to make my voice rhythmic, hypnotic. "Think about the way the waves keep moving against the rocks. Pretend you're walking on the water." My voice trailed off as I left, closing the door behind me, wondering how many nights a child can go without sleep before he dies. The hallway seemed to swell and contract like a bellows and my throat filled with a metallic taste. I closed my own gritty eyes, leaned against the wall, and swallowed several times in order not to be sick.

Downstairs, I flipped on an overhead light, filled the teakettle, and lit a burner underneath. The kitchen was a bright place, far less ominous than the cold bedrooms upstairs. Gas hissed out and the stove flame burned red, then a clean, hot orange tipped with yellow and blue. I opened the cupboard where Jack had hidden a bag of espresso beans in a tin canister behind the blender we never used. He drank coffee only when he had to, when he was changing shifts and needed to stay awake all night. And he tried to do it when I wasn't around, so I wouldn't have to suffer. But I was not so kind to myself.

Every morning before he got up I took the canister down, opened it, and breathed in its scent. I craved coffee in a desperate, passionate way, like heroin or cocaine. I fantasized about how my hand would curve around the warm cup, how the steam would dampen my face. I wondered if this was the sort of desire that made junkies sell their children for a fix. Jack insisted real drug withdrawal was much worse; secretly, I doubted it. Sometimes I imagined I was having full-scale hallucinations: bugs crawling on my eyelids or purple snakes slithering across the floor. But I never drank any. I knew the consequences of doing the wrong things during pregnancy, even if I wasn't sure exactly what all those wrong things were. I was determined never to do them again.

The window over the kitchen sink was black. With the light on inside, the houses behind ours weren't visible. Nor was the clothesline in our yard, where a red towel that had hung through three blizzards was now completely frozen with one stiff corner pointing down toward the ground. The world was noiseless at four o'clock in the middle of winter and my movements—putting the kettle on the stove, setting a cup down on the countertop, shutting the cupboard door after getting a tea bag—seemed to pop rudely in midair.

This was the eighth month of my third, and easiest, pregnancy. Even so, every change had taken me by surprise. I'd forgotten all about the inhuman bulkiness of this stage, the shortness of breath, the leg cramps. And the certainty that the downward pressure inside my body had grown so intense, the baby must be about to drop right out onto the floor. I had imagined this far too often: the infant in my mind falling headfirst and bouncing several times, its skull breaking open like an eggshell before the small body skittered to a stop.

Just yesterday, the doctor had assured me it was pinched nerve endings and not fetal distress that was causing the currents of pain to run down my legs. Of course, he was a neurologist, not an obstetrician, and I had met him only that afternoon. But I liked Barry Newberg more than my own OB; he seemed smarter and his conclusions made sense to me. The fact that I believed in him was one of the things keeping me up tonight. The previous afternoon Newberg had also offered a possible diagnosis for Edward, one worse than anything I'd ever heard before or been able to dream up on my own.

I sat at the kitchen table, using one hand to balance a mug of tea on the shelf of my stomach. The tabletop was clear but for a cellophane-wrapped library book and a thick sheaf of cream-colored pages held together with a large industrial staple. For a moment, my hand hovered above the book but I pulled it away and lurched up out of my chair to look for a pen instead. I found one in the desk we'd tucked into a corner of the living room: blue with a fine, wet tip, the sort I used to edit galleys at the newspaper. I took this and an afghan, which I wrapped awkwardly around myself, and returned to the table.

The questionnaire began, as these things usually do, with easy questions. Name, address, parents' names and marital status. Born:

March 12, 1988. Age: 6. Grade in school: 1st. Siblings: one, Matthew, 4 years old. Then I turned the page. *Developmental Milestones,* it said. When did he first smile? That was easy. I remembered the day, how amazed we were, Jack and I, that this three-week-old baby could look so wise and amused by two ridiculously young, awkward parents. But then the questions got harder. When did he roll over? Sit? Stand assisted? Stand unassisted? Eat with a fork?

A better mother would have all these things recorded in a baby book along with locks of hair and inky footprints. I had only flashes of memory: Edward sitting on the living room floor surrounded by pillows in case he toppled over, while Jack's friend Paul sat behind him on the couch and played a guitar. Jack extending one long finger for Edward to use for balance as they waded through a creek near our apartment. Was Edward eleven months old? Thirteen?

When Edward was an infant, I had showed his pediatrician the dark spots on his back and side during a well-baby checkup. After he withdrew, years later, I'd returned to ask if there could be any connection. "Mothers," she'd said, shaking her head, as if I were so silly to be worried about a little boy who'd suddenly stopped singing and begun chewing his clothes. That was back when she insisted mutism was just a phase he would grow out of. About six months later, she changed camps completely and decided he'd probably suffered some sort of brain damage. How, she wouldn't say.

Recently, we had been referred to Barry Newberg. Very expensive, well educated, and new in town, he'd already discovered that one supposedly autistic child actually was suffering from a yeast allergy and cured the boy overnight with a drug called nystatin. That story had spread like a forest fire among desperate parents like us.

The day before, we had sat in his examining room, Edward and I. And this man who couldn't have been much more than thirty read through every page of the medical records I'd brought while pulling compulsively on the dark curls over his forehead. I tried to match his stillness and be perfectly quiet, but the baby was jabbing around inside me and Edward had climbed from table to bookshelf. I tried to coax him down with a lollipop from a bowl on the doctor's long oak desk.

But Edward wouldn't even look at me. "He's fine," Newberg said, waving without lifting his eyes from the pages. So I stopped.

Then he started the examination. Heart, blood pressure. He paused for a minute after measuring Edward's head and I held my breath. Newberg wrapped the measuring tape around again. Edward, sucking on the lollipop, bobbed rhythmically like a toy on a spring so Newberg had to move with him. When the doctor glanced back at me, I thought he was about to say something so I waited, my throat tightening with fear. Instead, he walked over and slipped the tape around my head. Then he laughed. "Ah, good. It's not an abnormality. Apparently, big heads just run in the family."

The mood shifted, becoming almost jolly, and I had the feeling we'd escaped. Newberg pulled off Edward's T-shirt and began examining his body, which was muscular and strong. Nothing to worry about there. In my head, I began planning dinner: grilled cheese sandwiches and tomato soup, brownies to reward Edward for behaving. But then I looked up and saw Newberg studying Edward's back, just standing over it, looking down, and everything went still. Even the baby stopped moving.

"Would you come here?" he asked, his back still to me as he leaned over Edward, who had had enough and was fishtailing, trying to squirm away. "How long has he had those?" Newberg pointed to those cocoa-colored Rorschach splatters I'd brought to the attention of the pediatrician six years before.

"Since he was born," I said, trying to remember if this was true. "But they got bigger as he grew. They've been like this since around eighteen months."

Barry Newberg kept moving his index finger across the largest one, as if he were hoping it would rub off. Edward had stopped wriggling and was laughing silently as he always did when he was tickled.

The doctor had me put one hand on Edward's back so he wouldn't fall off the table and went into a closet to get something that looked like the Lite-Brite I'd had as a little girl—a box with a slanted, black screen in front. He flipped off the fluorescent lights as he walked back. Now we were both standing over Edward in the dark and Newberg turned on the box and shone it down. Its beam was purple and smoky except where it hit Edward's skin and there it was blue on the white parts, greenish on the parts that had been brown. My son's back looked like a map now: mostly ocean with a few small floating landforms.

Later, while Edward played in the waiting room under the receptionist's watch, the doctor took me into his office, where he put on a white coat, sat behind his desk, and told me the name of a disease that could explain everything that had happened to Edward. He said the words *calcification* and *brain lesions* and *deformity*. He didn't show me any pictures but instead gave me the questionnaire and instructions to take Edward down the hall for a series of blood tests.

"Try not to kill yourself worrying," he said quietly as he handed the forms across his desk. "I'm just being very cautious."

Diagnosis required a minimum of three irregular spots, he explained, each one at least an inch across—and that's exactly what Edward had. The bare minimum. Plus the loss of speech, insomnia, hyperactivity, the way his hand kept flying up in front of his eyes, and the eerie outbursts of uncontrollable laughter—all those could come from snarls of tumor that were sitting like roadblocks on the pathways of Edward's brain. Newberg rattled off the list of symptoms like ingredients for a recipe and all the time I just stared out his window at a patch of bright, sunlit afternoon.

After the appointment, I went to the library and found the only book they had that described the eight-syllable disease whose name I'd written carefully on the back of an old bank receipt from my purse. I checked the book out, but I didn't look at it then. Instead, I brought it home and set it on the table with the questionnaire inside. Now, alone in my bright kitchen, I reached for the book and let it fall open in my hands. What I saw made the air leave my body, only I didn't realize it until I found myself struggling to breathe.

The child in the picture was no more than five, a girl, I thought, though it was hard to tell. Her hair was sparse and wispy and there was a cabbagy bump emerging from the right side of her head, making it look as if she had grown a second, external brain. As if to balance this, her left ear had a series of tuberous growths that dangled like jewelry and her cheeks and neck were covered with a variety of pustules, some like large pimples, others inflated to the size of golf balls.

I imagined stroking the head of this little girl. Would the bumps feel squishy or firm? My hand crawled and before I realized what I was doing, I pulled it back from the page as if this would prevent my ever coming in contact with such a child. And all the things I had dreaded—Edward's ongoing silence; the pained and bewildered look in his eyes; the prospect of watching him grow into a teenager who rocked and stared into the palm of one hand while other boys his age were beginning to date and drive and shave—all of this receded as I saw his face and body erupting in a rapid time-lapse manner. Mottled outcroppings bursting out all over his smooth, perfect skin. The problems would still be there, underneath. But in addition there would be this horror: a permanent armor of fleshy, reptilian blight making him that much harder to hold.

At least, the way things were, people tended to forgive Edward his oddness and comment instead on his beauty. There seemed to be a place in their understanding for children who were mute but angelic-looking. What would happen to him if that, too, were lost?

The sky had lightened to a slightly grayer shade; when I raised my eyes to the window, I could see the corner of that long-forgotten towel sway in a sweep of wind. I closed the book and went through the medical section of the form, checking boxes quickly: no for a family history of cancer and heart disease, yes for alcoholism and diabetes. I made a note in the margin that Jack had been adopted and we had no information about his blood relatives. Then I began working on the more difficult questions: Did my mother have age spots? Did anyone in our family have soft tumors? A medical condition that involved calcium deposits? Unexplained thickening of the spine?

This disease was not, Newberg had explained to me, one for which there was a definitive test. Instead, it was more like a verdict a doctor might reach after reviewing all the evidence. That afternoon, I was due to return to Newberg's office, to see him alone and present him with all the facts before deliberations began.

Inside me the baby shifted, kneeing the lining of my body, rotating and settling against my right lung. I raised my arms over my head and stretched back for air. Upstairs, the floor creaked in stages as Jack moved, first to the side of the bed, then the hallway, and into the bathroom. Because I was listening for it, I heard the muffled thunk of the toilet lid as he flipped it up against the porcelain tank, the stream of his urine as it hit the water. I felt Edward turn over in his bed and squeeze his eyes shut, pretending to sleep even though the rest of the house was waking up.

I turned to the final page and faced the hardest question: *When did you first notice your child's symptoms?* There was only an inch of space in which to write my answer. One day when he was nearly four, when he went from a bright-eyed, laughing boy who talked in a high voice and asked *Why* nonstop to a silent zombie who looked as if his inner fire had gone out, turning him gray and cold and dead inside.

Three years, ten months, I wrote. After the next line, *List symptoms in order of appearance,* I dashed the words *withdrawal, insomnia, rocking.* I stared at my pen for a moment, then wrote another one: *desolation.* But before I rose, I shook my head and crossed it out with one broad stroke of ink.

Turning off the lights that were no longer necessary, I walked slowly up the stairs and down the hall. I pushed open the door to the boys' room. Matt was moving fitfully under his blankets, but Edward was sitting up in bed staring straight ahead with unblinking eyes. I went to him and put my arm around his shoulder but he felt loose and deboned, as if the person who used to occupy his body was already gone.

2

THE FIRST TIME I saw Jack he emerged through a haze of smoke and glittering dust, lit from behind by a string of colored Christmas lights.

It was afternoon, but inside the Main Street bar of our small southern Minnesota college town the air was a perpetually muddy shade of dusk.

I was sitting in a booth with a group of people I didn't particularly like—whose names I no longer even recall. Mariel, my roommate and best friend, had been awarded a Rhodes scholarship and gone off to Oxford the week before, leaving me alone. But then Jack was there, framed by lights and bottles, and he was all I saw. More massive than I had ever imagined a real man could be. He was perfectly proportioned, legs, arms, chest, and head all to scale; standing alone he looked simply large. But when Roy the bartender approached—slender but nearly six feet tall—Jack made him look like a child by comparison.

The girl who sat across from me waved and Jack tipped his head and nodded back at her. "Who is that?" I asked as I watched him order, holding up two long fingers in a peace sign.

"You mean Jack?"

I nodded. Apparently he had been ordering with the hand gesture: the bartender set two full beer glasses in front of him. Jack picked up the one on the right and drained it, then picked up the other glass and sat on a stool to drink from it more slowly.

"You don't want him. Not that way."

I swiveled to look at her. "Why not?" She was a girl who had slept with every one of the boys who sat around the table and I assumed she would tell me that she had been with Jack, too. I thought she was about to reveal some distasteful sexual predilection or fetish. Instead, she scrunched up her tiny white-powdered face and thought for a minute.

"Jack's not the kind of guy you date," she said finally. "He's the kind of guy you call when the one you're dating hits you and then Jack will come and kill him for you."

I laughed, mostly to cover the heat that swept through me, then stood. I hadn't touched my drink yet, but before I left the table I took the whole thing—an ounce and a half of cheap, oily whiskey—in one swallow. The girl reached out and tapped my arm. "I mean it," she said. "Jack is really different."

But of course, I could see that.

He was leaning on the bar now, drinking a third beer, or maybe a fourth, staring at the television overhead where a silent basketball game played through the watery gloom. I approached him and made my voice as low and strong as I could. "Do you have a cigarette?"

I must have been swaying a little because when he turned, Jack put a hand out to steady me. His palm covered the cup of my shoulder. "Yes."

We both waited and he kept his hand on me while he looked straight down into my face. One of his eyes was darkly blue, the other a pale, nearly translucent green. At first, I thought it was the whiskey I'd drunk, or a trick of the colored lights that glittered behind him. But when I focused hard, the contrast between them only became brighter. He blinked, as if he knew why I was staring.

"May I have one?" I finally asked.

"Yes," he said again, releasing my shoulder to pull the pack from his shirt pocket. And I remember even now exactly how the room swirled, lights and colors running together, when he let me go.

Jack had been orphaned twice, once when his biological mother left him at a convent outside Rochester and again when his adoptive parents were killed in a car accident when he was sixteen.

What he did was a mystery. There was an inheritance, but it was small. And most of it he'd spent on the degree in religion and philosophy that it took him nearly a decade to finish. People from around the college who knew Jack—and there were many, though none seemed to know him very well—said he'd been passing through, enrolling in classes, hanging out at the bar, working odd jobs and disappearing, often midsemester, since the late seventies. No one knew his exact age. Finally, I asked him.

"You're gray," I said one evening and reached up, making a V with my fingers so I could touch the two vertical stripes in his beard.

"I'm old," he said.

"How old?" I had been meeting him for a week, nearly every afternoon. We sat in a small booth of our own now, but he had never even kissed me.

He pulled out his wallet and for a moment I thought he had to check his driver's license in order to answer. But he was only ordering and paying for another beer. After it arrived he drank, then said, "Twenty-eight. In June."

"Oh." Under the table, my leg brushed his and even through two layers of denim, I felt the heat along my thigh.

"Disappointed?"

"No, I just thought you were ... um ... older." I whispered this, leaning in.

"I am," he said.

And that's when he kissed me, gently, as if he had never thought about it before but did it now simply because my face happened to be there.

We made love once in February, a dark, silent experience that made me feel as if my body were melting into the air. I had tried smoking pot, even hash, but never achieved the languid ecstasy my friends described; my muscles had relaxed, but there was a part of my brain that stayed alert, keeping watch in a twitchy, grandmotherly way. Now, for the first time in my life, my mind detached. Time passed. My thoughts bled together. And wherever Jack touched me, there was a rush of liquid fire that traveled the length of my body under my skin.

When he disappeared, in mid-March, just days before my twenty-first birthday, I quit attending classes. All my life, I had felt disconnected, at odds with the world, as if I were the wrong shape for the space that had been allotted for me. Mariel and I had shared this trait and it had brought us together, a friendship cemented by the fact that it was helpful for both of us to be with someone else who knew how this felt. But with Jack, for the first time, I'd had a sense of being whole and right—the way I'd heard other people describe the feeling of being home. When he left, my newfound equilibrium disappeared along with him and I sat in the bar from noon until well after dark each night, reading and smoking. I drank coffee until my legs shook and grew so thin my skin was rubbed raw where my bones poked through. I would have flunked out if my father had not intervened with the dean.

After the graduation ceremony, which I skipped, my parents picked me up and took me to their house and I stayed, sleeping and recuperating and applying idly for jobs, until Jack arrived. I can't say now if I knew he would come. But six weeks to the day after I went home to their sprawling lake home west of Minneapolis, Jack appeared at the front door.

He wore leather sandals and a plain cotton shirt and a long beard. Despite his height and his broad chest, he looked to my Catholic mother like Christ. I still recall the way she stood, gazing up at him much the way I must have the first time we met, her hand still on the doorknob, a puzzled, horrified, interested expression on her face.

"I'm here for Rachel," he said. And as I came forward, out of the shadow of the staircase where I'd been waiting, breathless, my mother simply nodded, let go of the doorknob, and stepped back.

I don't think anyone was surprised when Jack and I eloped, three weeks later.

I hardly remember what happened next, only the sense of well-being I had waking up every day with this man. We read the same books and talked about them obsessively, laughing and arguing, often staying up until three or four in the morning because we couldn't stop. Sex bled into everything we did; it wasn't separate from our life but one of the many areas in which we worked perfectly together. And there was a way he touched me even when we weren't making love that seemed to untangle my thoughts. Simply by running his fingers lightly over my arms, or placing one hand in the hollow under my ribs, he could draw pain or worry or frustration right out of me. Static left my body. I felt clean; I could breathe. This was something I couldn't explain—and therefore tried not to think about. But I was addicted.

Jack had sold his last motorcycle on his way to find me and we used that money for the security deposit and first month's rent on a tiny apartment in south Minneapolis. He took a job driving a cement truck for a commercial builder. I quit looking for professional work and began clerking for a natural foods co-op. I spent my days surrounded by exotic scents, lifting burlap bags of kidney beans, feeling them move and puddle like beads on my shoulder, pouring them into large plastic bins. For the first time in my life, I grew muscular. Though next to Jack, I still felt dainty.

We didn't intend to have a baby right away; nor did we do much to prevent it. We'd go through random episodes where we used birth control, then periods where we were swept up by each other's proximity. The fact that Jack and I could touch each other any time we chose was amazing to me, and in my adolescent mind it took precedence over the risks. So it was only two months into our marriage that I discovered I was pregnant.

I was sick a great deal in the beginning—penance for my greed and carelessness, I sometimes thought. Despite the fact that we could barely survive on what Jack made at the construction company, I quit my job because my sense of smell had become both more acute and distorted and the odors at the co-op made my nausea unbearable. The one thing I kept doing was their newsletter, a project that had been all but abandoned until I expressed an interest and began managing it like a school newspaper, collecting snippets from cashiers and stock people and the cheese buyer, then editing them fiercely. I was paid only in organic groceries, but given our situation this seemed reasonable.

Eventually, I grew so large and misshapen I had to wear Jack's castoff clothes, overalls and coats he had trimmed by a foot and hemmed. But Jack never seemed to mind. And when Edward was born, he appeared nothing short of magical: a strikingly beautiful and stoic baby with blond curls and huge, intelligent eyes. I think we became convinced having children made us stronger. Invulnerable, somehow.

I stayed home with Edward and spent my days dazzled by his serene Buddha-like presence. Throughout the day I wore him in a front pack and spoke to him as if he were another adult, often believing I saw understanding in his face. Sometimes, he would utter a series of soft, wet syllables that sounded like answers, but he almost never cried and though he slept far less than other babies, napping infrequently even in his first weeks of life, he would nurse contentedly for long, warm, quiet hours. We joined a playgroup through the co-op. There, I met other mothers like myself and we traded recipes and child care advice and occasionally babysat for one another. I left Edward only when I had to attend a meeting, because luckily my work on the newsletter had led to a couple very small commercial-writing jobs, paying ones, with an insurance firm and a large company that manufactured floor-cleaning products.

"Everything is working out better than I thought it would," my father said gruffly one evening when I dropped by to show off the way Edward, not yet a year and a half old, could recite the words to *The Cat in the Hat* and turn the pages on cue, exactly as if he were reading.

But then, I told them I was pregnant again. My mother flushed and stayed silent and my father sighed loudly, rose to kiss me roughly on one cheek, and held up his hands, as if in surrender. "Go ahead," he said as he lumbered out of the room, holding his newspaper. "Do whatever crazy thing you want. You and Jack always do. It's like logic has no bearing whatsoever on your life."

Then he was gone, which was just as well because there was no way to respond. What he said was true: with Jack, I felt safe and strong, exempt from the sort of mundane concerns other people faced. And watching Edward—his head bent over the book, small pink mouth forming the words while my mother looked on with awe—the wisdom of this seemed clear.

After Matthew was born, I assumed no questions remained about the life Jack and I had chosen. Our children were perfect: large like their father, and almost rudely healthy. While other parents in the neighborhood waited in pediatricians' offices, combating chronic ear infections and colds, we hiked through the snow, pulling our two on a sled behind us. They were like little storybook heroes in coats with pointed hoods, their bright, red cheeks and glittering eyes showing above knitted scarves. One look at this tableau—my rugged husband and princes for sons—and even my parents had to admit I had done well. The only missteps we made were tiny ones. All financial. Temporary, though occasionally when I sat down to pay the bills I would feel a stir of fluttery panic.

Around the time Edward was born, Jack had opened a small construction and home-repair company. His carpentry was fine, slow, and careful. People who wanted their turn-of-the-century lake homes restored called him and were grateful for his precision. But he seemed never to care for the money end of things: invoices went past due until

I found them and by then we would owe late fees and interest. Jack would special-order items for customers and then forget to charge them. I took control as best I could, but I had no experience. I'd grown up in a very comfortable home and never before considered what a person would do if there weren't enough money to pay for electricity, or rent, or food. It puzzled me that somehow, around us, other couples were making this formula work: earning enough money to cover their needs plus allow for extra purchases. Vacations, private schools, wide-screen TVs. Our income and expenses never quite matched up and no matter how carefully I shopped, there was usually a shortfall. But when I showed our accounts to Jack, he tended to look vacant and surprised, as if I were asking him to comment on a problem real but remote from him, such as global warming or Third World hunger.

One night I sat down and opened the blue bank register—which I kept balanced in neat orderly columns no matter how paltry the amount—showing Jack the two-digit sum we had to live on for the last ten days of the month. He thought for a moment, then slowly stroked my hair with one large hand. "It'll be fine." His voice was thick, like whiskey and sex. I felt the muscles in my forehead release, the worry sloughing away, as he passed his hand over them. "We'll work it out, honey. You know we will. We always do."

He was holding both boys, the baby sleeping along the length of his forearm, Edward perched regally on his knee and paging through a book that had glossy black-and-white photographs of wild animals. It had been Jack's gift to him on his second birthday the week before and the book's shiny paper was already worn thin at the corners from so many turns in Edward's warm little hand. Over and over, he returned to the page that showed African gazelles running across the savanna: noses pointing forward, tails flattened in back, dark bodies sleek as arrows.

I was torn between concern and relief on the night Jack told me his business was failing. It was May, the beginning of summer, a pink evening following a rain shower that had wet the sky so it seemed to glow. We were at the park near our apartment. Matt was in a baby swing that Jack pushed with his fingertips; Edward was squatting on the path, bottom sunk between pudgy knees, examining something close to the ground.

"I really think this is the best thing that could have happened," Jack started. He squinted at Edward, who was poking one finger down toward the dirt. "Hey, little guy, don't push the ants around, they're just trying to build a house." Edward's finger halted, a quarter inch above the dome of a miniature sandhill, and he grew perfectly still, remaining in this position as if Jack's voice had frozen him in time. "Good job," Jack called softly, and the words floated out like a ribbon through the soft lavender air.

I was leaning against the metal framework of the swing set and reached back to curl my hands around a pipe as thick as the heavy end of a baseball bat. The light was dimming in rapid stages. One minute I could see Jack's eyes but the next his face was only an impression above me—a skeletal outline with beard and hair and features roughening its terrain.

"But it's the beginning of summer." I held on tight, yet still it felt as if the ground were shifting beneath me in the wavering light. "You know business always picks up in June."

"Yeah, but . . ." Jack stopped and backed away from the baby to light a cigarette. I stepped forward to take his place and began pushing the swing with a flat hand. "Look, I'm no businessman." He tipped his head up and exhaled, wisps rising from his mouth and nose. "And the truth is, this place is starting to make me itch. The traffic and all the people. I've never been a city person. Maybe it's time for us to start over somewhere else, somewhere better."

There was something about the way those words drifted to me in the wake of the swing—Matt's small body arcing out into space but returning every time, Edward rising from his crouch and walking toward us, blond curls wafting in the breeze—that made them seem prophetic. By the time we gathered the boys and walked back to our apartment, Jack and I were already talking about Minnesota's North Shore, the length of which he had driven once on his motorcycle. A place he remembered as cool and wooded, peaceful, untouched.

Jack spent the next few weeks selling off equipment from the business to pay our way, and I took care of everything else: renting the U-Haul trailer and finding a residential hotel where we could stay for a month or so while we got settled. We set off on a particularly sticky day in late June. The softness of spring was entirely gone. It had stormed the night before, then grown warmer throughout the morning hours so the air felt thick, as if the molecules had swelled with water until they were too large to breathe. We put the boys in their car seats and directed all the air-conditioning vents toward where they sat in back. Jack drove. I closed my eyes for a long time and listened to the kissy sounds of the tires against damp asphalt.

"My parents think we're crazy." I said this aloud while thinking the word *stupid,* which was the one my father had actually used.

Jack said nothing. I opened my eyes and saw him looking straight ahead into a glittering lemon sun. Outside, the world had changed. Buildings had been replaced by trees, the highway winding through a vast greenness that started with the tall grass and extended into the sky on the points of fir trees as slender and rangy as the giraffes in the pages of Edward's book.

Miles passed. Finally I spoke again. "You didn't respond."

"You didn't ask a question." He continued staring out but reached with one hand to touch my hair and smooth it back, and even after he pulled his hand away I could feel the imprint of where he had touched my forehead. Like gold coins left where his fingertips had been.

Twenty minutes later, we stopped at a roadside oasis to fill up the gas tank and let the boys out of their seats to play in the grassy area behind where the semi-trucks parked. When I opened the door, there was a cool, clean, silvery rush. The air seemed thinner, as I imagined it would be in the mountains, and it had a faint, steely taste to it. I got out of the car and stood, the wind from a hundred lakes stirred into a single force around me. Suddenly I felt smaller than I ever had before.

Jack started the gas pump and stood next to the car, his elbows planted on the roof. When he saw me looking at him from the other side he smiled, straightened to his full height, and opened his arms wide. "Here's your answer," he said.

It was evening by the time we reached the North Shore. The sky was gold and rose and smoke-colored. We crossed a long bridge and curved around the base of a hill dotted with houses that jutted out of the face of the earth. To our right, the lake appeared and widened with every mile. Below us lights bloomed, the town of Aurora sparkling, cupped in the crevice between hill and water.

I looked up and saw a sign looming ahead. Its blue background faded into the dusk but there were bright white letters with the outline of a boat sailing across the top of them. From the backseat Edward spoke, though I hadn't known he was awake, nor did I know until that very moment that he could read.

"Aw-row-ra." The sounds were separate, each one tentative but clear.

Jack, who seemed not at all surprised, only nodded and answered Edward. "Yes," he said.

3

AT FIRST, AURORA was glorious. All through July, the air was light and cool and full of the empty blue scent of water. It was a novelty to make warm foods in summer, so I did—meat loaf or roasted chicken, baby potatoes crackling inside their red skins.

And after we had finished dinner and washed and dried the dishes, we would walk down to a shore covered not with sand but with glossy black rocks big enough for Edward to step on. Suddenly older and less babyish, he seemed to feel no fear. He walked out onto the lake—Jack trailing him a respectful distance behind—as far as the exposed tips of rock would allow him to go. Then he would stand, balanced on the water and looking like a boy-shaped cutout against the darkening sky. He would face the horizon, gazing toward a place where lake and air faded into each other, while Jack waited and I stood on the shore holding Matt and watching the gulls above Edward's head circle and coast and cry.

Then we would walk home, bathe the boys, and read them stories. And once they were snugly tucked into their beds, Edward on the top trundle and Matt curled into a soft ball in the bed below him, Jack and I would leave through the sliding glass door and stand on the deck to watch the sun set.

It was an August of the northern lights—the aurora borealis for which the city had been named. We stepped out into darkness that rolled like velvet unfurling with trails of burst-open stars. The colors weren't substantial, just faint watercolor streaks of blue and pink against a backdrop of deep, hazy plum. Jack caught me by the shoulders and held me against him as the cool breeze played with our clothes.

"It was the right thing to do." He lifted me, setting me gently on the rough planks of the railing, leaning against my body, holding me in place with one giant hand. "I think we've finally found our home." Jack slipped his other hand beneath my shirt. The upstairs windows were open an inch or two, so we would hear the boys if they woke up. But they didn't. And as Jack and I began to move together, I stared into the smooth blackness of space and felt us fitting ourselves into the nucleus of this new world. Our family. Our home.

Nearly every day, I took the boys to a tiny lakeside park with an old wooden play structure, peeling from years of sun and wet spray, the chains for all but one of the swings hanging loosely to one side so the seats pointed down toward the sand. In the beginning, the boys took turns in the one balanced swing while I pushed from behind. Then we would walk together to the edge of Lake Superior and I would imagine it was an ocean—but colder, darker, without the taint of salt. I would tell all this to Edward and he would stare intently, either listening and considering or simply letting the rhythm of all my words play over the lapping sound of the water. But after a week of swinging and talking, Edward was no longer content. All he wanted was to walk on the water.

The first few times, I stopped him. Jack wasn't there to follow him and I had to stay with Matt. I envisioned having to make a decision:

whether to put the baby down on a rock and let him scrabble for himself while I saved Edward from drowning, or watch my older son sink. Each time I held him back, Edward grew furious. He said nothing but tensed his body in my arms, straining toward the water, until I had no choice but to carry both boys back to the car. Finally, I let him venture out. The lake was calm, the tide a frothing tongue of water that rolled relentlessly but never crashed or peaked.

Bare-armed, his hair curling in the damp, sneakers gripping the rocks like suction cups, Edward began, carefully, walking out. Rock to rock. He was tall for three, so I could stand onshore and follow his solid form, moving across the water.

One day, a voice broke my concentration: "Aren't you worried he'll fall in?"

A blonde woman in overalls had appeared beside me with a little girl. And I realized in that moment that I hadn't talked to another woman, face-to-face, since the weekend before when I wrote a check at the grocery store.

"He never has," I answered. But at the same time, I felt my grip on Matt tightening. "We don't really understand it. He can just . . . do things."

"Hmmm." The woman rubbed her lips silently back and forth while the child butted her mother's knee occasionally with the hump of a shoulder.

"Oh." The woman looked down suddenly, as if she were surprised. "This is Ingrid." She smoothed her daughter's windblown hair and the little girl closed her eyes, like a cat being stroked. "I'm Carrie."

"Matt." I held forth the baby, who was curled up like a possum, hiding his face from the damp wind. "And Rachel."

I rearranged the blanket I was holding so it would cover Matt's head, and Carrie and I turned back toward the water, watching as Edward veered in a line that angled to the north, away from us. He stopped, some thirty yards directly out from a painted blue knob of wood that stood onshore: a bulbous thing over four feet high whose head was rotting softly from constant moisture and had the mashed-in look of a severely dented hard-boiled egg. I could not fathom its original purpose, but Edward treated it very seriously. He walked back to shore and touched the post, once, then swiveled precisely ninety degrees and came back to me.

"Ask him to play, Ingrid," the woman said. She nudged the girl's head with her hip and instantly Ingrid's eyes flew open. She had pink cheeks, the perfect porcelain features of a china doll. "Wanna play?" she asked Edward.

He nodded slowly and leaned in as if he were going to kiss her but stopped an inch short of her cheek and simply stared. Then he straightened and turned to look back at the blue post.

Jack had found work immediately, as assistant manager of a development project being built on the site of an old army barracks next to the airstrip over the hill. It was one of the few spots in Aurora with no view of the lake, but the owner insisted the city's population would double when the new paper mill—still just an open field with a sign announcing its construction—opened its doors; workers would flood into town desperate for good, cheap, convenient housing. That's why he was converting the old Quonset huts into town houses with white carpeting, small verandas, and wide, windowless living rooms that ran the length of each anterior wall. The job paid almost nothing, but it came with free housing, so we moved into an end unit where the stairs leading up to the two perfectly square bedrooms were oddly misaligned—like teeth prior to orthodontia. I told myself ours had been built before Jack took over. Surely standards would rise now that he was on the job.

Shortly after we met at the lake, Carrie invited us all for dinner. Their house was tiny but set on the end of a pier, a cottage full of shining wood: the floors, the moldings, even the countertops. Carrie's husband, Doug, taught art at the college that lay in the valley behind Aurora's steep hill. He wore an embroidered shirt with laces and three earrings in his left ear. His sculptures, made of clay and a heavy cast metal with a coppery sheen, were scattered throughout the house.

"Beer?" he asked when we walked in carrying the baby and a fruit salad.

"Of course," Jack said. Doug reached into the refrigerator and handed Jack a smoke-colored bottle. I watched my husband as he stood, dwarfing the elfin kitchen. Jack twisted off the cap with a quick swivel of one palm, tipped his head back to drink—a third of the bottle's contents in one swallow—and grinned down at Doug. "Jesus, that's good."

Doug had used a church key and was pouring his beer into a glass very slowly, squinting at it as if he were conducting an experiment. When he was done, it looked like a photograph in a magazine: six inches of chocolaty darkness, with a layer of clean, light foam. He raised the glass. "Scottish," he said. "The best there is."

By the time I'd put the fruit salad in the refrigerator and talked to Carrie for a few minutes, the men were sitting in the living room. There was music playing, the hollow sound of African drums and the high, thin song of a flute.

"I have two sections this semester, which is more than I like to teach," Doug was saying. "The kids are great but, you know, mostly they're just passing the time in my class. Looking for a couple easy credits. And it takes so much time away from my work." He waved in the direction of the pieces that stood on desks and bookshelves, the dining room hutch, and Jack nodded gravely.

The children sat a couple feet away in the little nook off the living room, a cathedral-shaped space with plenty of windows that Carrie had turned into Wonderland with glittery scarves, colored rugs, and an old wooden trunk full of puppets. I thought of our town house, its sharp corners and cheap white carpet. There was a pile of stuffed animals and toys in one corner of the boys' room. But their favorite was downstairs: a large plastic car, big enough for the baby to get in and paddle with his chunky feet. Nearly every day, Edward would open the door and hoist Matt inside, then climb on the roof and sit straight as a visiting nobleman while his brother scrabbled to maneuver the car in the circle from front hall to living room to kitchen and back again.

Now, Edward sat at Ingrid's side and watched her dress his brother in a baseball jersey with the number 24 and an apron. The sharp, exotic scent of cumin and red pepper floated from the kitchen along with a sizzling sound. I closed my eyes and imagined a house like this, just down the pier, with soft, cloth playthings instead of plastic ones and dark wood instead of white walls. I would walk downtown with Carrie to buy spices by the bagful, red lentils that needed to be soaked for two days, big yellow onions in papery husks. Our children would go to school together.

"So, Carrie says you just moved here." Doug's voice jostled me out of my daydream and I opened my eyes reluctantly. "What do you do?"

I was staring at a photo of Doug and Carrie's wedding—outdoors, on the beach. He was in a soft gray suit with no tie and she wore a crown of purple flowers woven through her shining hair. Jack and I had gone to a justice of the peace, worn jeans, uttered only the essential words while standing on the cement floor in front of his bench. When I turned to say "I will," there stood my new husband in profile, looking dark and otherworldly—his face made of sharp planes and lines and eyes of two entirely different hues. As abstract, it occurred to me now, as any one of Doug's sculptures.

"Right now," Jack said as if he were thinking and choosing his words very carefully, "I'm working construction for a big developer." He raised one hand, as if to erase the last word. "But what I love is saving old things. Back in Minneapolis, I had my own company, did restoration work. Some building. All vintage design." He stretched, looked at me and shrugged, then reached over to take my hand. "Business was good. I never mastered the money side of things, though."

I pressed my palm against his, enjoying as I always did the way my hand fit entirely inside. Doug hooted and ran one hand through his unruly hair. He reminded me of the theater boys in high school, the ones who'd worn long feather earrings and leather boots.

"Right on!" he crowed, holding up his glass and clinking it with Jack's nearly empty bottle. "If Carrie didn't handle the checkbook we'd be flat broke. But artists aren't meant to deal with that shit. Money has nothing to do with what we are. Man, sometimes I think it's what screws us all up."

Darkness had fallen. Carrie set three large candles on the dining room table and we ate in the dappled light of dancing flames and shadows. I drank a half glass of beer—my first since becoming pregnant with Matt—which made me limp and woozy. Halfway through the meal I ended up leaning against Jack's shoulder, listening to the chatter of our children and the tap of fork tines against ceramic plates, the haunting tattoo of drumbeats coming from the next room, and I remember thinking that I could stay happily suspended there forever. Perhaps the reason this moment stands out so clearly in my memory is that it was the last time I would ever feel that particular brand of contentment and hope. I think of it now as the end of youth.

Winter came early that year. It began with a snowstorm on Halloween: seventy-two inches in two days. We couldn't take the boys trick-or-treating. Snow fell until it covered the bottom halves of the windows—for a short while this was pleasant, like being sealed into the soft, white center of an ice cream cone. Mesmerizing and surreal. But then January came and for weeks the sky was the color of granite, the wind so harsh it scratched exposed skin raw.

And then we were poor. It had happened almost without my seeing, like the way a flower wilts and shrivels and dies. The first period, between Halloween and Thanksgiving, had seemed familiar. I thought back to the times when Edward was an infant and Jack had just started his business, when money ran short and I'd had to cash all the government bonds my grandmother had left me in her will. In those early years we wore our clothes until they were faded a uniform, fuzzy gray, and drove an old Volvo. That sort of poverty hadn't stopped us from buying books and movie tickets and organic baby food. There were steak dinners at my parents' house and always enough work coming in to provide us with a trickle of income.

But for the fact that my parents weren't in town, that's what it was like in Aurora at first. There was a temporary, surmountable feeling to our financial problems. We even met Carrie and Doug at the Mexican restaurant on Huron once, pretending we weren't terribly hungry and ordering carefully so when the bill came it could be paid with the $20 I'd saved back from the week's grocery account.

But since late November—when the developer had run out of money and told Jack one Friday that he no longer had a job and we were now, according to the contract he'd signed when he was hired, expected to pay full rent on our condo—we had been living like real poor people. We ate generic noodles and rice. We ran out of heating oil in December and didn't have enough money to pay for a shipment, so I had to go to a county office and apply for emergency assistance. I dreaded opening the mailbox, my stomach greasy with apprehension when I heard the mail carrier click the lid shut, because I knew it would contain nothing but bills we couldn't pay.

I'd quit calling my parents, in part because we couldn't afford it but also because I was afraid I would pour out my story, weeping, admitting that my father had been right. Instead, I wrote short cheerful notes, pretending I was too busy with the boys to talk. At any other time in our lives, I probably would have told Mariel the truth. But she had stayed in England, applied to graduate school, and had written just a few weeks before to say she was involved with a man she'd met in Trafalgar Square one Sunday—a brilliant young barrister who took her to Paris for weekends. I was ashamed. It appeared I alone had made all the wrong choices in life.

Jack worked as a drywaller, when he could find the work, and at night he went to school. The only thing Aurora needed, it seemed, was more law enforcement; unemployment had risen to 12 percent and the port authority was rumored to be controlled by mafiosi. When Jack went to the Jobs Advocacy Center that fall the worker there took one look at him—six foot six and so broad through the shoulders he could carry a hot-water heater like a keg of beer—and signed him up for police training. Now, the only time Jack was home was when he was sleeping. Or drinking. He'd switched to a cheap brand of beer and late at night when he came home too tired to sleep he would sit in the living room, staring at the television, opening bottles until he lost consciousness on the couch. I tried sitting with him, talking to him, but he was vacant; often he had to search hard to think of the words he wanted to use. Once, he said he hated this place. He still held my hand if I reached for him, but his fingers were limp. And his eyes were empty, recessed in dark pouches the dusky purple color of a bruise. Mornings, no matter how early I awoke, he was gone and I had to figure out how to fill the long, silent hours. The boys and I went to the county library nearly every day, because it was bright and warm and, best of all, it was free.

The building was shaped like a ship, perched on a pier on the western shore of Lake Superior, looking as if it were about to set sail. The children's section was bright, full of cloth books and the sort of stimulating, educational playthings I knew my boys needed. But even here, there were reminders of our situation. Tables by the entrance displayed "Friends of the Library" trinkets for sale: colored erasers and plastic key chains. Almost all the children would stop to finger these items on their way in and out. But Edward was fascinated—particularly by the things that were shaped like balls—and had begun crying loudly when I made him put back the toys he picked up. Twice, I'd spent a precious dollar to buy one, because I couldn't quiet him any other way.

For days, I'd been meaning to discuss this with Jack. Clearly, our older son was sensitive and he was picking up on the stresses in our home. It had occurred to me to take the boys to Minneapolis for a visit, but I was reluctant to drive the icy highways alone and loathe to show up at my parents' house beaten and in need of their help. Together, I was sure Jack and I could come up with a better plan, but lately he had been gone even more than usual. And when he finally came through the door, in from the dark and frigid cold, he looked numb with exhaustion. Each night, I put off our talk. In the morning, before we set off for the library, I put one of the toys I'd already bought into my pocket; if Edward made a scene again, I would slip it onto the table and then pick it up and hand it to him, pretending it was new.

It was a Tuesday in late January. We made it past the trinket table without incident and I led the boys to the children's section where Carrie was waiting. She was five months pregnant, wearing a pouchy pair of men's overalls along with thermal shirts and layers of wool scarves and shawls. She managed to make even this outfit look glamorous. Her face glistened like a pearl and I flushed, hot with resentment. Suddenly, it seemed cruel to me that while I was perpetually exhausted and worried, I'd been saddled with someone so perfect for my only friend.

I turned away from her and tried to swallow the ugliness of this thought. Carrie had done nothing to deserve it. Besides, I'd waited all week for Tuesday—because it was story-hour day. While Edward and the other children drank juice, ate cookies, and listened to the librarian read books, I would talk to Carrie about preschools, forgetting, at least for a short time, that we could never afford such a luxury. Then I would walk through the stacks, with Matt in the backpack holding a cookie or dozing against my neck, and assemble a stack of books to take home. Every night while I waited for Jack, I sat propped on pillows in our bed and read; it was only then, during the few hours when the boys were asleep and I was lost in a story about someone else's life, that I ever felt at ease anymore.

But for two weeks in a row, I had not been able to spend the hour looking for books because Edward had begun to cry as soon as the square, brown-haired librarian began herding the children toward the stairs. He refused to go, putting his arms around my leg and squeezing until it truly hurt. He made an endless humming sound as if he were screaming deep down inside where no one could see. This morning, I could hardly breathe as the clock overhead ticked toward ten.

Carrie and I were sitting on plastic chairs, red and blue ones, watching the children play in a cardboard castle. Ingrid, her long blonde hair adorned with seven or eight small butterfly clips that sparkled, sat Edward in a chair and announced, "You're the king." He said nothing but looked at her serenely—almost regally, I thought. "Hold this like one of those king things." She was two months younger than Edward and when they were standing she barely reached his shoulder. But she peered up and poked him to make him listen, then held out a toy bat that she gripped exactly like a scepter. He did not respond. "Here." She used her other hand to curl his fingers around the bat, but when she let go, he did, too. The bat clattered to the floor and he didn't look down.

"You're a dumb boy," she said, and moved away to talk on the phone in a toy kitchen.

At 10:03 A.M. the story-hour lady arrived. She was like a miniature version of the building itself, her small, stout ship of a body sailing across the children's section with the boys and girls trailing behind like dinghies. I put my hand on Edward's back and gave him a push in the direction of the other children. He turned and looked at me with a gray, cardboard face. Carrie tried to be helpful: she made Ingrid take Edward's hand and whispered that she should lead the way to the story room.

He went. Carrie and I stood, tensely watching their two blond heads bob away. Edward was taller than all the other children but he walked more slowly, dragging on Ingrid's hand and scuffing the toes of his tennis shoes against the carpet. Carrie clutched my arm and breathed out noisily as the children disappeared.

"See!" she said. "I knew he would do just great today."

We piled our coats and Matt's diaper bag in an out-of-the-way corner and walked toward Adult Fiction. I found three novels that fit my new criteria for late-night reading: literary but uplifting, engaging but never dark. It had gotten hard to find books that did not frighten me; everything had spiraled out of control so rapidly, I'd become irrationally certain my life would expand to include any new problems I read about.

I checked out my books and was on my way back to the children's section when I heard Edward, crying in the loud, ceaseless whine that had suddenly, about two weeks ago, taken the place of his speech. When I turned the corner, he was standing by the castle, and the librarian with the helmet of brown hair was holding on to the back of his collar. She brightened a little when I walked toward them, but in a vicious way.

She pushed Edward forward but held on to his shirt, facing me with her hands resting on his shoulders, as if she owned him now and was considering whether to give him back. "This child," she said loudly, "does not belong in our story hour."

Her voice, that one sentence, was like the loud cracking noise that happens seconds before a building collapses. I knew everything was about to crumble at my feet.

What she said simply confirmed what I had suspected, avoided, feared for weeks. I stood, trying to control my mounting panic, silent.

But the librarian seemed to interpret my pause as a question. "He walks around the room the entire time the story is being read," she broadcast. "He turns the lights on and off. When we ask him to sit down with all the other children, it's like he doesn't even hear us."

Two mothers with whom Carrie and I had once talked briefly about peewee soccer were sitting in chairs against the wall, staring at me, openly curious, wondering how I was going to respond. I realized Edward was still crying. I reached down and took his hand, pulling him forward, and at the same time the librarian gave him a little shove so he tumbled right into me.

"Don't try bringing him back for a while," she said. "At least three months." Still, I did not speak. This must have made her angry because she began stamping one blocky foot. "If I were you," she said. "I would get some help for him. There's obviously something very wrong."

If only she knew. For three days, he had not spoken. Not one word. He was round-cheeked and golden-haired but sometimes his whole face looked dead. He'd chewed holes in some of his clothes. Overnight, he would no longer let me hug him. The day before, I'd found him on his bed holding one hand in front of his eyes and turning it slowly.

The helmet-haired librarian started to walk away. Carrie came hurrying toward us, having heard the commotion, asking me what had happened. I tried to speak but something rose in my throat— either a sob or a scream, I couldn't tell. And I couldn't risk it. Our friendship had been forever spoiled by this day and somehow I knew that my life had changed, completely, in the past hour. I would never again believe in the fantasy of a home and a family like hers. I scooped up Edward and, carrying both boys, followed Helmet Head to her desk. "Where?" I asked. She turned, clearly annoyed that I was still there. "Where can I get help for him?"

"I don't know." She sat behind the desk. Even so, she appeared, at that moment, to be above me. "This is a library, not a social service agency."

I'm not stupid, I wanted to scream at her. *Or at least, I didn't use to be.* Instead, I took a deep breath and tried once more. "But the library helps people find things, right? We just moved here. My husband is . . ." I stopped. The librarian flicked her hand at me. My belly felt full of sand.

I turned, the boys swinging around my moving body like tassels, to get our coats and leave this place.

"Maybe he's autistic," she called after us, her voice loud but gentler than before. "If you ask me, that's the first thing you should check into."

"How?" I moaned.

She shrugged her shoulders. "Call the school district, maybe?" Already, she was staring at something on her desk. We had been dismissed.

I hated her. Yet, I did exactly what she had told me to do. When I got home, I looked up the number in the telephone book and called and repeated everything the librarian had said. I explained our financial situation and was given the first available appointment for Edward to see the district psychologist—in two months. Then I made toasted peanut butter sandwiches for Edward's lunch, sat down in the rocking chair with the baby sleeping on me, and cried. But my tears were angry, and crying didn't make me feel any better.

Later, I found Edward on the floor in his room, staring at the wheel of a toy car that was spinning around and around. I tried to read him a story, to prove the evil librarian wrong, but he just chewed on his sleeve and stared wordlessly out the window at the house next door. Finally, I picked him up and held him on my lap, trapping him inside my arms no matter how much he struggled against me. Near dusk, when Jack came home from work to change for class, he found us there, still clenched together.

4

WE LEFT AURORA the week Jack graduated from the police academy and returned to Minneapolis, where we lived with my parents during an interminably long, cold spring. My father made one phone call and we were issued medical assistance for disabled and chronically ill children. I kept the card in my purse but always felt dirty after touching it. Each time someone used a word like *disabled,* it seemed more and more to become the truth. I imagined Edward responding to the weight of these expectations: he had a label, a file in a county office somewhere, identification and records and bracelets and buttons and pins that stamped him defective. And so, he was.

In the evenings, sometimes he closed his eyes tight and squealed like an animal that had been caught. But the rest of the time he walked in circles of his own making, staring into the palm of his hand as he moved. He would eat hungrily but never at the table and always furtively, as if he were ashamed. His only point of connection with us came through string. He went through skeins of it, making loops around his own ankles and fingers and arms, then throwing the length of what remained on the spool, lassolike, around my arm or my mother's, Jack's enormous feet as he lay sprawled and exhausted in a chair. I worried that through his obsession, Edward would strangle Matt inadvertently, but I didn't want to stop him from binding himself, even in this unusual way, to his brother. So I trailed the boys during the hours they spent together, reaching in to loosen and unwind the string whenever Edward wound it around Matt's creased little neck.

I took Edward to a series of doctors during those months, and they threw out a glossary's worth of words: *schizophrenia, childhood disintegration,* and *brain damage OUO,* code that a nurse translated for me in a whisper: "of unknown origin." But each time, when I began with our long and complicated history—Edward's perfect babyhood and early language skills, his sudden dissociation in Aurora, the intermittent days of near normal speech—they would check their books and sigh and say he didn't really fit in one category or another. And when they said this, I knew the next step would be for them to send us on to someone else: another phone call, another three to four weeks of waiting, another appointment that gave me an irrational kind of hope.

Each time, I would ask about autism, shuddering because I could still hear the librarian pronouncing the word. If he had it, it seemed to me she had caused it somehow, putting a curse on him with her cruelty.

It had been six months since that January day and still, I hated her in a way I could taste as bitter and acrid as tar on my tongue. But when they turned to the *A*'s in their diagnostic manuals, all these doctors lined up against the evil story-hour lady. The onset was too late, they said. He did not pull away from us in infancy. He had none of the physical traits such as toe-walking and digital hyperextension; one sweet older psychologist with white hair demonstrated, holding his hands taut with the fingers bent backward so they resembled bird wings.

While I sat in waiting rooms, trying to keep both Matt and Edward entertained with coloring books and plastic toys, Jack searched for a job, taking tests in police stations and sheriff's offices throughout the thirty-mile-wide circle of the metro area, eventually finding one in what we both knew was the roughest, most dangerous precinct in the city.

"It's money," he said to me in bed that night. We slept on a foldout couch in the basement rec room of my parents' home, like teenagers only pretending to be on their own. Because Edward had begun wandering in the middle of the night, the boys slept in the room with us, on a mattress Jack had pulled off a bed upstairs and carried down three flights. "They're offering decent health insurance. And we could get out of here."

"People get shot there," I whispered. I didn't tell him I was already certain he would be killed. We'd lost all our money and our brilliant little boy had gone insane. Jack's death seemed like the next logical step.

He picked up one of my hands, which had been lying loosely on my hip, and pressed the palm into his bare chest. We were no longer so haggard as we had been over the winter in Aurora, but sex remained infrequent. Once, we had found each other by chance in the tiny bathroom off the laundry and he'd pushed into me while the boys watched television with my parents upstairs. And a few times, we had both been awake in the middle of the night when even Edward slept, snoring audibly beside us; but our lovemaking then had been tentative and quick. Jack seemed not quite himself and I was distracted anyway by the constant task of finding out the truth about Edward.

Most nights, we contented ourselves simply with lying next to each other, me in an old T-shirt of his that hung to my knees and Jack naked to the waist, wearing long, loose flannel pants. Now, he moved my hand back and forth, over the foot-and-a-half span of his rib cage; I could feel the muscles there, and the steady bass beat of his heart under every spot I touched.

"Nothing can hurt me." He sounded more sure than he had in months and this filled me with a sudden joy. I'd tried not to blame Jack for what had happened to our son, but the coincidence nagged at me. Our descent into poverty, Jack's depression, those long, cold, lonely days in Aurora—all of it seemed related to Edward's silence. Maybe this was the end, the way out: Jack would be valiant and we would be fine. I trembled with the pleasure of believing in him again. "As long as I have you and the boys and a home of our own." His mouth was warm against my ear. "I promise, everything will be good."

As soon as he took the job, this began to come true. Edward awoke clearheaded one morning and said a full sentence before relaxing back into a reverie that seemed more dreamy than disordered. We found a dilapidated 1920s-era house for a price we could actually afford in a school district that had come highly recommended. There was a lot of work to do, but Jack and I were eager to take it on: this house would allow us to leave my parents' basement and establish the sort of home we'd planned when we were first married—a small, vintage place with natural wood and a garden out back. Even the children appeared pleased, spending hours out in the yard with me, clearing weeds and stacking the loose bricks that lined the fence. Edward seemed aware of us for the first time since Christmas. I spent the first weeks in our new home blissful, washing down the musty basement walls with a bleach solution while the children napped, believing our new life would restore Edward the way Aurora had dismantled him.

My fervor died out with Edward's first regression. It was a morning like all the others, a clear summer day. Jack kissed me and left, brawny and handsome in his uniform. I baked muffins before the heat set in. But when I went to wake the boys, I found Edward lying curled on his side in bed, staring into the cup of his hand and sighing a persistent, rhythmic roller-coaster sound. Even when I picked him up and tried to turn his head, his eyes didn't unlock. He kept gazing away. He giggled breathily and closed his eyes when I said his name. And over the next two years, it went like this over and over again. Periods of clarity that never quite achieved normalcy, followed by spirals down in which new symptoms emerged and accumulated. But through it all, one thing seemed consistent to me: with each passing week, Edward was sleeping less and less.

Despite the legion of doctors who disagreed, he was called autistic as soon as he went to school. "I don't much care about his specific pathology," said the district's special ed consultant when I talked to her prior to his kindergarten year. She was firm but not unkind; she put her hand on Edward's knee as she spoke and kept it there even when he began pinching the skin over her knuckles so he could watch it turn white. "I have to find a way to support him in the mainstream classroom, and the only way I know of is to put a label on him."

She wrote down the name of a local pediatrician and tucked the paper into my hand. "Take him here. This doc works with us all the time. He knows what the system requires."

For the past year and a half, since he'd entered school, the system had required us to refer to Edward as a child with "pervasive developmental disorder," a category broader than traditional autism, the doctor had explained, so it would accommodate children like ours who didn't quite fit. And I'd used the phrase so many times, sometimes I simply believed it. But since the weeks we saw him miraculously and completely healed last spring, I'd refused. What Edward had was not pervasive; it could disappear like a puff of smoke and reveal a warm, real child underneath. There had to be another answer. I only hoped Barry Newberg hadn't found it.

As morning dawned in our kitchen that January day after my nightmare—the questionnaire still lying on the table where I had left it just hours before—the air turned suddenly, unseasonably warm. Outside the window over the sink, icicles sparkled in sunlight and dripped water from their tips; when I glanced at the thermometer that hung there it read 34 degrees. Behind me, Matthew sat in his booster seat, singing preschool songs as he ate his Cheerios.

Jack was on days until the end of the week and he stepped behind me, his leather belt creaking as he bent over my shoulder to say good-bye. I closed my eyes and leaned back for a minute, breathing him in. He smelled official, like wool and oil.

"I could call in sick." He had draped his arms over me and I looked down at the sleeves of his blue uniform, embossed at the cuffs with the letters *M.P.D.*, hanging over my turnip-shaped body. "I'll go with you."

"No." I relaxed into the space he made with his arms and the weight of his coat, but only for a minute. Then I straightened and made my voice casual. "You go. I'm going to drop Matt off at my mother's early and try to get some work done before I go to the doctor's office. I have deadlines later this week."

This was not completely true. I did have a deadline coming up, one, but the article had been written for two days and needed only a final proofread. The fact was, for reasons I didn't fully understand, I wanted to keep Barry Newberg to myself. Also, I couldn't picture Jack sitting in the doctor's office; in my mind he didn't fit in any of the chairs.

Before he left, Jack walked around the table to cup one hand around each of the boy's faces. Edward tipped his head, one cheek resting in Jack's palm, and closed his eyes as if he could finally fall asleep there at the table in his father's hand. Under the table, his feet stopped twitching. But Matt quivered with energy and grinned through Jack's fingers.

"Be good," Jack said. I couldn't tell which one he was addressing. Or whether, perhaps, he meant me.

"Daddy?" Matt held a spoon that dripped milk above his bowl. "What if I was twenty miles tall?"

"Maybe you will be." Jack had opened the door and he stood with one hand on the knob. Fresh cool air swept in. The baby turned and leaned an elbow into my ribs—a sharp, pleasant sensation. "You can be a giant, if you try."

Edward was humming, a tinny noise. Then he cleared his throat. "I will be a giant." His voice was sure and musical, though for days even his one-word responses—*no, yes*—had been raw. "Like my dad. He's very tall."

The three of us stopped and turned, stunned as we always were to hear Edward form words. He would appear to us like this, breaking through at odd moments, then retreat again so that it always felt like a sighting of a unicorn. I often found myself wondering later if I'd only imagined it.

After Jack left, both boys were silent but for the taps of their spoons against ceramic bowls. The refrigerator motor whirred; I ran water in the dishes in the sink and watched soap bubbles glisten with color in the sunlight. The phone's abrupt ring startled all of us. Inside me, the baby lurched, and I felt the boys jump behind me, heard their spoons clatter.

"Hi. I didn't wake you?" Mariel sounded breathless. By eight o'clock, she'd likely been up for three hours tending her horses. We'd chosen very different lives after college but lately I'd begun to see how similar the outcomes were. She, too, rose to feed and brush and love creatures who nuzzled her hand and whinnied but never spoke.

"No, I was up getting Edward ready for school." Despite the season, I pictured Mariel outside in a green field, drinking from a ceramic mug, her long ropes of dark hair lifting in a prairie wind. As if Iowa were a whole different world where spring had already come.

"Oh, right. Uh . . . are you okay? The baby?"

I looked at the clock, then down at Edward, who seemed to be counting something off using the same three fingers over and over. "Merry, can I call you back? I've got about two minutes to get him out the door."

"Yeah. I'm at my mother's new place. Do you have the number?"

"You're in town? Why?" I clenched the phone between my cheek and shoulder, moving around the table to put my hands on Edward's arms and coax him out of his chair. We walked to the back door and I began handing him his winter clothes, piece by piece.

"I'll tell you everything later." I'd been wrong, she wasn't out of breath. Her voice was tight and low. Controlled. "But one of the reasons is I was hoping we could get together."

"Don't you have classes?" Edward was struggling. His snow pants had twisted so the left leg was behind him. I hunched over him, feeling a twinge of tired muscles in my thighs, and saw that the pant leg was inside out.

"Winter break. And, uh, Scott's managing the farm."

I was on the floor now, my hand stuck up through Edward's clothes, tugging at the cotton lining of his pants. It had been six months since I'd seen Mariel. During college, we'd lived together and often, at night, she would drag her futon into my room so we could keep talking in sleepy voices as we lay in bed. But it wasn't enough. At least once a week we went to a vegetarian place in the basement of an old Victorian where we ate blue chips with black bean hummus and drank Turkish coffee, spending long hours arguing about world events and consoling each other over men. These days, our conversations took place mostly over the telephone but I needed them; once I'd fed Edward chocolate chips right out of the bag so he wouldn't make siren noises while we were talking.

"I have an appointment with Edward's doctor at two. And some work I should do . . ."

"Newspaper stuff?"

"Yes." Next to her title, associate professor, her conferences, and her papers on classical theory, both the doctor's appointment and my job sounded too small to discuss. I glanced up again; we were truly late now. "I can probably drop Matt off at my parents' house a little early if you can drive out this way to meet me."

Mariel sighed. "Thanks. I'll be at the bagel shop at eleven-thirty. You get there when you can."

I hung up. Edward was tilting his head, staring out the window at the sparkle of icicles dripping from the gutter. He looked thoughtful and I hated to disturb him but in the distance I heard the far-off sound of the school bell. I handed him his jacket, mittens, scarf, and hat; Edward put them on, one layer at a time. When he was done, he was as padded as a hockey player. If you didn't look at his hollow eyes, Edward still looked robust and strong.

A pair of stretched-out sweatpants hung on a hook by the door. I pulled them on, yanking the waistband up over my medicine ball of a stomach, but they kept rolling down. I was breathing hard as I picked up Matt and took him to the living room couch with a blanket, gave him his orange juice in a spill-proof plastic cup, and turned on the TV.

When I got back to the kitchen, I found Edward slumped in the corner behind the door. But he had put on his backpack without my asking. It was brightly colored with lions and bears from a Disney movie we'd seen that fall. In the theater, Matt had laughed and bounced in his seat; Edward faced the screen but his eyes had seemed to grow custard skins and his face was blank in the red light of the exit sign.

I glanced back through the doorway at Matt. He was chewing on the spout of his cup and watching the television calmly. Already, he was soaking up everything he saw: the fuzzy ABC's that danced across the screen, the skits describing up and down, the songs about skin color. At four, he could hold a pencil and write his own name. He could add small numbers. This should have proved Jack and I could raise a child right, but most of the time Matt's abilities seemed more like an amazing and undeserved fluke.

"You'll stay right there?" I asked again as I put on Jack's old motorcycle jacket and pulled on a pair of long leather gloves. Matt nodded without removing his eyes from the television screen where Maria and Oscar were arguing.

Outside the air was much softer than I'd expected, like an April breeze that had suddenly blown into January. I walked with Edward down the damp sidewalk in front of our house, across the street, and along the dirt path that cut across the park to the distant corner of the school yard. I could still see our house from here; I turned to look at the blank windows and make sure nothing had changed. Matthew hadn't run out in his footed pajamas, frantic because I'd left. The neighborhood was perfectly quiet, glittering in the sunlight. I knew we were very late, but time seemed to stop as I stood, looking at the silent world.

Suddenly dark clouds gathered on the horizon, rolling the way they do before a thunderstorm. The sky smelled like rain, which was impossible in Minnesota in the middle of winter. But the wind sharpened and licked wetly at our exposed skin. Inside me, a voice insisted: anything is possible.

Ten steps into the park, I was exactly halfway between our house and the edge of the school property. When I leaned over to kiss Edward's cheek it felt cool and smooth, like suede. "You go now," I said. But I held on to his shoulders. Finally when I took away my hands, he moved forward. I stayed and watched him until he got to the end of the park, squinting so I could keep his whole body framed in the circle of my vision. Blue coat, bouncing backpack, shuffling, booted feet. And a small, round head that bobbed gently, like a balloon tied to the end of an invisible string.

5

I MET MARIEL between classes during my sophomore year in high school. I was carrying a stack of books, hurrying to keep up with a throng of students that moved like one body. She was standing on the stairs, separate from the crowd, yelling to someone in a throaty voice so masculine that I had what I never could have known at the time was a purely chemical response. She was just one year ahead of me, a junior, but looked easily twenty-five. A gypsy earth goddess with round, pink cheeks and yards of kinky, black hair, she wore layered scarves that had glittery fringe along the edges and her earrings—crescent moons—dangled nearly to her shoulders.

She and I had been best friends since, and until I met Jack there had never been anyone else who knew me so well and loved me without reason. Mariel's family no longer lived in the house I passed on my way to drop off Matt at my mother's. Her parents had divorced shortly after she finished high school and then her father had disappeared. Merry heard one rumor that he'd moved to Las Vegas with a girlfriend, another that he'd gone to Belize and gotten involved in something shady—drugs or money laundering, no one ever said specifically. All we knew was that two years later, when he came back to Minneapolis for a visit, he was arrested and put in prison. He'd been released since, but Mariel said neither of them had called the other. She had erased him from her life, as if a human being could be nullified. Her mother still taught at the university and had helped Mariel get her position in Iowa, around the same time I was giving birth to Matt.

The road grew wider as I passed Mariel's old house and began rounding the lake. Yet, I always felt squeezed at this point, breathless. There was a two-dimensional quality to my family's neighborhood; it was picture-perfect and orderly. Even the accumulated snow—pocked and dirty on Jack's and my side of town—appeared fresh and sculpted. With its columns and strangely cheerful bright red door, my parents' house looked like a manor, sitting up higher than all the rest in the neighborhood on the curved end of a cul-de-sac. I stiffened and clutched the steering wheel, suddenly aware of my own hard weight pressing against the seat. I looked into the rearview mirror at Matthew in his car seat, a talisman against the way this place seemed to rise and tower above me.

I parked my minivan in the driveway. Back when I drove a sagging Volvo station wagon with Grateful Dead stickers on the back windshield, my parents' next-door neighbors had complained and asked if we would park it on the street outside their development. I was proud that at least this car could sit in front of their house, and angry at myself for knowing it.

I used my key to let us in. I was kneeling on the hard tile of the foyer, helping Matt take off his coat and boots, when my mother appeared at the top of the winding staircase, calling hello. As she descended, I watched from below and saw the age in her face. The skin on her cheeks was thin and transparent while the flesh on her jaw and neck seemed to have loosened and grown thick. I wondered when this had begun to happen. Had I been too distracted by Edward to notice that my mother was suddenly growing old? She hugged me and put her hands on the huge mound of my body. "Soon," she said. "Maybe by Valentine's Day?"

"Oh, God," I groaned. No matter how hard I tried not to, I always reverted to sounding like an adolescent here. "If it takes that long, I swear I'll slit my wrists."

My mother pursed her lips, but then she laughed. "I remember." She nodded as she led us to the kitchen, a room twenty-four feet long with arched windows. The table was set with a white cloth and her dessert china—gold-rimmed plates and cups and saucers etched with pictures of fruit. And my throat grew hollow when I realized she'd prepared for us, like we were company. I looked furtively at my watch: it was almost eleven o'clock. In thirty minutes, Mariel would be waiting for me. I imagined her peering out the window of the bagel shop, one foot tapping inside her riding boot.

"Sit. Eat." My mother waved toward the cake sitting in the middle of the table. It was a recipe her mother had handed down: rolled pastry with poppy seed paste spiraled through and an egg-white wash that made it hard and shiny. I'd never liked this cake, but every time my mother served it, it seemed to be the wrong time to admit I found it dry and sinister tasting. I cut a piece, took a bite, and choked twice as I tried to swallow.

Matt sat in front of his plate, crumbling the cake between fat fingers, making a mound of silty black stuff. I checked my watch again: Mariel was no doubt on her way to the bagel shop. My mother got up and went to the cookie jar, where she pulled out two chocolate-covered graham crackers. "Here you go, sweetheart," she said, dropping them onto Matt's plate. Each cracker made a small thunking sound that echoed through the kitchen.

We sat for a few minutes, chewing. Somewhere a clock ticked. "You shouldn't have a drug test after this, you know," she said conversationally, as if it were something we'd been discussing.

I was amazed. I'd had no idea she even knew what a drug test was, or how it worked. But for one panicked minute I wondered if she knew about the plastic bag hidden beneath a stack of sheets in our linen closet, infusing them with its sharp, green, woody smell. In the next moment, I recognized this as paranoia: my mother was only making conversation in the random, desperate way she always did with me. And I was being rude. "After what?" I asked, leaning forward as if I were intensely interested. The baby protested, pushing hard against me as my body compressed.

My mother held up a bite of cake and waved it at me. "Poppy seeds. They show up as some sort of opium."

"Mother," I said, opening my arms wide around my enormous stomach. "Who would test me?"

She laughed once, then cleared her throat as if she were embarrassed. "I don't know. I'm just saying, for the future. Barb's son was rejected for a job because his drug test turned positive after he ate poppy seed cake. This very cake—I gave her the recipe." My mother nodded twice, her penciled-in eyebrows tight, blonde hair bobbing with each movement.

I watched her face. "Don't tell me you feel guilty."

"Well, I did start the whole thing. I sent a cake over when she had her hysterectomy and he liked it, so I sent more. Then next thing you know, he was turned down for a job even though Barb really thought this might be the one." She paused and looked at her hands. "Raising children is hard."

"Mother." I put my hand on her arm and she flinched slightly, but I kept it there. "Barb's son is an art student who takes his poppy seeds with about a quart of rum and a couple grams of cocaine. I really don't think you're to blame."

She pulled her arm away and adjusted the sleeve of her blouse. "You always see the dark side, Rachel." She rose and began stacking our dishes, waving me away when I tried to help. "Why is that? We didn't raise you that way. Why do you insist on painting the world so bleak?"

I had no answer but simply watched as she worked, hands wrapping the leftover cake in plastic as neatly as if it were a package. Unlike me, my mother could not bear to stay angry or even remember an exchange of harsh words. Within moments, she was smiling at Matt, who had climbed down from his chair with chocolate-smeared fingers and lips. She wiped him off and turned back to me, fresh, all unpleasantness forgotten. "So, what are your plans today?"

"I'm going to meet Mariel." I stopped myself from checking my watch. "And then, I have a doctor's appointment."

She glanced at my body. "But didn't you just . . . ?"

"Not for me. For Edward."

"Oh." She folded her hands together in her lap. A reflex, though it always made me wonder if true believers could pray no matter where they happened to be, or who else was around.

I got up to leave, but suddenly the list of unanswered questions appeared in my head, lines of type with spaces after. I turned. "I'm wondering." I cleared my throat. "I'd like to ask you a few questions." I dug through my purse and pulled out the questionnaire. "This doctor thinks Edward may have a disease that causes tumors on the brain," I said bluntly, unfolding the sheets of paper on the table. My mother winced and sucked her mouth in, which made her look ancient, a waterfall of drooping skin. "It's not likely, but he thinks it's possible. I need to know if anyone in your family has had any of these things."

I handed her the sheet. There were boxes to check for various symptoms; three checks meant a family tendency, five a diagnosis. I breathed slowly as she put on her reading glasses and scanned the form, eyes moving from the top to the bottom and back up. Swiftly, the thought came to me that I would hate her if she checked five, even four. But I doubted she could do it, even if the checks belonged on the page, because she would hate herself, too.

A minute ticked by. "This one." She pointed to a section marked "Skin Discoloration." "I think . . . my aunt Mamie had some spots." My mother rubbed the back of her own left hand with the palm of her right. "Here." She rose suddenly and went to the hallway where I could hear her climbing the staircase, her rings tapping against the banister as she pulled herself along. I rinsed the plates she'd stacked by the sink and put them in the dishwasher before following her upstairs.

She was in one of the guest rooms, on her knees, hands inside the bottom drawer of a dresser that was neatly set with a lace runner and silver candlesticks. "My cousin Martin went through a phase where he collected old clippings. Newspaper announcements, things like that. At one point, he gave Grandma Mary a scrapbook full of them as a gift. I paged through it after she died, and I seem to remember she stuck some other things there. It's possible there are medical records of some sort."

My mother pulled items out one by one and set them neatly in piles on the floor. Holiday tablecloths with painted turkeys and elves, napkin rings, trivets and doilies. Eventually, she withdrew a leather-bound album; she straightened, opened the book, and began riffling through the pages. I peered into the drawer, surprised at what I saw. It was rare to find disorder in this house, but under the stacks of things was a pool of loose photographs, three or four layers deep, their surfaces so slick that when I touched one they all shifted, revealing dozens of others. Women with fleshy, clear-eyed peasant faces and scarves tied over their hair. Slim young men with hands clasped, watch chains looping from the pockets of their suits. Groups of couples lined up in front of lake cabins, smiling broadly. Fat children in wading pools.

I picked up a shot of my grandparents, Mary and Ted. They were at a table against the darkened windows of a restaurant or country club, talking to people who sat with their backs to the camera. There was a clutter of glasses and cups on the table. My grandmother was laughing, her head thrown back, a strange turquoise hat with a half veil perched precariously on top of her bouffant hair.

Then I spotted a picture of a man I recognized, though I could not recall where I had seen him before. I picked it up and brought it closer to my face, but this did not help me remember. He was a man around my age, perhaps twenty-five or twenty-six. His face was dark and sober, chin pointed, lips full. Though his hair was neatly combed—a smooth wave to one side over the forehead, trimmed high over the ears, small sideburns—it seemed ready to burst into something wilder, the way the fur on an animal's neck springs up when it is provoked. And his eyes, wide and nearly black, were lit with something that looked like fear.

"Who is this?" I turned, still crouched. It was too hard to get up. My mother had moved to stand by the door, the open book in her hands. She took a few steps toward me, then stopped.

"My brother Mickey," she said softly.

"The one who died?"

"One of them." And with that, the memories started streaming back to me. A photo that had hung in my grandmother's hallway—not this particular one but another taken from the same time period. The same man with a thinner face, a khaki uniform, a dog at his feet. And another, a black-and-white portrait of a ten- or eleven-year-old boy with an entirely different expression: round, clear eyes, smooth cheeks, and an easy smile. My mother rarely talked about her childhood and I realized, now, how little I knew about the boys who would have become my uncles.

"There was Frank," my mother said, as if reading my mind. "He died young, before I was born. And then there was Mickey." She gestured at the photo I held, then repeated, "He was my brother, too."

"How much older?" I asked, gripping the edge of the dresser to stand, still clutching the photograph in my other hand.

"Almost four years. He was just turning three when Frank died and my parents always felt . . ."

"What?"

"He changed then. My mother thought he had a lot of psychological problems because of what happened to Frank. They shared a bedroom and Frank took care of Mickey; I think Mickey worshiped him. Poor baby. One day, he woke up and the older brother he adored was just . . . gone."

"It was scarlet fever, right?" I asked. Bits of the stories I'd heard were coming back to me.

"Yes. Frank came down with it on a Monday and he was dead and buried by the weekend." She shivered. "My parents were so devastated, they probably never realized Mickey was suffering, too."

"Suffering how?"

She shrugged. "Later there were problems in school. He couldn't seem to concentrate. He was smart. I know he was. When he served in Korea the air force made him an air traffic controller, and you have to be smart to have that job."

"But what happened to him in school?"

My mother stared into the empty air, as if she were seeing a picture I couldn't. "He was an outcast in grade school, for one thing. He was handsome, but strange somehow, and the teachers thought he was dumb. The other kids didn't like him. I remember that." She took a breath and I was afraid she would stop, but she didn't. "And he couldn't read. I mean, eventually he learned well enough so he could read a newspaper, or write a letter. But he was old: fourteen, maybe? Early on, he had a really terrible time."

"Was it like dyslexia?"

"No, it wasn't that. In fact, he was amazingly good with numbers and directions. It was more . . ." She put one finger to her forehead as she always did when she was trying to put her thoughts into words. "Like he just didn't connect things somehow. Then in high school, things improved. At least, for a while. But later . . ." Her voice cracked and she swallowed. "After Mickey died, Grandma Mary told me she hadn't prayed hard enough. Because she'd used up all her prayers on Frank."

I studied every inch of Mickey's skin, what was showing in the photo, and it was clear: no patches or bumps. "And you're just telling me this now?" I tried to make my voice gentle, but the impatience cut through. "Didn't you ever think it might have something to do with what's happening to Edward?"

Just then, I heard Matt downstairs, calling for me. My mother looked startled, whether by his voice or my question, I couldn't tell. "No." She took the photo from me and stared into it just as I had, as if it might answer my question. "Truthfully, I never did."

FRANK

In 1935, Bruno Hauptmann was on trial in New Jersey for kidnapping and killing the Lindbergh baby. Amelia Earhart aborted her first attempt at an around-the-world flight when she lost control of her airplane on takeoff at Luke Field, near Pearl Harbor (which had no special significance for Americans, beyond being the place where Amelia Earhart failed to begin her landmark flight). And penicillin, which had been discovered by Alexander Fleming in 1929, was in the final stage of development but scientists had not yet found the formula for a stable commercial preparation.

Frank Donnelly was twelve years old. He lived on the north side of Minneapolis, close to the main boulevard where tall trees grew out of a wide center swath and formed arcs over the streets. His house was brand-new, a stucco A-frame with three bedrooms in back and a swinging door between the dining room and the kitchen. His father, Ted, was a jeweler, with clean, white hair and a slight stoop. Ted was very tall for the time—almost six feet—gentle and pensive. He worked long hours in his store and at home at a bench in the basement, peering through a set of monocles attached to the frames of his glasses. Frank's mother, Mary, was ten years younger than her husband—small and willful and quick to laugh. She cleaned the house with short, swift jerks of the dust rag and carpet sweeper. She volunteered at the church, serving funeral luncheons every Tuesday and Wednesday. She was a competitive bridge player—far more so than Ted—sifting quickly through her cards and playing them with the snap of an Atlantic City dealer.

Frank was tall and serious like his dad. He had medium-brown hair that he would wet down every morning with a comb dipped in water. He wore starched white shirts and stiff woolen knickers with knee socks and hook-and-eye lace-up shoes. He preferred reading to kickball (although he did quite well at the game and once got a home run playing in the alley behind his house) and had raced through every story ever written by Robert Louis Stevenson. He asked the librarian to recommend other adventure books but none, so far, was as good as *Treasure Island.*

Frank had skipped a grade and still he was at the top of his section at school. The nuns seated him at the front of the classroom and often pinned up his work—particularly his penmanship and math assignments—as models for the rest of the class. They never hit him across the knuckles with their rulers. In the lower grades they asked his sister, Eleanor, who was nine and already vain about her long, silky hair, why she couldn't be more like her brother.

The sisters praised Ted and Mary for raising a son so mannerly. And pious. Even kneeling with their heads bowed on clasped hands and their habits tented around them, they noted that he did not fidget during daily Mass. He was a good boy. A smart boy. A credit to his family, his school, and the Church.

Every afternoon, when Frank arrived home after school, he took his little brother into the kitchen with him. Mickey was not quite three, still wearing pullover jerseys, rubber pants, and hard-sided shoes. Frank would hoist him easily onto the countertop and talk to him while he fixed a snack: bread with butter and white sugar for both of them. Lemonade when the weather was warm, hot chocolate in the winter. Mickey's black jelly-bean eyes would follow Frank from the icebox to the sugar drawer to the sink. He loved this room because the cupboards were stacked three-high all the way up to the ceiling; when he looked up at the top, he got shivery and dizzy and felt like he might fall off his perch. But he knew Frank would catch him if he did. Frank would never let him fall.

Mickey couldn't say as many words as other children his age, but that was fine because he preferred being quiet and listening to Frank. He especially liked hearing about school—a glorious place. Frank told him about the ink pots sunk into holes in the desks, the new-smelling books filled with numbers, the gymnasium with its waxed board floor and blue wrestling mats against the walls. In Mickey's mind, the school was a castle. He could see the nuns, sweeping down the halls, two abreast, in full-skirted black habits. He knew that school was the place to become smart, like Frank. He wanted to go to school. He didn't understand why Frank had to leave him every morning.

December was snowy that year, even for Minnesota. Each afternoon brought a fresh shower of fat, wet flakes that covered the streets and rooftops with white. The air was quiet and full. Frank loved the snow. This was the one time of year he would spend hours outside, sledding down neighborhood hills on his Flexible Flyer, holding the steering rope in his bare hands, his cheeks reddened and chapped from the onslaught of wind as he flew down the hill.

But on a particular Monday afternoon early in the month, he walked straight home through the swirling snow. He felt tired, and his ears rang in the quiet. There was no snack for Mickey that day. No wild ride up the cupboards. Frank sat in the living room with a book and read until dinnertime. He ate little. Once, at the table, he put his head down in the cup of his two hands.

Mary stood up from her seat, felt his forehead, and said it was "warm-ish." She put him in bed early, tucking three quilts around him. His cheeks were streaked and fiery. Later, his father came in with a mix-ture of lemon and honey and a capful of whiskey steeped in boiling water that he told Frank to drink. Ted sat on the bed, silent, one large, long-fingered hand—so deft with the tiny inner workings of a watch—holding the hump of his son's knee through the thick blankets. When Frank had finished the drink, Ted turned out the light and told him to sleep well. The next morning, Frank woke up feeling empty and weak but much better. His face was white, but he pinked up a bit after he ate some toast and drank a glass of orange juice.

"Can you go to school?" Mary asked as she rushed around the kitchen, fixing plates, pouring coffee, and brushing the knots out of Eleanor's hair. "I'm due at the church at ten to serve for the Williams funeral."

Frank said he could go. He packed his satchel slowly with paper and pencils and his history book. He walked to school and sat himself gently in his seat. When Sister Magdelena called for attention and began the Lord's Prayer, he barely mouthed the words. The morning seemed endless. By noon, his neck felt as if there were two knobs growing inside it, under his jaw on both sides. The knobs made it hard for him to swallow and pressed painfully into his ears, too. His eyes were teary. His throat and the roof of his mouth were as sore as if they had been scraped with ground glass.

Frank hunched on a wooden bench after lunch, staring at his shoes and trying to decide what to do. He could not concentrate on the lessons. He seemed to be a beat behind everyone else: as if his body were going forward but his mind had been separated from it and couldn't catch up. Finally, midafternoon, he gathered all of his nerve and asked for permission to visit the office of Sister Mary Constance. He had only ever seen her once before, when he hurt his foot jumping off a swing on the playground. Now, once again, she towered over him, a black specter, the lower half of her face obscured by her wimple. She used large, rough hands to examine him. Pinching his chin between her fingers and thumb, she tilted his head back, felt his forehead, and looked in his open mouth.

"You don't appear to be ill," she said, speaking from the back of her nose. "Go back to your class for the rest of the day and your parents can decide tomorrow whether to send you."

Frank turned to go. But as he did, Sister Mary Constance saw the spots. Pustulant pinpricks of bright red dotted his arms and neck; when she lifted his shirt to check, she found they had exploded like constellations all over his chest and stomach. She did not utter a word. Carefully, she pulled his shirt down and tucked it back into his belt. Putting her hands on his shoulders, lightly now, she guided him to the small cot in the back of her office.

"I will send someone to the church for your mother," she said quietly to Frank.

Grateful, Frank laid his head down on the hard cot. He thought about his mother coming for him. He imagined her seizing her hat and coat and putting them on as she rushed out the door of the church. He wondered if she would make him ginger tea when they went home. He fell asleep wondering this.

By the time Mary reached the school, Frank was burning inside. His fingertips and palms were stigmatized with tiny blood spots. He was unconscious, deep in a dreamless sleep. His body shivered delicately as if from cold. She got him home with the help of Father Bernard, who carried Frank into the house and then drove off to Ted's jewelry store to bring him home. Mary put Frank into the double bed she and Ted shared; again she piled on the three quilts, then knelt beside him with a rosary laced between her fingers like a child's string game. *Hail Mary full of Grace.*

She did not move from the side of the bed, even when Ted came home and found the baby, Mickey, sitting on the floor and clinging to one of her feet. "Come on, Mary. You must get up and leave the boy to rest," he said. But she stayed. Finally Ted picked up Mickey, whose pants sagged low with wetness, and took him away. He changed the boy's diaper. In the living room, Father Bernard sat with Dr. Ross, who had just arrived and paused, his black-handled bag on his lap, to talk to the priest. Ted heard Father whisper, "Scarlet fever." He heard Mary muttering in the room down the hall. *The Lord is with Thee.*

Dr. Ross rose and went down the hall. He pushed through the bedroom door and glanced briefly at Frank lying lifeless on the bed, his face bright with flames of fever. The doctor smiled at Mary. "Well, I think we can do without a few of these," he said kindly, lifting two quilts from the bed. "Mary, why don't you bring me some ice. Crush it real fine, if you would, and put it in a bowl." Mary stood, her fingers still pinching their way down the row of beads. "And a few towels, dear," said the doctor. Mary went out the door, but turned to look at Frank as she departed. Dr. Ross shut the door behind her. *Blessed art Thou amongst women.*

In the living room, in the fireplace framed by Spanish tiles that they had been so proud to own when they bought the house, Ted built a fire. He stood next to the trifold screen that held the flames inside. One arm extended up, his hand flat against the brick chimney, he stared into the fire and smoked his pipe. Mary's youngest sister came to collect Mickey and Eleanor. All of Mary's sisters and brothers had offered to take the children, but Clara did not yet have children of her own so it was decided she should take them, in case they were contagious.

"Are you all right, dear?" Clara rushed through the living room, as if it were a crowded train station, and clenched Mary to her puffy breasts. She was just twenty-two, but already Clara had the clucky, wide-hipped appearance of a matron.

Mary shook her head. She clutched her beads. She felt a tearing inside her as she watched her two well children walk out the front door. *Blessed is the fruit of Thy womb.*

Dr. Ross was in the bedroom with Frank for a long time. Mary and Ted said almost nothing to each other. Ted stirred the fire with a long, black poker. Mary mated a basket full of thick, dark socks. Her rosary stayed wrapped in circlets around her wrist.

Sometime after midnight, the doctor came out into the living room and slumped silently into a chair. Within minutes, and without reporting a word, he was asleep, his head tilted back and his mouth open. Mary touched his arm, hoping he would wake up, hoping he would say something comforting. When he did not, she took out her ironing board and began on Ted's handkerchiefs.

At 3 A.M., the doctor awoke with a snore that turned into a grunt and then a start. He went to the bathroom and urinated. He washed his hands at the sink and examined his chin in the mirror. He walked slowly into the bedroom, snapping his suspenders into place in the hollows of his shoulders, but emerged quickly. His face was pale. Frank's dead, Mary thought, though she continued ironing. My child is dead.

"Mary . . . Ted," Ross said. Ted turned from where he stood, still watching the dying fire. "I think it's time to take Frank to the hospital." *Jesus.*

At St. Bridget's, nuns in white nurses' habits surrounded Frank. He lay on a rolling cot meant for an adult, his feet marking the length of his body only two-thirds of the way down from the top.

The surgeon who explained the procedure was young. He had slick dark hair and serious eyes. He looked like Frank might when he grew up. If he grew up. They would open Frank's back, the doctor explained, and massage his lungs manually. This had been known to work in extreme cases.

"And if we don't do this?" Ted asked.

"He might die," said the older, doctor version of Frank. "The fever is progressing very quickly and he's struggling to breathe."

Mary heard the promise in this. He might die if we don't do it, she reasoned silently, therefore he cannot die if we do. She grasped her bracelet of beads. "Go ahead," she said. "We give our consent." The surgeon looked to Ted, who cleared his throat and nodded.

At 8 A.M. on Wednesday morning the bell rang at Frank's school. His classmates, who were lined up outside three doors, filed in to the tune of a Sousa march. And a flock of blackbirds, heads bowed, circled Frank and rolled him into an operating room. *Holy Mary, Mother of God.*

At noon, Frank was out of surgery and in a private stall off the children's ward. His hands were lashed to the sides of his bed with straps, to keep him from falling out. He lay on a rubber sheet heaped with ice. His fever had reached 106 degrees and would not fall; his face and arms radiated red, hot vapors. Mary sat at his side, one hand parked inches away from his shoulder, afraid to touch him because she thought she might transfer more heat into his body. She had not eaten or slept. She smelled sour. Her hands had gnarled into large, knuckly claws, like the wicked witch's hands in Hansel and Gretel.

"Mary." Ted stood beside her. He rested his hand on her back, but she flinched it off. "You must get some rest. Mary! Let me take you home for an hour."

She did not answer. Her words would have been wasted. She could not leave her son, or he would die. She had to stay. She had to keep holding the line of his life. If only he were a baby again, and the other two were not yet born. If only she could pick him up and take him home and forget about this awful day, this awful night, this awful week ... If only she had not sent him to school.

She lowered her head to the bed and buried her face in the rough blanket, scratched it from side to side against her cheeks. Ted stroked her messy hair, and she let him. She knew there was an answer somewhere. If Frank woke up, he could give it to her. He could tell her. He could let her take back the day and just make her apologies for missing the Williams funeral. She would never again make the same mistake. She would know to stay home with her boy. *Pray for us sinners.*

Just past midnight on Thursday morning, in a dark crevice of night, Frank Donnelly died. His fever had risen to 108 degrees and his body had melted the ice he was packed in so quickly that his bed had turned into a pool of milky water. The red spots on his hands and legs and chest, instead of getting larger, had begun to fade, as if he no longer had enough blood inside him to fuel them. Frank's breathing became quieter, easier. His neck relaxed. His body released the disease and with it, his soul.

Mary was led away from his bed by two mannishly built nuns. They carried her between them. She did not make a sound. Ted, in a chair in a murky corner of the tiny room, cried quietly. Unnoticed. After a while he got up, went to the bed, and slipped his arms around Frank's body. It was still hot. The suture wound on Frank's back ran from a spot between his shoulder blades down to his waist, held tight with wide X's of heavy, black thread. His skin puckered pinkly at the entrance point of each stitch and wept tiny drops of fluid. Ted lay across Frank's body, rocking him. His white shirtsleeves became soaked from the water that streamed across the mattress.

At his aunt Clara's house in Robbinsdale, Mickey crawled into a linen cupboard in the dining room and sat on her best tablecloth, wrinkling it so that it would take her an hour in front of the mangle to press it before Christmas Eve dinner, weeks later. He held his knees to his chest. He felt hot; there was a pain in his head and his throat was squeezing shut. He sat in the dark, rocking back and forth, wishing for a butter sandwich. For his mother. For Frank.

At the hospital, Frank's body was anointed with oil. He was wrapped in a clean sheet. Under the sheet, he held the rosary that Mary had placed in his hands before the nuns came to take him away. *Now and at the hour of our death.*

Frank was buried on Saturday and placed in the Catholic cemetery next to his great-grandmother, under a stone that said, "Beloved Son and Brother." Mickey and Eleanor and their parents sat in the front pew under the huge ceramic Jesus Christ, hanging on the cross, feet entwined, thorns circling His head, blood flowing down His fingers. Eleanor was next to her father. Ted had one arm around her and he kept pulling her closer to him and whispering, "Hush now. Hush. Don't worry. He sees."

She wore what was to have been her Christmas dress—a dress that she would stuff into an old oilcan in the basement when they returned home. She looked up at Christ on the cross and saw Frank's face. She looked at the statue of the Blessed Virgin and saw Frank's face. She looked all around the church and saw Frank's face. At the wake the night before, her mother had told her she would never see Frank's face again. She cried, as much out of confusion as grief.

Mickey sat next to his mother. It was the first time in his life he had ever worn long woolen pants and a white-collared shirt. Just like Frank. He stared straight ahead, his dark eyes clear and vacant. He did not see Frank. He would never see Frank. Because his mother had sent Frank to school.

Mickey had awakened in the dark, alone in his room, that morning. Frank was not in the bed beside him. No one was in the bed beside him, but there was something in the room with him—a creature breathing green fumes and trying to snatch him from his bed. Mickey got out of bed on his own. He went to the doorway of his parents' bedroom and pushed open the door. The room was dark, but they weren't there. They had disappeared. Just like Frank.

Then he heard the voices. He heard his mother coughing . . . no, crying. She was choking on the words, yelling in a whispered voice. They were in the kitchen. Mickey slid his feet slowly down the hall. He waited outside the door of the kitchen. He knew he shouldn't be listening, but he didn't want to go back in his room, alone, with the monster that was ready to eat him and make him dead. Just like Frank.

"You're making yourself sick, Mary," he heard his father say. "You've got to think of the other children. You've got to stop this and get some sleep."

Mickey pushed the door open an inch. He saw his parents in the too-bright light of the yellow kitchen. He saw his mother's face twist up horribly. He saw her hit his father with one of her wide, ringed hands.

"It is my fault, it is!" She hit him again and again. "I shouldn't have made him go to school. If I hadn't made him go to school . . ." Hit, hit, hit. "He would still . . ." Hit, hit. "Be alive!" Finally, Ted caught her arms. He said nothing. His face was gray and old. He stood with Mary, her wrists locked in his hands, and they stared at each other.

Mickey turned away from the door. He went back to bed. The monster in his room didn't scare him anymore. He knew where people died: at school. He knew what had happened now. He knew that he should never go to school, or he would be made dead. Just like Frank. *Amen.*

In early February, Mary got up one morning, set the bacon on the stove to fry, put the coffee on to boil, and suddenly felt the room begin to tilt around her. She was sick that morning, and three more times that week. By late February, Mary was sure. And by mid-March, her doctor was, too. On Easter Sunday, at dinner with her parents and six of her brothers and sisters and their wives and husbands and children, Mary announced that she was going to have a baby. There was a silence, but it wasn't long. Then everyone laughed and cheered and congratulated Ted. The men wrestled him away for cigars. They told him how a new baby would keep him young—even at forty-nine. No one mentioned Frank.

Mickey, who had turned three during the dark week after Frank's funeral, could use the toilet now and he wore white buttoned shirts every day. He slept alone in the room with his monster every night and dreaded the day when he would have to go to school. He didn't understand why a baby was coming instead of Frank. But he never asked anyone about it. Certain things, he knew even at three, were never meant to be explained.

6

WHEN I RETURNED from helping Matt in the bathroom, I found my mother, still standing by the open dresser, staring down at Mickey's picture. Downstairs, the grandfather clock chimed the half hour.

"May I take it?" I asked, holding out my hand.

"This?" My mother held up the photograph but kept her eyes averted. "Why?"

I shrugged. But she handed it over without argument and I took the picture carefully, by its edges. "What was Mickey like? Did he have any unusual marks? Or, uh, odd behaviors? Any symptoms like Edward's?"

"I wouldn't have seen much of his body." She walked to the dresser and began repacking the drawer, her back to me. "We were pretty modest in those days. But of course, there were the times we went swimming." She squinted vaguely into space. "No. I don't remember anything. No marks. There were . . ." She paused, hands still for a moment, then continued. "No, nothing."

"Are you sure? Because if there's anything that could relate to Edward, I should tell the doctor." I tried to keep the impatience from leaking into my voice.

My mother moved slowly. "Just what I told you. Mickey was different: he was just a troubled boy. Not like Edward. My brother always spoke. He slept."

We both waited in silence while her implication, *Your son doesn't speak or sleep,* echoed through the air. And I felt the same shameful anger for my mother that I had directed at Carrie in the Aurora library, two years earlier. It seemed everyone was determined to point out how contrary my situation was, how unlike theirs.

"I have to go," I said, checking my watch for the dozenth time. Eleven-thirty-four. "Thanks for keeping Matt."

My mother turned to me, smiling. Somehow, while I wasn't looking, she had wiped her face clean again and erased all the sorrow. "That," she said emphatically, "is my pleasure."

After I got out of my parents' neighborhood, I sped most of the way into the city, to the place where Mariel and I always met. I paid to park in a nearby lot and rushed through the door, stopping just inside to glance at the woman who sat at our regular table. While I had changed repeatedly over the years since we'd lived together, stretching and shrinking, folds of skin collapsing again after each baby, Mariel had always remained the same: compact and strong. Until now. She still had the long, dark tangle of hair. But when she raised her head from the cup she had been blowing into, her cheekbones stuck out like arrows. She swallowed and sinew appeared in her long neck. She was hunched over on the chair, legs folded, looking like a prehistoric bird.

"Hi, sweetie." She stood and draped one arm over me, a long, hinged bone that bent stiffly to squeeze. "You look . . . huge. How are you?"

I held on to the back of a chair with one hand and unwound the wool cape I wore with the other. "Tired."

"I'll bet. Let me get you something."

I set my teeth and thought about eating; the poppy seed cake felt heavy in my stomach. "Nothing, I'm fine." I perched carefully on a wrought-iron chair with a seat the size of a salad plate. "So. What's wrong?"

Mariel slumped in her chair and sighed. I barely recognized this fragile woman, so weak and insecure. "It's possible," she drawled, "Scott may have a gambling problem."

The surprise of this caught my attention and a spark of interest flared inside me. For once, the problem was not mine, my marriage, my child. "What makes you think so?"

"Money." Her voice was flat. "A lot of it is just . . . gone."

"What do you mean? Yours? His? How much?"

"It's hard to say."

I picked up Mariel's cup and took a tiny sip. Her coffee was thick with sugar, unmelted so grains remained on my tongue and I sucked on them.

"Here." Mariel had reached into her purse and pulled out a sheaf of papers—receipts, credit card statements, canceled checks. "I need you to help me get through this. I stopped at forty thousand."

"Dollars?" The awful truth was that, for a moment, the sheer largeness of this number actually thrilled me. It was more than Jack and I combined had ever made in a year. I rubbed my forehead as if it were possible to erase these traitorous thoughts and leaned over to pull a calculator from my purse.

"That's why I love you," Mariel said, grinning so her wide, drawn face looked like a jack-o'-lantern's. "You're the only person I know who carries a calculator."

I bent over the papers and worked quickly, jotting figures and adding. There was, in fact, $83,000 missing. Spent, withdrawn from various accounts, charged as cash advances on credit cards, all in the previous twelve weeks. Mariel tightened as I added the figures, arms circled around her own body like she was using her hands to hold herself together. At some point, a cup of tea appeared in front of me and I drank it.

"Okay. I think this is the total." When I looked up into her frightened face, it reminded me of Edward's and I realized I had forgotten about him, about the doctor, about the weight of my own body, for a blissful half hour. Carefully, I shifted my weight in the chair. "But, ah, aren't these *your* credit cards? I mean, how did he get ahold of them? You're not married so he can't technically—"

"I gave them to him." The husky assertiveness was back in her voice, along with a defensive edge. "It's not like he stole them. He's been helping me run the farm for a year, so he had the cards for expenses."

"Oh." The last time we saw Scott, Jack and I were sitting in a restaurant where Mariel had invited us to celebrate when she received tenure. After dinner, the waiter discreetly set a leather folder between Scott and Jack but Scott had picked it up and tossed it to Mariel, saying loudly,

This is your deal, babe. Then he'd laughed and nudged Jack, like it was a great joke. "When did you first get concerned?"

Mariel was opening sugar packets and dumping the contents on the table—small, glinty mounds of white. "Well, the last time, it was less. In March, when Scott took a month off from work and stayed with me. There were some . . . issues."

"This has happened before?"

"Not exactly." She squirmed. "It was only like twelve thousand. He makes that in a week when he's got work."

Scott was a performance consultant, which always sounded to me like some sort of modern dance instructor but had, Mariel assured me, something to do with sales and marketing at big corporations. He wore silk shirts and a large gold watch that slipped around his wrist when he moved. However, for a successful businessman, I'd always thought he spent a great deal of time on the farm in Iowa.

"So what happened? With the twelve thousand?"

"He said he'd get help. So I took care of it for him."

"How?"

She sat up straight and gathered her hair at the back of her neck. Her voice, when she spoke, was hard. "I took a second mortgage on the farm."

That's when I felt a stab of real horror, for my best friend and for my son. Mariel was at home on that piece of rolling green land in a way she never had been in the city. She loved it there, and so did Edward. Even when he couldn't hear us, he seemed to listen to the animals; a lamb would quiver up to him on shaky legs and Edward's head would stop bobbing. He would look into the creature's eyes and hold out his hand. "How are you making the payments?" I asked.

"It's hard." Mariel smiled and smashed a sugar mountain with her fist. "Last month, I called my dad."

"For money?"

She nodded. "He still has tons of it. Bastard. He had it all hidden away while he was in prison."

"Did he give it to you?"

She shrugged. "Sure. He thinks it's going to make a difference. Like I'm going to forgive him."

I touched her hand, my throat filling with relief. The farm was safe. Though the thought of Scott occupying a permanent place there made me cringe.

"So." She sniffed and leaned back, looking more like herself, less cadaverous. "Tell me about the doctor's visit."

"I'm going in this afternoon to give him the whole history. He's mentioned one gruesome degenerative disease . . . but I keep thinking about the times Edward's gotten better." I worked hard not to sound like I was pleading, though Mariel, of all people, would know exactly what I was doing. "There have been days all along where he seemed almost normal. And that whole month a year ago last March, right after his birthday. I swear, I thought he was coming back, all on his own; like maybe turning five was the key. Then there was that period last spring."

She'd quit with the sugar, but I had started now—making anthills and tunnels through the crystals. "If he were really sick, if there were really something wrong with his brain or his nervous system, you'd think it would be, you know, steadier."

"That makes sense." It was Mariel the professor speaking. Reasonable, rational, mollifying. Her tone made me panic.

"I really think it's the sleep at the root of it all. If Newberg can just help us get him to sleep without—"

She put her hand over mine. Her nails were ragged and worn and as she stroked the back of my hand, I could feel the blisters she'd gotten from all the long-handled tools—rakes, hoes, shovels—she used on the farm. "You did what you had to do. Believe that. You're the best mother I've ever seen."

I flushed and swallowed. "Thanks."

She squeezed my hand once, then let it go. "Are you going to tell this doctor everything?"

It was the question I'd been trying to work out in my head all day, and the night before. I closed my eyes. "I don't know."

Aside from Jack and myself, Mariel was the only person on earth who knew the truth about Edward and what we did for him. To him.

Now, I wanted someone to tell me if confessing the whole story might help me save my son.

7

IT HAD STARTED on a cool, damp day in April, a little more than eight months earlier.

I was lying on the couch in the dim blue of dusk, dizzied by the way my vision had gone blurry and knowing exactly what it meant. I counted on my fingers: eleven days, maybe twelve. A pregnancy test might not detect it yet, but I knew.

The arguments we'd made for having another child wound through my head. We wanted Matthew to have help in case he should end up taking care of Edward. Jack used to say that would never happen, but after six months as a cop he'd seen hundreds of homeless men wandering the streets of Minneapolis in raggedy clothes, talking to themselves, staring at their hands in a way that had become chillingly familiar. At night, Jack whispered that he saw our son's face on vagrants as he read them their rights—blank eyes gazing off over his shoulder, letting his words rain down on them but not hearing.

And we wanted people to stop treating the boys like they were opponents in some sort of morbid life game: the smart one and the sick one. Out in the yard one day, I'd heard a neighbor ask someone whether Edward was the "boy with all the problems" or his little brother. By having a third, we would create a triangle of children rather than two points at either end of a straight line. It would be a more complex relationship, harder to categorize.

Also, Jack would say as he lifted the T-shirt I'd worn to bed, it would be nice to have a baby in the house again.

Now that it was a reality I was convincing myself all over again that we weren't crazy, shuffling and reshuffling the reasons for this baby, and that's when the phone rang—a shrill lonely sound in the waning light of afternoon. I sat up and lifted the receiver. The sun was low in the sky, pink and gold, behind the black skeletons of trees in our yard. "Hello?" I asked softly, careful of my own aching head.

"This is Harriet Nelson," said a clipped voice. It was Edward's kindergarten teacher, from the mainstream school I had insisted he attend. "I thought you should know, I was reading aloud today. But the other children were having trouble hearing me because of Edward. Don't you think it's time for him to see a doctor?"

The nausea crested and I paused. Harriet was like a storybook version of a teacher, in long pleated skirts and pearls. She was the one who had informed me, with pursed lips, that Edward couldn't stand on one foot during a game of Simon Says. I argued that he could but refused to, which seemed, in the end, to prove her point rather than mine.

Of course, she knew we'd been to doctors. They all had theories, but none of them could tell us how to stop the noises. Edward tended to be quiet while things were moving around him; he would curl in on himself and hold his hand in front of his eyes. But when his surroundings were tranquil, he often filled the stillness by howling. During naptime, read-along at school, when the house grew heavy and silent at night. Typically he would begin by humming, then move to more urgent canine sounds. Since Christmas, it had only gotten worse.

"I'm sorry," I said. "We're trying to get his howling under control. He *is* seeing doctors, but so far—"

"No, no, it's not that. It's his breathing I'm calling you about. Haven't you noticed how heavy and stuffy it's become?"

Had I? My mind played back miles of audiotape from the last month and I heard, as if for the first time, the background noise of Edward's constant snuffling. It was the sound of someone sucking through a straw filled with something thick, like a milk shake. But louder.

"I looked in his throat with a flashlight," Harriet continued crisply. "His tonsils are huge. They're actually meeting, blocking his airway. I just thought you should know."

I pictured her doing this, turning Edward's head up and peering inside him with her light. I glanced at the digital clock in the VCR; it was 5:38 P.M. and this woman was still thinking about Edward. I wanted to do something for her in return, perhaps invite her for dinner. I opened my mouth to ask but remembered just in time that I had nothing planned and probably would end up making scrambled eggs and toast—if I could stand the smell.

I thanked Harriet twice, hoping I sounded sincere. The darkening room was soupy and green by the time I hung up the phone. But then I sat, perplexed, because I didn't know whom to call. Edward had not seen a regular doctor since the one recommended by the special ed teacher, because he'd never been sick. Not a single fever or cold. It occurred to me that our failure to notice Edward could hardly breathe might be a sign we weren't ready to have another baby.

Suddenly, I had a nightmarish vision of the next nine months: fretting constantly that I was hurting the baby inside me, waiting to see if it would be born healthy. Then the years after that, understanding what most parents never have to—that a normal start is no guarantee. Children change overnight; they stop hearing your voice and laugh uncontrollably in the middle of the night but cannot tell you why. They eat pencils and rock and hit their heads with the palms of their hands. And then, just when you think nothing else can go wrong, their throats close off.

The room was nearly dark now and I felt weighted, as if someone had covered my body in the lead blankets they use in hospitals during X-rays. I could hear the boys in their bedroom, bumping the walls with their toy cars. Matt was making highway noises, probably moving his cars in circles. Edward, of course, was lining his up end to end. They would be content to play together this way until Edward ran out of cars for the chain and reached for his brother's. I listened. Edward was breathing a low, dragony sound.

I lay back down and waited for Jack to open the door.

"What if he's really sick?" I asked before he'd even had a chance to take off his belt and lock up his gun. I got up and followed him into the bedroom, pleased by the rhythmic sound of leather creaking as he swayed from side to side. A thought popped into my head and I blurted it out without thinking. "Oh, my God. There are viruses that could damage the baby."

He'd been unbuttoning his shirt but this made him look up quickly. "What baby? Are you pregnant?"

I sat on the bed, embarrassed. I never knew how to handle these occasions. "Yes. I think so. I mean, I'm almost sure."

He walked over and raised me off the bed, as if I were the child. And he hugged me hard. "Don't worry," he said. "She'll be perfect."

"She?"

"No doubt." Jack ran his fingers through my hair, grazing the tops of my ears, and finally my headache eased. A girl. I had never considered such a thing. But this could be the answer. Girls, I'd been told, almost never became like Edward.

After he changed into jeans and took a beer from the refrigerator, Jack went to his car and came back with his police flashlight—a foot-long aluminum club. He called Edward to the living room, pried open his mouth, and shined the light inside.

"Christ, she's right. He's breathing through a pinhole." Jack crouched and worked the flashlight around, inspecting from all the angles, leaning back to take long drinks from the sweating can.

The next day, I took Edward to the children's clinic, the one where he had failed a full battery of developmental tests at age four. And we were assigned to their newest recruit.

"Oh yeah, these need to come out immediately. We're going to charge you folks by the pound," the doctor said, winking. He pulled a roll of stickers out of his pocket and handed Edward two, pretending not to notice when Edward purposely dropped them from the table, then leapt down and squatted so he could watch the stickers waft to the floor.

Edward's name was placed on a waiting list for the first surgical cancellation. "Be ready to go immediately when I call," the doctor said. "I honestly don't think I've ever seen a set that big."

Three days later, Matt was napping while I sat in a chair trying to read words that wavered all over the page. Again the phone rang, but this time it was the receptionist at the doctor's office, telling me to hurry. A sudden rainstorm had come up—thick, black clouds pressed against our windows, hail pelted the roof, wind sliced horizontally through space—and a patient driving in from out of town had called to say he couldn't make it. If I got him there within the hour, Edward could have that man's appointment and his surgery slot the next morning. I had just enough time to retrieve Edward from school and drive to the clinic, if traffic was light.

My stomach rolled in time with the rush of air outside. I'd taken a home test and our third baby was confirmed. I went to the kitchen for a box of crackers and began eating one after another, pushing them into my mouth as I got Matt out of bed and began dressing him. I held out clean underwear, socks, and pants, using one hand to wipe away the sweat that broke out on my forehead every time a yellow wave like seasickness moved through me.

We put on jackets with hoods and raised them. On the way to the car, I hunched over Matt so the hail wouldn't hit him. The chunks were tiny, pebble size, spattering my back like raisins. It was ridiculous, I knew, but after the talk of unknown brain damage I'd grown acutely protective of both boys' heads. So far it seemed to be working with Matt: he knew all his numbers and letters. He spoke to us and laughed in the right places when he watched cartoons.

But just lately, there was one possible sign: Matt had been talking about falling cars in an obsessive way. Again and again he drew cars, bright blobs, always near cliffs, lying upside down in lakes of crayoned blue. He assured us each time, as if it were a mantra, that everyone inside the car had survived.

At the hospital they gave Edward a Winnie-the-Pooh gown that he wore like a tent, his wan face pale above the whirl of happy orange and yellow figures. A woman who introduced herself as our Child Life worker set him on her lap and read from a picture book about a swan with a sore throat who had his tonsils removed and felt so much better afterward, he was able to fly from the rooftop and rejoin his family. But Edward didn't listen. While she read, he pulled repeatedly on his sleeve, stretching Eeyore out of shape. I touched the fabric and it was stiff with a tight burlap weave.

He can't hear you when he's wearing something like that, I wanted to tell her. *And, anyway, he can't follow the words, or care about what happens to the swan.*

"Now, Mom and Dad can come with you while the doctor gives you the sleep medicine." The woman was bent over Edward, her nose very close to his face. Close enough to bite. Would he do that?

Jack and I were outfitted with papery blue scrub suits and stretchy gauze hats. We were not given masks. An orderly who looked as young as the boy who bagged my groceries trundled the gurney forward and we fell in step behind, shuffling in our paper slippers. Inside the operating room was maddeningly bright, like a planet that was too close to the sun. I remembered this from the delivery room when Edward was born, the point where they switched on all the lights and my pain became extended in the relentless flash of white.

"Count backward from ten," said a masked figure without preamble. It made no sense to me that his mouth and nose were covered when ours weren't. When he lowered the rubbery tentacle of the anesthesia machine to Edward's face, I panicked and grabbed for Jack's hand: we had never met this person. How did we know he was doing the right thing to our son?

Vapors slid into the room, a combination of menthol and diesel fuel. Suddenly, I thought of the baby inside me, breathing in these poisons every time I inhaled. I tried to hold my breath, stopping only to sip the air—as little as I possibly could—when I grew light-headed. An image unfolded of me, at thirty, sitting in a doctor's office with another damaged child, thinking back to this as the moment I ruined another baby's brain. Then, I heard someone counting.

I took a step forward to look at Edward, but he was saying nothing, only struggling against the hand of the masked man, trying to get out from under the evil black suction cup that was being lowered onto his face.

Still, the voice went on: *eight, seven, six . . .*

I stepped back again and saw Jack's fingers tracing the numbers on Edward's arm, heard Jack's voice lowering as the numbers descended, reaching one, saying zero, then in a husky whisper: "You sleep now."

But Edward *doesn't* sleep, I thought. What if anesthesia doesn't work on him either? What if they think he's asleep but he's really awake, paralyzed, screaming inside? Then I looked and saw him lying still with his eyes closed, breathing steadily and rhythmically as people moved around him, talking and setting up equipment. A laugh broke out somewhere along the perimeter of the room and sudden, angry tears started in my eyes. They should be paying attention to the work at hand, taking Edward more seriously.

Jack led me out and we went to a waiting room—a warm place with stale, rebreathed air, but I gulped it compulsively in an effort to give back to the baby what I'd denied her during the minutes we spent in the OR. A television played a soap opera and I tried to watch, but all the characters looked alike to me and I couldn't keep the story lines straight. My mind wandered and the room got hazy and suddenly I was dreaming of Edward on a rolling bed, forgotten, discarded in some dark closet in the basement of the hospital. Mute and alone.

Then suddenly a woman called our names and we followed her to a brightly painted children's ward, six beds long. Edward was sitting up in the last one, eyes glittering, his face smooth and pink. Beside him, holding a cup with a crooked straw, was a very large man wearing blue scrubs. He was as broad and tall as a statue, with blond hair sweeping across his forehead. And this colossus seemed absolutely overjoyed to see us. He shook our hands with gusto, engulfing mine, making even Jack's look normal size.

"You got a great kid here." He reached out with one huge finger and touched Edward tenderly on the forehead. "Eddie's a real smart little guy. Aren't you, Superman?"

The relief receded and my stomach began to churn: I hated this sort of cheerful game. Then I looked at Jack and saw a smile break across his dark face. He gazed at Edward and touched the same spot on his forehead the nurse had, as if it were a button you could press.

"I've never seen a kid wake up as nice as your son." The giant man eased Edward down onto his pillow and pulled up the blankets with hands that straightened, tightened, tucked, and smoothed in one long motion. "He just opened his eyes and said, 'Where's my mom?' and I told him you were right downstairs waiting for him to feel better and he said, 'I feel better now.'"

Jack's hand was on the hollow of Edward's neck, feeling for a pulse,

I thought, assuring himself he was really there, our son, speaking, making sense.

"That's not possible." I sounded hard. But the nurse didn't seem to notice.

"Yeah, I was surprised, too. Lots of kids feel terrible after a T and A. But I think Eddie was telling the truth. I asked him if his throat hurt and he said, 'Just a little,' so I gave him a drink of water. Then he told me he was okay and again, he said he just wanted to see his mom. So I had someone go for you."

I stared at Edward. He had closed his eyes and I realized I hadn't seen him look so comfortable since he was a baby. I crossed my arms and whispered, so I wouldn't disturb him, "Edward doesn't talk that way. He doesn't say that many words in a week."

The man looked like he might laugh. "Why would I lie to you?"

"Why would I lie?" Edward croaked, a turtle-ish sound.

It was echolalic, I started to explain. But then I stopped. Edward hadn't mimicked the intonation, or completed the phrase with exactly the same words.

"I'm hungry," Edward said then. "I would like for something to eat."

I sat on the bed and grabbed his hands. This seemed to scare him, but I kept pulling until he was in my lap and I could hold on to the real boy he was pretending to be.

Later, a lab tech came to draw his blood and afterward she handed him a red Popsicle.

"He can't have that." I began to recite the list: no artificial dyes, refined sugar, NutraSweet or MSG, new carpet, synthetic air fresheners, scented toilet paper, or dryer sheets. But before I could take the Popsicle, Edward had stuck it in his mouth and gone back to watching a Disney movie. I'd taken him to see the same film in the theater, but he had twisted away from the screen and flipped the cushion of the adjoining seat up and down until people around us became angry and we had to leave. Now, he looked up at the TV and laughed.

I glanced over at Jack, who was watching, too, and reaching to accept a tray from a large, gray-haired woman.

"You looked hungry," she said. Women were always feeding Jack, who, now that the enormous male nurse was gone, appeared as he usually did: oversize and slightly work-worn, gentle, watchful. He grinned at her and waved his fork before eating a piece of cake in three bites.

I was sitting right next to them, but Edward and Jack looked like people in a picture: a still life of how I'd always wished our life could be. If Matt were here, too, I thought, I would never want to leave this place.

Edward took codeine-laced Tylenol every six hours for nearly two weeks. At night, he slept. And after the first couple of nights, when I couldn't stop getting out of bed to watch him, I slept, too.

On the afternoon of the fourth day, I sat on the couch with both boys and read *Crictor, the Boa Constrictor*. "I would like for to have a snake," Edward said when I was done.

"Really?" I asked. If it would help, I was seriously considering it. "What would you name him?"

Edward looked at the cover of the book. "Crictor," he said, lying back on a cushion and closing his eyes disapprovingly, as if I were the one who hadn't been listening.

"I would name mine Oswald," Matt said. He snuggled close to me and whispered, "But they kind of scare me, Mom. Maybe I really don't want one."

Edward was still, eyes shut, like he was on display. "Snakes aren't scary." His voice was distant, as if it came from a place deep inside him. "There are many things that could be very scary. But they are never snakes, or animals, or cars."

Since he'd come home from the hospital, there had been several statements like this: truths about Edward that would suddenly tumble out. One of them, I was sure, would illuminate the last two years. I kept listening, waiting for the explanation. "What, Edward?" I tried to make my voice fluid and hypnotic. "Tell me about what scares you."

"I'm tired." He turned toward the wall and yawned noisily. Then I heard him snoring, lightly, and realized this was the miracle.

I picked up Matt, whose eyes had started to go glossy, too. "Nap?"

"I'm hungry," he said, laying his warm face against my neck.

We sat in the kitchen while he ate graham crackers. Outside, the sky was clear, transparent in a way that did not look real.

"He doesn't like talking or people or smells."

I stared at Matt. His cheeks glistened and his eyelids were half-moons, as if he'd gone into a trance.

"What do you mean?"

Matt startled a little at the sound of my voice and caught his body, as if he'd been about to fall. "You asked what he was scared of. It's when they all mix." He was fighting to stay awake and I put my hand on his shoulder to steady him.

"The talking and the people and the smells?"

"Yes. When they get all mixed up. He doesn't like that. It's like bad snakes to him."

When I put him in his bed, Matt fell immediately to sleep and then everything was quiet. The house felt enchanted. I tried to read but could not. So I sat in front of a muted TV, watching the screen shift and change, waiting to see what would happen when this spell wore off.

8

I TOLD THIS part of the story to Dr. Newberg immediately.

I'd left Mariel at the bagel shop and gone directly to his office in the very children's hospital where Edward had awakened from his surgery eight months earlier. Dr. Newberg sat opposite me. When I'd entered the room, he had shown me to a set of leather chairs in the corner of his office. "I never use that," he said, waving at the large desk that was covered with papers and open books. Newberg shrugged. "Too formal."

Now, he sat forward in his seat, eyes bright, waiting.

"I'm telling too much. Do you want to know all this?" My throat ached with longing. *Please say yes. Let me tell the whole story.* No one with the power to help Edward had ever taken the time to hear everything— to know that he was different from the way he appeared. I could still feel the child he was, before Aurora, underneath the shell of the one he had become. If I could convince the right person, maybe together we would be able to excavate the child inside. That is, assuming he did not have a fatal disease.

"I want to know everything. That's why we're here." Newberg leaned forward and put his hand on my arm. "But . . . I'm sorry, you must be uncomfortable. Do you need to get up, have a drink, or, uh, use the bathroom?"

I shifted on the smooth seat and imagined hoisting myself out of the chair, bulging stomach in the lead, while being watched by this delicate man. "No, I'm fine. Water, maybe."

He moved a little like a leprechaun, feet in small, black shoes that seemed to meet and click as he trotted toward the desk and picked up his phone. "Marie, would you bring us a couple of sparkling waters, please?"

She was at the door in what felt like seconds, smiling broadly not at me but at him. "Perfect," he said, taking the tray. "Oh, and tell Sarah good luck. We're all very proud of her."

He tipped his head toward the door after the woman had thanked him and gone. "Her daughter. Sarah. She's in the regional figure-skating championships this weekend. Very talented girl."

The mineral water gave off a metallic vapor as he poured. I sat silent, staring at my feet, my heart pounding with frustration.

He glanced at my face. "Not a fan of figure skating?"

I flicked my hand at the closed door. "It's just hard to hear some-times. Other people's children become violin players and debate cap-tains and figure-skating champions."

"And that's what you want for Edward?"

I pictured my son, grown tall, still silent, leaping and then landing, sending a spray of ice dust in his wake. Then spinning so fast his body became a blur. "Sure. That would be nice. Anything successful. Anything that isn't this."

Newberg had begun pulling on his hair again, drawing a strand down to meet his eyebrows. He had nice eyebrows: thick, but not sinister.

"I want him to be like he was, then, right after the surgery," I went on. "I had him then. He was back and I could talk to him and he knew me. But I couldn't even enjoy it, really, because I was so afraid it wasn't going to last."

The Sunday after Edward's tonsillectomy, we went to my parents' house for dinner and my father asked Questions. This was his game, one he created and played with me and my sister when we were children. *Who was the vice president under Abraham Lincoln? What's four times seven divided by two plus six? Which elements make up water?*

He had always asked Edward baby questions. *Where's your nose? What does a dog say?* Even so, Edward rarely answered.

I was helping my mother carry the meal to the table when I heard my father's voice in the next room: "Edward, point to the book. Do you know which one is the book?"

I put the dish down on the table and went to where my father sat in his chair, the two boys on the floor at his feet. "Harder, Dad. Go ahead. You can ask him real questions now."

My father screwed up his face, causing his entire bald head to wrinkle, and put a finger to his lips. "Sshhhh! You. Go back in the kitchen and stay out of this."

I looked at Edward. He was hiding, pretending to be his old self. His face was placid, but I saw a bit of tightening at the cheekbones. He didn't want to let on that he'd changed; he was that smart. "Really, Dad. You have to listen to me. He's better now."

My father made a sweeping motion with his hand. "Leave," he said. "I am the one in charge of the Questions."

I went to the kitchen, but stood just inside the door listening. He paused. Then: "Edward, what's four minus two?"

There was a long silence. I clenched my toes inside my shoes, so tightly they grew cold.

"Edward, if you have *four*"—I knew my father was holding up four fingers now, wagging them like tentacles—"and you take away *two* . . ." In my mind, I saw him fold two of them down with his other hand. I stood, sweating, praying.

There was a low noise that meant my father was about to speak again and then I heard Edward mutter, "Two."

At dinner, Edward used his fork and sat up straight, looking around the dining room. After the children left the table, Jack and I sat with my parents over dessert.

"He's better." I stared down into my tea. "Don't you think?"

"I think so." My mother cut another small slice of cheesecake and put it on her plate quickly, as if she were hiding it even from herself.

My father raised his glasses to the top of his bald head and stared at the ceiling, scratching the whiskers on his chin. We all waited. "Weeellllll . . ." He blinked for many seconds then lowered his glasses and looked at me. "I wouldn't get my hopes up if I were you. Edward's had up times before and they never held. I think you should be prepared to see him go back down again."

"This time is different," I insisted. "It's been days and he just keeps learning and putting things together. The surgery really changed him."

"I doubt it." My father sounded as if he were commenting on the state of the economy, whether the market would rebound soon.

It made my throat itch. I made a sound like an embarrassed laugh, for which I hated myself. "Why would you say that?" I cut another piece of cake, too, and began eating it. Fast. Barely tasting it but feeling the cream cheese smooth against my tongue.

My father reached over and took my hand. His was white and pillowy, far softer than mine. "I just want to save you some pain, Rachel. I'm trying to get you to look at things realistically. It's never been your strong suit, you know."

I looked at Jack and raised my eyebrows. His face darkened but he was silent; he finished his last bite of cake and pushed away from the table to go check on the boys.

. . .

I had a theory: that Edward's tonsils had been too powerful. They'd performed their immune function too well, fending off all invaders, from cold germs to mold spores to comet dust, and subsumed his brain with busywork. Once they were gone his mind had been cleared of static; he could think and talk and return to being the boy he was always meant to be.

Even Jack was skeptical of this explanation. He just wanted to enjoy having his son back and had grown impatient with my need to talk about how it had happened. Only Harriet Nelson seemed as interested as I was in the source of Edward's transformation.

"It's a miracle," she said the day he returned to school and said, without prompting, "Hello, Mrs. Nelson."

"Edward, how good to see you back." She picked at the beads of her necklace. "How do you feel?"

"Better," he said, looking straight up at her. "Like a boy, I think."

Her wrinkled face with its splotches of too-red blush had an almost youthful look of wide-eyed awe. She placed Edward in line, then came back to me for a moment. "I still can't believe it. I've never seen a change so complete." Her voice caught and she cleared her throat. "I think we're on the right track now."

9

MY HIPS HAD begun to ache and I couldn't sit any longer. I struggled out of my chair and walked to the window in Dr. Newberg's office. Outside, the sun had weakened and an oaky color was gathering along the tops of bare trees. A lone bird—probably a black crow, hardy enough to scavenge through the winter—circled slowly across the sky.

"Standing in his classroom that day," I said, turning back to face him, "it was the first time I didn't hate all the other kids, all the healthy ones who knew how to use scissors. Isn't that awful?"

He shrugged, got up, turned on a desk lamp. I returned to my chair and sat offstage, outside the circle it shone. "It didn't last," he said. Not a question.

I breathed deeply, in and then out. "No," I choked. The grief remained as sharp as it had been six months before.

"Tell me about it."

I looked at my watch. Jack was picking up Edward from his after-school program right about now, leaning over to help him buckle his boots. I pictured them shadowed, in relief against the gymnasium's light green walls.

"It was just like the first time. Only . . ." He pushed a tissue box toward me and I pulled myself tight. I did not cry in front of doctors. "Only this time, I knew what was happening. I watched it, one sign at a time until he was . . ."

"Like before?"

I looked down at my lap. "I can't tell." I was hungry and needed to urinate, but the desire to keep telling my story was stronger. "I can't remember anymore who he was when."

Edward stopped taking codeine on the twelfth day after surgery. For a short time, he stayed suspended in rosy-cheeked wellness, talking to us over dinner, coloring pictures with Matt as they lay on their floor together before bed. Then one night a week or so later, I heard him up in the bathroom at least five times. At breakfast, his skin had begun to go a familiar gray.

It was a warm morning in May. Matt and I put raincoats over our pajamas and walked Edward to school; along the way, I pointed out a walking stick on a leaf but Edward looked away, swinging his head from side to side. When we reached the playground, he ignored the children who called his name and batted away the arm of a little girl who ran to hand him a ball. I delivered him directly to Harriet, who took him by the shoulders but said nothing when I looked at her. I wheeled around, picked up Matt, and stalked all the way home.

Once inside, I called and left a message on Jack's voice mail. I was sobbing. *Edward is slipping back, I don't know how to hold on to him.* When Jack came home that afternoon, he went straight to Edward's room. Ten minutes later he came into the kitchen, where I was furiously tearing lettuce, took a beer from the refrigerator, and stood drinking it, looking at his feet.

"You saw it, didn't you?"

"He's not . . . as good as he was." Jack still wasn't looking at me.

"He's right back to the way he used to be." My abdomen felt sore, as if the baby were already growing rapidly, stretching it. I tried not to smell anything but it was raining and even the countertops gave off a dead, plastic odor.

"Not completely . . . I don't think he's quite as bad." Jack pulled out a pocketknife and began cleaning under his fingernails with the blade.

Stop doing that, I almost screamed. *Stop pretending!* Instead, I told him I felt sick and asked him to get dinner for the boys while I went to bed. Hours later, I roused myself from the messy tangle of covers and went downstairs to find Jack at the table playing a board game with the children. I stood in the doorway, wondering why the scene made me so uneasy: everything was in place, the dishes drying in the wooden rack next to the sink, kitchen gleaming. And my family was gathered, this man with two beautiful boys. Then I realized what was bothering me: Matt, the younger, knelt on a chair alone, eagerly reaching to push at the plastic bubble in the middle of the game board and pop the die inside, moving his pieces from hole to hole. But Edward, the older, sat on Jack's lap, listless, face sagging so that it seemed misshapen from my point of view. It was Jack who was moving his hand, propping it on top of the bubble, exerting pressure to make the game pop, manipulating Edward's fingers so he would grasp the red game pieces that were his and move them along their track.

The following afternoon, I called the surgeon to beg for a prescription for more codeine. My heart was racing, my voice high and thready.

The receptionist put me on hold. Then the doctor himself was on the phone, explaining in a kind, uncle-ish tone of voice why he couldn't give me more drugs for my son, that codeine was a highly addictive medication, that it would not truly help him.

"But he was better!" I begged, not caring if I humiliated myself. "It wasn't the tonsils. It must have been the drugs. He could sleep with the drugs; he could think! There's nothing else it could be."

The doctor's voice got calm and he asked if I had a pen and paper. Satisfaction filled my throat: I had convinced him; he would do what I asked if only I would write down a prescription number, the name of a pharmacy. "I want you to call Barry Newberg," he said, then gave me the number.

"Yes," I said, writing down what he told me. "Fine. And he'll have the drugs? He'll be able to prescribe?"

"He's the best pediatric neurologist in town. He's not taking new patients right now but I'll call and ask him personally to see Edward."

Something broke inside my chest and I made one hoarse awful sound. The doctor's words began again in my ear and I couldn't stop them. "My son went to school with him. With Barry. He'll do this for me."

Then he did something that startled me. "Rachel?" he said. I hadn't realized he knew my name and it stopped me. He seemed to know it would and he said it again, speaking very slowly, as if to a child: "Rachel, I need you to listen to Barry. He knows about these kids. Really. You must find a way to accept Edward's disability and get on with your life."

All afternoon, I held the paper on which I'd written Newberg's number. I sat with Matt watching videos while Edward knelt on the hardwood floor to the side of the TV with a pack of playing cards. Over and over he tossed them all up in the air and watched them fall— listening to the whiskery sound they made against one another as they settled—and laughed. Up and down, at least forty times in a row.

When Jack came home, I pulled him into our bedroom and shut the door. The scrap of paper, still clenched in my hand, was damp with sweat. "He won't give us more codeine!" I whispered. "They don't understand, Jack. They'll never understand. No one believes he was better. We have to figure this out by ourselves."

"Fine. We'll figure it out. But do you think I could take off my boots first?" Jack sat heavily on the bed and groaned. Dark patches of fatigue on his face made him look old and sullen. I felt him wanting to get up and go to the kitchen for a cold beer.

"No! This can't wait another minute! You told me he'd be better, that this could never happen again. But I'm watching it. He's disappearing right in front of me and I'm trying to hang on to him and I can't. I can't!"

I'd been breathing hard and fast; light-headed, I slumped onto the bed next to Jack and he took my hand. "Okay, Rachel, listen." He talked to me just like the doctor had—soothing me as if I were a child, as if what was happening to Edward were my exaggeration of the facts. "I'm going to change my clothes. And then we'll talk about this. But you've got to calm down. It's not like we're going to be able to solve anything tonight."

Rage rose inside me, choking me. I knew I was being unfair even as I formed the words, but I couldn't have stopped them any more than I could have stopped a train with my body. "Oh no, you're right. We should both be like *you*." Hissing, I pulled my hand out of his. "Always pretending things are going to get better, being surprised and disappointed when they aren't, waiting for other people to supply the answers."

Jack made a low animal sound. He leaned over, tugged off his boots, and threw them at the wall, where each one left a long black mark. "Oh, so you have the answers? Then, please! Enlighten me. Tell me what you've come to with your perpetual chatter and entire days spent worrying about something that might or might not happen. What?" He stood, his face twisted, so tall over me even in his socks I was glad he'd taken his boots off after all. "What? Spit it out! Tell me now. What the fuck am I supposed to do?" His words kept cutting off at the ends, as if he were being strangled.

"Get him some drugs." It was easier to be calm when Jack was yelling.

"What do you think? I'm going to walk into a pharmacy and say, 'Give me some codeine or I'll shoot you?'"

"That's not what I meant."

Jack rocked on the balls of his feet, as if he were flexing some long-trapped muscles. The air suddenly got quiet and he peered down at me, interested. "What *do* you mean?"

I'd been thinking it all day but didn't know if I'd actually say it. If I explained out loud, that would make it my idea alone. I sat on the bed where Jack had been before and stared at the pattern in the quilt. "You know . . . There are things you can get that most people can't. . . ."

"You're going to have to be clearer. I want to make sure we're talking about the same thing."

"Marijuana." I said the word like an old lady swearing. "Start there. See what happens. Maybe he'll sleep again. Maybe he'll . . ." I stopped and put my fingers to my forehead because something had started to buzz there. "Relax."

Jack sat next to me then, hope washing across his beaten face. "Do you think?"

"I read an article the other day, about a teenager who takes it because he has Crohn's disease and it helps his digestion." I could still see the photo of the kid in the article, a strikingly handsome, grinning hockey star with dark curly hair. One arm flung around his mother's shoulders. She had saved him. "People are taking it for cancer, AIDS. You've said you'd buy it yourself if one of us needed it."

"Yeah." Jack nodded slowly.

"So." I shrugged, suddenly braver. "One of us does."

He picked up my hand and I leaned against his shoulder. "It's just pot," I said into his blue officer's shirt. "You used to smoke it all the time and nothing bad ever happened. Right? Besides, you can find some that's really pure. Just make sure it's not tainted with anything." I couldn't stop talking. Then I remembered this was exactly how it went when we would get high together: I rattled on and on while Jack grew quiet. "It can't be worse for him than never sleeping. And it might help. We wouldn't have him smoke it, just . . . eat it or something."

"Tea." Jack was rocking me a little. "I could make an infusion."

"Yes." That sounded better. More refined. Less horrifying. I closed my eyes, burrowed into his chest, and said it. "An infusion."

· · ·

The room was silent. No matter how many times Barry Newberg pulled on the hair over his eyes, it didn't straighten. Again and again, it sprang back.

I hadn't meant to tell him this part of the story. I hadn't decided not to, either. All day, I'd thought I would stop before I got to it, look him in the eyes, figure out if I could take the risk. But talking in that shadowed room felt like skiing on a moonlit night: a gentle slope of reason, one thing sliding easily into the next, my body so weary I'd ceased to notice anything but the slow tumbling down. I sighed.

"So did you?" His head was tipped down so I could barely see his face.

There was still time to lie. Buttery light from the lamp was reflected in the window—a shower of brightness that blocked out the dark.

"Yes," I said. "We did."

It took Jack less than a week to do what I'd asked. This time, he pulled me into the bedroom when he came home from work, shut the door tightly, and handed me a clear, plastic bag half full of weedy fiber, seeds, and tiny flowers. It even looked like tea. I stood near the window, turning the bag over in my hand, examining it in the waning light.

"Was it hard? To get it?"

Jack shucked off his boots, bowed down to the floor, and lined them up neatly; for three days, both of us had avoided looking at the black marks on the wall. Easing his belt open, he arched his back and spoke in the strained voice of a stretch. "Nope. Couldn't have been easier."

"What are you saying?" I kneaded the bag and it gave off the green smell of a college dormitory hall.

"Nothing." Jack's face was open wide, like a baby's. "It *was* easy. Too easy." He shrugged. He'd unbuttoned his shirt now and was scratching at his neck where the polyester rubbed against his skin all day. "The only thing is . . . I had to deal with Simmons."

"Oh."

Bob Simmons had been Jack's shift supervisor when he first joined the department. A sergeant with white hair, a wet-looking face, and a belly that rode out ahead of him, tilting from side to side as he walked.

"How far into the drug business is Simmons? I mean, was that a good idea? Does this put you in the middle of something . . . criminal?"

Jack glared at me and the tiny muscles along his jawline began to twitch, little cricket wings of tendon that flexed in and out. "Yes, dear. I'm a police officer who just bought drugs from the dirtiest cop I know to give to my six-year-old. I would say that definitely puts me in the middle of something 'criminal.'"

We waited until ten o'clock. Then ten-thirty. Jack wanted to go to bed, but I was still hoping Edward would fall asleep on his own. It had been a week and his eyes looked like blank holes. But he was staring at the ceiling when I checked on him again.

Jack was in front of the news, not watching. "Still awake?"

I nodded.

"Okay." He stood. "Either I'm going to sleep or I'm going to make the stuff into tea. You decide."

"Why me alone?"

Jack lifted one hand and slapped himself on the forehead. "Christ! Fine. I'm going to bed."

"No!" I was still on the stairs, looking over the rail. I turned to go back up again. "Make it. I'll go get him."

I brought Edward down and he sat at the table, legs hanging from his chair like dead things. He hummed a metallic sound that changed frequency with no particular pattern.

Jack was ready. He walked over from the counter, holding a glass of yellow-green liquid. It smelled like weeds, iron, salt, and old garbage. Edward turned away and buried his nose in the sleeve of his pajamas.

"Time to drink!" Jack said heartily, as if he were buying rounds in an Irish pub.

"Shouldn't one of us try it?" I asked. Like the Secret Service, I thought, one of us should drink a little in order to check for contamination in the drug.

"Which one of us?" Jack was hunched over Edward, wrinkling his own nose at the smell. "You're pregnant and I get drug-tested every two weeks."

Jack put the cup to Edward's mouth and I paced around the far side of the table, watching. Edward took a tiny swallow and gagged, turning away sharply. "I know." Jack rubbed Edward's back with his free hand. "It tastes like shit. I'm sorry. You have to drink it. Afterward, you can have anything you want."

I flew around the kitchen opening doors, looking through every cupboard to see what we might have, what would tempt him. There were no chips. No frozen pizza. No crackers and only a tiny bit of Swiss cheese. Nothing to satisfy a case of the munchies. What kind of parents were we?

Barry Newberg laughed and I realized I'd actually said that out loud. Night had fallen. My watch said five-ten but the midnight sky said something else, thick, black, and timeless.

"Did he drink it?"

"No. Yes. Some." I fidgeted but it didn't help. "I need to use your restroom."

He rose and took me to the hall, pointed to a blank wooden door. When I returned, he was lying back in his chair and had removed his shoes; he wore beautiful socks, knitted argyle. "Did it help?" he asked without raising his head.

I sat. "Maybe. It seemed to, at first." Everything, I thought, seemed to help at first. "He got down a couple sips that first night and then we waited. I could swear he slept for a few hours. I tried to stay awake myself so I could watch, in case he had some sort of . . . reaction. I was in his room, but I must have fallen asleep at some point."

I looked at Newberg, who now had shed his tie as well as his shoes. He was looking less and less like a doctor, more like one of the neat, clean-shaven boys from high school that my parents had expected me to marry. "And then?"

I shrugged. "We had him drink a little more the next night. It was awful. He hated it and he cried. We felt like monsters. But he fell asleep around two and it seemed worth it. So we kept it up." I stared at the wall and saw the scene in our kitchen replayed five times, like still photographs on its surface. "Then in the end it didn't work and it was horrible and we stopped."

"How long ago was this?"

I stared at him for a minute, wondering if he might be going to pick up a pen and write down my answer, or reach for the phone to call the police. But he stayed in his chair. I sighed. "It was May."

"And since then?"

"He's gone again."

"How so?"

"Inside himself. Weird. Vacant. He never sleeps, can't talk to us. He swings his head around all the time in a way that just makes me want to . . ." I spoke through gritted teeth so even though I didn't finish the sentence, the message was clear. I was a terrible mother.

"Always?"

"No. It's never always. There are times. We went to visit my friend Mariel in June—four or five weeks after he withdrew again. She has a farm in northern Iowa. Edward loves it there and he tends to perk up, even just getting in the car to go." I was remembering as I spoke, seeing the suitcases we used, the piece of toast Matt was gripping when I buckled him into his car seat, the rush of yellow dashes on the road in front of me. "While we were on our way, this time, he said the oddest thing. He hadn't spoken, really, in days. But this was so clear."

Newberg had been looking a little drowsy, but now he brightened and sat forward a little. "What was it?"

"A space between the signs, Minnesota and Iowa. I'd pointed it out before. But this time as we were driving through Edward suddenly said, 'This is the nowhere place.'"

"This is the nowhere place." Newberg said this just like Edward would—not a question but an echo.

"I thought"—I slid my wedding ring up and down my finger—"it was pretty abstract. I mean"—I looked up to see his response—"he got this concept. He's not stupid. He knows things."

"That's important to you."

Alarm gathered in my throat. I'd thought this man understood. "My son is in there, locked away. I know. I saw him when he was younger, before this started, before he couldn't sleep and he started looking . . . haunted all the time. It's not that it's important, it's just what I feel. It's my job to remember and figure out how to get him back to what he used to be."

Newberg was silent. His face was the same and I couldn't tell what he thought.

I sat up straight and said loudly, "Also, there was his story."

10

DURING THE LAST week of the school year, there was a reading by the students of Harriet Nelson's kindergarten class. Edward brought home a handmade invitation in his backpack and I wondered who had helped him write the words and color it in. It said the children would present their own stories on Wednesday afternoon and there would be refreshments afterward.

I hadn't heard from Harriet in a few weeks. For about a month following the surgery, she'd sent letters nearly every day telling me about Edward's accomplishments, then lavishing enthusiasm despite the fact that his progress had stalled. But the notes had stopped coming the same week we first gave him the marijuana tea.

As I dressed Matt for the reading, he told me a story about a frog and an anteater who became best friends after fighting over the choicest insects in their part of the woods. Then he hugged me and said I looked pretty and we walked, hand in hand, all the way to the school.

Edward's classroom was full of tiny chairs. It was hot and the mingled smell of cookies and glue made me queasy. Children read in turn. All but two of the stories were about family vacations. There was a strange, frail little girl whose plotline was surreal—one sentence about turkeys, the next about war, nothing leading to anything else. Edward went last.

I stared down at my lap and hated myself for feeling embarrassed. Matt sat up straight, the perfect size for his chair. He tugged on my shirt. "Look, Mommy, it's Edward's turn."

Edward sat at the front of the room in the "reading seat," a large oak captain's chair with arms, his head drooping to one side. Harriet placed a book in Edward's hands but he let it fall to the ground; I heard him saying something—a string of muttered words—over and over under his breath.

"Edward, may I read your book to the parents?" she asked.

He didn't answer. I squeezed Matt's hand too hard in order to keep myself from getting up and walking out, going as far away as I could go on foot. Harriet cleared her throat.

"Cry is a boy." She looked at me. The parents around me shifted. One man looked at his watch, picked up his coat, and left quickly. But Harriet read on: a story about a boy who looked for flowers in the middle of a crowded, noisy city. "He does not feel like he can ever find the flowers, and this makes him sad. But then his mom helps him look for the flowers and she shows him and he sees pink and green and yellow ones under a wall. Then Cry feels happy."

When the other children had finished their stories, there was applause. But at the end of Edward's there was only a stunned silence. Harriet stood, pursing her lips. Edward appeared not to know we were all there, watching him. He slid down in the chair, his head moving back and forth like a metronome. The woman seated next to me put her hand on my arm and asked, "Is he your son?"

I nodded. She said nothing else but kept her hand out, touching me, for a few seconds longer. Then Matt stood and walked to Edward's chair, put his face directly in front of his brother's, and said, "I liked that story."

That's when people began to clap, politely at first and then with a burst of energy. Matt pulled Edward out of the chair and toward the table, where they both stood, eating cookies.

I waited until the crowd of parents had thinned and went to Harriet, who was still holding Edward's book in her hand. "How much of that was him?" I asked abruptly.

"All of it. Edward told me the story; I wrote it down." She sighed. "It was during that time. You know." She stopped again and caught her breath. "The week after he came back from his surgery. When he was well."

She sat, then, in the reading chair, the book on her lap, her speck-led, veiny hands clutching the wide arms, creases under her eyes giving away how tired she was. "I'll admit, I've done a lot of work with him lately to get it . . . ready. For today. But in the beginning, the story itself, the part about the flowers, and the picnic." She looked up at me. "And the mother. That was all him. I remember him telling me, being so cer-tain that Cry really couldn't *see* the flowers and then, suddenly"—she raised her hands to the level of her shoulders and thrust her fingers open in a quick starburst—"there they were. Right in front of him."

As he helped me on with my coat, Barry Newberg said, "I don't think Edward has brain lesions." He said it casually, as he might have said at a party, *I don't think I will have any wine, thank you.*

If it had been Jack standing behind me, I would have crumpled with relief and let him hold me up. Instead, I locked my knees and swayed.

"No horrible disfiguring disease?"

"I can't be sure." Newberg tucked the coat over my shoulders and stepped around to face me. Smiled. "I'm sorry. They teach us in medi-cal school never to say anything is one hundred percent. But the history you describe sounds like something else. What, I'm not sure."

We both waited. Somewhere, a clock ticked. Jack and the boys were eating dinner now; or maybe it was later than I thought and they were getting ready for bed. The wind had picked up, making a low, sad noise outside. "I'll tell you what: I'm going to schedule a sleep study and while we're at it I'll get an MRI, take a look at his brain so I can give you ninety-nine percent certain. And to be thorough, I want you to get those family histories—everything about your direct relatives, inherited diseases, learning problems, psychiatric disorders, and as much of your husband's as you possibly can."

I nodded. After the weeks of worry and research, finding Jack's birth parents seemed an easy assignment. I thought of the photo of Mickey that was inside my purse; that, too, seemed like a key.

Newberg slipped into his shoes and picked up his own coat but didn't put it on. He opened the door and ushered me into a dark hall;

at the end, the buttons for the elevator glowed against a silver plate. We rode down together in silence.

"Where is your car?" His voice was almost brusque and I realized he must be tired and hungry, too.

"It's in the ramp . . . but I can just go—"

"No. You can't." We entered the blue light of the garage, heels tapping on concrete as we walked to where my minivan was parked. "Someone from my office will call you early next week to schedule the sleep test." He was squinting at a concrete wall, as if looking through it for his own car.

"Thank you." My voice was stiff. "I appreciate your time."

"No. No. It's interesting. Your son, your story . . ." He was still holding his coat draped over one arm, one hand in his trouser pocket, jingling his keys. "Don't worry. I have a feeling. I shouldn't say." He glanced away. "Just—don't worry."

Then I was standing, listening to the quick taps of his feet walking away. I climbed into the driver's seat and pulled the seat belt as wide as it would go so I could wrap it around me. I clicked it closed. Then I put my forehead to the steering wheel and sat in silence. Minutes went by. My feet grew wooden with cold.

"God." It came out a croak when I finally said it, my voice like Edward's, so unused to praying I sounded as if I'd just awakened. "Please. I swear, if Edward can be all right, I don't care about anything else." I drew a long breath and exhaled the rest in one long stream. "Whatever you want. I don't care. Take it all: Jack, our marriage, the house, Mariel, my job, all our money. Anything but the children. Let them all be perfect and healthy. But I truly don't care about the rest of it. And Jack doesn't, either. We'll never want another thing for ourselves. Just help Edward come back to us. And stay."

My fingers ached inside my gloves; in a minute they'd go completely numb. Finally I said, "Thank you." My words floated on the frigid air like smoke.

Then I turned the key, engine, heater, and radio all switching on at once. And I drove slowly and deliberately along dark, curved highways all the way home.

HELEN

THE FALL OF 1940 was unusually warm. Throughout October, trees burned orange and red on the boulevard in front of Ted and Mary Donnelly's house. On Halloween evening, children ran through a wet 70-degree breeze that ruffled their capes and rattled loose windows.

Most mornings, the *Tribune* was full of headlines about a war in Europe; German soldiers had invaded Poland, forcing Jews into ghettos. Armies were gathering in France. But in Minnesota, downtown businesses were thriving. Ted had added a salesgirl in September, because his bookkeeper predicted it would be a record year for Christmas sales. With Helen to help customers and talk to the ladies who came in and browsed to fill their afternoons, Ted could keep working, making brooches and ring settings at his bench in back. But it took its toll.

Ted would be fifty-four in March and his shoulders had begun to ache from the hours he spent hunched over the close work. At night, Mary rubbed his back with hot oil and brought him aspirin, but they never talked about the fact that they were raising a four-year-old when many of their friends already had grandchildren. They didn't discuss things they couldn't change; also, they both knew Susanna had saved them after Frank's death. She had saved their marriage and their faith.

On the other hand, they talked about Mickey often, searching for ways to reach him. It had been a difficult school term already; Mary had been called in twice to discuss his failing grades. Sister Theresa Marie said Mickey was a smart boy who didn't pay attention to his lessons. Mary pursed her lips tightly when she related the conversation to her husband, not mentioning the other thing the nun had said: "He's nothing like his brother. Frank was such a good boy."

Ted tried to spare Mary, too. For instance, he didn't tell her about the squirrel he'd found in the backyard in June, flat like the ornamental tail on a coonskin cap, the tread of narrow bicycle tires running the length of the animal's back. Ted had smoothed its fur back and looked into one blank watermelon-seed eye. He knew he should find Mickey and ask him how the animal died, tell him that all God's creatures deserved decent treatment. Insist that the boy confess whatever it was he had done. But Mickey hardly spoke these days and the thought of fighting through that silence made Ted feel beaten. Instead, he had laid the squirrel's body carefully in a small grave he'd dug under the peony.

Days later, Ted would wonder how he missed the beginning of the Armistice Day storm. He had been working intently, fretting about Mickey, and by the time he looked up from his workbench, it was close to four o'clock and the air outside had turned the color of a bruise. Helen stood at the front window, watching a sweep of white flakes that brushed the road outside like an enormous plume.

Ted walked out, one hand massaging his sore shoulder. "When did this start?"

"Not so long ago." She was still facing the street. "There was rain for a bit. Then this sudden wind and sleet and now . . . snow." She said the last word softly, as if in apology.

"Well," he said. "I suppose we should close up, in case it gets bad." Yet, they both stood, silent, staring as the snow thickened into long wet-looking flakes that fell at a slant. Then there was a sound. It began as a moan and rose to become a whistle that pierced the air. Ted turned to Helen but dark had enveloped them so completely he could not see her expression.

"Not to worry." His voice was low but he moved quickly. "We'll just leave the deposit until tomorrow. Why don't you get your things and I'll see you to the streetcar."

To enter the swirl of snow and darkness and wind was like swimming in a pitching sea. He had never touched her before, but now Ted kept a tight grip on Helen's elbow. They had gone only a few yards when the world seemed to turn on its side: an icy wind drove into Ted's back and the storm rushed straight ahead like water from a fire hose. It was, he thought, as if he were suspended from the sky looking down.

They kept their heads tucked, chins to their chests, as they walked toward the corner. There were no car noises, no people they could see. A few voices floated in the distance but they were so faint and hollow as to seem ghostly. Pulling on Helen's arm like a rein, Ted stopped and they paused for a long moment, blinded, two people caught inside a pocket of wetness and white and cold. He bent toward Helen and found her ear with his lips. He worked to shout, "We better head back. Take shelter in the store."

He was mindful of the turn. Everyone in Minnesota had heard stories about farmers who froze to death during blizzards. Dizzy and disoriented, they would move in too many directions and lose their sense of place, turning away from the path they'd walked between house and barn every morning for decades, succumbing to the snow, often lying down just yards from their own front doors. Rotating his body slowly, Ted steered Helen until he was nearly sure they were facing back toward the store.

They trudged, arm in arm now. The snow was packed hard near the ground but new drifts rose, loose and wet, to the middle of their calves. When Ted's foot ran into something solid, he assumed it was a piece of ice; then the thing gave a little, like a peach. Ted let go of Helen and bent down to touch the person who lay in the snow. His hands were so frozen, he couldn't feel the texture of the shirt but discerned the general outline of an arm. Standing with his feet planted, Ted gripped and pulled up with all his strength; both of his shoulders lit up with pain. Once he'd righted the body, Ted reached again for Helen, grabbing her almost roughly, and dove headfirst toward the sand-colored building now receding into a cloud of snow.

At home, Mary stood at the window. Suddenly, midafternoon, darkness had descended along with the storm. When six o'clock came it looked little different outside than it had three hours before, but her anxiety quickened because this was the time she expected Ted home. Typically, he walked through the door at five-forty, but she had tacked on twenty minutes for the snow. She knew it wasn't enough, but holding off her worry had become more difficult than simply wallowing in it.

The children were in the back playing a board game, Eleanor trying to distract the younger two from the storm so they wouldn't be afraid. Susanna, at four, was a quiet, fearful child by nature. She was happy and quick to learn, like Frank in that way, thank God. But too content to play alone at home, dressing dolls and muttering gently to them rather than running through the alley with the other children, who yelled and hooted as they kicked soft, rubber balls.

Mickey was quiet, too, but in a more troublesome, pent-up way. He seemed both older than his classmates and completely bewildered by them. After Frank's death, Eleanor—seven years older than Mickey—had taken over mothering him. Mary was grateful, even though it made Mickey even more remote from her. She had borne him as she had the other three, yet she often felt afraid with him, as if there were no connection between them, no way to understand or help this child.

Secretly, she had watched him approach groups of boys his own age and seen their circles tighten against him rather than break apart to let him in. She'd felt her heart flutter so hard inside her chest she thought it might take flight while he slunk away, head hanging, mouth set hard so he wouldn't cry. But she had never said a word to him because she had no idea what to offer her only remaining son.

Frank, the child who taught her about boys, had drawn people naturally—teachers, older children, the babies of her friends. He gave off an aura of warmth that filled the rooms he entered. But Mickey was different. As a baby, he had been large and serious but normal in all respects. Perhaps it was when Frank died, or even before that, when something happened to make Mickey different.

But earlier this afternoon, miraculously, she had broken through to Mickey. When the storm swept in and the wind began to howl, he had disappeared and Mary found him an hour later sitting in an old chair behind the bookshelves in the basement. He was staring at his own knees with eyes so intent they were nearly crossed.

"There you are now! What are you doing down here in the cold?"

He kept his head down. "I don't know."

Normally, this sort of vague response would upset or even infuriate Mary. But today she'd coaxed him upstairs and convinced him to help her make cookies. And for a time, they had laughed and baked, sending up clouds of flour as the rooster clock counted off the minutes overhead. Afterward, the two of them sat at the table eating cookies and drinking cold milk—two glasses for Mickey, who had already started to grow lanky. The boy needed a hearty snack, Mary thought, because they would not have their evening meal until Ted arrived.

Mickey sat at the table, still tasting the sweet muddy chocolate in the pockets of his cheeks and staring up at the bank of cupboards where he'd once spent afternoons with Frank. His mother reached out and patted his hand and for once, he did not pull away. Her touch was gentle, not scolding. He felt the stirrings of a safety he hadn't known since the night Frank went away.

But after that, the afternoon had gone on too long and become very dark. Mary seemed to let him loose again and become lost in her thoughts, pacing the living room and lifting the curtain often to look outside. She thought Mickey was playing with his sisters but really he stood in the hallway, inside the crook of space by the attic door, watching her finger her rosary beads and mouth the words to prayers. When the door finally burst open at 7:45 and Ted stumbled through with two shivering wet forms clinging to him, Mary said, "Thank you, God," slipped the rosary into her apron pocket, and walked toward them, arms open, beads shifting and clicking against her hip.

But instead of leaning shyly toward her, Ted had bellowed for the first time in all the years Mickey could remember: "Something to eat. Now!" Still standing in the foyer, wet flakes dripping from the brim of his hat, Ted held a fat, rumpled-looking man upright with an arm tight around his shoulders as if they were about to dance. A pretty girl stood next to them, on her own now but dripping water all over the floor from the ends of her hair. Mickey's sisters came running and he joined them, entering the living room in a rush as if he hadn't stood quietly, watching the whole scene.

"Eleanor, quick! Bring your father a cookie." Mary's face looked blank, perplexed. Mickey had never seen her so quiet. Together the whole family watched, curious, as Ted took the cookie Eleanor handed him and fed it in small pieces to the man whose face was gray as stone. It was, Mickey thought later, like seeing a real miracle: the man's cheeks had bloomed pink again within a few minutes of eating. His father had been like Jesus when he healed people in the desert. But if he had this power, Mickey wondered, why couldn't he have done the same for Frank?

Over supper, Ted explained how he and Helen had found this man, Dick Murton, lying on the sidewalk as they headed back to the store. He was weak but could speak well enough to tell them that he was diabetic, that he had taken his insulin and needed food or he could die. Dick's car was parked in the lot next door, but he lived in St. Paul and could not possibly make it home. There was no food in the jewelry shop and everything downtown had closed.

"So." Ted had changed into dry clothes and a comfortable pair of house slippers. He leaned contentedly against the soft padded back of his dining room chair and looked at his family gathered around him. "I had no choice but to drive us here."

Helen, too, had changed. She sat huddled in a long skirt and blouse of Mary's that hung loose around her waist but did not reach to her wrists or ankles. Her blonde hair had dried and was clipped back so it fell in a mass of curls down her back. Mickey was trying to listen to his father, but he couldn't help wondering how it would feel to pick up one of the strands of Helen's hair and draw it straight. Would it pull back against his fingers like a rubber band?

Before he began eating, Dick cleared his throat and reached into the wet coat he'd slung over one corner of his chair. The Donnellys and Helen sat speechless as he pulled out a hypodermic needle and a small vial, lifted his shirt, pinched a roll of flesh, and stuck himself. Mickey watched with a particular mix of fascination and horror. Dick's fat stomach was covered with fine brown hair, like moss, and he jabbed the needle in it with a small sigh, as if he were relieved to feel it pierce through his skin. Mickey stared, waiting to see if blood would drip out when the needle was withdrawn, but the man pulled his shirt down too quickly. Though he was facing away from her, Mickey could feel his mother breathe out silently, the air around her slightly electric as she struggled to contain her distaste.

But as soon as the needle had been stowed back in the man's coat pocket, Mickey shifted his attention to Helen. He'd met her once before, at the jewelry store downtown. And she had smiled at him like one of the ladies from church. Now, suddenly, she looked more like one of Eleanor's high school friends—small in his mother's clothes, strands of loose hair falling down around her face, green eyes darting as if she were afraid to say anything in the presence of so many adults. She ate slowly and carefully and though Mickey was hungry he found himself imitating her, raising his fork at the same pace.

He was only halfway through his meal when he heard his mother gasp and turned just in time to see her catch Susanna, who had fallen asleep at the table and begun to slide off her chair. Suddenly, everyone realized how late it was. While Helen and Eleanor cleared the dishes, Ted got up and went to the front hall closet and Mary left to put Susanna in bed.

"Coffee?" she asked when she came back to find Dick and Mickey sitting alone at the table. "Or maybe you'd prefer to get right to bed."

"Nah, a little coffee'd be nice," Dick said, stretching out his legs. Ted had returned, holding his pipe in one hand, a tobacco pouch in the other. His eyes were ringed blue with fatigue.

"Mr. Murton is having coffee." Mickey could hear the irritation in his mother's voice. "Would you like some, too, dear?"

"Certainly." Ted sighed. By this time in the evening he should be smoking his last pipe and reading the evening paper so that at ten-thirty he'd be ready to rise and change into one of the nightshirts Mary kept fresh and ironed. He would brush his teeth and—because his beard was so light—shave for the next day. In five years, he had not deviated from this routine.

"Feeling better?" he asked as he sat down again at the head of the table.

"Much." Murton pulled a package of cigarettes out of his shirt pocket and motioned for Ted to pass his lighter down. "Glad you and your girl found me. This diabetes is a wretched thing. Doc says I might lose a leg someday."

Ted nodded and drew on the pipe stem. "I'd like to call your family so they won't be worried. But Mary says the lines are down."

Dick made a backhand motion. "Not a worry. My wife passed last year and God never saw fit to give us any children. So it's just me."

"Oh. I'm sorry." The room was quiet. Ted puffed gently on his pipe, sending out a blue vapor that folded over on itself then vanished into the air.

"Work keeps me busy." Dick crushed his cigarette out on a bread plate and reached for Ted's Zippo to light another. "I'm an insurance man. And I put in twenty hours a week at the church." His chest swelled as he said, "I'm a deacon at St. Francis. You're Catholic folk?"

Ted nodded.

"I could tell. Stopping to help me the way you did."

Ted paused. Mickey looked at his father. Often, he'd noticed, Ted would pause in conversation because he took time to think about what was being said, what it meant, before responding. Many people took this as a signal to barrel on.

Mickey slipped off his chair and crept out of the dining room as Dick lit another cigarette and began, "Now the Jewish people are very different . . ."

When Eleanor turned from wiping out the sink she found Helen standing on her toes, putting dishes away in the cupboard, and Mickey watching her intently from just inside the swinging door.

"Time for bed," Eleanor called out and Helen jumped, looking back. But Mickey knew this was directed at him and he edged toward the broom closet, his back pressed against the wall.

"Did it stop snowing?" He had no idea why he asked this, or why his voice sounded so high, but both young women seemed to think it was a reasonable question; Eleanor lifted the curtain over the sink and they all three gazed outside. The glass was a shiny patch of black with crystals glittering through. Mickey thought they looked like diamonds sparkling on dark cloth, like the rings he'd seen on display in his father's store.

"It's beautiful, isn't it?" This was the first time all night Helen had uttered an entire sentence and even Eleanor seemed surprised. But she answered: "Yes, it is. But it looks cold."

Mickey listened and heard the creak and whistle of the wind, so constant he had grown used to it, like the whir of a fan in his room on a hot summer night.

"There's no way we're going to school tomorrow. Can't I stay up a little while longer?"

Eleanor considered. Maybe because her face was so beautiful she appeared older. People often treated her like a grown woman, especially men. But at nearly fifteen, she was not yet accustomed to making decisions, only upholding the tenets of the household. Their mother kept events running smoothly on course; shopping, dusting, and laundry each were done on a particular day of the week. Bedtime rules were rarely broken.

"We could play cards." Even Helen looked surprised that she had suggested it. Her face colored, but she went on. "That's what we did at Katy Gibbs when we had time between classes. Canasta or spades. I'd be happy to teach you."

Eleanor looked at Mickey and saw the longing in his eyes. "I know there's a deck in here somewhere," she said, opening a drawer.

Mickey had never known you could stumble into something so suddenly wonderful. The kitchen was warm against the howling wind. At some point, Eleanor rose from the table to make hot chocolate and Helen inched her chair over to teach him more about the game. "Arrange your cards like this," she said, brushing his hand with her fingers as she took the fan and began sifting the cards so the suits lined up: red hearts with red hearts, and the upside-down black ones she called spades together in a line.

She smelled like lilacs in summer and Mickey breathed in gulps. No school tomorrow meant he would not have to face the Latin teacher who had kept him after class last week and made one long, angry red mark on the sheet where he'd been reworking the day's declensions.

And he would not have to hide from Marcus, the boy on the playground who had been pinching him so hard there were bruises all over his chest. Best of all, he would be here in this house with his parents and sisters and Helen. It was as if a party had erupted out of nowhere and for once, he was invited.

Eleanor shook a handful of white sugar into the saucepan of milk and slipped in two bars of dark chocolate, stirring so the mixture wouldn't scorch on the bottom of the pan. She was watching Mickey, his face smooth and soft in the bright light coming from overhead, looking for the first time in her entire memory a little like Frank's when he was this age. It seemed that Helen had brought about this change and Eleanor wished suddenly for a friend like her—someone older who could teach her how to wear the heels her mother said were too risqué, someone she could tell about the man in a sailor's uniform who had asked her to meet him at the library on Thursday.

The three of them barely noticed when Mary and Ted and Dick Murton filed one by one into the kitchen. Mickey and the girls were too busy laughing over empty cups, crusted with dark flecks on the rims, and cards scattered over the tabletop.

"Goodness! It's nearly midnight. Off to bed with you!" Mary said, even while she took note of her son's happy smile and clear eyes. She walked quickly to him and squeezed his shoulders. It was as close as she had been able to get to Mickey in months. "You must be so tired, dear." She was still touching him but had turned to face Helen. "You'll room with Eleanor tonight. The bed is a double, more than big enough."

Now it was Eleanor who clearly felt lucky. She was smiling at her new friend. But in the same moment, Mickey was seized by a terrible thought. He glanced warily at his mother and then at Dick, who stood leaning against the counter, arms crossed over his chest.

"Mr. Murton will sleep in your bed." Mary smoothed Mickey's hair as she spoke; still, he felt as if each strand had stiffened and stood up. "We'll make up a place for you on the floor."

"Hate to put you to the trouble," Dick said to her. Then he looked at Mickey. "But I'm an old man. I wouldn't be able to get up off the floor."

It happened so fast: while Mickey was brushing his teeth and changing into his pajamas, someone—almost certainly his mother—arranged a nest of blankets on the rag rug next to his own bed. Mickey could hear the girls murmuring and giggling in the next room, as he crawled under the covers and settled his bony body carefully against the hard floor. Before turning out the lights, Dick Murton set a full glass of water and a plate of crackers on the bedside table; he took off his watch and put it there, too. Then he reached into his mouth and pulled out a wire that had two teeth attached to it and laid them out next to the watch. He smiled and there was a big space in his mouth. "Good night."

Once the lights were out, Mickey listened and he heard the man breathing like a car, hunkered, idling in the cold. "I saw you watching her, boy." The voice came suddenly out of the darkness and Mickey jumped.

"Excuse me?"

"The lady from your father's shop. I saw you looking at her. She's a very pretty girl."

This hung in the air, which had grown tight and stale. Mickey thought he could almost see the man's shape in his bed, but not quite. "She is. Pretty, I guess."

There was a silence and Mickey willed himself to sleep. Tomorrow he could get up and eat breakfast with Helen and Eleanor and maybe they would make pancakes. They could reshuffle the cards and begin another game. Maybe this man would stay away during the daylight hours, or Mickey could learn to avoid him the way he did Marcus.

"You know what a sin is, young man?"

Mickey swallowed. His throat seemed so small he felt he had to open his mouth in order to breathe. "Yes, sir." He thought about Frank and the way he had died; the nuns at school said he was a good boy, baptized and faithful, and he went to heaven because he didn't have sin.

"Looking at a girl like that, someone older and a little too independent, it's the way you start down the road. You don't want to be doing that. Not at your age, son. You're so young and already having impure thoughts."

Mickey didn't know what *impure* meant, so he tried to remember what he'd thought when he looked at Helen. But all he could be sure was that she'd seemed clean and she was nice to him and she smelled of lilacs. This couldn't be sinful. But terror was building inside him, because he'd done something that almost certainly was. He hadn't wanted to do it. When he'd found the squirrel lying on the sidewalk, looking as if someone had ridden over it with a bicycle and squeezed some of its life away, he thought he could save it. He had hidden it in the rosebush in back and checked on it every day, even tried to feed it once—a twig and then, when it didn't even respond, a piece of cheese. But in the end, it had looked at him with frantic eyes and made tiny wheezing noises and Mickey hadn't known what else to do, so he had used a rock, gently grinding against the animal's tiny head.

He hadn't expected the crunching sound. He dropped the rock and ran and vomited in the alley and later was too afraid to go back and see what he'd done.

"Do you ever touch yourself, young man?" Mr. Murton's voice seemed to be coming out of a tunnel. Mickey wanted to put his fingers in his ears but he didn't know what would happen if the man heard him moving: he might jump up and turn on the light and catch Mickey sinning. "Looking at girls is one thing, it's something you have to train yourself to control. And you have time. But if you ever touch yourself, there is no coming back to be saved. You will burn in the fires of hell and never see those good people who raised you ever again."

Mickey freed his arms from the blankets and flattened his hands to the floor, six inches from his body on either side. He did not want to touch himself by mistake in his sleep. Outside the storm raged, but his room had grown so close and hot he could imagine he was already in hell. He wanted to ask Mr. Murton how he could make it stop. He wanted to promise that he would never look at Helen again. But he couldn't form the words and then, from the bed, he heard a loud snore.

Mickey saw red marks in the darkness. Around him, the air began to trip and spin and then a chunk of it broke loose and pressed itself hard against the side of his head.

He closed his eyes tight and waited.

11

_____

IN THE WEEK following my talk with Barry Newberg, January eased.
The light increased a few minutes each day, and it grew stronger and
yellower. The temperature climbed to 30 degrees most afternoons. I
found a rhythm that had been missing earlier in the month and was
able to return to work, concentrating in a way that had been impossible prior to my confession in the doctor's office and my secret deal
with God.

I'd quizzed my mother over the weekend and heard a story about
the Armistice Day blizzard—details she had put together from her
memory, her mother's stories, a late-night talk she'd had once with her
brother, and a letter from a woman named Helen. Certain connections were occurring to me now: the silence of young boys seemed to
be caused by fear. Mickey had been troubled, too, but eventually he
learned to speak and function in society; he went on to get married
and father a child. And his death—however it actually happened—
was tragic. But it didn't appear to be the direct result of Mary's early
mistakes.

Seated in a restaurant on a Wednesday afternoon, I realized I was
relaxed. Hopeful even. The same could not be said for my companion,
though it never could. Eric was nothing like the other men I knew—the
ones I grew up with or the one I married. He was small and blond,
always neatly dressed, quick-moving and easily distracted. He paused
and cleared his throat every time he was about to speak, then issued his
thoughts in perfectly crafted paragraphs.

There's corruption in recycling, he told me shortly after I met him.

His voice was low and fierce. *All that carefully separated glass mixed in with the garbage. I've seen this. It's being hauled away and destroyed. These people are breaking their contract with us, all of us who are carefully washing out bottles and cans. For nothing.* Despite his intensity, Eric never looked directly at me when he spoke. It was as if he thought eye contact would be too intimate, or rude.

I'd been working at the newspaper for two years. In fact, I was the one who had found an anonymous garbage hauler willing to admit his company was landfilling recyclables—my first headline story. But this was the first time my editor and I had ever sat down to a meal together.

We were at a small, private table near the window in a new restaurant uptown. Eric slipped his napkin out of its ring and spread it across his lap. I tried to do the same, but I had only two or three inches of space to work with; finally, I folded the napkin into a triangle and tucked the long edge under my huge stomach. Eric's face reddened, but he smiled.

"You're almost ready, aren't you?"

"So ready." I took a drink of water, sloshing a few drops onto my blouse. A huge, galumphing walrus of a person who had trapped this tidy man at a table. "My doctor says it'll be another three weeks, but I swear I won't go that long. I can't. If I do, I'll kill someone, most likely him."

Eric leaned toward me, his eyes crinkling so it looked as if he had the imprints of tiny pitchforks extending out from the corner of each one. "I've never really known anyone who went through this."

"Never?" The waitress brought a basket lined with cloth and set it on the table. I reached in immediately and broke off a piece of bread, showering the table with flakes. Eric handed me a dish of whipped butter. "You were . . . married?"

"For a couple years. We never had children." Eric's hands were folded in his lap. I couldn't understand why he wasn't eating; Jack would have worked his way through the breadbasket by now and held it up to ask the waitress for a refill. "We never even considered it." Eric stared out at the other tables and laughed nervously. "I can't remember why. It just never came up."

He lifted one hand and put it on the table. I wondered what he would do if I touched it, held it. Slowly, he pulled a piece of bread from the basket and put it on his plate. Then he left it there, as if he'd lost interest in the few seconds between reaching and setting it down. I tried to recall if I'd ever seen this man eat.

Eric's regular restaurant critic was on vacation and we were filling in. It occurred to me I was the perfect cover: people might think we were married, about to have this baby together. It wouldn't be impossible. Eric was fifteen years older than I, but young-looking. Fit. Successful. I chewed and looked around the restaurant at businesspeople, clearly accustomed to white tablecloths and sparkling glasses that were kept constantly full. They probably wondered what Eric was doing with someone like me.

He had been in Vietnam. When he returned to Minneapolis in the early seventies, he wrote a series of award-winning human rights articles for *Time*. Everyone who knew him back then assumed he would become a famous journalist, traveling the globe to report on war and squalor. Instead, he took this job as features editor of the newspaper. I liked to think it was because he believed he could do more good here, at home—maybe especially because I was the paper's consumer advocate, a throwback to the sort of journalist Eric himself had been twenty years before.

I wouldn't have called us friends, but lately I'd begun wondering exactly what we were. He called me at home to discuss story ideas. In the office, he often sat on my desk. At night, when I couldn't sleep, sometimes pictures of Eric would pop into my head and in them, he was always doing something he would never do. A handstand. Cutting off the tip of his own nose with a scissors. Kissing me.

These images had begun around the fourth month of this pregnancy, as my hormones were cresting—the lushness that had twice before driven me toward my husband, rooting for him every night like some lusty animal—but I had stopped turning to Jack after the events following Edward's surgery.

Since the night of Edward's last "infusion," we had been careful with each other at home, polite but quiet; and the current that had connected us since the moment we met had all but disappeared. There was a dull flatness to our interactions now, as if we'd both collapsed and become as two-dimensional as paper dolls. I would still get a surge of warmth from time to time when Jack smiled at me from across a room and I recalled the rawness of him hitching up to the bar all those years ago. But I only felt this from afar. Up close, all I could see when we were together was that night in our kitchen when Jack and I sat by, power-less, while the life drained out of our son all over again.

At first, I'd fought the images of Eric, batting them away as if there were something heroic about denying them. But lately, this hadn't been necessary. Edward wasn't sleeping at all and I'd been up night after night, too frantic to have inappropriate fantasies about Eric. It was the only advantage to this misery that I could think of.

The waitress approached. "Hello. I'd like to recommend our house salad. Mixed greens, fresh vegetables, and a creamy lime-and-serrano dressing."

Eric looked as if he were trying to swallow something bitter. "You don't have French?"

She shook her head.

"The house salad sounds wonderful." I handed her my menu. "That, and the risotto."

Eric scratched his cheek. "What's risotto?" he asked, eyes round like Edward's.

"It's a small grain—" the waitress began.

I cut her off, putting a hand on Eric's arm. "You can try mine. Just order one of the others, maybe the duck-and-feta linguine, and we can split them."

Suddenly I realized how bossy that sounded. I glanced at Eric but couldn't tell if he was angry. Then he smiled. "Whatever she says."

Now I really felt like we were a couple.

I dropped my napkin and had to lean over to get it, cutting off my air. Eric bent at the same time and our eyes met, inches from the floor. "I'm sorry," I said, straightening.

"About what?" He'd actually started eating. Breaking off small unbuttered shards of bread and putting them in his mouth.

"The . . . You know. Taking over like that. I didn't mean to."

Eric looked down at his tie and squinted, as if he'd just noticed he was wearing it. "I imagine you have to."

"Have to what?"

"Take over. Take care of things." It was the closest he'd ever come to commenting on my personal life.

Six months ago, when I told him about the new baby, he was silent, though I could tell from the way he turned away quickly and began marking galleys that he wanted to say something. The next day I told Mariel, who had stared at me for a full minute, then said, *You will never stop making your life impossible, will you?* And I knew what Eric had been thinking.

The waitress came with our salads and filled the moment of awkwardness. I began eating, thinking about how to describe the dressing, which was a very nice combination of lime juice, hot pepper, and something buttery. Eric took a bite and choked. He coughed several times into a closed fist and drained all his water, then asked for mine. "Hot!" he breathed.

"I think it's fine. Give it a good review."

Eric nodded and pushed his plate away. "What I meant before was that it seems like your whole family relies on you . . . and now." He waved his hand toward me. "One more."

"Oh. I suppose. I end up with a lot of . . ." But I had no idea how to name what I had. Eric waited, then began talking about an editorial meeting scheduled for the following morning.

"I won't be there. I told you last week."

His eyes wrinkled again as he concentrated, trying to remember. I looked away so I wouldn't start thinking about what he might look like in the morning, how quiet his apartment would be, how easy it would be to lie under the covers with him and drift. "I'll be at the sleep center. With Edward."

"Ahh. That's tomorrow. Good." Eric got the same frightened look every time he saw or heard about Edward. I couldn't tell if it was concern for Edward, for me, or for himself. But something spooked him.

"It's possible I could come in. After." The waitress came, took our salad plates, and set down bowls of pasta.

"No need," Eric said after she left. He picked up his bowl and handed it to me. He winked. "Go ahead. Split them for us. And just stay home tomorrow. I can handle the meeting."

"Thanks." I handed his bowl back, neatly divided now, risotto on one side and linguine on the other, like perfectly matching half-moons.

12

———

AT EIGHT O'CLOCK that night, a technician showed Edward and me into a dim, blue room. There was a thick shade on the window and the sort of heavy, steel door that secures bank vaults—smooth and gray with no cracks around the edges. I wondered if they would lock us in and the thought made me panic. This was a tomb.

"That'll be yours, I suppose." She motioned toward a bare cot, propped on the floor on short foldout legs. "I'll get you a blanket and a pillow." Then she looked me over. "Hmmm. You're not going to be too comfortable."

"It's okay." I lowered myself to the cot and it sagged like stretched-out rubber. The lime-and-pepper dressing that had tasted so good at noon was simmering in my stomach. I wondered if I'd packed Tums. "I'm not comfortable no matter what I do."

"No, I can see that." She stared at my bulk, the curve of what should have been my stomach resting on my knees. Yet, this woman was even bigger than I was—tall and so uniformly broad her breasts, waist, and hips filled every pocket of space within her white smock—packed into a powerful, cylindrical body that moved as one solid muscle, like a dolphin's tail. Her hair was pulled back, covered with a colorful cloth cap.

"Up here, young man." She patted the bed and Edward climbed up slowly. She pulled out a squishy bottle with a cone-shaped nozzle on top and shook it upside down. In her other hand, she held a long plastic stick that she used to probe Edward's head and hold the hair down while she squirted. Each dollop of gel came out with a spider-crunching sound. "Hmmm. Can't find . . ." Her stick scratched back and forth against his scalp. Edward sat perfectly still.

"Okay. That part's done." She put the bottle and stick down on the table next to his bed.

Edward looked at her from eyes so sunken they seemed to have melted back into his head, like the evil Nazi's in *Raiders of the Lost Ark*.

The woman turned to me. "How long has it been?"

"Twelve days." *Twelve days. Twelve days.* Even without Edward's echolalia, the phrase resounded inside my head.

One of her feet was tapping in a soft, rubber-soled shoe, making tiny suctiony noises. Rhythmic, hypnotic, like little snores. "And you?"

I looked up. She was smiling insistently, the way my mother did when she was most worried. "Maybe five. The last few nights, I've been in his room."

"You both need sleep." From anyone else this would have been insulting, infuriating. But this woman seemed to be offering a new solution. "He'll get it here." I opened my mouth to tell her she was wrong, but she held up one hand in a stop motion, like a traffic cop. "I know, you don't think he will. But it happens every time. People come here after they haven't slept in days and they just . . . do. You'll see."

With one hand, she pulled a tangle of wires from a placket on the wall. I hadn't noticed them before; she appeared to have conjured them like a magician's flower bouquet. Her other hand went to Edward's face, grasped his chin, turning his head so he was looking at her. "I'm going to attach these to your head. It won't hurt, but you have to leave them there. Okay?" He blinked, then nodded. One by one she found the disc on the end of each wire, checked the label on its back, and pressed it flat into a circle of gel.

When she was done with the left side, Edward had become a bizarre futuristic clown, color-coded cords twirling like licorice whips from one hemisphere of his head. Before she could move to the other side of the bed, he rotated so she wouldn't have to walk around. She turned and squinted at me. I could read her name tag: *Nora*.

"I read his chart." She was back to work already, gripping another handful of wires with shiny discs. "It said A-U-T-I-S-T-I-C."

"Yes."

"I'd disagree." Nora spoke into Edward's hair as she reached for wires and pasted the discs on with her forefinger. "We get a lot of them through here. Sleep problems are common. . . ." She looked at me. "Though, I'm sure you know that."

I nodded. Waiting.

"Done," she said.

Edward bobbed his head, testing the tension in the wires. He looked natural like this. I could imagine the currents from his brain traveling out, so strong they would make the wires rigid. Perhaps they could measure what I felt pulsing out of him all those nights he lay awake. The way he could hum, in perfect sequence and key, notes he'd heard only once. Or find his way through the hospital corridors, turning before I nudged him, as if he'd divined our destination and was pulled toward it by a gentle magnetic force.

"What did you mean?" I'd built up the importance of Nora's answer in only a few seconds. I wanted to hear her say there was hope. "You disagree with . . . the diagnosis?"

"Oh, never mind." Nora unwound gauze from a spindle next to Edward's bed, wrapping it around his head until the wires were hidden and it looked as if he were wearing a large white beehive.

"What? Tell me." I sounded about thirteen, insistent and surly.

Nora shook her head. "Nope, I talk too much. Get myself in trouble all the time. The docs here keep telling me to stop giving medical advice. So." She pressed her lips together; they were big and rubbery, like pink gum erasers, and I wondered what it was like to kiss a mouth like that. This made me think of Eric and I quickly looked down at the cot.

Nora yanked the wires roughly and they came from the wall all at once with the sound of tearing Velcro. The ends were attached to a huge plug that she inserted into an electronic box on a rolling stand. "Here." She placed Edward's hand on the metal rod and pushed from behind. "See? You're mobile now."

Edward got up and grabbed the rolling apparatus, steering it smoothly. He took a series of quick steps—more nimble than I'd seen him in days. A short, pale shaman dancing around a shiny pole. Under his white turban, he grinned crookedly. He already looked rested, which made no sense.

"I'm hungry." These were the first clear words he'd spoken in days. Nora raised her eyebrows; she patted Edward on the ear as she left.

"Lights out at ten," she called back over her shoulder.

We walked through quiet, carpeted hallways. Edward shoved the rolling stand so it flew ahead of us, wires growing taut, then ran to catch up with it before he disconnected. And he laughed once, a natural laugh. In the cafeteria were metal shelves filled with treats: brownies and cakes and doughnuts. Edward chose a peanut butter cookie the size of a saucer. I took a slice of pie, dark chocolate under whipped cream. I remembered my mother telling me why hospitals always have good desserts: because sugar consoles people who are suffering.

For once, though, we were not. Under the fluorescent lights, Edward was ghoulish with his dark-ringed eyes and wrapped head and leering smile. But I didn't care. In between my lunch with Eric and now, I'd had dinner with Jack and Matt. The coolness of the pie was working against all the acid in my stomach. I'd spent my whole day sitting at tables, eating with boys. And they all needed me. For a moment, I felt blessed.

It seemed like an opportunity—one I should not waste. "Sweetheart," I said. But Edward stared straight ahead, taking big, cracking bites of his cookie. "Edward," I tried again. And this time, he swiveled his head to look at me. The wires clicked and shifted. "Do you remember anything bad? Did anyone ever . . . *do* anything to you?"

"That library lady hurt me." It was so startlingly clear. The answer, here in this wonderful alien place. Rather than being simply a cruel woman, she was evil, an abuser—the true cause of Edward's break with reality. This made perfect sense.

"How?" I put my hand on his, but he pulled away and used his thumb and forefinger to trace the length of a single cord.

"She made the colors spin," he said, as if in a dream. "Those colors shouldn't be together."

"What do you mean?"

"She had a twister and she would make it go around. She showed it. Up, like this." He held up his hands, as if in surrender, showing me how the librarian had displayed the twisting colors. "It hurt my eyes and then I looked at the lights. She got mad."

I sighed, sharply disappointed that the evil helmet-haired woman had not tortured him outright. "Did she hit you?" I tried once more. So much would be explained if it were her fault. "Or shake you? With her hands?" I showed him mine, clenched like claws, and made a frantic push-pull motion.

Edward shook his head. "Daddy did."

Suddenly, my stomach was ice-cold. I looked around wildly to see if anyone sitting near us had heard, but we were alone in the cafeteria except for a table of women in pink scrubs sitting ten yards away.

"When?" I combed my mind, thinking through the times Jack had been alone with Edward, whether he was drinking, what his mood was when I arrived home. I had never seen Jack threaten a woman or a child; I slapped him once during an argument over money, early on, and when I raised my hand to do it again he simply caught my wrist and held it so gently I relaxed into him and continued the fight in a whisper, eyes closed, my head lying against his chest.

"When?" I asked through clenched teeth. "What did Daddy do to you?"

Edward paused, and I was afraid I had lost him. But then he looked at me disapprovingly. "Making me drink," he said, so clearly the phrase might have come from a machine that recorded his observations. "I did not like that tea."

Still queasy, I slumped over my own enormous form in the chair. Images hurtled through my mind: the last night we tried giving Edward the infusion. Jack and me, standing over him in the glaring light of the kitchen. Edward's face gray and then green as he began to choke, looking as if he were going to stop breathing. Jack making a sudden, furious sound, grabbing Edward out of his chair, lifting his small body and rubbing, shaking, pounding lightly on our son's back until he vomited and relaxed and the natural color returned to his skin. The two of us sitting at the table, huddled with Edward's body straddling both of ours, sharing him, rocking him, staying there for hours despite the mess on the floor and the darkening night. Swearing to each other we would never do this again. And that we would never tell a soul.

13

FOUR NIGHTS AFTER the sleep study, back in my own bed, I drifted through the layers of a chaotic, Technicolor dream, suddenly realizing I was wet. And cold. My bare calf grazed the sheet and the faint scent of salt water drifted up.

I stared into darkness at what would be the ceiling if I could see. I knew what this was. I'd been afraid it would happen the night we were at the hospital, but then the only strange occurrence was that Edward had slept, just as Nora had predicted he would. That night broke the cycle: I quit waking at three-thirty, and I was pretty sure he'd gotten at least three or four hours' sleep each night since.

Even as I thought this, I could hear him shifting upstairs. Long, careful movements that I knew from experience meant he was wide-awake. Again. I took a deep breath and stretched, extending my limbs and holding them rigid. To anyone who was watching, I would look like a bug on its back. A huge bug with a dangerously swollen thorax.

I sighed and moved my legs, wincing as I brushed against the wetness. Sitting up on the side of the bed, my back to Jack, I said, "I think it's started."

He didn't answer. He was lying face-up, snoring, which explained the dream: I always had a lot of these—surreal visions that moved in the choppy way of an old Super-8—when he was sleeping out loud.

Placing my palms flat on top of the bed, I pushed myself up and off with a hard thrust to clear the mattress. Once I was vertical, the trickle became steady. I went to the dresser for a change of clothes. Underpants as round and roomy as a knapsack, sweatpants (drawstring missing), and a white men's T-shirt, size extra-large. In the bathroom, I peeled off an outfit that was identical but for being saturated from the waist down. I used a washcloth to clean myself, steadying my bulk with a hand on the sink's edge. Then I dressed and went back down the hall to the bedroom, where I poked Jack awake.

He yawned and stretched like a bear. "Should we call them?"

I picked up my watch from the table at my side. It was five-twenty. "In about ninety minutes, rush hour will start. They could be caught on their way here. We could get caught on our way to the hospital. On the other hand . . ."

"I'm not worried about the hospital." Jack reached out and put his hand on my body, kneading a little as if he'd been cooking what was inside and would be able to feel if it was ready. "We can get there in ten minutes, easy, going the back way."

Then I felt something—a pain so vague it hardly counted, like someone tightening a wide, cloth belt under and around my belly for twenty seconds or so.

"That was one, wasn't it?" Even a monitor might not have detected a contraction so weak, but Jack could feel it. I put my head on his shoulder and closed my eyes, felt my face go warm with a flush of relief: in birth, the connection between us suddenly had returned. I would have my husband back, at least for this day. "Much as I hate to say it, Rae . . ." He sighed and kissed my head. "I guess we'd better call."

Twenty-six minutes later, my parents knocked on the front door. Jack had been timing them on his Mickey Mouse watch because since the contractions had stopped he'd had nothing else to do. "Not bad," he said as he walked toward the front hall. "This means he only went eighty."

"It's fucking freezing out there," my father announced as he stepped in the door, bringing with him the fresh, starched smell of snow. "Get coats. Warm ones."

"Well, you're going to have another baby!" My mother followed him in; her voice was bright but her eyes sagged and pillow wrinkles still striped her cheeks. She touched her hair into place, set her purse on the floor, and stood, one gloved hand resting on the back of Jack's oversize armchair, the other holding the small cloth kit she carried with her supplies—insulin bottles, glucose meter, syringes. "Don't worry about the boys. We'll be fine. You just get going and be sure to call us when there's news."

"No need." I said this from the middle of the hug my father had leaned over to give me. His unshaven jowls, wide and cool as salad plates, prickled against my cheek. "Nothing's happening now."

He straightened, still wearing his hat, the checked one with the English brim. Underneath his coat, I saw the lapel of his blue pajamas. "You're not in labor?" He turned to Jack. "So why the hell did you get me out of bed at five o'clock in the morning?"

"My water broke." For a moment, it occurred to me they might not believe me, that I'd have to stand and prove it somehow. "It seemed like labor might be starting and we didn't want to wait too long. But now . . ."

I looked up and, despite the morning light, my father appeared in darkened cutout like those old profiles of Alfred Hitchcock, the three-hundred-pound bulk of him set squarely between me and Jack. I couldn't catch Jack's eyes, but I saw his form as he raised his head and shook it slightly, long hair brushing his shoulder, then walked behind my dad and into the kitchen. There was the cowbell rattle of him lifting a frying pan from the rack behind the stove, the soft mouth sound of the refrigerator door being opened, the whoosh of a burner as it was lit.

"Susanna?" My father was still looking at me. "Where did Jack go? What's he doing?"

My mother went to the doorway of the kitchen. "Well, Abe, it looks like he's making an omelet. Jack? Are you making an omelet?"

Butter sizzled, sending off a sweet, smoky scent. I heard the delicate tap of eggshells meeting the edge of the counter. Six times. "Yes, I am. Would you like one?"

My mother smiled, considering. Jack was an excellent cook.

"He's eating?" My father took his hat off, looked up at the ceiling, and wiped his forehead. "He's eating *now*? This is crazy!"

"Please, let him eat." I was trying hard not to laugh. That could make my father angry and if he stormed out there would be no one else to stay with the boys. My mother always went with him when he left, lifting her eyebrows slightly in apology, never mentioning the incident again. "Please. He won't have time later, and we were told most fathers who faint in the delivery room do it because they're hungry."

Jack poked his head out of the kitchen. "Doctor's orders," he said, waving a spatula. "They're worried no one could pick me up if I fell over." He waited. I waited. Then my father smiled. "Omelet, Abe? Tomato and Cheddar. I have fresh basil, too."

I felt something tug inside my abdomen and I grimaced, trying to decide what it was.

"You are in labor, aren't you?" My father began to pace. "You just don't want to go to the hospital for one of those insane female reasons."

"I'm not. I wish I were, but I swear I'm not." My cheeks were hot.

"I think you should go anyway." This was my father's vice president of General Electric tone and it made me furious. I wouldn't leave this house now if the baby's head started to emerge from between my legs. I plotted it in my head, how I would rip the shower curtain from its plastic rings, throw it down on the couch, and give birth right there— efficiently and heroically, without yelping or complaining. He couldn't do that. I stared at him, hoping this message was beaming from my eyes.

Jack had entered the dining room with a plate and was sitting at the table, spearing a large chunk of tomato and egg with his fork, using the back of his hand to blot his mouth. He hummed as he ate.

Suddenly I was confused. What if Jack didn't know what he was doing? What if I was being irresponsible? What if my father was right?

He'd bent over to retrieve his hat and when he straightened, his face was firm. "You're making me too nervous. I just can't take it. Go. Now. What harm could it do?"

I imagined the potential harm: our embarrassment when we were sent home, my discomfort as we looked for a place to wait until my body was ready to cooperate, the possibility that I'd be hooked up to monitors and injected with something.

I looked at my mother, who had remained by the kitchen door as if she were still waiting for her eggs. "Well, you better go then." Her eyes shifted away. "It'll probably work out just fine."

Jack had finished eating and was holding the plate on his fingertips, fork balanced on top, a loose, dreamy expression on his face. When my eyes met his, he shrugged.

I debated whether to take a stand or cave in. But before I could decide, my father slapped the hat back on his head. "I'm getting out of here." He strode toward the front door and jerked it open. "I can't stand this." He glanced at my mother, who had moved and was standing, leaning against the dining room table, looking as if she were steadying herself on a rocking boat. "You deal with them, Susanna. I have work to do."

14

Not long after my father walked out the door, I had two jagged pains. They didn't have the shape of contractions—that arc of tightening and release—but they were close enough that Jack insisted it was time to leave. The sky had cracked open, gold and gray, and the streets shone. We sped down the highway, just minutes ahead of rush hour, and I held on to the door handle as Jack steered around a cloverleaf. But the moment we crossed the threshold of the hospital parking lot, the spasms vanished and my body again became blank and stubborn. I envisioned myself sentenced to a hospital bed: strapped to a fetal monitor, hooked to an IV, the long hose and needle of an enema bag coming at me. I begged Jack not to take me to the maternity floor just yet.

It was cold out, but not painfully so. We walked, hand in hand, on the grounds of the enormous hospital building and for the first time in months, I felt at ease with Jack. As mismatched as we were—a plump rabbit alongside a stately dinosaur—we stepped in sync. Halfway into the second loop around, I stopped, leaned against a wall, and breathed.

Jack looked at me and squinted. "Not a contraction?"

I shook my head. "Legs."

He nodded and slipped one arm around me, lifting until the downward pressure eased.

We moved slowly after this but finally reached the entrance again and went inside to warm up in the lobby. A few minutes later, the sliding glass doors opened with a whisking sound and a familiar-looking woman walked in carrying a large plastic tote bag. She was tall, sturdy, and muscular. If only I could recognize faces.

She stopped. "You having that baby?"

"Yes," I said. Then, "No. Well, not quite yet."

She shifted her bag from one hand to the other. There was a hot-pink feather boa coiled on top—the kind drag queens wear. I glanced up at her. She was one of those women who easily could be a man impersonating a woman. She caught me looking. "Uh, this is my husband. Jack."

He shook her hand. "Hi," he said. He was no help at all.

"Your son's results are in." Her hand was still in Jack's, but she was squinting at me. "Doctors have been talking about them for a couple days."

Nora! Her face clicked into focus. I imagined the little cap she wore, the white uniform. "Talking about what?"

"Well, they were a bit unusual." She pursed her lips. "I'm not supposed to say more. But . . ."

"But what?"

"I think you should come with me." She started toward the elevators, then turned back. "If you're sure you're not going to have that baby on us?"

"No big deal." I laughed. "You've got beds up there. And Jack's seen two born. He can deliver if I start to go fast."

"Sure." Jack nodded his head, mouth set with confidence, like he was agreeing to manage a big construction job.

We took the elevator up. It was seven o'clock, and people in the sleep center were just awakening. Nora went to the nurses' station and made marks on the tapes coming from a dozen machines. "Good, nothing big happened while I was out." She nodded at us. "You two, wait here."

She was back a few minutes later, bending down and rooting through her bag so the top items spilled over the sides. I couldn't stop myself: I started to ask her about the boa. That's when I felt the first real contraction, a hard squeezing, inside, down low, then a solid wave of pressure that traveled up and made my entire midsection a hard shell.

"That was one, wasn't it?" Jack asked softly. He was standing a full four feet behind me, not touching me or watching my face.

"How could you tell?" I whispered, turning.

He shrugged.

Nora pulled a thick, folded pack of papers from her bag and flattened them on the counter of the nurses' station. "I was looking at this just last night." It was actually one continuous length of paper with perforated seams between sections, blue lines running horizontally across the pages. Like waves, they were shallow in some places, very high in others, so the crests nearly ran off the top of the sheet. Nora flipped through the pages, folding them accordion-like in her left hand. As she went through them, the blue became more jagged, like the ocean during a storm, waves coming faster and faster, peaking in sharp triangles rather than rounded arcs.

"There." She pointed. This page was covered with blue ink. "That's your son. Asleep."

"Wow." Jack was bent over the page. "That doesn't look very restful."

I breathed through another contraction, quietly. Through my nose.

"Come." Nora swept the report off the counter and carried it, a long piece trailing behind her like a train. I could see her onstage, dressed like Liza Minnelli. "The doctor should be ready by now."

She showed us into an office with soft, leather-padded chairs around a conference table and we sat. I was worried about leaking on the leather, but I said nothing. Nora sat. Then she got up and opened a side door. "We're ready."

A ridiculously young man came in, hair in cowlicks, white coat askew, face creased. He sat at the table. "Coffee?" he asked Nora. This doctor made Barry Newberg look like a senior fellow.

"In a minute. We've gotta get these people out of here. Can't you see? She's going to have a baby."

The doctor's eyes widened and he looked suddenly more alert. He couldn't have been more than twenty-eight. Working in the sleep center, probably still an intern, he probably hadn't delivered many babies. "Now?" he asked.

"Soon," I admitted.

"How soon?"

"Very soon," Nora interrupted. "She's got that look. Why don't we just start?"

He cleared his throat thickly. "Okay. The truth is"—he shot a look at Nora, who nodded—"we've never, ah, seen an EEG like your son's. We've all looked at it, compared it with the data we've got and it . . . just . . . doesn't appear like any . . . other."

He looked at us as if he were expecting an attack.

"Yes?" Jack leaned back in his chair. "This doesn't surprise us."

"It doesn't?" The young doctor reached to his throat as if to straighten a tie, but his fingers ended up waving in the air because he wasn't wearing one.

"No. We've always known he was different." Jack gazed at the pictures on the walls—photographs of sunsets from all over the world—as if he'd already heard enough and was beginning to tune us all out.

"Have you looked at the EEGs of autistic children?" I sat forward. I was just seconds postcontraction, so I knew I had a clear two minutes ahead.

"Hundreds," the doctor said.

"Thousands." Nora raised her hand and grinned. "I'm a lot older."

"Does this look like any of those?"

The doctor shook his head slowly. "No, which is what we were expecting to find. But . . ."

"This spot here." Nora tapped her finger on the page she had showed us before. "It's not a seizure. That's the unusual part. There were *no* seizures. In autistic kids there are almost always a few small ones. But what this shows is about thirty times as much activity as a typical person would have during that phase of sleep."

"So he's thinking more?" Jack sounded almost bored. As if he knew all this and was reviewing it only for our benefit. "He can't sleep because his brain is more active than most people's."

"It would appear . . ." The doctor stopped, looking perplexed. I felt sorry for him and wished someone would bring him his coffee. I would have done it myself if I hadn't felt another wave of pain starting.

Jack stood. "Thanks." He held out his hand and the doctor stood, too, to shake it.

"Wait!" I didn't mean to shout, but I was just counting through the last iron clench of my abdomen, panting a little. I held up my hand. "So, what do we do?" I asked after the pain had passed. "How do we help him sleep? Brain activity or no, he seems to need the sleep. God, I need the sleep. Please."

Nora waved at the young doctor. "Go ahead. Get caffeinated. Have a shower." He tipped his head gratefully. "I'll finish up here." She looked down at me. I wasn't trying to hide my labor any longer; I was doing full-scale Lamaze breathing, in through the nose, out through the mouth. She slipped an arm under my elbow and lifted me off the chair in one fluid move, as if I didn't weigh nearly 180 pounds. "We're going to get you to Labor and Delivery."

"But. What about . . . ?" The contractions had grown fierce. Talking made me choke and I felt as if I had to concentrate in order to avoid being sucked down into the pain.

"In a minute." Jack was on the other side of me now and they were steering. I lifted my feet off the floor at one point and they kept moving, bearing me up between them.

Then the pain was gone, completely, and I could walk again. I put my feet back on the floor. "Okay. I'm fine." I looked up at Nora. "Now, tell us. While I can listen."

We got in the elevator and Nora pushed a button. The metal doors slid closed and it was just the three of us, plus the baby straining to get out. "There's nothing the docs can recommend," she said. "Not and keep their licenses. But I don't worry about that. I'm a loudmouth by nature. And no one pays any attention to what I do."

"I've got another minute and a half here." It came out bitchy. But Nora grinned.

"Okay. Unofficially, I'm letting you know about melatonin. It's not approved. You'd have to get it on your own. You'd have to assume the risks." She shrugged. More and more, this woman reminded me of Jack. "Understand, I'm not recommending it. Officially."

"Understood." He nodded. "We're pretty open to nontraditional treatments. So where do we get it?" I felt the hair-pulling sensation that meant a contraction was coming.

"Almost any health food store. It's a hormone. Bovine, I think. Unregulated. Could be full of impurities. I'd do a little research on brands. Choose carefully."

Insulin once was made of bovine hormone, too, and it saved people's lives. Twenty years ago, my mother would have taken it. I opened my mouth to say this—and then it hit me. Not just pain, but the feeling that the baby's head was there, pressing down, about to burst out between my legs.

"Oh, my God! This baby is coming." I leaned against the metal railing at the back of the elevator and screamed. Envisioned her shooting out of me and skittering across the floor, hitting her head on the doors. That's when they slid open.

"Relax." Jack moved slowly even now. But he knew what to do. He got behind me, took my shoulders, and leaned me back against his chest; without the force of gravity it seemed possible to hold on to the baby for a few more seconds. "Women don't give birth in elevators in real life. That's only on TV."

Nora laughed. "I'll get a wheelchair." She stepped out of the elevator, still chortling. My heart was pounding.

"Breathe," Jack told me. "The baby needs air."

Nora trundled the chair over the metal threshold of the elevator and they sat me down. The pain had vanished again. There was only a ghost of the pressure imprinted where her head had been, inside, against my pelvic bones. The labor suite was close and it looked less like a hospital room than one my mother had decorated: pale blue walls, eyelet curtains, and spread. Nora and Jack lifted me together, onto the bed.

"I shouldn't be on the . . ." I gestured down at the white bedcover.

Nora rolled her eyes. "Honey, they don't have anything in this place that isn't one hundred percent washable."

Then the pain came again and the baby's head was pushing so hard I could feel membranes tearing inside me and the last thing I heard was Jack saying, in a voice that was much louder than his real one, "When my wife says now, she *means* now."

And three minutes later, just seconds after a doctor I'd never met stepped through the door still pulling on his rubber gloves, Grace arrived.

15

THERE IS NO shower as good as the one right after giving birth. And I knew this would be the last one, so I took my time.

My mother had come and was walking with the baby, no doubt showing her to every laboring mother in the hall, while Jack sorted out all the forms we hadn't filled out on the way in. I made the water so hot my skin turned red and showed marks from the spray. Nine months of nausea, breathlessness, and pain—disappeared in an instant. And with that wonderful absence, a small wise-looking girl. I had promised God I would give up everything, yet at this moment it seemed as if the world were righting itself. I imagined Edward's slim body appearing in the vapor from the shower, wavering, breaking apart.

I stepped out, dried quickly, and wrapped a towel around myself. It was nice to fit in a towel again. I was in a single room—Jack insisted on my having privacy and I let him, even though I knew we shouldn't be paying the extra $50 a day. I got into the bed, still damp, and the room darkened slightly. Looking up, I saw my father filling the doorway, as if he'd transported himself from the front door of our house—my last vision of him—to this place. He edged into the room, staying close to the wall.

"Where's the baby?" I asked.

"Your mother . . ." He gestured toward the hall with one hand. "She'll be back." He paused. "I don't understand why you did this. It seems crazy to me."

I knew immediately what he was saying: the third baby. We were inadequate, unstable parents with one blighted child and no prospects for success of any kind.

In that instant, my euphoria was gone. I looked down at the sheet, which was white and clean, and I wished for sleep. "We thought about this very carefully." Tears gathered behind my eyes. "He's a good husband. He's a good father."

"He is a good father, one of the best I've ever seen. In many ways, better than I ever was to you." He looked up at the ceiling. "But. He just doesn't have what it takes to get ahead. Ambition. Or drive. Follow-through. I don't know, something. It just isn't there. He'll be nothing more than a beat cop the rest of his life."

I was thirsty and my plastic pitcher was empty. All I wanted was a cold glass of water and some sleep. "Do we have to do this right now?"

My father held up his hand. "Hey, I come in peace. I just had to say this. I hate . . ." He paused. It was the first time I'd ever seen my father swallow back something he meant to say. "You're never going to have enough to support a family of five."

"You don't know that!" I squirmed under the covers.

"Look." My father was holding his hat again, turning it around in his hands. "You're going to need money."

"No."

"Yes." His voice rose, trumpeting over mine. "Face facts for once in your adult life. You and your husband don't have what it takes to raise three kids and I do. I'll help you out. For a while."

We stared at each other, his eyes strangely frightened in an old face.

Jack walked in during the silence, Grace wrapped in a blanket, tiny against his muscled forearms. "I think she's hungry." He handed her to me, kissing my forehead as our hands touched around the baby. "Abe." Jack nodded.

My father pushed off the wall and came to the side of the bed. He reached out with one smooth white hand and pulled the blanket away from the baby's face. "Well." His throat hitched and he cleared it. "She's perfect. A mitzvah." He held his hand out to Jack. "Congratulations," he said.

"To you, too," Jack said, smiling. Over my bed, over the body of the girl, their hands met. And clenched.

The afternoon was long. Grace lay in a clear, plastic bassinet next to my bed and made humming noises. So far, she didn't seem to be a sleeper.

The boys had been and left. Matt had tried to grab the baby's face with his little fingers so he could turn it to kiss her. Edward looked vacant but then he brought the back of one of his hands to rest gently against her cheek for a brief second—like a butterfly's wing brushing her, then moving on.

Now there was a light knock at the door and Eric cleared his throat before walking in. He came directly to the bed, handed me a wrapped triangle of floral paper, and retreated quickly. I imagined there were roses inside, dark red, announcing his love. "I hear you did well." He walked around my room, peered inside the bathroom. I wondered if it was clean.

I had no makeup on and was trying to remember if I had brushed my hair after the shower. "How did you hear?"

"Your dad. He called, afraid you'd lose your job if you didn't come to work. I told him this was a good enough excuse to take a few days."

"And you came."

"I had to make sure you were okay to write. I thought you could do some quick proofreading for me while you're just lying around in the hospital." He smiled and I smiled back.

"Do you want to hold her?"

"God, no. I've never held anyone. Ah . . ." His face reddened. "You know what I mean."

"Come on. Sit down." I patted the spot next to my legs.

He moved silently in his leather jacket and faded jeans and when he sat down on the bed, I felt my whole body shift toward him. I was warm with hormones and coffee and the lunch that tasted as if it were the first thing I'd eaten in years—every flavor of the hospital food snapping like a color inside my mouth. It didn't seem wrong at all to seduce my boss with this new baby.

I leaned over him to lift her out of her bed. "Here."

Eric held his hands up, palms splayed. "No. Like this." I tucked Grace into my left arm and used my right to rearrange him so his elbow was crooked and ready. "Now." I settled her into his arms and pulled the blanket back, just as my father had done hours earlier, to show him her lovely, elfin face.

"You're directing me again." He was almost cradling her, rocking a little.

"Yes, I am. And you like it."

His face darkened. "She's really beautiful," he said. "Do you know yet if she's okay?"

I positioned myself so I was looking over his shoulder at Grace. The three of us might look like a family this way. "She seems fine."

"I mean," he shifted around, wrinkling the sheets, moving closer to me, "do you know she isn't like your son? Can they test her?"

Now, my throat felt like a guitar string, winching tighter. "No." I reached for the baby and Eric gave her to me. I checked her, hating that he had said any of this while he was touching her. Jack would never have said something like that, or even thought it. But I might. I remembered Edward's hand against her cheek and guilt washed over me.

"Edward doesn't have some sort of disease that shows up on tests. He's just . . ." I reached for a word, the sort of word Jack would use. All I could see was Edward's raccoon eyes staring at me. "He's better, in a lot of ways." I squeezed Grace too hard and her arms flew up in the defensive baby move, the one that makes them look as if they're reaching up to catch baseballs.

"I'm sorry. That was rude. I shouldn't have said anything." Eric hunched over the side of the bed, elbows planted on his knees. "It's just, I would hate to see you take on any more. You're already dealing with Edward. And Jack's problems."

Something buzzed in my sinuses and at the bridge of my nose. For one crazy minute, I was certain Eric and my father had been talking about us.

"I don't think of it that way," I said firmly. But this wasn't true. Recently, I had begun thinking of it: if I'd waited to marry someone like Eric in my midtwenties, we'd just be having our first baby. Grace. We'd have enough money to go out to dinner. He'd always have a job. But there would be no Matt. No Edward. Just the three of us, sleeping and eating like people are supposed to do. The thought of the boys' disappearing, never having been, made my throat nearly close with panic.

Then I looked at Eric, sitting so close to me in his clean shirt and pressed jeans, a silver watch strapped precisely to its spot, centered just above the knobby bone on his left wrist. And I thought, He would never understand. It came to me in a sentence, like someone had spoken the words inside my head. *He thinks Edward is broken.* Suddenly, an image of Scott popped into my head: all of us at Mariel's farm, him with his watch, gaudier than Eric's—heavy and gold, with two rings circling the face. Also a cell phone and a constant self-satisfied sneer, turning away to take a call, ignoring us, ignoring her. Something fierce rose inside me, making my face flush and my heart pound. These men were nothing compared with my husband.

Eric turned his head and looked at me. He blinked and rose slowly. "She's perfect, and she looks well behaved. Remember what I said: you're welcome to bring her to work with you. When you're ready."

I nodded. "I'd like to take a few months," I said. "Stay home with the children for a while. If that's okay."

Eric leaned down as if he were going to kiss me, then set his chin on the top of my head for a moment. "Get some sleep," he said into my hair. "You're going to need it."

After he left, I sat with Grace for a long time, rocking her back and forth as Eric had done. I stared at the door and once I might have whispered, *Good-bye.*

16

DESPITE EVERYTHING I'd felt, I was restless and irrationally lonely after Eric left. I missed him and the whiff of the outside world he brought with him. The euphoria of birth was subsiding and I'd grown tired in a faded, itchy way. But I felt virtuous, too. I had promised God I would give up everything—my career, which certainly wouldn't be helped by my taking an extended leave, and the phantom relationship with Eric that had been my only private vice. It was a reasonable trade. Neat, in fact. I found satisfaction in adding up the columns and knowing I had paid my debt. I was the wife of a law officer, the mother of three; it was time to become a real adult, an honorable woman.

When we arrived home, on the afternoon following Grace's birth, Jack carried her into the house, where my mother waited with the two boys. Each of them was holding something and Matt immediately ran toward Jack, bouncing back off his knees, holding up the stuffed monkey he had chosen and pushing it as high into the air as he could. Jack knelt. Matt dusted the baby's face with the toy and she sneezed.

"You, too," my mother said, giving Edward a pat from behind. I sat on the couch and watched him walk toward Jack, purposefully but with his eyes trained on the floor. When he arrived, Edward stared at the baby for a full minute before raising his left hand, the one that was not holding something, and touching one of her eyes.

"Careful," said Jack. He moved Edward's hand to her cheek. "Do you have something for her?"

Edward raised the giraffe he held by its long neck. "Horse," he said, and dropped it on Grace. My heart sank.

"It's a giraffe, honey," Jack said, tucking it into Grace's blankets. "See the long neck."

"No." Edward looked up and that's when I noticed both things in his eyes: another sleepless night, but something else, too. Something like the look before someone winks. "It's a horse."

I looked again and saw, plainly, what I had missed before: despite the elongated neck, this animal had a horse's face.

By the weekend, three days later, it felt right and natural to be a family of five. But I was exhausted and by Friday night it was all I could do to sit in the living room, watching TV with Grace on my lap.

Jack stood in the middle of the room, holding a white bottle of melatonin; he had his glasses pushed up on top of his head so he could read the tiny print on the label. "I'm going to give it to him." Grace, still awake, waved her arms at the sound of his voice. Jack grinned and waved back at her before walking up the stairs.

I could hear him talking to the boys. The water running, stopping, running again so they could brush their teeth. Matt's feet pattering quickly across the floor above my head. Edward's limp-legged shuffle as he moved from the bathroom to his bed. He had not slept since the night before Grace was born.

"Under your tongue." Jack's words floated down the stairs. "Now swallow."

He came down a few minutes later, ducking automatically so he wouldn't hit his head on the doorframe. He looked at his watch. "It's nine-seventeen. I'll check him at ten."

"Fine." I refused to get my hopes up. We waited, sitting side by side on the couch, not speaking. The television program I'd been watching ended at nine-thirty. I turned off the TV with the remote, opened my shirt, and began feeding Grace. Jack rubbed my back. Grace sighed.

At 9:52, Jack jumped up. "I'm going to look." He was bouncing on his toes.

"You were going to wait." *Not yet, not yet.* Inside my head, I was begging for a few more minutes of hope. *Just a few minutes longer.*

"I can't stand it. I'm going."

Jack walked up the stairs. I lifted Grace and set her against my shoulder so her warm face fit into the hollow of my neck. She sucked little fish-mouthed kisses on my skin. Five minutes passed. The house was silent.

When Jack came down the stairs this time, he forgot to duck. I was watching, startled, thinking he might be hurt, but only his hair grazed the top of the doorframe. He came toward me, head straight, tears leaking down his face in two straight lines.

"He's asleep." He stood in front of me, very straight and tall, as if he were in school giving a speech. "Really asleep. I sat by his bed and just kept sitting there, thinking he'd move, or something. But he didn't. And I could hear him breathing. He and Matt, both sleeping." He sat next to me and stared straight ahead. "It's real."

I felt numb. Nothing had been lost, nothing but a fraction of the trust between Jack and me. And the lilt of hope I'd attached to Eric, which had been an indulgence anyway. Just one of many distractions I'd used to escape the fear that had filled me since that day at the Aurora library. Now, for the first time in two years, that cold terror began to melt. I took a breath and stared, searching for a response—whether to Jack or to God, I wasn't sure—but there was none. I told myself I would call Nora in the morning, probably cry as I thanked her. But right now, there was simply nothing to say.

I eased Grace down so I could look at her face. Her eyes were closed. I settled her in on the side closest to Jack and leaned back against his chest, burrowing us both inside his arms so it was like he and I were holding the baby together. We sat this way for more than an hour, listening to nothing but the wind rattling branches against the windows and the steady, quiet breathing of three sleeping children.

BO

IN EARLY DECEMBER 1952, President-elect Dwight D. Eisenhower went to Korea for three days. The war in that country had been raging for two and a half years, but quietly and without the wild patriotism of previous wars. American soldiers shipped out and were swallowed up by a country ten times more foreign than England or France; this was a place tucked between Communist Russia and the islands of Japan, full of people—enemies and allies alike—whose faces were entirely different from the freckled and blond and black-skinned American boys who moved through them wearing olive fatigues and carrying M1 rifles.

It even looked like the landscape of some distant planet: rocky hills against a pewter sky to the east, rolling terrain with dirt fields and glossy rice paddies to the west. And in winter, a constant, bitterly cold, somehow visible wind that swept down the peninsula like a train gathering steam, all the way from Siberia.

Eisenhower's conclusion was that the war was not working. This was no Nazi Germany with evil combatants who identified themselves even in the way they walked. Here there were enlisted men milling, growing nearly as restless as the prisoners of war they guarded. The man who would be president returned to the United States determined to renew diplomatic efforts to end the war. But ten days later, 3,600 internees on the island of Pongam-do organized a mass revolt; guards fired on them, killing 85 and wounding another 113. And the war only intensified as winter descended.

Mickey had been on a small, hidden air force base outside Yongju since July. And after arriving he had become a completely different person from the one he'd been in Minnesota. During the day, he learned the science of flight. A test he'd taken at the conscription office had determined something about him; the officer who'd tallied the results had excused himself and gone behind a closed door, then returned to tell Mickey he had a rare gift for "spatial relations." They would make him an air traffic controller. After twelve years of failing tests in school, it was nearly impossible for Mickey to believe.

But now, he did believe what the test had showed. Sitting in the tiny hut where the radio equipment lay amid a tangle of strings and cords on a rickety desk, Mickey understood everything he was told by the departing controller. Like Susanna, whom he had watched glance over her spelling lists once and then earn all A's, Mickey immediately understood everything he was being taught—the way you had to factor wind speed and direction into an aircraft's landing plan; the fact that a pilot had to drop his armament a fraction of a second before he reached the target he intended to hit, in order to account for the acceleration between that action and the bomb bay's actually opening. It was as if all this knowledge was already inside him. All Mickey needed to do was listen once to the homebound soldier's instructions and it was magically unearthed.

Nothing but baseball had ever come to him this effortlessly. And even that, astonishing as it was, had not been enough.

Mickey's brief turn at athletic stardom had come out of nowhere. As a child he had been friendless, wandering the alleys alone most afternoons, ashamed because he often gave the wrong answers in class and was whipped with the sisters' rulers. His knuckles were perpetually raw. The school felt cold and dank to him even in spring—a place with too much noise and movement, too many nonsensical rules. Faces in the hallways blurred together, like a stream of laughing clowns passing him on a train. He felt hungry all the time. And he never forgot that this was the place where Frank had gone to begin to die.

At the end of eighth grade, Mickey failed two of his exams and there was a question, up until the last week, as to whether he would graduate along with his classmates and move on to the high school. Father

Bernard let him go because of Frank; he didn't want to cause the Donnellys any more grief. But Mickey knew he hadn't deserved to advance. He didn't belong with the boys who moved easily around him, calling to one another, shoving, jostling, clustering to talk in hoarse whispers. When he passed them, he kept his head down and stared at the cracked tile floor. His mother wanted him to become a priest and Mickey had begun considering it, though he felt no connection to God.

One afternoon, the summer before he entered high school, Mickey found an old baseball and glove in a box in the garage. They had been Frank's. He lifted them to his nose and breathed, wondering if the leather still held his brother's sweat. Then he slipped the glove on his left hand and nestled the ball inside. For the rest of the day he had walked this way, sometimes slipping the ball out and tossing it back and forth, catching it neatly in the glove so the sound it made was a solid, hollow little thwack. He caught Frank's ball hundreds of times that day and began throwing it higher; by evening, he was pitching it yards into the soft, damp, darkening sky and each time he would simply extend the glove and the ball would return to it. He never dropped the ball, not once, not even when the sun disappeared and dusk glistened and he couldn't trust his eyes to follow the white sphere among a backdrop of planets and stars. Never in his life had anything felt so natural and right.

By the time he began ninth grade, the boys in the neighborhood had noticed Mickey—his arm, his unerring movement toward the ball. They told the coach, who called Mickey from his math class on only the third day of school and asked him to try out. He handed Mickey a bat and pitched to him, slowly at first and then faster; out of thirty pitches, Mickey hit twenty-one, his body moving toward the ball in one long, smooth pivot, his arms extending like wings to move the bat, his mouth setting with silent satisfaction each time he heard the pop of hard wood against leather and twine.

Coach Halloran claimed he'd never seen a boy begin playing at fourteen. The other players were boys who had been practicing since they were in the primary grades, beginning as stumpy children in short pants, hitting a ball off a steel post driven into the ground. With those boys, even in high school, Coach still yelled out instructions for each move: *bunt, run, stay on base, you knucklehead.* But when Mickey was at bat, or on the pitcher's mound, the old man would stand to the side, scratching the white fringe of hair around his bald head, or rubbing absentmindedly at the belly hanging over his cloth belt and leggings, never saying a word.

Mickey wasn't close to any of the boys on the team. Throughout grade school—before he'd been discovered—they had tormented him, turning away on the playground, snickering when he answered questions incorrectly in class, counting with nods of their heads when he was being struck with the sisters' rulers. When he joined the team, suddenly they wanted to be friends and shrug away eight years of cruelty. But Mickey wanted no part of them. The only boy he allowed in, James Huber, was too young to have participated.

When James began following the team, the year he was in eighth grade and Mickey was in tenth, it was in a relentlessly quiet, polite, nearly subservient way that made Mickey both pleased and angry. There was something eerily familiar about James that unsettled Mickey. But James was always there, ready to carry bats, offering to pitch balls for Mickey, running after the wild ones that flew into the woods surrounding the baseball diamond at the park.

"He's going to be a major leaguer," Coach told Ted after a game Mickey's junior year in which he had batted in seven runs. Coach had clapped Mickey on the shoulder when he said this, then pointed to a seat at the very top of the bleachers. "When scouts come, they sit up there. You watch, son. One of them's goin' to come for you someday." A little ways down in the stands, James Huber sat with a group of boys from the freshman class; they were still cheering and whistling and calling Mickey's name.

"You think so, do you?" Ted asked, sounding uncertain. On the way home, he had asked Mickey, "A career in baseball. Is that what you want?"

Mickey had shrugged. "I don't know." He gazed out the car window, watching the trees along the road recede into the gathering gloom of evening.

"It seems to me," Ted said slowly, "you can't just want to play, you also have to want to win."

That was the night Mickey realized how much his father knew, not just about gems and gold prices but about him. Later, when the scouts came and went without inviting Mickey to try out for their teams, it did not come as such a great disappointment. It might, Mickey admitted to himself now, have even been a relief. But his mother and sisters continued to believe he would be a great player someday.

"I don't see why you can't at least try for a scholarship," Mary had told him the month he was to graduate from high school. "Eric Halloran said there was a chance."

"Sure he did." Mickey's voice was an adult's now. Steady, even if he still felt uncertain. "Coach wants to see his name in lights, the guy who discovered the next great home run king. But I'm not that. I'm ten seconds slower than the worst guy in the major leagues and most of them are four, five years older than I am."

"So you try. You stay here. You play on a college team and get your degree. You don't go off to some place no one's ever heard of to fight someone else's war."

"Mary, Mary, dear." Ted sounded tired. "Harry Truman says this is our war. It's for the people of the world. For democracy. He would be fighting for what's right."

Mickey didn't know if the war was right, but for the first time in his life what he himself was doing felt worthwhile. Like real movement after years spent aimless, stranded in a place where he never fit.

Each night in Korea, he lay awake, his head full of diagrams and trajectories of planes he had steered but never seen. He had lived a life of regular bedtimes. Back home, he would lie awake into the early-morning hours night after night and drag through the day following, feeling gritty and dumb from the lack of sleep. But here in this sandy, deserted land of rock and hills and open air, his body seemed to need almost no rest at all. He might fall into bed when the other men did, ignoring the rough fabric of the mattress pressing upward through the limp sheet. But sometime after midnight he would awaken, alert, feeling as if he'd just experienced some brief, benign surge of electricity. The sky was always pale, never the blanket of darkness he knew back home but a constant glow of near-dawn. His body seemed to shut off its understanding of time and operate in a new way—like a machine constantly idling, ready at any moment to throttle back up to maximum speed.

It took him until August to realize he could get up, that no one would come to fetch him, prod him to take an aspirin or drink warm milk before getting back into bed. For the first time in his life, he was able to read with ease—alone, sitting on the ground under the sulfurous illumination of a Coleman lantern. Against the backdrop of the blank eastern horizon, in a country where most people spoke in a series of undecipherable staccato bursts of long and short sounds like Morse code, English suddenly made more sense.

And he began writing letters. *You asked if there was anything you could send and I shur would like more books,* he told his mother. He couldn't explain the way, suddenly, his thoughts flowed fairly easily through the pen and onto paper. *I like Zane Grey and Louis L'Amour but whatever you can get is good. Don't worry a lot, xcept I know you will. I'm okay and eating fine.*

By the time fall came, Mickey was sleeping even less: two or three hours at most. That's when he began to walk. At first, he stayed within the perimeter of the encampment, a small oblong that he might circle twenty times. He grew lean. Before long, his uniform—which had fit him perfectly when it was issued—was loose, swishing around him like a woman's skirt. He'd developed the habit of checking the spaces between his ribs with his index fingers, pressing them in and feeling with fascination and horror and pride the lack of flesh there, the hard, knobbed ridges of bone. Like a wolf, he'd grown rangy and wild. Inside him, there was a rhythm like a faraway drum whose cadence told him to stay watchful, keep moving.

One night Mickey set off, heading toward the charcoal silt and rubble of the distant hills. As he stepped across the camp's border something came out of the dimness, sweeping down from a great height, and grabbed his arm with a strong, certain grip. Mickey gasped and yanked away from the thing, then began to fall. But the hand that had accosted him was joined by another and together they caught Mickey, gently and easily, like a man taking hold of his dance partner after twirling her. "Stop," said a low voice. "You're gonna trip the alarm."

His heart drumming furiously, Mickey righted himself and breathed the dusty scent of the mountains. Facing him, looking down from a face that loomed like a big, dark moon, the man was still holding Mickey's arm—as if he'd simply forgotten to take his hand away. Mickey had never felt the skin of a black man before; he'd always assumed it would be leathery, like a lizard's hide. But if he were to close his eyes, this man's hand would feel like any other, like his father's. Though larger, and maybe even softer.

"Identify yourself, soldier." Mickey saw the black-and-white brassard worn by military police wrapped around the other man's arm.

"Second Lieutenant Mickey Donnelly," he said. Then added in a small voice, "Sir?"

The MP grinned then, a flash of white teeth, and let go of Mickey's arm. "None of that *sir* shit; name's Bo. But you're gonna have to tell me what the hell you're doin' out here this time of night."

"Man, if you want to walk," Bo said after Mickey explained his insomnia, pointing into the distance at the rim of pearly light that kept him awake night after night, "you're goddamn well gonna have to walk with me. I'll keep your white ass protected." Bo stamped the butt of his rifle on the packed dirt for emphasis and Mickey felt the thrill of adolescence, of hearing a man use the words he'd thought but never said, speaking in a voice so strong and confident that they sounded as powerful as the words of a prayer.

They walked together that night, and throughout the next months, right into the coldest season Mickey had ever known. Nights, he would put on all the clothes rationed to him, then throw a blanket over his shoulders, like an Indian poncho. Bo wore a torn rag of flannel around his head and a winter-weight coat, but otherwise his uniform had barely changed from summer. On his hands, he had army-issue gloves from which he had cut the top half of the right index finger slot.

"You Minnesota boys ain't so tough in the cold as a person woulda thought." He shoved Mickey sideways, the impact warming the spot on his shoulder where Bo's elbow touched. Mickey felt a childlike satisfaction bubbling through him. He'd never had a best friend before. He was in awe of the fact that every night they could meet and walk through long stretches of silence, yet speak to each other—when they did—in short, clear sentences without the bewildering falseness of conversation back home.

It was January before Bo mentioned his brother.

"Rex told me about the nights," he said, breaking ten minutes of trudging, the crunch of heavy boots on snow, and the wind that moved through the mountain crevices in sheets of sound. "He wrote and said, 'long about this time, the world starts to seem the same all over. Just a lonely dark place."

"Who's Rex?" Mickey had thrown the blanket all the way over his head, so the question came out of it as if from a tent.

"He was my brother."

"Was?"

"He dead. War killed him. The last one. Fact, that letter was the last one I got before the telegram for our mama, January of forty-three, tellin' her he was gone. No body, just disappeared forever."

"Where?"

Bo stopped. Closed his eyes for a moment and nearly smiled. "Africa," he said. "Funny, ain't it?"

"No." Mickey shifted the blanket from his head to his shoulders, felt the cold settle on his scalp like a cap. "I'm sorry."

"Yeah. Me, too. Me, too." Bo rubbed his chin with his exposed index finger. The nail was white as a pearl against his dark skin, the size of a small watch face. Then he started walking again and Mickey automatically moved, too.

"Funny name for a kid from Detroit. Rex." He was panting a little. Bo's pace had picked up since he mentioned his brother and Mickey had to skip in between steps in order to keep up. "Like an Englishman."

"Really?" Bo grinned. "That's a good one. He'da liked that."

"So why Rex?"

"He was Reginald, after our daddy. But they was six Reggies on our block, and another couple on the next one. Town just couldn't take another, so when he went off to school . . ." He squinted into the distance, snow glowing on the hills as they rose against the dark sky. "I suspect it was Mama thought of it. She was the type to know about fancy names and such."

An idea cracked like light inside Mickey's head. "So you're . . . Beauregard. Aren't you?"

"Now don't you be tellin' no one." He thumped Mickey's back. "I don't want to have to take you all out." Bo tossed the rifle he carried from hand to hand, as if it were a baton.

They turned to the south when they came to the small red flag marking the edge of the station's perimeter. "They left me home," Bo said, his voice small as if he were talking to himself. "Said I was the man of the house since my daddy was dead. Took my little brother."

"How old was he?"

"Seventeen . . . just shavin', still cuttin' his face wide open every time."

"And you?"

"I was about your age: nineteen, nearly twenty. Had a job at the furniture store, movin' heavy things. My mama needed me. Least that's what they said."

Numbers flashed in Mickey's head, the way they always had. Never in columns but in spaces that seemed to have dimension. He couldn't do the math neatly, only estimate fast. "But that means you're almost—"

"Yup. You're speakin' to an old, old man. Be thirty years old my next birthday."

"They wouldn't call you up." Mickey saw another picture in his head: the letter that had arrived at their house in Minneapolis, marked *Official Government Correspondence, U.S. Military,* exactly four weeks after his graduation.

"Nope. They didn't call me. I called them."

"Why?"

"Shoulda been me, the first time. Shoulda been me fightin' that war in Africa, gettin' killed there. Seemed like the only way to set it all straight. Give God another chance." Bo looked up. "I keep tellin' Him

He can have me, too. Mama died. She don't need me. Ain't nobody on this earth would lose too much sleep over my bein' dead."

Mickey shivered and pretended it was from the cold. "Were you close? I mean, did you know Rex well?"

"What kind of a crazy question is that?" Bo peered down at Mickey. "He was my brother. Of course I knew him. Who don't know his own goddamn brother?"

"I didn't." Mickey found a thread on the blanket's edge and worked it between his thumb and one finger. The weave was so tight, it unraveled with a tiny snapping sound as each knot came unjoined. "I was three."

"He die?"

Mickey nodded.

"Maybe you was lucky." Bo's voice came out soft, sleepy almost. And the men walked on, moving back toward camp now, the flat-roofed buildings lying squat in front of them, boxes containing rows of sleeping men and boys. Many of them, Mickey thought, brothers. A few minutes later, Bo spoke again. "Nah, I guess I was wrong. Be better to know your own brother."

Mickey said nothing and the sky whitened with predawn light as they walked toward camp and the men, who were only beginning to stir and awaken into the cold, still air.

In spring, tiny, tight buds came out on the trees lining the hills. Within a few weeks, a heavy, wet heat settled in stealthily and the air around the rice paddies moved in shimmers of rose and yellow. Mickey routed American planes each morning, working first on graph paper, then over the headset with pilots all over South Korea.

Often, when he was alone and awake in the early-morning hours before dawn, frantic to tell someone about everything that had changed, Mickey would fill five or six tissue-thin airmail sheets with his spiky handwriting and send them to Eleanor. He told her about Bo, about his own surprisingly strong body, about the way the lights of the tiny bombers glittered through the dusty nights. Eleanor had boys of her own now, and a marriage in which Mickey detected bleakness, though he couldn't say exactly why; she wrote back on heavy paper that bore her name engraved in gilt script at the top, like a fancy menu. She reported nothing about her own life, only that their father looked tired and old and their mother was attending Mass daily, praying for Mickey to return; she signed her notes simply, *Love*.

He realized then the fear his mother must feel, imagining Korea a wild and foreign place. So he wrote to his parents and Susanna religiously, every week, two-page letters containing the funny comments of his bunkmates, news of the change to summer uniforms, summaries of the movies they'd watched in the mess tent after dinner, paragraphs about the surprising boredom of war.

When the first envelope came from Susanna, he opened it expecting the sort of chipper note she'd been trained to write: *We've had several days of rain, but the sun seems to be peeking out this morning. . . . Mother bought a new rosebush for the garden, American Beauty, and Dad's been digging the hole this afternoon, no doubt wishing you were here to help.* But this was different; she'd written about James Huber. *I've been out with him three times since May. But we always end up talking about you. There's something sweet about it, but strange, too. And I can't imagine marrying him, though I know that's what everyone is thinking.*

Mickey hadn't thought about James in a long time. During his senior year, before the big game with Central High, they had spent several weeks in the field behind the school, volleying the ball back and forth until it was only a small white spot rising in the dusky evening sky. One unusually sticky night, they had gone into the locker room to shower off afterward and Mickey tried to respond appropriately as James prattled about his own plans for high school, baseball, a career in the majors. Over the years, he'd developed the ability to appear interested even when his mind was full of the abstract darkness that overtook him whenever he was not running at full speed. Then there was a moment when the sound of James's voice stopped and Mickey realized he must have erred—failed to hear a pause that required a grunt or a nod.

They were toweling off and Mickey had dropped his to the floor, was leaning forward into the locker his mother kept full of fresh changes of underwear. He backed out to look at James and saw on his face a mixture of something he had only seen in church, a vapid, prayerful expression that made him turn red-hot for reasons he could not name. To this day, he had never told a soul.

Now, holding Susanna's letter, Mickey considered the boy he'd abruptly stopped meeting at the ball field, whose calls he'd quit returning, and pictured James standing next to Bo—a faint, white shadow of a man twice his size. And Mickey wondered, idly, if the two met whether they would even know how to speak to each other.

In May of 1953, Mickey was told he would be sent home by year's end. His first-year term was nearly up and when he went to Seoul to reenlist, he was given a physical and an eye exam.

"Good Lord, son," the tiny army doctor said as he clicked new lenses into the black viewer. "You say you've been directing planes?"

Mickey nodded. His throat was dry, a feeling he remembered from every math test he'd ever taken. He was failing this exam, too; it was clear from the way the little man kept rifling through the back of his padded box, looking for thicker and thicker discs of glass.

"It's your lucky day." The doctor chuckled in a way Mickey knew was meant to be kind. "Not only do you get these . . ." He handed Mickey a worn pair of horn-rimmed glasses that were chipped in several places and looked as if they'd been worn by someone else—someone engaged in heavier combat. Mickey wondered what had happened to their previous owner. "But you also get discharge papers, effective in June. We can't have you bringing in planes." He clapped Mickey on the back and laughed again. "You go back stateside, I'm not sure you should even be driving."

Mickey knew it was useless to explain: he didn't use his eyes nearly so much as he "saw" the way the planes traveled inside his head. The pilots were safe, would be safe even if he were blindfolded. He opened his mouth to speak but closed it, remembering the nuns' tight lips and twitching rulers when he insisted he had arrived at the right answer for an algebra problem without having any idea how he got there.

Over the next several weeks, Mickey's walks continued but his pace slowed. Summer was coming and settling over the brown moonscape of the base with a heat that made him feel thick and immovable, as if he were caught under layers of dust. His body was adjusting and he had lost the wolflike toughness of his early days. Now, he lived in limbo, caught between dreams about planes crashing midair and sharp but strangely artificial memories of Minnesota—the dusty-smelling rafters of the church basement, the baseball field on a pale twilit night in May, snow swirling in cyclone clouds in the backyard on Christmas morning. All truths, but snapshots that appeared without people in them, like empty movie sets.

He lay on his cot, staring at the flat ceiling of the barracks, his body settling into the sagging springs. Mickey missed the sharp points of bone and had been avoiding mirrors, dodging the round face that stared back at him. He seemed to be turning back into himself, despite Korea. His body was resuming its Minnesota shape: bulky shoulders, a slightly sloping torso, rosy chipmunk cheeks. Little by little, the person he had become was disappearing and the one he'd fled was coming back.

Bo had noticed and begun calling Mickey "Fat Boy." They still walked, but Mickey felt an emptiness between them now. It was like extra air packed in the spaces between their two bodies—the distance from Minneapolis to Detroit. Maybe, Mickey had to admit, from white to black, Catholic to Baptist, twenty to nearly thirty.

Now that he was slated to return, the letters from home were coming at a faster rate. Mary wrote to tell him about Eleanor's new baby, the third boy, and their Memorial Day trip to her sister's cabin. Next year, she said, you'll be with us. Won't that be grand? Susanna wrote with the news that James had asked her to go steady, then disappeared when she declined; back home, Mickey had never heard this sort of close confidence from his sister but suspected that once he was stateside again, they would return to being awkward with each other.

His father had written only once, to ask what he planned to do once back home. *My observation is that it's harder for you boys than it was for the World War veterans. I'm sorry to say it, but the country isn't quite as proud. And jobs aren't so plentiful.*

Mickey turned over and felt his stomach roll like custard against the stiff blankets. He sucked in his gut and thought about Mary's Memorial Day picnic dinners. Baked beans in brown sugar, floury white rolls, strawberry pie. He salivated. No one else was in the barracks. Tuesday afternoon. Mickey had been on the radios all night, so he alone was not working; he alone had time to sleep or write letters. The room, ten beds long on each side, echoed with the stillness of a deserted war.

He reached down and touched himself, once. His body had changed back in this way, too. For his first entire year in Korea, Mickey hadn't felt this need. Now, he ached again each morning, and even while the rest of him was growing soft, his cock was red and hard. He closed his eyes and thought about graph paper with pencil marks, showing where the planes were headed. He pictured the dead North Korean soldier he'd seen lying across the road, a bubble of purple-white intestine poking out of the wound in his belly. Nothing worked, though. Mickey grew warmer. He shifted and his hand found its grip—four fingers curled loosely, moving, slowly and without a particular cadence at first, and then, as if a machine had taken over, regulating the process in swift, rhythmic jerks.

Just as he was about to give in to the pressure that was building, as so often happened, Mickey heard the voice of Dick Murton. *But if you ever touch yourself, there is no coming back to be saved. You will burn in the fires of hell and never see those good people who raised you ever again.* Suddenly, the movement, the touch of his own hand, was painful. He rose off the bed all at once, jackknifing his body to stand, so frustrated he felt tears beginning to gather in the corners of his eyes. He paced the long aisle of the room and imagined dying boys in the empty beds. Heads bandaged, guts leaking, blood dripping down the length of an arm. Other than the dead Asian man on the road, Mickey had never seen war's carnage. It was like a story he'd been told, a fairy tale about what war was supposed to be. What had happened to Bo's brother, perhaps with a spear, deep in a darkened jungle: that was war. But everything Mickey had done, his experience, had been cowardly. Without real suffering. His own brother, at twelve, had died a more heroic, more senseless death than Mickey had ever seen.

He stood in the center of the room and prayed to leave his own body. Not to die, not exactly. But to shed this human skin that grew weak and deceitful, no matter what the thoughts he tried to keep, ordered, like flights and vectors and compass points, in his mind.

He itched under a loose shirt and lifted it to scratch, looking down at his pale belly with its patches of long, dark hair. Not long ago, he'd imagined there might be a similar job waiting for him at home. He would spend his life directing airplanes, understanding their patterns, sitting in a darkened tower all night watching their red lights flash then leaving his post before dawn each morning to walk across fields and hills. Land that, in his fantasy, looked a great deal like Korea.

He had sat down to write to his family at least half a dozen times, wanting to ask, Could you find out where I might go? How does a guy find work in air traffic? He imagined Mary, wearing a blue dress and hat, clutching her pocketbook, walking determinedly across the tiny airstrip in Minneapolis to find the man in charge. Or, he thought, she might not believe he could do it.

Mickey had tried to ask on base, but once trained he'd had no contact with the men from his division. That was their plan: to leave him behind, an expert in flying surrounded by young, reckless pilots, a few guards, and a cook. Now they were gone and Mickey had no idea whom he might contact to find them again. Or if they would even talk to him. Chances were, even if they did they would look over his service records and see the note about his eyes.

His captain hadn't panicked, had, in fact, taken three weeks to come up with a replacement. But in just nine days, Mickey would spend his last shift in the small closet where his radio equipment lay on a chipped wooden desk. After that, he would never again begin a night with new paper, a soft pencil, and the satisfying weight of the headset covering his right ear.

"What are you going to do back home?" he asked Bo that night as they shuffled, kicking up clouds of dirt.

"Go back to the furniture store, most likely. Not much else I know how to do."

"Do you have anyone back there, in Detroit? Family? Or a girlfriend?"

"Nah." Bo shifted his rifle and looked up. "Had a girlfriend for a while. But she just . . . I don't know, dwindled away. She's got three kids now."

"Wish it was you?" Mickey asked.

"You'd think." Bo scowled. "But I don't. Some men ain't meant to settle down, I guess. I love kids, wish I had some nieces and nephews, but I'm not ever gonna . . ." He stopped and shook his head.

"Never?" Mickey stopped. "That's a lonely life, don't you think?"

"The way I see it"—they were walking again and Bo was looking away, as if Mickey had already gone home and he were traveling the perimeter alone—"it's a lonely life no matter what you do."

"C'mon, that's pretty trite."

Bo turned suddenly and Mickey backed away, realizing for the first time in months how much taller the black man was. How dark his face became when he wasn't smiling.

"Okay, college boy. What the fuck does that mean?"

"I never went to college." Mickey's voice was surly, covering his fear. "I couldn't get in."

"Yeah, right. Tragic. So what's it mean?"

"What?" He was stalling.

"Trite."

Mickey opened his mouth, but he couldn't think. Words swirled in his head, but there weren't two he could string together in a definition. "It means, uh . . ."

"Stupid?"

"No, more like"—he reached hard and grabbed the only word he could find—"simple."

"Uh huh." Bo started walking again, his long legs moving in strides Mickey couldn't match unless he jogged. "So I'm simple."

"No." Mickey panted. He tried to think how this had started. But the air felt close around his skin and there was a knot in his lower back. Korea had changed and he no longer fit. "It's just, my parents always taught me there are ways to rise above. Family, you know. The Church."

"Your parents did, did they?" Bo stopped sharply and faced him, eyes angry and curious. "And it worked? The Church? You been fine because they gave you this magic way to rise? That why you walk all the damn night?"

It seemed to Mickey as if the threads holding his thoughts together tore at this point. He felt, or imagined, a shower of sparks in his brain. "No," he said, not certain which question he was answering.

He was still trying to figure it out while he watched Bo's back, retreating in the dim light as the big man walked away from him.

The morning he was to leave Korea dawned the pink of a magnolia blossom, the light near the horizon a translucent misty green. Mickey's skin prickled inside his civilian clothes. Ted had written again, to suggest Mickey work in the jewelry shop when he returned. It would, his father argued, give him time to figure out what else he might like to do. Mickey became breathless when he thought about the buildings and skyways downtown, but he could come up with nothing else. Nothing real, at least. The only thoughts that came to him had to do with pitching baseballs or trying to guide a plane through the narrow streets. He imagined objects flying, bouncing like pinballs off brick towers, street-lamp posts, and windowsills. Shattering glass, causing shards to burst and glitter and fall, landing at his father's feet.

His mattress was rolled up and he had left his navigation manuals lying next to it on the bare springs. When the army jeep pulled up to take him to Seoul, Mickey grabbed his bag. Bo was sleeping somewhere across camp. It was not until that very minute that Mickey realized he had no idea where. He was silent as he climbed into the jeep and threw his satchel in back.

"Going home?" asked the driver as he turned the wheel and sped out of camp, so fast all the buildings and mountains melted together when Mickey looked back.

It took him a minute or two to answer. When he did, his face remained tight and sober. But he worked hard to make his voice light, appropriate to the occasion. "Yep. Going home."

The driver nodded, fooled. Mickey sat back and closed his eyes, suddenly leaden in his seat, letting the landscape and the airplanes and the thin mountain air simply drift away.

17

MY MOTHER HAD reminded me several times that I should take my daughter to visit Eleanor. We'd never been close and I could count on two hands the number of times I'd met her children, my cousins. But lately my mother and her sister had been talking on the phone, having lunch, even going to movies together. It was as if, after fifty years, they'd decided to become family again because they were all the other had left. I liked Eleanor, her wit and her statuesque Lauren Bacall carriage. But I'd been too absorbed in the new baby, Matt's need for a nearly adult level of stimulation, and Edward's reawakening after a month of sleep to think of doing anything outside my own small sphere.

Then, one brisk March afternoon my mother called and suggested I meet her at Dayton's, where there was a sale on winter linens. She wanted to buy new quilts for the children. It was there, standing amid the bedding displays with their dust ruffles and shams and small heart-shaped pillows, that she mentioned Mickey's letters from Korea. "It was terribly cold there." She fingered a white eyelet comforter threaded with pale pink and yellow ribbons that she was considering for Grace's crib. I pulled at the end of a pink strand, discreetly checking to see if it could come loose in the night and strangle the baby. "Isn't that surprising? He went over from Minnesota, but he said that first winter he'd never been so cold in his whole life."

She shivered as if still feeling sympathy for her older brother and slipped on a pair of reading glasses to look at the washing instructions on the comforter's tag.

Ever since that day in her guest room when she'd given me the photograph, my mother had begun mentioning Mickey more often, talking about him easily, as if he, like Eleanor, had recently returned to the family circle. "And he couldn't sleep while he was overseas." She let out a short, light laugh, still examining the blanket, turning it over to run her finger along the stitched edge. "Funny. I never made the connection before. Mickey wrote to Eleanor more than the rest of us. Writing was hard for him, so it shows how lonely he must have been. Anyway, she seemed to feel Mickey was different when he was over there: he wandered in the middle of the night, lost a lot of weight . . ." Her voice trailed off, then picked up brightly: "Maybe that's the secret: I should stop dieting and go to Korea."

Grace was asleep when we arrived home. I lifted her portable seat from the car, carrying it with a still, stiff arm so as not to wake her, and set it in the middle of the living room rug. I left the three heavy plastic bags stuffed full of soft quilting in the trunk of my car and immediately picked up the phone to call Eleanor.

I'd heard all the stories about my aunt's early marriage: her Frank Lloyd Wright–style house, the swimming pool, the diamonds and parties and martini shakers on the sideboard, constantly in use. Also, her husband's chronic affairs and their divorce after twenty years of marriage. Still, it was hard to imagine. For as long as I'd known her, Eleanor had lived in a two-bedroom ranch north of St. Paul—a tiny, perfectly rectangular place with heavy, lined curtains on the windows and the smell of stale ashtrays, pot roast, and lemon-scented air fresheners. Eleanor was nearly seventy but other than her cheeks, which were so deeply lined the rouge she put on made dark furrows in the crevices, she was still lovely. Tall with thick white hair and a regal way of walking, she seemed too big for the house. And for her husband, a small, happy man named Bob who had been her milkman when she was married the first time.

The next afternoon I dressed Grace in the playsuit Eleanor had sent and drove over the river to her house. My aunt picked up the baby immediately, turning her around in sure hands. She'd had five children of her own, and fourteen grandchildren so far, yet I had never seen someone look so delighted to see a small, round face poking out of blankets. "You are a beautiful girl," Eleanor said to Grace, in a tone as level as if she were speaking to a teenager, or a show horse. "Nothing like your grandmother. What a scrawny ugly baby she was."

I settled back on her couch, enjoying the freedom of having no one lying against me. "My mother was small?"

"Tiny. Five pounds or so. It's probably because our mother was so sick over Frank's death when she got pregnant. She didn't have much to give." Eleanor was batting Grace's hand lightly with her own.

"Do you remember when he died?"

"Of course I do." She answered so abruptly, I looked up to see if she was angry. But she was still smiling down at my daughter. "It was one of the most awful days of my life. Until . . ." She sighed. "When Mickey died, that was even worse."

"I want to know."

Now she looked up sharply, tucking Grace into the crook of her arm. Down the street, there was the low, grinding sound of a car turning, then nothing. I hadn't realized how quiet it was until then. "What do you want to know?" she asked.

"About Mickey. Everything. I understand he had . . . problems."

"What sort of problems?" She was tough, staring at me with sharp eyes.

Years of interviewing had taught me not to fill the silence by talking. I waited, breathing slowly, and sure enough, after a couple minutes, Eleanor began to speak.

"He had some. These days, they'd probably call him depressed. But he had reason to be—young boy like that lost his brother and then his mother and father had a new baby. Somehow he got lost and . . ." She turned a deep shade of red, even the smooth parts of her face blending with the rouge.

"What?"

"My parents were good people." She spoke slowly. "But even they couldn't hide their feelings. Mickey was never . . . Well, he wasn't Frank. I think my brother lived with that burden all his life."

"He had trouble in school." I stated it as if I knew, then realized I had only a sentence or two from my mother upon which to base this.

But Eleanor was nodding. "He did."

"Like Edward." Inside, I was pleading: *say yes*. It surprised even me how desperate I was for someone to claim my son.

But my aunt paused for a long time, looking thoughtful. She tipped the baby gently and raised the bundle of her to one shoulder. Eleanor swayed, lips pursed. "No," she said carefully. "I never thought of it like that."

Inside, my composure was crumbling. Every time I got close to an explanation, it evaporated. Edward had been taking melatonin, sleeping regularly for only a few weeks, and already he'd bloomed—his face bright, his eyes clear, skin smooth and pale and unlined. But he was still quiet. He spoke now, but awkwardly and with his head averted. I needed Eleanor to tell me how to reach him, what her parents had done. Whatever had worked I would duplicate. If she could outline the mistakes they'd made, I would do the reverse.

I struggled to keep my voice from rising. "Look at the similarities. Didn't it start around the age of three? Mickey withdrew just like Edward. He didn't do well in school. But he was smart. He grew up to be a functional person: he worked, he got married, he had a child."

Eleanor was patting Grace's back with long, veined hands. "Yes." She stopped the movements and Grace stirred. "He also died. I would think you'd want to hear that Edward is different."

I stared at Eleanor and she met my gaze, locking her eyes with mine; I had never before realized how very unlike my mother she was. "You think he killed himself?"

"I think it's a distinct possibility."

My body was still distended, flabby after birth, and I sat there feeling messy, as if I were spilling everything onto Eleanor's couch—worries and questions and excess skin. Grace had fallen asleep on Eleanor's shoulder and I was jealous: I needed something to hold on to now. "But that's the sort of thing we could prevent. We've managed to get him sleeping. If it were just a matter of his feeling . . . depressed. Then we could help him."

"You're sure about that?" Her voice was crisp but not unkind. There was a moment of silence and I heard the soft tick of the mantel clock.

"Here, take this darling baby." She handed Grace to me and I caught her quickly, awkwardly. But she slept on. Eleanor rose and left the room. When she came back, she was holding a stiff, old-fashioned shoe box stuffed with envelopes and a clothbound book, some bits of tattered yellow newspaper.

"I want all this back," she said, a warning in her voice. "It's all I have from him. But I think you should read these before you assume your son takes after my brother . . . and whether you want him to."

18

THERE WAS SOMETHING about having actual documents that seemed auspicious. Like an archaeologist, I was certain I could unearth history and truth from these artifacts. I drove home feeling satisfied, with Grace, exhausted from the attention my aunt had showered on her, sleeping softly in back and the box of letters on the seat next to me. When I stopped at lights, I would glance to the side and imagine the answers buried inside, glowing dimly, just waiting for me to dig through and find them.

That night, I set Eleanor's box by a chair in the living room and poured a glass of wine. I said nothing to Jack: this seemed like private work, better kept mysterious. Hadn't my son written a story that predicted I, his mother, would help him find the flowers? Part of the magic might lie in my working alone at this point—without doctors or teachers or even Jack—to figure out the final solution.

But as I sat and read, the wine quickly forgotten, I grew confused and slightly, irrationally angry. Mickey's letters, the few there were, told me just enough to know I should be worried either way. They were full of misspellings and grammatical errors, but conversational—not at all the halting mixed-up formality of Edward's new speech. The early notes seemed almost jolly. But the ones he'd sent during the spring of 1953 conveyed a repetitive bleakness, especially when he wrote of returning to Minnesota: this was a man who appeared to have lived in dread, not of war but of his life back home. I thought about my conversation with Eleanor, the pain that had drifted across her face when we talked, and realized he'd probably told her things no one else knew. I wondered if she felt guilty because she hadn't been able to save him.

The cloth diary had been hers, a yellowed mosaic of household notes, addresses and recipes, as well as thoughts, recorded in the distinctive wet-looking script of a fountain pen. One of the only things I found that interested me was a sentence written about twenty pages from the end. *Talk to Ruth about M. Must make an effort.* This was followed by a mundane list: golf, women's club, garden center. I puzzled over this for a while, finally putting everything back in the box and stowing it in a trunk with wide buckle latches that Jack had salvaged and set in a corner of our living room because he thought it looked like a pirate's treasure chest.

There was something in Mickey's life, I told myself, that would someday help me figure out how to reach the real Edward—the boy whose brain worked at thirty times the rate of everyone else's. It was simply a matter of looking at the clues in a number of different ways until I was able to crack the code.

By fall, Grace was a chattery seven-month-old, crawling from room to room with an unusually low-to-the-ground platypus gait. And Matthew, already a voracious reader at four, needed glasses; he chose green-rimmed spectacles because they looked like the ones worn by the characters entering the Emerald City in *The Wizard of Oz.* In preparation for second grade, I'd taken Edward back to see Barry Newberg three more times over the summer, looking again for the breakthrough that would allow him to enter the school an entirely healed child. Though the doctor seemed pleased with Edward's progress, he offered us less on each visit and stayed in the examining room for a shorter time.

"I think the medical work is done," he'd said in August, one hand resting on the doorknob as he prepared to leave. "It's time for you to get him the therapy he needs: occupational, sensory work, maybe some good old-fashioned tutoring to bring him up closer to grade level."

By mid-October, I'd revised my theory: Mickey might be part of the answer. There was an element of him in Edward—something mysterious and reclusive and too easily hurt. But there had to be another strand: Edward was the sum of my history and Jack's. If we put the two pieces together, maybe we could work the rest of the puzzle.

On a dusky late afternoon I stood leaning against the wall of the bedroom, half expecting the breeze that blew through the screen to bring in the color of the sky: orange melting to rose over the landscape of roofs and trees and power lines outside. Jack was dressing slowly, his large body in silhouette canted toward the open window. And at first I was quiet, watching.

My husband's face was tight. He clipped his tie under the points of his collar and reached for the belt lying open on the quilt my grandmother had stitched and tied with small blue flowers made of yarn. His belt was hung with weapons: revolver, Mace, retractable nightstick, and the heavy black flashlight that could be turned, held by the bulbous end, and used as a club. The leather creaked as he lifted it, paraphernalia swaying like charms on some huge, medieval bracelet. Jack fastened it around his waist and straightened, hands on his hips to balance the gear, shoulders twitching inside the polyester uniform he once said felt like greased wool, slick and prickly and hot against his body. In this uniform, his size became almost grotesque: six and a half feet of darkness.

I'd learned not to talk much before a night shift. Jack was usually silent as he dressed. After work, when he sat down to eat the morning meal he called supper, we might say a few words.

"I'm not afraid of the guys in the cage," he'd told me a couple days before. "It's the ones sitting next to me . . . more and more, lately." Then he shook his head, a small movement, and drew in a long breath. "They scare the hell out of me." He smiled, showing his perfect teeth. But I knew he was serious.

I closed my eyes and let the wall hold me up for a few minutes, listening to the sounds Jack made: old floorboards groaning under his feet, equipment shifting as he moved.

I had been up in the night with Grace, and after she was fed I'd spent an hour sitting beside Edward's bed, trying to figure out what remained to be done. He had spent months sleeping, which still seemed like a miracle. The fact that he could say good morning dazzled me, and throughout the last slow, sun-soaked weeks of summer I clung to the hope that once he was surrounded by other children, he would be stimulated or provoked sufficiently to emerge.

In that same time Jack and I had become closer again, but in a slightly different way from before. Police work had made him rougher, darker, even more silent. I found it more and more difficult to talk to him. But when he began touching me again after Grace's birth there was a rabid edge to him that was new, coming in from outside our life together. And I liked it.

I had planned to return to work part-time after the boys were settled in school but somehow the months had stretched on. Eric had quit calling and the newspaper had become a shadowy memory tied up in my mind with the epoch of Edward's sleeplessness. Then it was summer and I couldn't bear to waste the days when we could be swimming or going to amusement parks or visiting the zoo—all the things Edward had missed out on, activities I was hopeful would transform him into a happy, resilient kid, no different from other children his age who'd slept regularly all their lives.

But on the first day of the new school year, after walking through a shower of lemony sunshine with Grace in her stroller and a boy on either side, I had entered Edward's classroom with its dancing construction paper signs and the truth came rushing at me, as cold and forceful as a sudden wind.

The other second graders were lined up at desks with notebooks on which they had printed their own names. They carried pens with the nonchalance of bank tellers about to sign off on a large deposit. The girls wore tiny jeans and thick-soled shoes and in some cases even earrings. The boys wore the faint dirt stains of the soccer field on their knees. Edward moved alone among them with a startled expression on his face and a lilting gait.

Since that day, the golden feeling I'd had since Grace's birth had begun to drain away. Each afternoon when I picked him up, Edward shuffled out of the school slowly, staring down, his forehead knotted, his eyes crossed. Often I heard him muttering. Speechlessness had given way to constant streams of words that made less and less sense as his vocabulary grew. He seemed to have little idea how new words were related to the few he'd known before; he used them at random and chanted questions for which there were no answers. *Can I, maybe, in a moment, for the teacher to like me?*

As often as possible, he spoke in numbers. Though he could not yet write them, he understood. Like a computer, Jack said. Edward sometimes uttered strings that I believed a mathematician would be able to decipher: a series of prime numbers, perhaps, or an elaborate code. Surely this was a gift, handed down. Finding its donor seemed necessary to helping him use it.

I opened my eyes and shifted my spot against the wall. "Will you look for her today? Please?"

Jack undid the flap on the black pouch at his hip and counted out six blunt-nosed bullets in one hand. I watched, fascinated and repelled as I always was—the way I felt once as a child when I watched one insect eat another.

"Jack?" He picked up his wallet and keys from the top of the dresser and walked toward the door.

"I said yes." I could hear him jogging through the hallway and down the stairs, running away from me even as he answered.

I followed him to the kitchen. By the time I entered he was already holding the bread bag and reaching into the cupboard for the peanut butter. I leaned against the counter; same position, different room. "You've said yes before."

"Well, this time I mean it. I still think you're crazy. There's no reason. Looking for my birth mother is nothing but a waste of my time."

"Come on. Aren't you even slightly curious?"

"You know how I feel."

I considered the truth of this. I knew what he said but had always found it hard to believe Jack really didn't care about his own history. His adoptive parents had been dead twelve years when I met him and beyond the tiny piece of the inheritance that was left after his random attempts at college and the wrecked carcasses of three vintage motorcycles, nothing remained of them but an antique pie safe, eight feet tall and made of a sturdy, golden oak, that now stood in our kitchen. It had five rows of stacked cupboards with leaded glass windows cut into the two upper doors, wrought-iron latches, and a recessed wooden board that could be pulled out.

Jack said he saved this one piece of furniture because his mother loved it and because she would slide the board out and use it to make his peanut butter sandwiches. He told me little else about his parents— only that they had been good people, quiet, very Catholic. And they waited for a baby for fifteen years before finally adopting him when they were both nearly forty.

"I had a mother, a good one." His voice was low. And it wasn't until he said this that I realized he was standing at her pie safe, six slices of bread laid out on the board in front of him. "I'm not going to go looking for a backup now because she's gone."

"But, Jack, this is different. You're not looking for you. It's for Edward. Your biological mother can tell us. For sure."

He wheeled around toward the table, gripping three sandwiches in his left hand and a glass of milk in his right. "I can tell us . . . tell *you*. For sure. He doesn't have some gruesome, disfiguring disease. He's sleeping now. He's learning. It's just going to take some time."

"He doesn't have time. The school wants to pull him out of the regular class."

Jack finished the first sandwich in three bites and took a long swallow of milk. "Why?"

I'd been working toward telling him since Edward had arrived home that afternoon, a note in his backpack from his teacher, a young woman who had none of Harriet Nelson's desire to reach him. "The new teacher says he's detracting from the 'general academics' of the classroom. She claims she has to spend too much time repeating and redirecting; she can't teach the others adequately."

"Bitch." Jack had finished eating and was fidgeting with his hat, long fingers drumming across its taut crown. "Does she know what he was like last year? He just needs time to catch up. Is that too much to fucking ask?"

"Apparently so." I tipped my head to listen for Grace, who was napping in the living room, but heard only the low hum of the boys, who were upstairs playing with Matt's chest of toy cars. No doubt Edward was enacting for his brother, again and again, the descent of a car into water. Matt's fascination with the repetition of this drama was one thing the boys could share. Sometimes they moved to the bathroom and filled the sink to make it more real. "Also, she wants to begin teaching cursive this year and Edward can't even print yet. She called in a specialist, an occupational therapist, who says he has 'fine motor dysfunction.'" I imitated the prissy, terse prose of the teacher's letter.

"So what exactly does that mean?" He rose and poured himself a cup of the morning's coffee, getting a mixture of scorched syrup and grounds because I'd already drunk most of the pot while he slept through the long hours of afternoon.

"They say he's incapable of holding a pencil or a crayon. He's seven years old and he's never written his name. He can't color a picture." I shrugged. Once in a while, I'd feel myself crossing over into the well-ordered camp of the school system and begin quoting from the diagnostic manual, using their explanations and multisyllabic labels. In a way, it was easier than always wondering, always justifying. If I joined the experts against Jack, at least I knew exactly what to say. "His development is atypical, disordered. Clearly there *is* something really wrong."

"It's all bullshit and you know it." He took a gulp and grimaced, then took another. "This kid climbs to the top of bookshelves and windowsills. Christ, I found him up there one day." Jack jerked his thumb at the flat top of the refrigerator. "He puts puzzles together. He buttons his clothes. He's talking more and more. They're all insane. His hands work better than yours!"

I looked at mine: rough, with slits of red nested in the wrinkled joints. I reminded myself again that I should wear gloves when I washed the dishes, the diapers, the floor where Edward dropped all the food he didn't like. In the same moment, I knew I never would. "That isn't saying much."

Jack took one of my ugly hands in his and it disappeared. "Don't believe them." He hunched so he could look into my face. "They're wrong."

I stood on my toes so he wouldn't have to stoop so low and touched his face. "God, I miss the beard."

Jack rubbed his own cheek. "Yeah, me, too. Next year. Once I'm off patrol I can grow it back. In fact, I'm thinking of going into narcotics so I can look like my natural self. Dirty and hairy. I might even have to stop showering. For the job, you know." He grinned and for just a minute, the old Jack flashed from this sober, clean-shaven face.

Then he laid his hands along the space between my neck and shoulders and I felt the energy sparkle through me, rushing toward his fingertips. I closed my eyes again and let my mind go blissfully blank.

This was the one thing I'd never discussed with anyone, not the doctors, not even Mariel. When Matthew had an asthma attack the year before, Jack had placed his palms, flat, on Matt's small chest. He remained still while he did this but when I touched one of his hands it was hot with a strong, galloping pulse—bursts of blood running like a string of beads through the soft fold of skin between his thumb and first finger. And while I watched, Matt's body relaxed and he began to breathe.

"Maybe I'm the biological child of an Indian medicine man," he said that time. Hopeful. "Or some Aztec tribe of healers. That would explain my coloring. Somehow I got lost, thrown into this culture where I don't belong."

And while it was all true—Jack's skin was dark year-round, as if he were constantly under a midsummer sun; one of his eyes was piercing and green, the other an opaque blue—I wasn't really a believer. How could I be? No matter what he tried, Jack had never been able to restore Edward completely.

Sometimes I fell asleep while he grazed my arms and back at night. But lately, whenever he touched me he started right away with firm pressure, sliding his hands down my body and slipping one between my legs while the other circled around to hold me firmly from behind. And the current in my body would become something else, an electric field that made me as likely to come from a long, slow kiss to the back of my neck as I was when he actually penetrated me. Later, I would be confused about the order in which events had occurred: when he entered me and which way I turned. I could awaken minutes or hours after making love with Jack and have no idea where to find my underwear, or, if it was dark, which way I was facing and how to find the door.

After eight years of marriage, I still didn't understand Jack at all and that was what I loved about him. Also, these days, what I feared.

A few days ago, at a party, Jack's partner, Danny, had informed me that Jack was growing careless around the other men. Danny told me about the call they had answered in north Minneapolis, in a neighborhood where even the houses with families living inside had boards nailed over the windows. There was a small black boy, maybe three or four years old, dressed in light clothes with no shoes, lying on the dark, ice-covered street, cars swerving around him. No one knew how long he'd been there; the few people they questioned couldn't say whose child he was. Three officers were standing over the boy already when Jack and Danny arrived; one of them had covered him with his coat. But Jack insisted on lifting it and touching the child himself, running his fingers up and down arms, legs, neck, and chest to make sure he wasn't revivable.

This, Danny warned me, was one of the reasons the others disliked Jack. They thought of him as odd and soft. Unprofessional.

"I'll find her today," he whispered, leaning down so his breath was hot against my neck. "I promise. And he'll be fine."

I heard the door close behind him when he left but I remained in the kitchen, drowsy, leaning against the stacked cupboards, my shoulders rubbery and warm. By the time I heard Edward let out a high, sharp *no* and opened my eyes, the room was hazy, filled with the dim, brown light of evening in autumn.

19

ONCE JACK WAS gone, the house seemed desolate. I thought about calling my sister, who lived in North Carolina with her husband—a very highly paid computer executive who had begun to bald exactly like our father. But Elizabeth would be cheerful. In my mind, I could hear her voice saying firmly in an eerie echo of my mother's, "It's not so bad. Why must you always make problems?"

I picked up the phone and quickly dialed Mariel but as I'd feared, there was no answer. I listened to her mechanical voice, saying she and Scott were out and I was welcome to leave a message, that they would get back to me "promptly." I hung up just before the insistent beep started. I'd left three messages over the past month and she had never returned a single one.

In August, Mariel had called me sobbing early one Saturday morning. It was one of the few days Grace had slept past six o'clock and I was still lying in bed, enjoying the quiet, when the telephone rang. "He's dead," she finally choked out after I asked her again and again to slow down, tell me what was wrong. "I woke up this morning and found him lying on the floor."

I conjured up a picture immediately: Scott, after suffering an Elvis sort of demise. His body bloated with sin—drugs, alcohol, food, pornography—sprawled out on the wide oak slats of the floor in Mariel's turn-of-the-century farmhouse kitchen. He'd been on his way to the refrigerator for a midnight snack, perhaps. A triple-X-rated video on pause in the VCR in the next room, a bottle of vodka sitting open on the table beside him—no glass or ice, he just drew directly from the neck. In my daydream, Scott's face was distorted but his hair still perfectly parted and swept to the side.

"Oh, my God, what happened?"

"He was in the barn," she said, breathing between the words. Of course, I thought; it was the pressure of living his lies day after day. This could be the best thing for her—a neat disposal of this man I'd been watching bankrupt her. "Scott had to carry him to the car so we could get him into town. But he was already"—she hiccupped a sound— "gone."

I fought a twinge of disappointment and sat up, rearranging the jumbled covers and adjusting the receiver against my ear. Jack was in bed beside me on one of his rare weekends off. He moved, arms and legs like a long, slow windmill, then slid out of bed all in one gangling motion. He stood at the side of the bed, naked, dark hair with glints of silver swirled over his chest and forearms. "Coffee?" he whispered. I brought my hands together, tented as if in prayer, and nodded.

"Wait a minute," I said as he stumbled into a pair of flannel boxers and left the room, edging around Grace's cradle, which we had wedged into a space near the door, scratching his stomach and yawning. "Who died?"

"Nigel." Her voice had the rusty tone of grief, or hysteria. Then she said again, "He was just lying there, on the floor."

We hadn't been down to the farm since Edward had begun sleeping. I told myself it was because I didn't want to disrupt his routine, but the truth was, Mariel hadn't asked us. Up until midsummer I had talked to her at least twice a week but the conversations had been largely about the counselors she and Scott were seeing three times a week in Des Moines—they were a husband-wife team who had gone through cocaine addiction and bankruptcy together and remained married. Now they counseled couples in their living room for $120 an hour; they also sold a line of herbal health products that Mariel said had helped Scott relax.

I tried to remember her mentioning someone called Nigel. A farm-worker, perhaps. Though even that would not explain her hysteria; aside from Scott and me, Mariel kept a cool distance from the world. Suddenly I realized: a student! This must be one of Mariel's thesis advisees, out on the farm for a weekend of study. I imagined a scene out of Flannery O'Connor—the young man, slight and blond, surrounded by hay and dust motes, swinging from a rafter where he had hanged himself with a noose made of coarse rope.

"I'm so sorry," I began. "I don't think I ever *met* Nigel, but—"

"Yes, you did." Her voice was hard, suddenly. "He's the one who swiped at Matt last spring."

Vaguely, an image began to take form in my mind. A cat, tiger-striped with frizzled fur and a belly that swept the ground when he crouched. He'd had sharp claws that Mariel said she left alone because his job was to catch mice. When he'd scratched Matt's hand, Mariel had scooped him up and held him like a baby, scolding him in a voice so loving he nearly went to sleep in her arms.

"We'll just keep the kids away from Nigel," she'd said. I remembered now; I did hear his name, that one time.

"I'm sorry," I blurted. "Of course I remember him. I just didn't recall the name. It's unusual. Very British. I really am sorry, Merry." Even as I spoke, I was wondering: What am I supposed to do? Do you make a Bundt cake in a situation like this?

She sniffed. "Thanks. Scott's out right now digging a grave under the willow. He's been really great. He tried to revive Nigel, even gave him mouth-to-mouth." I caught the laugh before it escaped but could not stop picturing Scott's wide man's mouth over the cat's whiskery, lipless chin.

"Well . . . that's good. How's he doing?"

"Okay." She sighed. "There've been a few rough spots lately. A couple slips."

"Slips?"

"You know. Old behaviors. Pete and Maxine say it's going to take twice as long for him to unlearn bad habits as it took for him to get into them."

"Do you ever wonder if it's worth it?" I hadn't meant to ask. The question simply materialized. "Living with someone?"

"Yeah, honestly, I do." She sniffled again and I heard her blow her nose. "But then I look at my mom. Her life. It's so empty. At least you and I have families."

Just then, Grace rustled in her blankets and made a sound like a hamster scratching through cedar chips. She began to mew and smack her lips. Jack came in with a mug that he set on the floor next to the bed. Then he lifted the baby out of her bed, expertly wrapping her as he walked the few steps to where I sat, and handed her to me. I pulled up my nightshirt and Grace latched on with the suction power of a tiny vacuum, milk running through my body in a warm rush. Yes, it was worth it. I felt ashamed and grateful to Mariel and had been about to open my mouth to say so when she spoke again.

"That's why Nigel's death is hitting me so hard," she was saying, her words echoing a little through the euphoria of the baby's strong pull at my breast. "Scott and I have worked so hard to get here and create a home with our animals and now . . . it's such a devastating blow. The grief you feel. It's just like losing a child."

I had been taking a sip from the mug, stretching to the side as I drank so I wouldn't spill on Grace, and it took a moment for this sentence to work its way through my lazy satisfaction with the baby and the chocolaty taste of Jack's dark coffee. But when it did, my mouth filled with something bitter. I cleared my throat and searched my mind for something to say but found nothing. Nothing but a revolving image of Grace, then Matt, then Edward lying on a barn floor, unmoving, each with a bloated purple tongue.

I thought of the dozens of times I had sat across a table from Mariel, or huddled over the phone at night, weeping about Edward. About the terror I felt that he would never be normal, that he would continue to slip further away. When I began to invent bizarre, hysterical explanations—that he had been possessed by a demon, or that he actually *had* died but some freak of biology was propelling his empty body through the motions—she was the only person I told.

Mariel had never wanted children. She was so certain, she'd had a tubal ligation at twenty-four, the year after she divorced the young Londoner she'd married impetuously while at Oxford. I was the one who drove her to the hospital and waited during the surgery, then took her home, wrapped her in blankets, and made her toast. I was proud of her decision. Though I never said so, I thought the deal we'd made was that we would both love my children above all else. Certainly above cats.

Breathing carefully, as if I were trying to mask my presence on the phone, I returned to the image of Mariel's dead Nigel. A small orange and white body, lying on its side. I didn't know what I was going to do until I did it. As Grace released my nipple and turned with a scrunched-up face to stab the air with one tiny fist and fart gently into my palm, I dropped the phone onto the soft surface of the bed and reached out with one finger to press the button that would cut off the call.

20

IN THE TWO months since, I'd relived that conversation over and over. Mariel and I had quit speaking for a week back when we were nineteen, but that was over a boy—a beautiful runaway we met at a dance club who, as it turned out, was gay. That time, we made up over hot fudge sundaes, laughing at our own insecurities and promising each other we'd never fight over a man again. Now, she wouldn't even take my calls. I dialed once more and listened to her message begin, *Hi, this is the home of Mariel and Scott,* then hung up.

The thin light of afternoon was waning and the house had gone silent. But when I went into the living room, Grace was fidgeting, building up to a squawk. I picked her up and trudged up the stairs to change her diaper, then glanced into the boys' room and saw Matt sprawled, sleeping, across his bed. I carried her back down to look for Edward and found him on the floor of the slanted sunporch the boys used as a playroom.

Edward was turned toward the wall, holding a shiny transparent disc filled with distilled water and glitter—a piece that he had pulled off one of Matt's abandoned rattles and now hid in a different spot each day. He stared at the "rounder," as he called it, and spun it, watching the spangles fall like an endless comet's tail. His eyes glittered in reflection and his cheeks looked warm and damp.

"Come with me," I said. "You're going to write your name."

He raised his eyebrows and stared, as if I'd said something ridiculous. "Why?"

"Because . . ." Grace began to fuss and I shifted her to my other hip and jiggled her with my hand. "Because your teacher thinks you can't."

Jack had thrown a half-eaten sandwich into the disposal side of the sink, where it lay bloated, bulging with water. I slipped Grace into her bouncing baby seat and shook a few Cheerios out onto the tray in front of her. She'd had solid food only once before, but I needed her to be occupied. I cleaned out the sink, wiped the table down, and sat Edward in the chair where Jack had been earlier. Then I opened his backpack and took out the letter from the school. Two pages of type on heavy white paper. I turned them over, so the paragraphs naming Edward's disability were hidden, and handed him a ballpoint pen. He let the barrel rest in his cupped hand, rolling gently against his palm.

I sat in the chair next to him, turned so I was facing his side, took the pen back in my left hand and with my right, I mashed the fingers and thumb of his right hand together. They were limp as string and stuck out of my fist like a bunch of flower stems. "Pay attention!"

I threaded the pen into the crevice between his first two fingers and wrapped his thumb around it, holding it there with the pressure of my own. Then I started the motions.

E. I made the outer bracket first, starting at the top right side, then crossed it with the middle line. I wondered if this was right. Would this program his brain for the letter *E* or confuse him with its awkward cornered shape? Inside my hand, Edward's was falling back toward his lap, as if weighted. I gripped harder.

D. I pushed him down through the line from the top, so hard the point of the pen broke through the paper at the bottom. We returned to the top, to make the round sweep of the *D*'s belly, and suddenly I felt something catch: he was completing the lower half of the curve. I loosened my fingers and let him glide to a stop, just millimeters short of the base point of the line.

I tipped his head down and stroked his coarse curly hair, as yellow as sunlight but thick and wiry like a buffalo's mane. Grace made a happy chirp and showed me the Cheerio stuck to her tiny index finger. "W," I whispered to Edward, guiding his hand down, up, down, and up again.

We began the A. I lifted his hand, squeezing so the pen wouldn't fall from his grip, moved it to a point that was level with the bottom of the other letters and began pushing up. Suddenly, he went limp. Then the pen stopped moving and Edward stared dumbly to the side, his body beginning to rock, his face gone soft. Waves of panic pounded through me. Then I saw the shiny rounder still in his left hand. It had been there the whole time and now he began raising it to his eyes.

"No!" I wrenched him upright, grabbed the disc, and threw it across the room, where it made a moon-shaped dent in the plasterboard wall. Grace's eyes followed the thing as it flew, then returned to me, wide and round as quarters.

"You're going to do this." I pulled on Edward's right hand but he kept it tight to his chest. So I yanked harder, cracking the tension from his arm.

"Don't." It was a whimper. "Mom."

My heart was pounding, my breath ragged and filled with tears. I turned Edward's arm over and looked at the perfect whiteness of it. He stared at me with fear and then interest, a lighted design on his face as he watched me panting, regaining control bit by bit.

I knelt on the floor, my knees like rocks against the cold tile, and pulled him into a hug. And it was while I rested there, with my face in the warm hollow of his neck, that a complete circle appeared as if it had been projected onto a blank screen in my brain. I pulled away, smoothed the paper on the table in front of him, and picked up the pen. Putting it in his hand, gently, I closed mine around the outside.

I stood behind him this time and led his hand through a round curve and the swoop of a tail. A cursive *a*. I stooped to look into his eyes, which were transparent. But when I opened my grip, he kept a wobbly hold on the pen.

The last two letters took only seconds: straight lines made from top to bottom and rounded swirls that met the lines in expected and acceptable locations. When we were done, his name marched haltingly across the white sheet, the *W* and *R* higher and darker than any of the other letters. But it was there, in the world. *EDWaRD*.

I held him, my arms looped around his shoulders, and rocked with him, looking out the windows into a night sky so dark it had a nearly reflective sheen. "Now." I said this softly, into his ear. "You do it."

I put my hand around his again and pushed left, down, right, feeling a dusty hopelessness. What was I proving? And to whom? Then I felt the movement start: acceleration, independent of my hand. Like the floating planchette on a Ouija board, suddenly come to life. I let go of his hand.

Copying calmly now, his movements became more certain and fluid. I could hear him breathe. There was a strand of saliva, like spun thread, dangling from his mouth to the paper. He wrote his name seven times in descending blocks, one below the next, each line becoming more solid as they filled the space down to the bottom of the page. On the fourth, for no reason I could imagine, he made the letter *A* with lines instead of arcs, a clear point joining the two slanted sides at the top.

Upstairs, I heard a bumping noise and the squeak of Matthew's door opening, hurried steps in the hall and his voice, calling for me through the fuzzy darkness. I touched Edward's back lightly and rubbed a soft circle there. "I'll be back in a minute," I said. "Watch your sister."

I found Matt in the bathroom, his face streaked red. He was trying to peel heavy, wet clothes off his body. "I peed in the bed," he said, his eyes large and bright with shame. "I'm sorry." And I hugged him right through his wet clothes, marveling as I always did that he knew to squeeze with his fat, fleshy little arms and hug me back. Together, we pulled his clothes off and put them in the hamper. I ran a warm bath and left him in it singing, so I could hear him and know that his head was above the water, then went to the bedroom to change my own clothes. A chill wind was sweeping in. I pulled on sweatpants, a flannel nightshirt, and thick, wool socks. When Matt was done with his bath, his hair washed and plastered to his head like a cap, I dried him and gave him a pair of footed pajamas, telling him to come down for dinner when he was done.

I walked down the stairs, flipping up the wall switches as I went so I moved from darkness into light. And I imagined Jack experiencing just the opposite: stepping out of the bright neon-lit diner where he stopped each night to eat. Hitching up his belt so the weight was more bearable, tugging his hat firmly over his head as he did before he left the house. I saw him walking out into darkness, blending with it, moving silently through the damp, windswept streets.

When I reached the kitchen, I stopped in the doorway. Grace had fallen asleep in her seat, her head lolling against her right shoulder. On the countertop, the stacked aluminum canisters I inherited from my grandmother gleamed in the bright light. Edward had shifted to the right, to the second piece of paper: the second page of the letter telling us he was disabled and could not hold a pen or write his name. His head was bowed over the table, his mouth pursed in concentration.

At the top of the second sheet was the same word, written several times in strong lines and curves: *EDWARD*.

Below it, stacked like tiles, were other words: *FLOUR, COFFEE, BOUNTY, JIF*. And, at the base of them all, like a pedestal drawn in block ink: *WHIRLPOOL*.

21

EDWARD WROTE NONSTOP for three days. I don't know what he did at school, but at home he would point to objects, not with his finger but with his head. "Spell it," he would command, tipping in the direction of whatever he wanted to know. And I would answer: *S-T-E-R-E-O; I-R-O-N; U-M-B-R-E-L-L-A*. Then he would write whatever I said, nodding to himself and glancing at the object between letters, as if he were seeing it for the first time.

It may have been this that kept him from noticing his father never came home. Once, he said "Dad?" and I thought he was finally asking about Jack but he only wanted to know the letters, both the *D* and the *A* from his own name, symbols he knew well now, and he printed them over and over again. On paper, on walls, in the margins of the library books I'd borrowed to read to him at night.

When Jack didn't return from work the morning after Edward wrote his name, I was oddly unsurprised. I got Edward to school and went through the morning routine with Matt and Grace. Diapers, juice, a walk under trees heavy with flat, brightly colored leaves. Pushing the stroller through shadow and bright sun spots, I went through my options again. I could call the station; I could wait. There were only two. Each time, I convinced myself it was looking for her that had delayed him. He'd stayed so he could use a police computer and do the research more efficiently. I imagined he might be on the phone with her right now.

Then there was work to do. I made Matt's lunch and nursed Grace while he ate, then loaded the stroller again for the walk to his afternoon kindergarten. As the sun peaked and then turned overhead, sliding infinitesimally westward, I sat alone at the dining room table. Grace was asleep. There was a ticking sound coming from somewhere in the house. My left hand lay on the table and I stared into its palm. It was like snakeskin, smooth and dry and worn.

I picked up the phone and dialed Mariel's number once more. This time, I listened to the entire message. After the beep, I took a breath and said, "Uh, hi," then hung up quickly and rubbed my forehead until it felt bruised. I was relieved when Grace made her waking noise and the circle of tasks resumed: another diaper change, feeding, then time to pick up the boys from school. And afterward there was the flurry of papers from backpacks, pictures to be admired. For an entire day there had been no other adult voice in our house and as the afternoon wound lazily down and a cool, clear grayness settled over the house, panic finally gripped me.

I switched on the TV and settled the boys one on either side of Grace, who was propped on pillows on the living room floor. She sat elevated, between her brothers, a modern-day Cleopatra with fat cheeks and a bald head.

Of course, by the time I dialed the station, he was, apparently, already out for the night. "Do you want his voice mail?" the dispatcher asked. "Or if it's an emergency, I can transfer you to the sergeant on shift."

I shivered, imagining Bob Simmons sitting at his desk, pushing his greasy hair back with one thick hand. I knew he wasn't, in life, as repugnant and oily as I remembered. I'd met him once and he shook my hand in a perfectly pleasant way. It was only after Jack's stories that his character became, in my mind, like that of the villain in cartoon westerns. I knew he'd handled the marijuana Edward ultimately drank; I shuddered whenever I thought of how he might have opened the bag and stuck his cigar-size finger in to stir up the buds and leaves.

"No. Just, ah, can you give me Danny Torkelson?"

There was a dead space, then the high-pitched voice of Jack's partner using words nearly identical to Mariel's, telling me he was out, to leave a message.

"It's Rachel," I said quietly into the phone. "Call me back, okay? Soon." Then I hung up without saying good-bye.

I had barely set the phone back down when it rang. I grabbed it, imagining first that it was Jack, calling to explain, then in the next second that it was Mariel—she'd heard my attenuated message and wanted to tell me she missed me, too, or she hated me and never wanted to talk again. But it was my mother, calling to ask about Edward. "Was the teacher impressed when he wrote his name?" she asked. "Does she believe you now?"

"I . . . uh . . . I never talked to her about it."

"But you were so excited when you called last night. I expected you to be in there first thing this morning, having him demonstrate."

I almost told her about Jack. The words rose in my throat, *Mother, I think my husband is gone,* but I swallowed them back. Instead, I made my voice hard. "Oh, what would be the point? It seems like no matter how much better he gets, she's still intent on proving there's something wrong with him."

"Oh." She laughed a short, nervous note. "You're in one of those moods again. Well, just go to bed; kiss your children and curl up next to your husband. It'll all be better in the morning."

"He's not here." My voice was dead-sounding, even to me.

"Oh, that's right. He's on nights. All the better then. You can take a good book to bed, something nice and comforting, not one of those depressing things you usually read."

"Okay." She was in her kitchen. I could hear water running, her radio playing the slippery chords of "Hey, Jude" refashioned into a piece for synthesizer and saxophones.

"Hey, Mom . . . ?"

Her cupboard doors made no sound when they closed; all the doors hung straight. And her coffee was weak but it was always on, always there. I thought about getting in the car and driving over, dumping the children out on my parents' king-size bed, three little travelers riding an enormous raft. I would leave without a word and climb into the canopied four-poster in my old room, shutting the door and pulling the shades, making it so dark I wouldn't be able to see my own fingers if I held them in front of my face.

"Yes?" There was the whisking sound of a hose rolling out, then the tinny spatter of water on metal. She was spraying the sink after scrubbing it with cleanser.

"Do you think he's getting better?"

She paused for just an instant too long before answering. "Of course I do." If I hadn't been so numb, I'm sure I would have felt her hesitance cut me, the way it always did.

It was 4:13 A.M. when the phone rang again. I'd been lying in bed with the light on, trying to trick myself into falling asleep by keeping myself awake. But it wasn't working.

"Hey." Danny's voice was as thin and high as a young girl's, though he was nearly thirty-five. Standing next to Jack, he always looked like a teenager, his chest narrow, hips slim, face fresh and innocent under a floppy hank of shiny, gold, rock-star hair. "Sorry it took me so long to get back to you. I got your message a couple hours ago, but it's been a crazy night and we're, you know, short-handed."

"It's okay." I kept my voice low, so as not to wake the boys. At least there was that, I reminded myself: Edward could be awakened now. "I just wanted to ask you a couple questions."

"Well." The word was like a squirm. "I don't think there's anything I can tell you that Jack wouldn't tell you himself. How is he, by the way?"

I paused, debating how to answer. Finally, I decided. "Missing."

"Christ." Danny sighed. "Well, I knew he'd be upset. What's he doing? Did he go out drinking afterward?"

"Probably," I said. Then, "After what?"

"After he was . . . when's the last time you saw him?"

"Night before last." It was Thursday morning now. I counted back in my head. "Tuesday, I guess. He left for his shift. He hasn't been back since."

Danny groaned. "Okay, I see. Listen, I really have to go. I mean, I thought this'd be a short call and I have reports to fill out. But I get off at six and I can look around for him, if you want. I mean, I will. I'll look for him."

"Wait!" I yelped, forgetting about the children. On the other side of the wall, one of the boys shifted and bedsprings wheezed. "What happened? Just tell me."

"Yeah, fine. Jack got canned." The harsh street lingo sounded ridiculous delivered in Danny's reedy voice. "Simmons came down on him hard and I gotta get going because he's watching me now and if I have any more to do with this, or with you, he's gonna have my head, too."

Then he hung up and for the sixth or seventh time in the past twenty-four hours, I found myself holding the phone, listening to nothing but emptiness on the other end of the line.

22

SATURDAY MORNING. It had been four days since Edward learned to write, four days since my husband disappeared. I stood at the sink, drinking coffee, staring out the window. The air was clear and bright, flooded with sharp light, full of the sounds of fall. A lawn mower puttered from a distant street and next door there was the scraping and rustling of dried leaves as the neighbor boy raked. I couldn't remember if we owned a rake—Jack usually took care of the lawn—but decided if we didn't I would buy one. The boys would love jumping in leaf piles.

Behind me, Edward and Matt still sat at the table. I'd awakened naturally that morning, after sleeping deeply for the first time in days. And they'd been sitting in the kitchen already when I came down the stairs carrying Grace, their heads bowed over Edward's work.

"He spelled me!" Matt said, pointing to the paper that lay between them. "Then he made *brother.* And *pancake.* Can we have pancakes for breakfast?"

I looked over the paper as I settled Grace into her chair. *Matthew* and *brother* were spelled correctly; the word *pancak* was missing its *e.* I bent and kissed Matt on the neck in the place that made him shrink and squirm and giggle. I did the same to Edward but he remained still, only brushing at the spot afterward as if a fly had landed there.

"How did you know how to spell these?" I asked.

Edward was silent, still writing, stacking words in neat columns.

"I told him." Matt looked back at Edward. "Baby! *B-A-B-Y.*" He looked at me shyly through Bambi lashes. "I can't remember how to do *Grace.*"

"How did you know all these other spellings?" *You just turned five,* I almost said. *Everything is backward, upside down.*

Matt shrugged. "So can we?"

"What?" I'd lost my place, momentarily lifted away by the cool breeze that sifted through the window screen.

"Have pancakes. For breakfast. Not yours, not that yucky kind with oatmeal. The kind from the box, like Grandma makes."

Grace crowed and maybe it was that, or the scent of the coffee now beginning to drip, or the fact that the four of us were balancing the room perfectly at that moment. The golden light I'd known after Edward's first few nights of sleep began to puddle inside me again. "Of course," I said. "We'll all have pancakes. Even the B-A-B-Y."

It was afterward, as I stood staring outside, that Jack pulled into the driveway. Our plates, coated with syrup, were stacked on the counter and I was running warm water, filling the sink with bubbles. I watched as he got out of the car, dropped his keys into his pocket, and stretched, as if it were any Saturday. I began rinsing the plates as he walked toward the house. Heard him open the front door, drop the newspaper on the floor inside. When I turned, he was standing in the doorway to the kitchen wearing a shirt I didn't recognize: *Leo's Auto Body*, it said on the front. And there was a crude drawing of a car with muscles underneath.

"Hey, guys," he said and waved at the children.

"Daddy!" Matt ran at Jack, who bent to pick him up and held him for what must have seemed to Matt like minutes. He clung to Jack, throwing his arms around his neck and burying his blond head in Jack's neck.

Jack made a sound that reminded me of the cry of a bird at night, but it was so low I doubted anyone else could hear it. He carried Matt back to the table and reached down to place one hand on Edward's head. Jack's palm covered the curls like a cap. "What're you doing, honey?" he asked.

"He's spelling!" Matt bounced on Jack's arm. "Mommy taught him how to write and now he likes it."

Jack sat slowly, carefully, protecting some part of himself. His back or his knees, I couldn't tell. "Let me see." He tugged on the paper gently and after staring at him for a moment, Edward released it.

"Wow, this is . . ." Jack looked at me and I met his eyes, one blue, one green. For the first time, I saw the hollowed-out darkness of exhaustion that ringed them. "Amazing," he said. His voice caught. I poured him a cup of coffee and he wrapped his hand around mine and held on for a minute when I gave it to him.

The children and I went for a rake and Jack got into bed and fell immediately to sleep. By the time we returned from the hardware store, they were ready for lunch. Then we raked all afternoon and the boys leapt and scuffled through the scratchy leaves. Matt's cheeks were bright with allergy but somehow Edward managed to remain pressed-looking; he would emerge, dignified, from the pile after each jump. Whichever boy appeared, Grace would cheer from the backpack I wore. Finally, I felt her head heavy against my shoulder and knew she'd fallen asleep.

By four o'clock, I was tired and angry. I'd kept the children out of the house long enough and my hands ached along the palms from where I'd been gripping the rake. We went into the house, letting the screen door slap closed behind us. Jack was sitting in the living room; he'd been watching us.

"We should talk." I was swaying from foot to foot, keeping Grace lulled in the backpack. My feet hurt and suddenly I felt dizzy, turned on edge, and drenched through from the sun.

"I guess. What about . . . them?"

"Well, I don't know, Jack. Since you've been gone I decided to keep them around, feed them and try to keep them clean and all that. But if you've got another idea, I'm all ears."

He looked at his feet and sighed. I half expected him to rise and leave again, the door closing like punctuation. *The end.* This time, it's for real.

"Look, why don't I order a couple pizzas and we'll get the kids settled, then I'll tell you. Everything."

"Do you think that's a good idea?" I asked. Genuinely this time. "Ordering pizzas, I mean. You just lost your job, right?"

"Right."

Even though I'd known what Danny said was true, my stomach clenched at hearing him confirm it. "So why don't I make them some sandwiches and fruit?" His eyes were wild and I softened a little. "They don't need pizza anyway. We had a big breakfast."

Then I handed him the baby and he held her and rocked, though he wasn't sitting in a rocking chair. Together, they sat in the big recliner while the sun settled, large and pink, behind bare trees and I fed and bathed the boys. When I came back the room was entirely dark but I could see the shape of Jack, continuing to move his body back and forth like a metronome though whether it was to soothe the baby or himself, I couldn't tell.

"What happened?" I asked as I unbuttoned my shirt and reached for Grace so I could nurse her.

"You mean Tuesday? Simmons happened. He came into the squad room while I was on the phone with . . . her. There was an emergency call down on Hennepin; everyone who wasn't already out was going. I just needed a couple minutes to explain, you know, why I was calling and arrange to meet her. Or something."

He looked at me intently. "I didn't want to."

"I know."

He sighed again. "And she didn't want to. Didn't want me calling like that, barging into her life. She made that very clear."

I looked down at Grace, wondering how a mother could ever feel that way, then imagined her in thirty-six years, a woman I'd never met, never held, and understood exactly how a mother could hate that dark space of not knowing so much she never wanted to meet it head-on.

"I'm sorry," I said, and meant it.

Jack shrugged. "Didn't surprise me. I just wanted to get the whole thing dealt with and over. So I told Simmons I needed five goddamn minutes and he exploded. Fired me on the spot."

"Did you finish the call?"

Jack laughed dryly. "Yes."

My thoughts were knitting together slowly. It had been a long day and my head felt thick with dust. "But this doesn't make any sense. You're a civil servant; you have a union. You can't be fired for making a phone call."

"I wasn't."

I waited. He wasn't going to make me ask. I would sit in silence for an hour if that's what it took. Finally Jack spoke again.

"About a month ago, I watched Simmons beat the crap out of a homeless guy. And I did nothing. Nothing." He looked straight down at the floor and for a second I expected to see tears falling in a stream—as if he were some giant gnome in a fairy tale whose rough exterior had broken wide open. But when Jack raised his head, his eyes were flat and empty.

"He'd been wandering in the traffic on Lake. So we were called out. I can't remember why Simmons had to go. Danny was tied up, or something. Anyway, this skinny guy was out there in filthy clothes and he kept looking up at the lights, sort of spinning around right in the middle of the street."

Jack sat back. He was seeing it again in his head. Grace had nodded off, my nipple locked gently in her teeth, milk dripping from the corner of her mouth. I pulled her away gently and handed her to Jack. He leaned back and placed her blanket on his lap, like a napkin, so he could rewrap her.

"I went out and got him. I had to pull him in, through the traffic. And he was stronger than he looked. But I got him into the car. Then Simmons got out and stood there, like he was in charge. Which he was." Jack looked at the floor. "So I stepped back and Simmons asked the guy what he was doing out there. But the guy didn't answer. Then he asked the guy what his name was." Jack twitched his head from side to side, as if he were trying to shake something off. "And I saw, through the window, I saw the guy lift up his hand and hold it in front of his face, like this."

I knew, even before he did it, exactly what Jack would show me. The sudden movement: palm twisting toward the face, fingers splayed, eyes riveted on the center of his own hand. Sometimes Edward would mutter strings of syllables when he did this; most of the time, he just stared.

"And the next thing I knew, Simmons was whaling on him. It happened so fast. He just sort of slid into the seat next to the guy and started beating him with his own . . ." Jack choked and had to stop for a moment and I was glad. "Simmons used the guy's own hand at first and made him hit himself and then he went at it for real and socked him in the stomach a few times until the guy puked. And that must have made him really mad, the mess and the stink, because then . . ." Jack closed his eyes.

"Did he kill him?"

"Jesus, no. He's not stupid. In fact, I doubt he left a lot of marks on him. By the time we took the guy in he was really worked over but the truth is"—Jack made an evil chuckling sound but I forgave him; I knew he'd taught himself this and used it when he had to—"he didn't look a whole lot different than he did when we found him. Dazed. Sick. Crazy."

"Why did Simmons do it?"

"Who the fuck knows? Fight with his wife, lost a bet on the Vikings? Could have been anything. That's just the kind of guy he is. Sometimes."

I listened to Grace breathing, to the toneless hum of the fan I'd turned on in the boys' bedroom upstairs.

"I did nothing," Jack repeated.

"So you were fired because you didn't stop him? He himself fired you for not stopping him?"

"Not at all. He probably thought I was a risk. I knew. I saw him lose control. Eventually, I might say something. In fact . . ." Jack stared at the fireplace as if he might be able to concentrate and conjure up a sudden blaze. "For the last week I've been thinking about making a report." He shifted his eyes to mine and held on. "That guy could have been Edward. And I let some asshole beat him up just because he couldn't say his name. Ever since"—Jack shrugged—"I guess I felt like I couldn't be here with you and the kids if I stayed quiet. And I couldn't hang on at work if I didn't. So one night, after the shift, Danny and I went out and got a little wasted and I said something. Stupid."

My face was hot. "Danny! You think Danny told him what you said?"

"Or not. Who knows? He's a cop. His dad was a cop. That's what he cares about, not some vagrant who heaves all over a senior officer."

"Dammit." My throat was fluttering, open and closed, with anger. "I called Danny. I trusted him."

"And he's the one who came and found me. Dragged my sorry ass out of the bar where I'd been sitting for two days. Made me take a shower and gave me these clothes."

I couldn't help but smile. "Where did Danny get clothes for you? He's about Edward's size."

"Can't tell you that. He just found 'em. That's who he is: cop, through and through. He's going to protect the badge first, then do whatever he can to clean up people like me: drunks, deadbeats." Jack smiled again. Using one finger, he traced Grace's eyebrows.

"Okay. So you fight this. We hire a lawyer. You can't be fired for threatening to turn someone in for brutality."

He was still tracing, shaking his head. "I wasn't, technically. I was fired for buying drugs."

This time, my throat actually closed for a few seconds and I had to work to breathe. "What?"

"Surely you remember." His words sliced the air, each one equally sharp.

"But you bought that stuff from Simmons. How can he get you on that?"

"Easy. He set it all up back then. I don't know, maybe he does this with everyone. Just in case. He has a few bills with my fingerprints on them, and the dealer is ready to swear I bought directly from him. He did a good job. He's got the report all typed up and filed and the department believes it. They won't press charges—to avoid the headlines—if I just go away quietly. If not, I'm a felon. I go to jail, never get another decent job in my life."

I groaned. "You hungry?"

Jack stood and lifted Grace to his shoulder. "Always."

Somehow, just moving to the kitchen made me feel better. The solid, looming tower of the pie safe with its multiple doors and wrought-iron latches. The shiny appliances. Edward's papers lying on the table along with Matt's latest drawings of cars submerged in water. I put the water on to boil and lit the gas burner—a satisfying whoosh of fire—busily making tea and a plate of cheese and crackers. When I had everything arranged I turned to Jack, who sat alone now. He must have stopped on his way into the kitchen and left Grace in her cradle.

"How much severance do you get?"

He made a zero with his thumb and forefinger.

"Okay. Have you looked for other jobs yet?"

"Well, I asked the guy behind the bar if he needed any professional beer tasters."

I swallowed and struggled to keep my voice low. "This is not funny."

"No. It's not. But you've only heard half the story. There's more."

"There's more," I echoed. Strangely, this affected me like good news though I was fairly certain it wasn't. Yet, I was interested again. And maybe we could quit talking about his losing his job.

"I went to see my . . . uh . . . Joan. That's her name; the woman who gave birth to me."

"And?"

"And she says there's no way Edward could have a genetic disorder. No history of it on her side or my father's." He seemed to gag on the last word. "To be precise, what she said was, 'We don't got no people with disgusting tumors all over the place.'" His voice was a monotone, hitting each word with emphasis as if it were its own sentence.

"Oh, God, Jack. Your mother."

"That was *not* my mother," he said fiercely. "My mother was a good person. She would have loved our kids no matter . . ." He rose and began pacing. In eight years, I had never seen him pace. "But this woman. She was like six feet tall, maybe three hundred pounds, living in this tiny hovel off Powderhorn Park with her 'boyfriend.' Jesus! The filth, the clutter, the smell. She's just one step up from the guy we picked up off the street. She's . . ." He stared out the darkened window over the sink, standing in the same place I had stood each winter night when I was pregnant with Grace. "Trash."

"I'm sorry," I said.

"Me, too. Sorry she is. Sorry I know it. Sorry I ever met her. Makes me itch, just thinking about her blood in mine. In them . . ." He shivered and sat. Jumped up again and loomed over me. "But you haven't heard the best part. About him, my father."

I didn't want to look at Jack anymore. This was difficult, because he was standing very close to me and I could feel his heart pounding, just inches away.

"He was a neighborhood kid. Knocked her up when they were both sixteen; she'd known him all her life but they didn't have a relationship or anything. No intention of getting married or, you know, *keeping* me." He snorted. "He found someone else, though. Some woman from St. Paul who moved in with him. Joan's not sure if they ever actually got married, though the papers called her his wife."

"The papers?" I lifted my head slowly and saw nothing but disgust in his eyes.

He answered like someone who'd been hypnotized. "The newspapers. In the articles. Whenever he was arrested for beating her up, or kiting checks. Once, I guess, he tried to run a scam on old ladies but he was stupid about it and got arrested right away. Then, of course, there was the article when he died. We saw that one, a few years ago, after the bar fight at Moby Dick's. That guy who went through the plate-glass window out front? That was him. Dear old Dad."

Just then, an image of Mickey appeared in my mind. Mickey as I had constructed him. He was a hero; I saw, now, how important that had become to me. I needed Mickey to be thoughtful and haunted and fine, because I had assigned him to be the model for Edward and because he was my uncle. His blood ran through mine.

"I'll tell you this." Jack walked away from me and stood by the window, looking down at his own hands. He spoke softly. "My father was no Indian medicine man."

JAMES

By the fall of 1959, Mickey had been back from the war for six years and the country was changing. Fidel Castro had assumed power in Cuba. *Some Like It Hot* was playing in the theaters, and *Goodbye, Columbus* had become a bestseller; suddenly, people were talking openly about things most wives and husbands wouldn't have discussed behind closed doors in the past.

In Minneapolis, the Lakers had gone all the way to the NBA Finals, only to be beaten by Boston. Though he went through a few weeks of focusing all his attention on the basketball team and became swept up, briefly, in a feeling of community spirit, Mickey still did not feel like he was home. Sometimes, at night, he dreamed of a pale open sky curved over glistening rice paddies and low-lying hills.

When he'd first landed at the Twin Cities airport, his mother had cried and hugged him and told him she'd expected him to die in Korea. She had prepared herself for it, imagining over and over the knock at the door and the face of the young soldier who would be standing rigid on the front step.

His father had said little but seemed almost tearful with relief when Mickey rose at seven o'clock a few days later and dressed for his first day at the jewelry store. He had meant for it to be temporary, but somehow the days had become weeks and then months. Mickey found himself constantly wondering at the glut of extraordinary comforts in this life: fresh towels that his mother had laundered and hung outside in the sunshine to dry, a mattress whose springs were hidden beneath layers of soft padding, the lightness of carrying with him only a wallet and a ring of keys.

At his father's suggestion, Mickey enrolled in a course at the gemology institute but it turned out it wasn't stones he liked, it was watches. The smooth, oiled insides, ticking every second the same as the last—or if they weren't, waiting for him to set them right. The cogs and springs inside a watch face made sense in the same way planes had when they flew across that perfect dome of sky. When Mickey began spending hours absorbed in this work, Ted was elated. He bought a new, upright display case and added a line of high-quality timepieces. He sent Mickey to a monthlong seminar in Chicago and had business cards waiting for him when he returned that said, *Mickey Donnelly, Watchmaker.*

A year had passed, and in spring, at precisely the time Mickey was beginning to think about looking into college, or perhaps a flight school where they took a more enlightened view than the military toward perfectly capable, nearsighted controllers, he met Ruth at church. She was eighteen with smooth dark hair and a shy smile. Ruth had just graduated from high school and begun working as a clerk in her father's insurance firm downtown. It was logical that she and Mickey would gravitate toward each other. They had lunch a few times over the summer and when Ruth wanted to buy her brother a sweater for his birthday in September, she asked Mickey to meet her at Dayton's men's department to try it on.

Being overseas had given him something—not just confidence but a foreign status that suited him. People expected him to be different from other men, rougher, more brooding. All of the things that had made him worrisome as a child now fit the character he'd become, so when he put his hand on Ruth's hip as she stood in front of him, fussing with the buttons on the sweater he was modeling, she didn't object. Mickey had never had a girlfriend, nor had he visited the women Bo told him about in Seoul. He knew nothing except what he'd read but this didn't matter at all with Ruth, who gazed back at him with frightened eyes, as if he were the wolf and she Red Riding Hood, but never backed away.

Before long, their families simply assumed they would get married and Ruth, timid in most other ways, began hinting that she assumed so, too. She'd been out shopping and seen a china pattern she particularly liked. She wondered if Mickey had thought about how many children he would like. She needed to tell her father if she would be leaving the office so he could look for a replacement. Or perhaps Mickey would not object to having a wife who worked?

It was winter. They had been going out for more than half a year and Mickey's life had settled into a predictable course: during the week he sat on a stool next to his father, a jeweler's monocle strapped to his head, peering into the tiny universe of watch workings, looking for the one broken tooth or spring that had caused the entire mechanism to grind to a halt. On weekends, he took Ruth out Saturday evening and saw her again the next morning, each Sunday, at church. Afterward, they would go to her parents' house for dinner, where Ruth's mother— a thin, silent woman whom Mickey had never once heard laugh—had begun automatically setting a place for him.

For a man his age to be living at home seemed odd, but he could come up with no reason to move. Susanna was still there, too, and she seemed perfectly content to help their mother with dinner every evening, then watch television or go downtown to see a movie with one of her unmarried girlfriends. Twice, Mickey had considered moving out, but the first time he had looked at a few bachelor apartments and found them depressing and cavelike, filled with what appeared to be used office furniture. The second time, he'd inquired about rooms for rent and had run into a landlady so very much like his mother he imagined living in her home would be like an uncanny mirror image of his current life.

It was at this point, looking back, that Mickey lost track. Somewhere, he must have proposed to Ruth or at least agreed to the marriage she seemed to expect. Wedding plans had taken another several months, during which he had felt a quickening of the slide that began when he was sent home from Korea. It was as if he were watching his life, controlling nothing but the sprockets of watches. Then there was the wedding three and a half years ago and the early months of marriage, during which he'd groggily adjusted to the small discoveries he made about Ruth: that she spoke to her mother multiple times each day, that she looked down at her hands with pursed lips whenever he attempted to tell a joke, that she sighed nearly inaudibly when he turned to her in bed at night.

Shortly after, he'd begun lying awake again and feeling the itch to walk. To move.

Though they were going to his parents' house for an early dinner that night, Mickey took the late lunch. Helen went first, then his father. It wasn't until one-thirty that Mickey opened the door to the shop and stepped out into the afternoon sun. He liked it this way: after the midday crowds had died down. Walking down Nicollet, hatless, he could feel the warmth on his scalp in contrast to the cool October breeze. He stopped for a moment, closed his eyes, and pictured Korea. The flat, gray sandy ground, mountains green in the distance, evening drooping its belly of clear brown light between them.

He checked his watch and then his stomach, realized he wasn't hungry, and took Sixth Street up to Hennepin Avenue, toward the bridge. It took him only four minutes to reach the river; he stood for a moment and scanned the water, a still and muddy green. On the other side of the Mississippi, the Gold Medal Flour sign loomed over a sprawling cement-colored mill. The scent of dust and heat and grain floated toward him.

Mickey crossed the bridge and kept walking, first past the granaries and a series of warehouses with barred windows. Then into neighborhoods where the houses grew close together. He thought about Bo back in Detroit, living in a house like this small pink one on the corner, perhaps married now like Mickey, working at a job in a city where the buildings rose and leaned toward one another and closed off the sky. Mickey wanted to call him but he knew such things weren't done. And as if to keep him from making that mistake, his own mind had clouded over everything he knew; Bo's last name had faded from his memory, becoming a jumble of consonants Mickey knew was nowhere near right.

He came to a street he did not recognize and paused, squinting into the distance, then checked his watch again. He was already halfway into his lunch hour and probably should turn back. But as he swiveled on the heel of one wingtip shoe, Mickey looked up and saw the sign, set so it jutted out from the rounded corner of a brick building: HUBER FUNERAL HOME. Mickey's memory clicked backward, as if through a series of file cards. He'd never met James Huber's father but recalled stories about the charismatic mortician—a ladies' man who wore a red carnation in his lapel every day and took new widows gently by the hand as he showed them oak and mahogany caskets lined with real silk. His mother remarked once that she'd never seen such a short man draw so much attention from women, not to mention one who touched dead bodies all day long.

From the outside, Huber Funeral Home did not look like the sort of place Mary's friends would go to grieve, or to pray. It was nothing like their church, which was as cold and noble as a castle—stone walls and stained-glass windows, a ceiling so high it was nearly invisible from the pews, and a crucifix made of beams as thick as a man's waist hanging over it all. This building was small, mud-colored, and squat, and it seemed to lean slightly to the south. Mickey peered in the front window and saw a large room lined with long shadows. There was no one in the space. It looked dusty and still . . . preserved, as if everyone had left it suddenly years ago but forgotten to empty it, or turn it into a restaurant or a grocery store.

Then, as if he'd willed it, there was a man in the back of the room. He walked forward and, before Mickey could step back and begin walking again, pretending he'd only stopped to shake something out of his shoe, the man swept open the door.

He had blond hair carefully greased back over his ears and a small mustache. But in every other way, Mickey thought, James looked exactly as he had at sixteen.

"Mickey Donnelly? Is that you?"

Mickey looked at his feet, then remembered he was a grown man now. More was required of him. He raised his head and tried to hold it steady. "Hi. I noticed the sign." He pointed up. "I remembered your name and . . . wondered."

James laughed. "And here I am. Where you'd least expect, I suppose."

Mickey shrugged. "You're working in your father's shop. I'm working in mine. It's not so surprising."

"No?" James's eyebrows quirked over his eyes. His mother might call it a devilish look if she were to see him, Mickey thought. "Maybe not in your case."

They stood for a moment on opposite sides of the door—James inside, his shoulders in shadow, Mickey still outside in the midafternoon sun—and just as Mickey drew a breath in to say he should be getting back, James said, "Come in! Come in! No sense in our standing here." He stepped back and the dimness seemed to swallow his body. Mickey stepped over the threshold. Next to James, he felt as big and bulky as Bo.

Music drifted out of the speakers. Not organs; Mickey listened. It was "Mack the Knife." James's face reddened. "I listen when I'm here alone...." He waved a hand around the room. "Bobby Darin helps liven up the place."

Prices were displayed on the caskets, small signs with gilt lettering. Mickey stared at one that read $900 and gasped. "Expensive to die these days," he said, not realizing until the words were out of his mouth that he was criticizing another man's business.

But James smiled. "Maybe that's why we don't have too many takers. People seem to prefer staying alive, spending their dough on other things."

Mickey began walking and noticed his shoes made no sound against the deep dark carpet underfoot. He tried scraping his feet as he went but every movement was silenced by the room. Suddenly the walls looked thick, fibrous, with something like the skin of a swamp weed. Mickey's heart began beating faster and he picked up his pace, moving toward the back of the building as if he had a purpose.

If James thought it was strange, he didn't say so. He loped alongside Mickey to the opening from which he'd emerged a few minutes earlier. "Come back for a cup o' joe?"

"Ah." Mickey looked at his watch again. "I really . . ."

"Nice," said James, taking Mickey's wrist in his hand and examining the silver Elgin. "Classic. One of yours?"

"I worked on it. My first. It's the one I learned on, so my dad told me to keep it."

"I hear you're good." They had moved through the door and into a surprisingly bright little kitchen without Mickey's even realizing it. He sat in a worn, wooden chair much like the ones he and Ruth had at home—a cast-off set from her parents' basement—at a table covered with a flowered sheet made of thick vinyl.

"You hear?"

James nodded. "I keep up. I knew you were back, working at the jewelry store. I've been meaning to come in and see you but then I look up one day and"—he made a wide gesture with his arms—"here you are!"

Mickey was quiet. He tried to remember what he knew of James. Susanna had never spoken about him after the war. And Mickey had never seen him around. He hadn't thought to wonder why Susanna went out so little; she seemed content to work each day in the clerical department at a brand-new mechanical computing company called Control Data.

Mickey had been staring at his hands. Now he looked up and saw James watching him. Perhaps it was rude to sit without speaking. Mickey cleared his throat. "How's business?"

"Pretty dead." James laughed from where he stood near the cup-boards. He plugged an electric percolator into a wall socket then walked over and pulled out the chair next to Mickey's. "Sorry. We just wait for suckers to come in and ask that question. The truth is, it's bad."

"I'm sorry to hear that." Mickey crossed his arms. According to his watch, he should be back in the store right now, taking off his suit jacket and settling back to work at the bench.

"Partly it's the neighborhood. It's really gone downhill in the past couple years. And then, it could be me, too." James looked directly into Mickey's eyes and held them. "Maybe some people don't like the idea of me touching their loved ones."

It was warm in the small kitchen and Mickey's back was beginning to itch under his jacket. He yawned then pulled himself up straighter in the chair. "Can't see why that would be. I'm sure you do as good a job as any."

Mickey was suddenly very sleepy, his forehead prickling with heat.

He needed that coffee. Then he planned to make his excuses, say his father was expecting him back, and escape into the cool autumn afternoon. He started to say something, gesture toward the pot, but just then James sat forward so their knees were almost touching and blurted out, "So you haven't heard the rumors?"

Mickey shook off the pall he'd been under, his body coming alert in an animal way. James's clear, wide eyes were staring at him so piercingly, he looked down to see if they were shining beams onto his clothes. There was nothing there, nothing but the rough weave of his jacket rumpled over his chest. Mickey yanked the coat off and tossed it onto the back of another chair. He shook his head. "How about that coffee?" He tipped his head toward the pot that had quieted but gave off a thin curl of dark, sweet-smelling steam. "I could really use it."

James jumped up. He poured two mugs and dumped several teaspoons of sugar into one of them. He turned to Mickey and grinned. "I like mine really sweet. You want anything?"

Mickey shook his head. "Just black."

When they sat facing each other again, Mickey felt completely different. Sharply conscious in a way he hadn't been since his last night on the radio in Korea, watching the glittering wing lights of tiny planes arc and dip against a black velvet sky through the glass of the tower window. He took a sip from the cup James had given him and burned his tongue. Still, it was better than anything he had tasted since coming home.

"What rumors?"

James was no longer looking at him but had tipped his head down as if to study the roses that repeated across the tablecloth. "About me. And girls. Your sister?"

Mickey thought hard. People's relationships so often were like a puzzle; you had to figure out the rules and then apply them to the situation. But he wasn't very good at working them out and often, as with Susanna, he just allowed himself to be ignorant. She was a smart girl. She had a job. She seemed perfectly happy living with their parents, helping her mother put on big holiday dinners, sitting with them at church on Sundays.

"My sister mentioned you in her letters . . . uh . . . years ago. I was in the service." He pointed, knowing, though he did not know how he knew, in exactly which direction Korea lay.

"I remember," said James quietly. "We used to talk about you quite a bit."

"She said that." Mickey nodded. He drained his cup and stood up to pour himself more. "She also said you two went out and that you asked her . . ."

"To marry me?"

"Jeez, no!" Mickey sat down again. "To go steady."

"Oh. I did that, too. Earlier. I guess . . . yeah . . . that would have been while you were overseas."

Mickey thought about Susanna, her cheerful attitude toward his wedding. The way she had talked to Ruth, as if she didn't notice his fiancée's coolness but felt like they were family already. The blank expression he sometimes glimpsed on her face right before she smiled. "So you're in love with my sister?"

James fidgeted with the spoon from the sugar bowl, trying to balance it on his index finger. "Not exactly. I mean, I like her. A lot. I would have been happy to marry her just because . . ." He had found the spoon's center of gravity and it teetered now on the tip of his finger. Both men watched it, and waited. "I want to be married. To have a home and children. I want to have a life. You know?"

Mickey did know. He felt a brief flash of anger. "What are you trying to say?"

"Hey, don't get sore. It isn't Susanna's fault. She's great. And she was right to say no. She deserves a real husband, not someone like me."

Now Mickey was confused again and his blood was racing because of the close, warm air and the sense that time outside was passing too quickly as he sat in this small bright room with James. "I thought . . ." He stopped and tried to think of a way to unsnarl his thoughts but couldn't. Finally, he reverted to the truth. "I thought you were talking about me. My marriage."

There was a long silence and Mickey closed his eyes. The room had become like a train, moving away from the rest of his life, and he wanted it to stop.

"I don't know about your marriage. I know about me. My proposal to Susanna was wrong." James shook his head. "It was probably sinful. Because I never could have felt about her the way I should have, the way I felt . . ."

Mickey opened his eyes and saw the way James looked at him and he understood something he never could have put into words.

"Is it the same for you?" James asked. There was hope in his voice.

The coffee, drunk on an empty stomach, was beginning to burn in his gut. Mickey shifted in his seat and cracked his knuckles, considering what James had asked. He thought about the baseball field and how running was like breaking out of the sealed space he occupied inside his head. He thought about Korea, about the long, brown nights and the way he could breathe there. He thought about Bo. Then he pictured Ruth in the pink skirt she'd worn the first time he met her for lunch, at Woolworth's, and the way she had made it plain to him that it was time for her to find someone, just as it was time for him.

"No." He spoke as if he'd been asleep for a long time, the word croaking gently in the bubble of the warm room where they sat. "It's not the same for me."

James folded his hands, focused on them, smiled briefly. Bravely, Mickey thought. "I didn't think so," he said.

"I wish . . ." Mickey surprised himself with this, the words coming even before his own understanding of what he felt. "I wish it were. That would be easier, maybe."

"Don't be so sure," James said roughly. He blinked several times, then his face softened so he looked exactly like the boy who gamely chased an afternoon's worth of fly balls and brought them to Mickey in a burlap bag. "How is it for you?"

"It's like . . ." Mickey concentrated and his head began to buzz with the effort. But he knew in the end he would not find the right way to say this. "I don't fit here. Anywhere. I can't stand still and I can't move fast enough to make it work. I get up every morning and I do the things I think I'm supposed to do. But it seems like it's only a matter of time before everything around me will start to slip away."

• • •

Later, sitting at his parents' massive dining room table after Ruth had made her announcement, Mickey looked back on the afternoon and it wavered in his head like a television show he'd watched but forgotten large parts of. Full of Mary's pot roast and mashed potatoes and a second glass of beer, he felt almost contented. The day slipped away—his nervousness and embarrassment over telling everyone about the baby, the urge to keep walking the way he had in Korea, the odd look his father had given him when he didn't return from lunch until a few minutes after four o'clock.

Susanna stood and began clearing the dishes. "No, no. You sit," she'd said when Mary and Ruth started to rise. "You're talking." And they were—talking about christening gowns and whether Eleanor might finally be done with her maternity clothes and ready to pass them on. Mary patted Susanna's arm as she walked by and mouthed the words, *Good girl.*

Susanna backed through the swinging door to the kitchen, a stack of dirty dishes in each hand. Mickey watched her go. He'd noticed how babies brought women together and how, more and more lately, his sister was the only single person everywhere she went. He thought about what James had told him and it came back to him, all in one piece, like a scene he had actually watched unfold.

They were walking uptown, James and his sister, on a dusty Sunday afternoon two years before. He was just back from minor league try-outs, explaining to Susanna that baseball was not going to work out for him after all. And then he had made a proposal. Not the sort of proposal she must have imagined: a man in a suit with a bunch of roses gripped in one nervous hand, a love that felt as strong as Ted's for Mary. This was more a business proposition. He had found no one, James said, and neither had she. But they had a history together, a respect and admiration for each other. Didn't she want children? he asked, and Susanna said, yes, she did. "Well then," Mickey pictured him saying, eyebrows crooked as he stared down into Susanna's trusting face. "It's the perfect solution."

"She said no." James had grinned when he told Mickey this. "Just like that: no way. I know this is going to sound strange, but it made me kind of proud of her."

No one at his parents' house seemed to notice when Mickey excused himself and stood, pulling the last few remaining dishes from the table. He went into the kitchen the way Susanna had, backside first, and found her standing over a sink of bubbles, her face flushed and moist from the steam.

"I could really use a Coke," she said, as he set the stack of dishes down on the sideboard. "You want to split one?"

"Sure." Mickey reached into the refrigerator and pulled out a bottle. He walked to the wall where the bottle opener hung and tapped the metal cap off, took a swig, and handed it to her.

She raised rubber-gloved hands from the water, took the bottle from him, and drank twice before handing the bottle back. "Thanks." But Susanna didn't go back to washing the dishes. She stood with her head tipped to one side and stared at Mickey until he grew uncomfortable.

"What?" He swung up to sit on the countertop and held out the Coke bottle. "Do you want more?"

"No, it's just . . . you look different. Not so tough. When you came back from the war there was something . . ." She shrugged, sounding almost bored. "It's like you've finally settled in. Mother's been praying for that, you know."

Mickey hunched forward in his seat on the countertop, gazing down and spinning the wedding ring on his left hand. Suddenly he felt very small, the bank of cupboards once again towering above his head. He knew Susanna meant well but settling in sounded something like dying. She turned and look at him quizzically, then walked forward a few steps.

"It's wonderful news, about the baby." She spoke gently.

"Yeah. I've always wanted kids."

"Have you?"

Mickey was puzzled. He tried to think back. "Doesn't everyone? Isn't that what you're supposed to want?"

"I don't know." For a minute, Susanna looked confused, too. But then her face smoothed and she smiled broadly. "Of course everyone wants a family. It's a wonderful thing, the best. You're very lucky."

"I know." Mickey's feet swung like a two-year-old's. "You ever think about it? I know you've had offers."

Susanna narrowed her eyes at him. "I think about it. I'm sure it will happen when the time is right. Or . . ."

"What?"

"Well, it's ridiculous really. I've already said no."

"To what?" Mickey jumped down and the room spun in a way that was vaguely familiar. He felt a little drunk, though he'd had nothing since dinner but Coke.

"I was offered a job in New York."

"City?"

"Yes, can you imagine? It would be way too big for me and too far away from home and now . . ." She waved her hand toward the door, the dining room, toward Ruth and her parents. "Of course, I'll want to be here for you and Ruth and the baby."

"That's not your job." He heard himself, his harsh tone. "You should go."

"What business is it of yours?" She laughed, which is what she did whenever she was nervous. "I don't want to go. I want to stay here." Susanna untied her apron and smoothed out the front of her dress—a dowdy, conservative garment, Mickey noticed, very much like the one their mother wore. "Maybe I will take someone up on his proposal, get married the way you did, start a family."

"Don't!"

Now Susanna looked afraid. He remembered her as a baby, when he was awkward and prodding and always afraid of hurting her. "Look, I didn't mean to shout." Mickey rolled the empty Coke bottle in his hands and his wedding ring clinked rhythmically against its thick glass ridges. "I just think . . . It isn't what you might imagine, this getting married because it's . . . time. And if you have the opportunity to go to New York, I want you to consider it. Can you? Still?"

Susanna nodded. "My boss's boss is starting a new division out there next month. He still needs good programmers. The job is mine if I want it."

Mickey looked up and it seemed that the doors of his mother's kitchen cabinets might go on forever. Ruth's voice rose excitedly in the next room and he thought that he had never heard that sound before. Under his feet, the kitchen floor was hard and he swore he could feel the pull of gravity under the soles of his feet.

"I think you should go," he said softly, closing his eyes in an effort to make the world stop expanding. "Walk through the city. Look at all those buildings. Write and tell me if it isn't something to see."

23

Throughout November and December of his second-grade year, Edward continued to write. In fact, it became his passion. Each day after school, he would sit at the kitchen table with a piece of paper and a pen and Jack would feed him words, never tiring, always starstruck by the sight of our son making letters on a page.

Autumn was long—damp and windy and bitterly cold but without the snow or the clarity of air that I associated with winter. Jack slept mornings and drank afternoons. Holding a beer in one hand and Grace in the other, he held court in the kitchen. He'd let his beard grow long and tangled and he had a new wild lostness in his eyes. But both boys seemed elated their father was home. From the moment he returned from kindergarten, Matt almost never left Jack's side.

At night, Jack would go wherever the temp agency sent him: to unload boxes at a plastics factory or fold shirts for a dry cleaner. He'd signed up for the graveyard shift and there was always dirty, tedious work to be had.

After Jack lost his job on the force, I had returned to work part-time, but often I made interview calls and wrote from home in the mornings when the house was quiet, sitting at the same table where Edward would compose his spelling words in the afternoon. Grace, a happy baby, played with blocks and spoons at my side, content as long as I tuned the stereo to a disco station she particularly liked.

When I started back at the newspaper, Eric said only that he wanted me to make it in for meetings. We were standing in his office, just days after Jack's firing.

"A few things have changed," I told him. I was wearing a dark linen dress from before my last pregnancy that was so tight around my chest and waist, I felt as if I'd been bound. The chair in front of Eric's desk was piled with papers and magazines and I thought about moving them, folding myself down inside the tight sheath of my dress, and telling him the whole story: Edward and the marijuana, Bob Simmons, Jack's biological mother. I took a shallow breath, then glanced at Eric's face and saw a flicker of something—impatience, I thought, or disgust. I remembered the hospital, and what he thought of my life.

"I'd like to work from home," I said, not quite as firmly as I'd planned. But Eric just nodded, made a few comments about my responsibilities, then turned to pick up a sheaf of galleys and a red pen.

I could not imagine why he took me back. My title was senior editor, but the stories I worked on were increasingly small and dull—domestic articles about how to stage a house for sale or make cleaning products out of white vinegar, a listing of local apple orchards where families could pick their own fruit. It bothered me, but what I wrote wasn't nearly as important as keeping the health insurance the newspaper provided for all of us, staying close to the children, figuring out what would come next. Every afternoon, while the boys milled through the house snacking and sorting through their school papers and watching TV, I puzzled over our bank statements, transferring bits from the tiny savings account I'd hoarded over the years when Jack and I were both working.

And after I was done, the bills paid and dinner started, I would go into our bedroom and close the door, pull the box my aunt had given me from my closet shelf, and sit with Mickey's letters and Eleanor's journals scattered around me on the bed. This time, I read everything carefully and in order, putting the story together slowly. What I didn't find in Mickey's own words, I imagined: the way he must have felt leaving Korea, his painstaking work at the jewelry store, my mother's curiosity about him when he arrived home in his dress uniform, manly and numb. The days passed quietly and, for a time, I felt pulled away from the other four, as if Jack had taken over my space in the house and I had escaped to another world.

There were times I lived inside the era of Mickey and my grand-parents, Helen, Eleanor back when she was glamorous, and my mother long before she knew I would be born. I found myself wondering how they would respond to the things I encountered: Jack's drinking in the early afternoon, shortly after he awoke; Matt's questions about why Daddy didn't work as a policeman anymore. Mary would protect her husband at all costs, I decided. And this, clearly, was a trait she had passed on to her daughters. But what, if anything, did their blind loyalty have to do with Mickey? Was it possible he might have been saved if the women who supposedly loved him weren't so focused on their own marriages?

It was bitterly cold the month Jack took up running. He did it as he did everything, silently and with abandon. He ran in the rain and the snow, miles every morning. I would hear him, before dawn, letting himself in after he worked the night shift on some barren loading dock across town, changing into his sweat suit and going back out into the still dark. We had an austere winter of this: work on opposing schedules, small school activities, a tightly controlled life. Then, early in spring, everything changed.

First, Jack met Drew. Running side by side on the path around Lake Calhoun, they recognized each other. Drew was a banker who had called the police when his wallet and keys were taken at his gym, Jack the officer who responded. Jack had given Drew a ride home that day, waited for him to get the spare key from his wife, then taken him back to his car before the thief could figure out which one to steal. When they met again by the semi-frozen lake, Drew didn't ask why Jack wasn't on the force anymore, he just offered him a job manning the desk in the safe-deposit vault.

This suited Jack, I thought. He metamorphosed overnight into a man who wore plain dark clothes and a goatee that he trimmed to a neat point. And it suited me, too: I found I liked the rhythm of a regu-lar workday schedule. Though my byline still appeared in the news-paper, my job continued to diminish, the twenty hours' worth of work I was supposed to do each week decreasing to about ten. But now that Jack was bringing in a salary again, I could relax a little.

My responsibilities with the children eased around the same time. By her first birthday, Grace was eerily self-possessed. She was tall for her age, with thick, kinky hair more like Mariel's than mine, and she spoke as clearly as a five-year-old, without the babbling run-ons of babyhood. Unlike Matt, who had seemed satisfied to cuddle and read with me until the day he went off to school, Grace was always staring out windows, talking animatedly to store clerks when we went out. So I put her in day care three mornings a week and began freelancing, using my credentials at the newspaper to introduce myself, pitching articles to magazines. One job led to the next; there were a few lesser-known national publications that called me on a regular basis to help with local stories. And it was while researching one of these—an article about charter schools for an education quarterly published in Washington, D.C.—that I found out about brain gym.

On a pale blue morning in March, I drove to a school in northeast Minneapolis, not far from where my mother, Mickey, and Eleanor had lived as children. It was moist and windy outside, last fall's leaves rotted in clumps and stuck to the sidewalks. The air smelled faintly like yeast. Houses in this part of town were twice the size of mine, towering three-stories, but they had broken porches, plywood covering the windows, and most seemed to have been marked up with huge pencils: there were broad gray streaks in unlikely places, along the roofline or between the upstairs windows.

The school itself was made of brick that had shifted, so the mortar was crumbling and the building appeared moth-eaten. The address, 897, was carved into the stone above the doorway in fancy calligraphy. But the steps leading to the front door had big bites taken out of them.

Inside, the halls teemed with children who walked like soldiers. Most of the students were black; some wore eye patches and others carried squishy balls that they squeezed rhythmically. Noises echoed off the concrete walls.

The principal was a small man with a nervous hopping gait and wiry gray hair. He took me on a tour, talking the whole time in a low voice. One classroom was covered with blue mats on which gangly grade schoolers crawled on their hands and knees—snaking lines of overgrown toddlers with their heads down, chanting as they inched along. Another had enormous colored discs that whirled and metronome sticks that bobbed; a young woman at the front of the room used a conductor's baton to prompt the students to follow the objects with their eyes. At the end of the hallway, six teenagers did complicated-looking jumping jacks, hands crossing to the opposite shoulders instead of rising in the air.

Inside me, a queasiness began. Our tax dollars were being funneled into this place where poor children were made to look like monkeys. I breathed, trying to control a rising wave of anger, and made notes describing the peeling paint, the slovenly look of the teacher who was down on the floor, crawling in dirty jeans and a loose pullover at the front of his classroom.

"Seems ridiculous, doesn't it?" the principal said as we headed back to his office.

"Yes," I managed tightly. "But I'm sure you have your reasons."

"We do." He nodded. "Our kids can read."

"And they couldn't before?"

"Most of them, no. Seventy percent of the students we take are severely dyslexic; the other thirty have a variety of behavioral problems, some mild brain damage. Our method *looks* like voodoo, but it's been working for twenty years."

I looked at him. He was short enough that I could almost meet his eyes straight on. "Then why have I never heard of it?"

"Because"—he smiled and opened the door to the front office, ushering me in—"people think we're nuts."

Inside, posters on the wall showed side views of children's brains with arcs and stars connecting the various parts. There was a curved counter with two women behind it, talking. One of them—a fat, pretty young woman with dark hair and smooth pink skin—came forward and shook my hand, introducing herself as Kathy, the school's physical therapist.

"A real physical therapist?" I asked bluntly.

"State certified," she said, holding up her hand as if she were saying the Pledge of Allegiance. "I swear."

"Why does it work?" I had dropped my notebook on the counter and was leaning against a wall, acting casual, picking fuzz balls off my sweater. But my mind was racing.

Kathy paused before answering and I realized she was waiting for me to pick up my pen. I reached for it too late. She had leaned over, settling her round face into the palm of one hand. She looked kind, soft and motherly, though I suspected she was around my own age. We could have been friends. "You have a child?"

I nodded. "Three. But one who—"

"We think the movement and the cross-patterning carves new pathways in the brain. Skills that were lost or never learned have bridges to cross. And suddenly, a child can read, or speak, or tie his shoes."

I saw Mickey walking across Korea, Jack running around the lake, Edward spinning the rounder in front of his eyes. "Have you ever"—I cleared my throat and looked around. The principal had left, but the other woman was listening. I lowered my voice—"worked with a child with autistic symptoms?"

"Yes. And it didn't go very well." She waited while I took this like a punch. "He was profoundly autistic and we never knew if the therapy was ineffective, or he was just too withdrawn to participate."

"My son is mostly out. I mean, he's verbal. He speaks and, basically, he functions. But he's just not completely . . . right."

Kathy pursed her lips. She reached for some cards and began flipping through them, sorting, her eyes trained down. "I'm not sure there *is* a completely right." Each time she pulled a card she snapped it somehow, making a sound like blocks of wood being knocked together.

I flushed and stammered, angry that she had caught me in this mistake. "I don't mean that. I mean . . ." I stopped so I could choose my words more carefully, for my audience. As a journalist, I should know how to do this. "He's not comfortable. He's frustrated because there are obstacles in the way of his learning."

"You're frustrated, too." She put the cards down and went back to staring at me from the cup of her hand. This woman was smarter than I was, and she seemed determined to prove it. I almost left. Instead, I laughed.

"Yes," I said.

She smiled and pulled a clipboard from underneath the counter. "Then let's get him signed up."

24

WHAT CAME NEXT was a stretch of monotonous contentment.

We enrolled Edward in the school's summer program, but after filling out the paperwork Kathy had given me, I saw that the appearance of the school was deceptive: for the children who lived in the immediate neighborhood, full of drug blight and poverty, it was free. But for people like us, who wanted to transfer in from elsewhere but wouldn't dream of moving there, the cost was $10,000 a year. And we made too much money, by a few hundred dollars, to qualify for any kind of financial aid.

Compared with most of the families whose kids attended the school, Kathy explained, we were wealthy. Jack's salary, while low, was at least consistent. And I had a respectable part-time income, as well as sporadic checks for freelance jobs. Yet even if I took Matt out of swimming lessons and kept Grace home instead of sending her to day care, there was no way we could pay the full tuition.

Halfway through the summer session, Kathy made me an offer.

We had become friends. She was, it turned out, a bit younger than me—around my sister Elizabeth's age. But she seemed like an authority, someone who could attract Edward's eyes and whose direct questions he answered more often than not.

"I'll come to your house, Wednesday," she said one week when I dropped Edward off in the crawling room. "I'll teach you how to do a modified program and you can keep it up at night when regular school starts up again."

She arrived just as she'd said she would, in time to have dinner with us. But afterward, while I cleared the table and washed the dishes, it was Jack she trained. We never discussed it and I didn't interfere, though I watched from the kitchen doorway and wondered what had passed between them. I wondered again later when Kathy, pulling self-consciously at the stretchy clothes she wore on her oversize body, sat down to have coffee with me and tell me about my own husband.

"He's gifted," she said. "A real natural. I tried to talk him into changing careers, coming to work at the school." Then she actually blushed. I watched her carefully, noting with curiosity how she touched her hair when she spoke. I would have been willing to believe it was only his hands—somehow resurrected as healing instruments, out of necessity and happenstance—that she admired. But this was something else. There was value being assigned to Jack. A woman should be more than happy with this, I imagined her admonishing me: a warm house and enough money and three children and a husband who touches with such extraordinary care. Even if one of those children is not quite right, it should be enough.

Of course, she didn't say any of this, but I'm fairly certain it's what she was thinking.

Then it was fall. Matt started first grade and Edward went into third, walking taller and saying more. But his grammar was splintered, his syntax upside down. He had an odd predilection for the word *of* and he used it in almost every sentence.

"The water all of the bathroom floor stopping those needs," he would say when the toilet overflowed.

"I am of the boy hurting for my knee," when he ran into something.

He could pass for a regular kid with people who talked to him only briefly. He said thank you when a delivery driver came to the door and handed him a package. Reported accurately his age and grade when we met one of my parents' neighbors in the grocery store. The day he called me a Big Butt because I told him he couldn't have a cookie, I gave him a short, motherly lecture on respect; but later, when I told Jack, we both laughed and then we cried.

So many words were missing. Words most children learn when they are three, four, five years old—the time that he was gone, inside his own head. He was trying to fill in the gaps, but his progress was painfully slow. Word by single word, I couldn't imagine how he'd ever get the job done.

"What does *behind* mean?" Edward asked me that spring. "*Toward? Able? Wider?*" I would tell him, but his eyes would remain cloudy and unfocused as I spoke. Using strings of words to define the ones that had escaped him often seemed to make him more frantic and confused.

Sometimes he would simply make up words to fill in for the ones he didn't own. He spoke tentatively and slowly, just as he did everything else: face tipped so his round blue eyes met the sun, or the ceiling, or some distant point in the air. Hands swimming, looking for a place to take hold.

But the routine in our house remained the same. Jack went to work each day dressed in a dark blazer, carrying not a gun but a walkie-talkie and a can of pepper spray in the loops on his belt. I wrote articles on everything from dog training to insurance law. I drove children to school and babysitters and karate lessons. Over time, I forgot about Jack's biological mother and the letters I'd stowed under my bed. I even, for a brief time, joined the PTA.

And each evening, when he came home, Jack would kiss me and change his clothes and take Edward downstairs to the room he had lined with carpet samples and flash cards and metal spoons and they would do their dance, hands to shoulders, eyes moving to make the lazy eight of infinity in the air, while chanting. "*Toward. Able. Wider.*" All the words Edward did not know that Jack had recorded throughout the week for exactly this purpose. Their voices would drift up through a vent in the floor and I would stand, drinking my after-dinner coffee, looking out the window at the changing seasons and feeling a vague tugging sense of loss.

There were nights when I longed perversely for the utter blackness of Edward's early years. I'd never told Jack, never told anyone. I actually missed the desperation and could not figure out why the sky never seemed to grow as dark anymore. I felt empty where once there had been a sense of inviolable purpose. In the past, Jack and I had been entirely devoted to making our son well. Now, days slipped by filled with nothing but grocery shopping, vacuuming, and small decisions about what to have for dinner, which television show to watch. And Edward's language skills improved, miraculously, as he crawled and leapt and recited his words.

In our bed, after he had finished going through the brain gym exercises with Edward, Jack's fingers would trail up and down my arm without effect. Since the day he had met Joan and found out who his father was, shed his police uniform and surrendered to an ordinary banker's life, Jack's crackling energy seemed to be entirely gone. He could still carve a wooden spoon out of a block of wood, or change the oil in the car. He could bring our son out of himself and teach him to think. But the power he once had over me was slipping away.

25

THIS TRANSITION PERIOD lasted exactly fifteen months and then it was as if a curtain lifted to reveal a whole different life, suddenly completely grown-up and staid.

Occasionally, *Newsweek* or the Associated Press would assign me to a small story that was unfolding in the middle of the country. I began traveling for work, walking relentlessly through the streets of Chicago, St. Louis, Milwaukee, Detroit. And my job at the newspaper simply dwindled away, the workload diminishing until I could no longer justify picking up my paycheck every other Friday. Eric had become involved with a woman it seemed he might marry and all the old ease between us had been replaced by a stiff formality. I had to call him and leave several messages in order to resign and when I did finally go into his office, to turn in my office key and badge and all my files, he shook my hand quickly but kept his eyes averted.

In the summer of 1997, my sister gave birth to a baby girl, April, and I went down to Raleigh, to a home so identical to our parents' colonial, I kept looking for the differences and cataloging them—a table that wasn't familiar, a bathroom with a separate shower and tub instead of a combination—in order to remind myself where I was. It was a far better visit than I had expected. For years, Elizabeth and I had had a guardedly cordial relationship, acknowledging the fact that we had nothing in common except our genes. But now she was a mother and I was a woman with enough money to dress well and go out for lunch in nice restaurants, which meant, I suddenly understood, she no longer had to feel guilty and I no longer had to feel ashamed and out of place.

I returned to Minneapolis after several days of holding and rocking baby April, and my own children looked like strange giants in comparison. Edward was slim but suddenly quite tall, Grace just two and a half but already a brazen child with the wild, long hair of a mermaid. Matthew—an unusually broad-shouldered and serious boy—had grown far larger and older than other children his age, and it was during this summer that Jack and I finally ceded to the principal's request to advance him a grade. Now just a year behind Edward in school, Matt became, against my wishes, a voluntary adult. I worried that the boys' roles would reverse completely now that Matt had skipped ahead, envisioning Edward as a runner who had started a race long before his brother but was left in a plume of dust by the first turn around the track.

However, when the school year began, no one else seemed bothered by the proximity of Matt's class to Edward's. In fact, the boys looked surprisingly natural together as they set out each day, Matt a head taller and twice as strong as most of his year-older classmates, Edward gliding dreamily through the clusters of raucous children waiting at the corner bus stop.

On a Sunday afternoon in December, six months after my trip to Raleigh, Elizabeth called to tell me her mother-in-law had died and they were coming back to Minnesota for the funeral. They would stay at our parents' house. But our mother and father were vacationing in Europe and she would need help with the baby the night of the visitation. Jack and I discussed it and decided it would be good for the children to attend, to learn about the death of an elderly person in a benign way. So on Tuesday, after dinner, we all dressed in dark clothes and climbed into our minivan.

Winter had settled in that afternoon, with a cold so still it carried sounds for miles. The bark of a dog, the scrape of a shovel on sidewalk. We coasted slowly past storefronts decorated with twinkling bulbs and silver streamers that danced in the clear, soft dusk. When we parked and got out of the van the air smelled white, as if it were coming directly from the moon hanging low in the sky. Full, I thought as I looked up. Then no, not full, but nearly so. One sliver of the bottom edge was faint and blurry, fading into the slowly darkening light.

Edward stepped down onto the concrete, stopped, tilted his head and adjusted his nose like a divining rod. He sniffed. "Snow." His eyes fluttered shut as he spoke.

Matthew, hunched behind Edward in the van and waiting to get out, put one hand on his brother's back and pushed gently. He could easily have forced Edward out of the way, but he never did.

"C'mon." I slipped my arm around Edward's shoulders and pulled him along. "It's freezing out here."

The five of us walked through double doors, bringing the clean scent of winter into a room filled with melting candle wax and lilies and aftershave. Inside, there was a low hum of dull conversation, embarrassed laughter, the rattle of necklace beads. Organ music muttered in an adjacent room.

Jack walked off carrying Grace, who sat perched on his arm like a thirty-pound bird. He had claimed her in the car on the way over; she was his human shield against small talk.

Matt and I stepped into the coatroom and when we came out Edward was gone, his purple ski jacket lying on the floor. We searched for several minutes before we saw him in the visitation room, kneeling on the padded bar in front of the casket, hands folded, head bowed. He must have stood in line to do this; there were about a dozen people waiting behind him.

Edward rocked and prayed for a full minute, then raised his head and reached one hand into the casket. I sprinted toward him, breaking into the line, saying "excuse me" over and over as I nudged people aside. When I reached the casket I was out of breath and Edward turned to squint at me disapprovingly before he went back to stroking Dolly's dead arms and hands.

"Don't do that, sweetie," I said.

He turned again to look at me, his round eyes pale and large and clear. "Why not?"

I had no idea how to answer.

He stood in line twice more to kneel and pray, then touch the cold, loose skin of my sister's dead mother-in-law. After his third trip Edward simply remained up in front, lurking among the tall crosses and floral arrangements near the head of the casket and poking his blond head out to stare at the snaking queue of mourners.

Edward's expression was sober and weary and wise, as out of place on his small body as a lion's head would be. He stood with his hands clasped in front of him, leaning a bit to one side, thick, golden hair shining in the candlelight. I watched from the back of the room as people mistook him for one of the grieving family members—a grandson, perhaps, or a nephew. One after another, they walked up and grasped his hand, particularly the tottering, elderly ones.

"I'm so sorry," they would say.

"She was a good woman," insisted a few of the men, pumping Edward's hand up and down.

"Yes, she was," he answered softly. "Thank you. Peace be with you."

His face was serene, unchanging. One woman smoothed his hair and another touched his smooth, round cheek. He looked a bit offended, but I was pleased to see that he didn't pull away.

Matt had stationed himself in a corner to read. He squatted and balanced a book on his knees, his wire-rimmed glasses flashing in the bright lights of the viewing room. Jack was sitting on a sofa in the lobby where we had entered. He was trying to retie the ribbon on Grace's ponytail but every time he gathered her hair together behind her head, strands spiraled out of his hands like coiled springs.

"Would you take care of this?" He let go and Grace's hair fell around her head like Santa Lucia's crown.

"Sure. If you'll go watch what Edward's doing." I pointed to the doorway.

Jack rose and bowed slightly. He wore black pants and a linen shirt, his goatee giving him a sleek, dapper 1940s air. I missed the old Jack in his Jesus clothes. But I was certain that, to the outside world, he was now a far better-looking man than he had been in the wild years before. Nearly six foot eight in his best boots, his tie like a two-foot streak of roadway running down his lean chest, my husband looked like a leviathan moving among the elves. People gave way when he strode through, parting swiftly to make a path. I pulled a hairbrush out of my purse to work through Grace's hair and by the time I finished, Jack was back. He sat.

"Do you think we should stop him?" I asked.

Jack shrugged. "He's not doing any harm." He began playing a game with Grace that looked like a cross between pat-a-cake and thumb wrestling. Her hand fit like a fifty-cent piece in the hollow of his palm. "Maybe he'll be an undertaker when he grows up. He'd be good at it: he likes quiet, he likes order. Let's let him practice awhile."

Suddenly Elizabeth appeared and held out the soggy bundle of her daughter. April had fallen asleep and she weathered the transition from her mother to me without even opening her eyes. She settled into the hollow between my shoulder and neck, breathing warm animal-cracker fumes into my face. I walked closer, my arms heavy with April, to watch Edward conversing with strangers. Though it had been several months since he'd begun speaking in complete sentences all on his own, each day I was still amazed.

For so many years, I had pictured his tiny body dangling over a bottomless cavern—Jack and Matt and me hanging on to him, hauling him, painfully, dragging him back over the rocky edge to safety. Then he returned to us. But he remained different, marked by whatever had happened. It was as if he'd been in some foreign country for a long time and now, even though he was able to communicate about other things, he couldn't tell us anything about why he left, or what the other place had been like. And occasionally he would travel back, vanishing for a brief period right in front of our eyes.

. . .

Edward greeted another band of mourners. I saw an old man hobble up using a cane, reach into his pocket, and pull out something that he tucked into Edward's hand. A coin or a piece of candy, I couldn't tell. Without looking at it, Edward dropped the item, then reached out and took the old man's cane. Edward held it in both hands, found the center, lifted it and placed the cane on his head, where it teetered but stayed balanced.

"He's Puck," Jack had whispered to me just the month before, in a moment much like this one. "He's just not like the rest of us. He's here to stir up trouble and make the world a little less real." The old man laughed and I smiled into April's hair.

Now my mother's cousin appeared in line, as if out of nowhere. Tall and red-haired, far better dressed than the rest of us in a dark suit with a vest and a watch chain, looking slim and forty-five even though he was well past sixty. He didn't belong on this side of the family, but Martin was a deacon. Perhaps, I decided, he thought he should attend not as a relative but as a representative of God himself.

Then I remembered that it was Martin who had provided the book of clippings I read back when I first became curious about Mickey. But the scrapbook had been a big disappointment: page after page of First Communion cards and wedding announcements, funeral notices and obituaries. Apparently even before he left the seed corn business to dedicate his life to the Church, Martin had been enthusiastic about these rituals.

He walked to the casket and knelt on the padded bar in front of Dolly, a woman he may have glimpsed once three years ago, across the room at Elizabeth's wedding reception. He crossed himself, looked intently at the rosary beads that were looped through her hands, then was silent for a moment or two before he stood. Edward was right there, rocking from foot to foot, awaiting condolences.

But Martin must have disappointed him. Soon after their hands met, Edward began to bend back and away, flexing his hands the way he always did when he was nearing an edge. I walked slowly toward them, jiggling April against me to distract her from the swell of noise as we entered the room, stopping about two yards from Martin's broad back.

"You're Edward, right?" I heard Martin ask.

But Edward didn't answer. He was stretching and trying to look over Martin's shoulder. Hoping, no doubt, to catch the eye of a more dramatic and appropriate mourner.

"Hey!" Martin grabbed Edward's shoulder in one cupped palm. "How old are you now? Eight? Maybe nine?"

Edward stopped rocking, shrugged the hand off his shirt, and looked at the floor. "I'll be ten in eighty-seven days," he said. Under his breath, he whispered the refrain: *"eigh-ty-se-ven days, eigh-ty-se-ven days."*

"So, you're here for your aunt and uncle." Martin clutched him again, putting his right arm around Edward's shoulder and giving him a huggy little shake. "And I hear you have a brand-new cousin, too!"

I wanted to step in, but I was anchored under the baby. If I were to approach him while he was already being pawed, there was a chance Edward might whirl away quickly and throw me off-balance. I couldn't risk this while holding April. I looked frantically for someone who could take her, but I was surrounded by frail, old people who might drop her.

Then I realized Matt was watching. Across the room, Jack was talking to Dolly's oldest son and I saw Matt go to him and tug at his sleeve, then point in Edward's direction.

By then, any one of us could tell in a glance when Edward was beginning to grow that hot, stiff crust that meant people were getting too close. Jack hurried over with Grace trailing him at knee level and extended his right hand so Martin had to remove his arm from around Edward's neck in order to take it. They were in the midst of saying hello and shaking hands when Edward suddenly cleared his throat.

As if on cue, the hymns stopped playing and Bette Midler began belting out "You Are the Wind Beneath My Wings." Edward gazed up, angelic, with pale, blue, unblinking eyes and an expression both rapt and serious.

"Hey!" He barked the word exactly as Martin had just a few

moments ago, his voice so loud and strong it carried over the music, throughout the room. "Hey, Martin! Do you ever feel like you might enjoy dressing up as a woman?"

We all stood still against the backdrop of casket and flowers, Bette Midler's brassy voice moving around us in waves. No one in the room made a sound. Martin's face darkened and he pulled his hand slowly out of Jack's, putting it into the pocket of his suit coat as if he were slipping something valuable into a case. He stayed still, staring at Jack. Waiting.

I jerked forward, carelessly squeezing the baby to my chest as I said, "Martin!"

April reacted as if I had struck her. She let out a startled, high-pitched scream then began crying in long, ragged breaths. "He didn't mean . . . ," I shouted. But I couldn't get through the wall of April's voice and she kept moving her head in front of mine so no matter how I twisted, she was blocking my view. Fortunately, her initial scream seemed to function like the opening bell at the stock exchange: the one that means *Regular business is now in session.* Slowly, the other people in the room politely resumed their conversations.

By the time I got April quieted down, Grace had wandered away, chewing the loose spaghetti of her hair ribbon, with Matt trailing her. Martin was tight-mouthed, staring at my husband, who stood gazing into the air above the casket, hands shoved into his pockets, swaying back and forth. Jack appeared to be humming. Martin turned to me and shook his head, raising his hands as if to say, *I give up,* and walked away.

Edward clearly had lost interest. He was eyeing the corner nearest the door and I knew he was plotting his escape from this place. He was tired of it. The room and the people and Martin's silence in the wake of his question—all of these had pushed him over the horizon of his own enjoyment and into his next, more solitary sphere.

Mrs. Doubtfire was the only movie Edward had watched that entire year. It had become his habit, or rule, to do only one thing at a time. The year before, for a few weeks, he had counted emergency-exit doors in the buildings we visited; he could tell us the exact location of each one, and what the signs on the latch paddles said. (Most of them said, ALARM WILL SOUND. That always gave him a shiver.) But these days it was Robin Williams in a dress.

Before *Mrs. Doubtfire*, I'd spent an entire summer taking him to children's movies, trying to expose him to all the culture and experience he'd missed, but the whole time we sat in the theater, Edward's eyes darted around. I could feel it happening; they kept landing on my face, his attention scattering like bits of confetti. Before long, I would be checking Edward more often than I was looking at the screen and he would be staring straight ahead, gulping air, making a big show of watching intently, though he was really just making faster, smaller movements with his eyes. Afterward, I would quiz him: What was the main character's name? Why did he follow the girl to California? What happened to his father? Edward could never answer a single question.

In other people's homes I'd see groups of boys, with arms like elastic bands and faces full of large teeth, watching ribald comedies meant for adults. Laughing in the right places. Always understanding. Then I would panic and push Edward harder, shouting rapid-fire questions until he got that glazed look that meant he'd stepped out of his mind for a while.

Sometimes when we were watching together, Edward would manage to come up with one lucid element of the story. "They went back in time on a bird," he would say. But that would be all. As often as not, his clearest observations would have to do with a minor character or a part of the plot that was used as filler; he'd follow some nonessential story line about the neighbor whose garage door wasn't working, but miss entirely the pivotal points at which the hero fell in love, or died.

Until *Mrs. Doubtfire*.

One afternoon at the YMCA, I was coming from the gym, descending the stairs, wiping the sweat off my neck with a small towel. Edward sat in the open, tiled area at the bottom in front of a wide-screen TV. ·And he was watching *Mrs. Doubtfire*—really *watching*. I could see it in his face, the easy way his eyes rested on the screen. Then he laughed. I was headed down, into the pool of light where he sat, intending to pick him up and take him home. But I stopped. I sat on a cold concrete step and watched him through the bars of the stair rail for the rest of the film. I hadn't felt this way since the night he'd finally slept after thirteen straight nights of pacing his room.

On the way home, in the car, I kept pulling at Edward with my eyes, and inside my head I heard a throbbing rhythm. "Tell me about *Mrs. Doubtfire*." I tried to sound casual.

"I think that's my favorite movie," Edward said.

I breathed in and it hurt. For just that minute, he sounded like a perfectly normal boy.

"What happened in the end?" My jaw clenched as I waited for the answer, but Edward's voice came through without a hitch, no eye-darting, no frowns. "He got to see his children. Daniel loves his children so much he was even willing to dress up like Mrs. Doubtfire to see them."

Edward coughed twice, two even beats with a rest between them, as he always did. Then tipped his head to the side and crossed his eyes. I was losing him. But he went on, without my prompting. "Some parents want to keep their children with them so much they'll do anything to be with them."

It had begun to snow while we were inside the funeral home, small bits of lace that drifted out of the sky and hovered, briefly, before settling to the ground. Jack was reflected in the dark transparency of the van's windshield, his black shirt blending with the color of night so his face appeared to be floating, like the one in the wicked queen's magic mirror. Against the backdrop of night, sitting straight at the wheel in the dim watery light of the van, even his real self, with body attached, looked grave and slightly sinister.

He pulled out onto the street and I watched the light change, heard the tick of red to green. Behind me all was silent, as if the children were holding their breath. "Why didn't you say anything?" I asked. "It wouldn't have been so hard to explain." Then I had a vision of Martin, shoulders freckled and broad in a backless, organdy prom dress, and began to laugh. "I mean . . . Jesus! He must think we're insane."

"Jack. You can call me Jack when we're alone together." He winked and my heart skipped a little, the way it always did when the old Jack surfaced for a moment. When I would remember what a lovely, unstrung man he used to be.

I stopped laughing and drew my knees together and we rode through the pause. "Why didn't you tell him about *Mrs. Doubtfire*?"

"Why do you care so much?" Jack began fiddling with the knob on the radio, his attention divided between the dashboard and the traffic outside. "What's the big deal?"

"You know what the big deal is."

A full minute went by and neither of us spoke. I looked back and saw that Grace had fallen asleep and Matt was looking hazy behind his glasses. Edward was alert but focused somewhere inside himself, eyes clouded in refusal to see the world outside, unaware and uncaring about anything we might say.

"Even now," I whispered to Jack, "I constantly have to make the case for Edward. Every day, I'm trying to convince people he's capable so they'll give him a chance. The school, his doctor. My parents." Jack's head was still pointing straight ahead, but I could see his eyes go to my reflection, wide and mocking. "No, you don't hear it. They're just so sure he's, you know, still faltering all the time. None of them see that he's okay now, just how he is."

Jack sighed. "So? They don't see it. We do. We know he's fine just the way he is. That's all that matters."

I took a breath and spoke without meaning to say it. "Do we?"

The van was rocking gently, crunching the snow as Jack drove slowly. I laid my head against the seat. Outside, Christmas lights were strung along rooflines and in trees and as we passed they grew tiny tails that streaked blue and silver and yellow and red against the sky. It occurred to me that I hadn't eaten since morning, and though I'd had no alcohol, either, I suddenly felt pleasantly, woodenly drunk. "Sometimes. I'm just not sure it was enough, the trade. I think I should have been more specific."

Jack reached out to take my hand. "What trade?"

"Your job, your mother, Mariel, our money, our marriage, everything. For Edward." I heard my own voice as if from a distance. My speech had gone rhythmic and dreamlike, monotonous. "I promised God He could take everything else away from us if Edward was okay. If he didn't have the tumors—that awful disease he was tested for back when I was pregnant with Grace. If he wasn't completely autistic, all locked away."

"You what?"

"I said I'd give up everything. Well, that's not true." I smiled. I loved the movement of the car, so gentle but fast enough we were never really in any one place. "I said *we* would give up everything. I knew you wouldn't mind."

"No. I wouldn't. But I don't think . . ."

I waited. "What?"

"It just doesn't work that way. I don't believe God took away my job and made my mother a crushing disappointment and wrecked your friendship with Mariel as some sort of quid pro quo. I was a lousy cop—at least with the law-and-order stuff. My mother was always a skank, even before I found out. And Merry's just a fuckin' nut." He shrugged. "Sorry. I don't think your bargain with God caused any of those things. Besides, we're still together. We have jobs and the house and more than enough to eat."

But your hands? The way you used to touch me? I thought to myself. That was the worst part. I didn't say this, however, because I didn't want to hurt him. "What if it did have an effect?" I began instead. "If everything that happened was because of what I promised: Simmons and your job and finding out about your parents and my losing Mariel. Was it worth it?"

"Of course it was! How could you even ask?" Time had grown dense. It seemed like years since we'd left the mortuary but according to the dashboard clock, we'd been in the car for only eight minutes. "We're still together. All the kids are fine. What else matters?"

"But that's the thing. It was worth it, I agree. But if I'd known He might take me up on it, I would have asked for Edward to be . . ."

"What?" There was an edge to Jack's voice.

The drunken feeling was growing more pronounced so that now,

my words had gotten thick and stuck together. I had to think very carefully. "I would have wanted him to be more . . . comfortable. And just,
I don't know. Real. Or something."

"Normal? Is that the word you're looking for?"

I thought about this, saw the word printed with capital letters in my
head; I imagined slicing through them from top to bottom with a knife,
trying to determine what *normal* really meant. "No." I was honest. "That
makes it sound boring. It's just . . . I always thought when he came back
to us he'd be the person I imagined when he was that happy, perfect
little baby. The one I pictured him becoming. Remember how he smiled
all the time, and how he talked, right from the beginning, using all those
nonsense sounds like they were a language only he knew?"

Jack nodded and the floating head in the windshield nodded back.

"That's what I was thinking of when I talked to God. Only I didn't
say so. I only said I wanted him back and now he's so . . ." I sighed loudly
and leaned my head back. "I guess I never knew there was so much
space between where he was then and the rest of the world. I didn't
think we would pull him back only to a certain point, that a person
could end up stranded forever in this . . . nowhere."

Jack turned to scowl at me. At first, I thought I'd become so inco-
herent my words hadn't come out clearly enough for him to understand. But that wasn't it. He swiveled back to the view outside and sped
up a little, running a yellow light, skidding softly along the curb in the
snow. "How the hell could you be married to someone like me for
almost ten years and still not understand that?"

Of course, I did. I'd never admitted it, even to myself, up until that
very moment. But I'd known for a long time that Jack was stranded,
too. And the farther the other children and I moved into the world
where he and Edward didn't belong, the more we risked leaving them
behind. What if I could only bring one of them with me? I wondered.
Each time Edward had faltered, Jack became more conventional: he put
on a uniform or a suit, he shaved and worked and organized our days.
But when Edward had showed signs of recovering, Jack began to fade.
I leaned back in my seat, half asleep, these thoughts drifting like
streams of smoke that curled around one another in my mind. Who

would I choose? I asked myself, too leaden in my seat to squirm even though I knew the answer. I would let go of Jack if I thought I needed to in order to reach Edward. I had already done it a dozen times. The only thing that had kept us whole was that Jack had hung on to me.

I reached out and found Jack's hand without opening my eyes. His fingers closed around mine and if he was surprised, he didn't say anything. From the back of the van, I could hear Edward singing in a whisper: *"There's something happening here . . ."* It was a song that had come out more than twenty years before he was born. He'd heard it once, on the radio, when he was seven, and still remembered every word. *"What it is ain't exactly clear . . ."*

Snow crystals glistened against our windows. We slid to the side while rounding a corner and Jack removed his hand from mine to grip the steering wheel. He was driving slowly, peering out the side windows to look for a highway exit sign, winding in and out of residential streets. Minneapolis was full of neighborhoods like this one—rows of neat, compact bungalows with pop-up dormers lining the boulevard while bare trees touched their branches overhead. In the glow of a streetlight, I saw a burly man in a parka, sitting in a plastic lawn chair in his driveway. There was a shovel next to him, lying in a sheet of snow, but the man was perfectly still.

I'd awakened a little. Not enough to trust my voice, but enough to know Jack was lost. This, too, was new. Along with his healing touch, he seemed to have misplaced his sense of direction.

"I'm going to stop and ask him for—" Jack began, but then his words suddenly broke off and we were floating. I saw that Jack's hands on the wheel no longer guided us. The van spun counterclockwise a quarter turn then drifted sideways, and we headed straight for the curb and a giant oak tree. The air was empty and white. And the accident, as it began to happen, seemed graceful and right. We all drew in our breath and held it—except Edward, who continued singing, softly.

I watched Jack and saw him do something that looked backward. He jerked the steering wheel to the left, crossing hand over hand and pulling it farther, until he could turn it no more. And just as we were about to soar over the curb and into the tree, the nose of the van changed course, like a dog that has caught a new scent. We spun a bit more, closing a circle, skidding harder this time, less gracefully, until the van finally was still, pointing back in the direction from which we'd come.

We sat for a full minute, none of us speaking. At some point, Edward stopped singing. Across the street the burly man had leapt out of his lawn chair and was standing in his driveway. Jack slumped over the steering wheel and when he spoke his voice was dampened by the fact that his face was buried in his sleeve. "In case you still want to know, the reason I didn't say anything to Martin was because I was just really enjoying the moment."

His head was still down and he had begun to shake. The man in the driveway was stretching his head forward, trying to peer through the dusk. What he couldn't see from across the street was that Jack was laughing so hard, I worried for a moment he was having some sort of seizure.

Edward resumed his singing at exactly the point where he'd left off, as if the interruption had been planned. "*I think it's time we stop, children.*"

Jack snickered and fell against the horn, which let out a short bleep. Then I heard Matt behind me, laughing like a high, faraway echo of his father. "*What's that sound? . . .*" The question was well timed but Edward's voice was dreamy, completely unperturbed, and the next line of the song danced through my head, even though he didn't sing it. The man in the driveway had begun to pace, moving his head from side to side as he tried to get a view inside our van. I reached over Jack, rolled his window down an inch or two, and shouted, "Sorry! We're fine."

The man nodded and shrugged and I opened my own window, stuck my head out, and looked up. Snow crystals drifted, sparkling, in a cone of yellow light from a streetlamp and for a moment, I was dazzled. By the time I pulled my head back into the van, the man was moving toward Jack's window. As he walked, he pulled the leather glove off one hand and reached inside his jacket to pull out a long, brown cigar. He slid it under his nose, side to side, snorting the scent deeply.

"Sand truck should be through soon to take care of that black ice." Then he transferred the cigar to his glove and lowered his bare hand, working it through the three or four inches of open window to shake Jack's. "Smoke?"

Jack raised his head. I could see where there were wet tracks of tears through his beard. "Excuse me?"

"Would ya like a cigar?" The man bounced the end a little. "Looks like you could use one."

Jack paused for a minute. He'd always been a smoker, but never in front of the children. He must have decided this seemed different. "I think I will," he said and rolled the window all the way down. "Thanks."

The man handed Jack the cigar, then took another one from inside his coat. He and Jack bit off the ends and spat them into the street, almost in unison. I was always touched, and slightly jealous, that grown men could bond like this over body emissions: saliva, blood, urine.

The man lit his cigar and pulled on it until the tip glowed, a round, bright spot of orange. Then he removed it from his mouth and poked his head into our van, smoke leaking from his mouth. "Wife won't let me smoke 'em in the house anymore." He craned around, looking into the back of the van, and waved a little. "Hey, kids." In the hood of his coat his head was so large, he had to make his hand flat and turn it sideways to fit it in alongside his face; and all he could do then was wriggle his first two fingers like antennae. "Coming from a party, all dressed up?"

"A funeral!" Grace shouted. "Dolly is dead."

"Oh, sorry." He pulled his head out and plugged the cigar back into his mouth. When he stepped back and stopped blocking the open window, cold air streamed in and quickly filled the car.

Edward suddenly sat forward. "Did you know her?"

"Your friend Dolly? Nah. Probably not. I knew a Dolly once, but she died a long time ago."

"Dolly wasn't our friend. She was our grandmother-in-law. Do you know what that is? That's your uncle- or aunt-in-law's mother. In this case it was our uncle-in-law. Our aunt's husband, actually." Edward sat back again, firmly, but he kept staring at the man. "She was a good woman, you know."

"Sure she was." The man said this quietly. He shuffled his feet in the snow and it made a dry, popping sound.

There was a pause and then Matt began laughing again. It sounded so out of place in the silence and the aftermath of the skid, I felt compelled to explain. "He's, ah, overtired, I think." Suddenly, everyone but Edward was looking at me.

"Mom," Matt shouted, in a voice that was louder than it had to be. "You *know* why I'm laughing."

The man leaned back in the window. "Why's that?" he asked Matt.

"Because, my brother asked our grandma's cousin if he . . ." Suddenly something weary crossed Matt's face, flattening it. He pulled his lips together and I saw him look back at Edward. "Nothing," Matt said to the man. "I was just making a joke."

But the man was interested. He pushed his head in again and eyed Edward. "Hey, what'd you ask him, little guy?"

"I asked him," Edward's voice was stiff as cardboard, probably because he hated being called by anything but his full name, "if he thought he would enjoy dressing up like a woman."

The man's eyes crinkled, but he didn't laugh. Instead, he reached up and pulled his hood back. His hair was wiry and gray and he ran one hand through it. "Hmm. That's an unusual kind of question, don't you think?"

"Maybe." There was a buzzing sound under Edward's voice and I realized he was humming a single note in the back of his throat while he spoke. He was going to disappear again very soon. I'd become good at reading the signs and knew he'd hang on until the end of this conversation. "Some men do, you know. They're called *trans-ves-tites*"—he gave each of the three syllables equal weight—"and they like wearing bras and dresses. I know that's true." He stared at the man, as if he'd been challenged.

"Yup, you're right. I've heard that, too." The man rubbed his jaw, where there was at least two days' growth of silvery whiskers.

"It's from *Mrs. Doubtfire*," I began. "He's watched it a number of times and in it—"

But Edward broke in. "No, Mom, being a transvestite is different." The humming in his throat was growing louder, like the steady background buzz of a faulty telephone connection. "Daniel, who was played by Robin Williams, didn't *want* to dress up like a woman. He had to, to see his children. But there are some men who do it just because they want to. Do you understand the difference?"

This time, everyone's eyes were on me. Even Edward's. Jack's hand touched mine and I felt a tiny electric pull. "Do you understand, babe, or do you need me to explain it to you?"

The man caught my eye and winked, then went back to Edward. "So why'd you ask your cousin that?"

Edward tilted his head and thought for a few seconds then said softly, as if the man were hearing his confession, "I'm not sure I like that cousin." After another pause, he cleared his throat three times and emitted a sudden peep, flashing his crooked half smile at the man. "Also, I thought it would be very funny."

With that, Edward was done. It was as if he'd never spoken; he closed his eyes and resumed singing: *"Young people speaking their mind . . ."*

The man leaned against Jack's car door, puffing on his cigar, and smoke wafted around him. He grinned through clenched teeth and jerked his head in Edward's direction. "Hell of a smart kid you got there."

I couldn't help but smile back at him. Jack was smoking and Edward was singing and Grace seemed to have fallen half asleep. I looked back at Matthew, who had relaxed, sprawling comfortably in his seat.

Then I turned toward the window and saw that I had been wrong earlier. The moon was full that night and it hung higher now and heavy in the cupped black sky, a perfect white disc that was pale and blank and beautiful.

26

It felt as if Jack and I had made a silent pact the night of Dolly's funeral. We were satisfied, committed to the pattern we'd somehow happened upon even if it wasn't the easygoing, eccentric hippie life we'd both imagined. At least that's how I saw things, and judging from Jack's behavior—the way he transformed gradually and without resistance into the sort of serious businessman my parents had hoped for and encouraged him to become—he seemed to feel the same way.

Two years passed and I continued working, making contacts, focusing mostly on political stories. I was developing some confidence, a distinct voice. Sometimes, I would read my own articles after publication and they would sound surprising and smart, as if someone I admired had written them. Grace was in half-day kindergarten now, and it began to seem possible that I might find a staff position when she started first grade. A career job, something with a national magazine in New York or Washington, D.C. Though when I mentioned my ambition to Jack, he scowled.

He had been promoted twice at the bank, first from the vault to assistant chief of security and later—after I pointed out that he worked for a chief who was only five years older than he was and a lifer who would never leave the post—to become an officer in the mortgage department. He chafed in the sales job. Jack loathed wearing a tie and talking about money all day. But if he drank a little more than he ever had before—and in a vacant, sedentary way that was new—I tried to ignore it, believing he would grow more comfortable as time went by and the rewards of our more responsible life came to bear.

We had money for the first time in our lives, enough to go out for dinner on weekends and take family vacations. I would never, I vowed to myself, experience the shame of going to my parents for a loan ever again. For Jack's forty-second birthday, in June, I'd already booked a trip to Glacier National Park on the train and asked my parents to take care of the children for an entire week. It nagged at me that Jack might prefer to take them with us, but even now we couldn't afford this. Also, since reading the entire contents of Eleanor's box—the letters from Mickey and diaries and newspaper clippings and Christmas cards—I'd begun thinking more and more about the secret to marriage.

Eleanor had died the previous year, of lung cancer that was diagnosed only two weeks before she slipped into a morphine coma. And though I'd always intended to return the things she had given me, once she was gone I didn't know where or to whom. Surely her second husband would have little use for our family artifacts, and my mother still avoided painful reminders of the past. So I kept them, an accidental inheritance. After her funeral, I shook the entire box out on the bed and reread every single word.

Mary and Ted, who loved their children fiercely and grieved over their sons forever, who worshiped a God I would never even know, still valued each other most. That was how they made it through the deaths of their sons, in the end. It wasn't their faith in the Church but in each other. I wondered if Jack and I were becoming a couple like them, bound together by the son who continued to veer in a solitary direction no matter how we clung to him, and by the life we'd built.

In a very different way, I learned, my parents' marriage was also forged in sadness. It was my mother herself who finally told me the story about how she and my father, and by extension my children and I, actually began.

Perhaps what loosened her enough to talk was the strangeness, the fact that she and my father had come to my house for dinner. It had become a point of pride with me that after a dozen years Jack and I finally had a stable home and enough leeway in our grocery budget to buy a prime rib and a nice bottle of wine. This was the second time I'd insisted on hosting the Sunday meal and afterward, when Matt and Grace left to play computer games with Jack, and my father had taken Edward aside for a game of chess, my mother began telling me about New York.

"Your father was my boss," she began, her hand curled around the stem of her wineglass. My mother rarely drank. "And he was as foreign to me as he would have been if he were an African. Older, you know. And Jewish. I had never"—she paused, considering for a moment—"never really known a Jew before in my life."

"Was he a good boss?" I poured what was left in the wine bottle into my mother's glass.

She smiled softly, her eyes nearly crossing with the memory. "Oh, so good. So kind and decent and smart. Everyone . . ." She stopped and fixed me with her eyes. "*Everyone* who worked there said he was the most brilliant man they'd ever met. One of the engineers told me Abe Goldman could read code almost as fast as the computers our company made, about twenty times faster than anyone else in the country."

"So?" I coaxed. "You fell in love with his mind. And then you married him."

"I did," she said. "I fell in love with him but then I left him. I quit. I was going to move back home and forget all about him. I couldn't marry a Jewish man. There was no way I could do that to my parents, and I'd told him so."

"Then what happened?" I spoke gently, afraid of startling her into silence.

She drank, set her glass down, then picked it up and took another sip before answering. "Then my brother died. I was packing up to leave, that awful night. And I went to bed but I couldn't sleep. I thought it was because I was so heartbroken over your father." She looked at me, her eyes as wide as Edward's. "The phone rang around three-thirty in the morning and it was Eleanor telling me. After that, the whole question of religion seemed so . . . meaningless." She sighed. "My brother had convinced me to go to New York. It was as if he wanted me to find something there. And I did."

MICKEY

In 1961, the weather turned wickedly cold with the new year. For the first two weeks of January, people walked the streets of downtown silently, heads down, holding their breath and taking the air in small sips, trying to keep from filling their lungs with frost. By the third week of January, Minneapolis had been more than 20 degrees below zero for twelve nights in a row.

Mickey ached with the cold. He felt it in his hands, as he worked each day. The shop was heated, but there was no way to keep the bitter edge of wind from seeping through the cracks in the door frames and concrete walls. He sat in back, hunched on a stool, his wool greatcoat draped over his back like a horse blanket. Lately, whenever he opened a watch back, prying off the disc with a penny, his pulse would speed up and his shoulders tighten with fear.

Around the time the cold had settled in, the wheels and cogs had stopped making sense. It had happened gradually, like eyesight that worsened each day. And it had been accompanied by foreboding, a sense that his own life had become completely foreign to him. The bone-chilling air reminded him of Korea and he was jarred whenever he raised his head to see the plain white lines of Minneapolis under the banks of snow.

Often he would slip into daydreams. He was the age now that Bo had been back then, and he would picture them walking through the hills together, shoulder to shoulder, matched in height as well as years—for in Mickey's fantasy of postwar Korea he grew taller as well as thinner. And Bo stayed exactly the same, never getting older but waiting through all the intervening time for Mickey to catch up.

Usually, if he set his mind to it, Mickey was able to muddle his way through a watch's workings, moving from one sprocket to the next, cleaning and resetting and fitting the works back into order. But occasionally the mess of teeth and springs would be too much for him to decipher. Once, they'd even seemed to move on their own, waving like sea algae. This was another one of those. A large dull stainless-steel Timex whose insides were taunting him. Mickey slipped it into a small envelope that he sealed and marked with an X. Helen would tell the customer it was not worth the price of repair.

He stood and gripped his coat around him, moved to the front window, and looked out at Nicollet, wide and clean and swept, still decorated with silver tinsel and red satin balls that twirled in the sunshine, left over from the Christmas parade. These days, few customers came in. The newspapers had published a police advisory asking people not to venture out unless they were going to work or conducting other necessary business. And Mickey finally had convinced his father to stay home until the cold broke; at seventy-four, Ted had begun to rattle a little when he breathed.

"It's deceptive, isn't it?" Helen leaned on a glass counter, her chin propped on her fisted hand. "So beautiful and quiet. It looks like you could just put on your boots and take a walk through all that white snow."

Inside, Mickey howled. To walk, he wanted to tell Helen, was all he wanted. Like a drunkard wants a drink. Instead, he turned to her and smiled. "Davy sure liked the parade. It's nice the weather held at least through the holidays."

"He's my sweet boy." Helen sprayed the glass with Windex for the third time that morning. She wiped in wide, sure circles. "And nearly two. Isn't it about time for you and Ruth to get started on another? I need a baby to rock at your parents' Sunday dinners."

Mickey grinned, for real this time. He couldn't help remembering Helen on Armistice Day, soft and shy and dressed in Mary's clothes, sitting at his parents' kitchen table, dealing cards in the same efficient way she cleaned the countertop now. For years, Helen had lived in his mind along with Marilyn Monroe and Rita Hayworth. During the war, he had carried her picture inside him the way other men had their girl-friend's photographs stowed in wallets and footlockers; she was untouched. Always young. Seeing her for the first time when he arrived stateside—her broadening hips and ruddy face, gold wedding band and plain, gray skirts that zipped in back—he'd felt mortified and then vaguely amused. This, he decided, was retribution for men's idle, sinful fantasies; God did have a sense of humor after all.

Instead of becoming his girl, Helen had become the closest thing he'd ever had to a friend since Bo. Age and marriage and the disappointment of never having a baby of her own had made her sharp, willing to say the things other people weren't. It was Helen who told Ted the china he carried was outdated and insisted he add a line of the popular Hummel figurines—even fifteen years after the end of the Second World War, Ted had resisted selling anything from that country. But Helen prevailed, and she'd been right. She sometimes joined Mickey for lunch, never asking but inviting herself. She would follow him out the door, staying a few paces behind until he'd walked a block or so, then dash up and tuck her hand into his arm, leaning her head into his shoulder.

"Take me to Peter's Grill?" she'd say. "It's Wednesday. Barbecued pork sandwiches."

At home, Ruth touched Mickey only in response. Only in bed, at night, when the room was completely dark and the talk of the day was over. But even that had become very rare since David's birth. And Ruth had never once laid her head on Mickey's shoulder or held his hand. She was a good mother, neat and orderly; Davy always had clean socks and freshly combed hair. But Ruth never grabbed their son and hugged him hard, the way Mary did. Mickey saw his mother's hands, the ones that had so terrified him as a child, now reaching hungrily to love his boy. She must have done the same with him, if only he could remember.

He exhaled and a spot of steam, the shape of a large egg, appeared on the window. Then it began to fade, disappearing in fractals, and he watched it vanish. Turning back, he saw Helen staring at him.

"Tired?"

"Yeah. I've been up a couple times at night to start the car and let it run." He smoothed a hand over the bristles of his crew cut and suddenly was embarrassed in front of Helen, realizing he was getting too old for a military-style buzz.

"Roger's been up starting ours, too," she said softly. And paused.

"It's just . . . I have trouble getting back to sleep," he explained. But he didn't say: *Afterward, I stand at the door of the garage, looking outside, praying for a break in the cold. I want so badly to walk away. To start off down the path that leads to my house and keep going, putting one foot in front of the other, until I reach something: an ocean, a mountain, a city, a giant crack in the earth.*

For two years, he had had a secret. Two or three times a week, in the middle of the night, he would rise and leave the house, walking under moonlight, through snow, on sultry summer nights so still and humid he could barely breathe. Some nights, he thought about Bo. Or about Eleanor, locked away in the palace of icy glass where she lived with her handsome husband, always smiling and fashionably dressed but staring at him from glazed and empty eyes. Other times, Mickey imagined Susanna's life and saw her taking an elevator straight up to the top floor of a fifty-story tower, high heels tapping as she walked down long, tiled corridors, surrounded by those large machines he'd seen in movies, trembling as they churned out streams of ticker paper and printed cards.

Once, he'd walked as far as Crystal Lake; on another night he'd gone east along the river and passed downtown, continuing on as if he were going to St. Paul. Or New York. But every time, he turned around and went back home. Because of Davy. When the boy was born, a nurse had put him in Mickey's arms, in a white towel that had been draped over his head and around his tiny hips like a nun's habit. Mickey had looked down into his son's scrunched-up face and felt nothing but fear. He sat, the baby an insubstantial weight against his knees, and wondered what to do. Then a low burn started in his chest. He looked again into the face, no different, no less wrinkled and dark and primal than it had been moments before, and he felt a connection so fierce it startled him. It was like a magnetic force gathering in his blood, every heartbeat seeming to tug him toward his son. Mickey tightened his grip and the fear grew even stronger. What if this child were to slip on the ice, or fall out of a tree, or come down with scarlet fever? When the nurse, an Irish girl from the east side, came slouching back down the hall on her white gum-soled shoes, she had to pry the baby out of Mickey's arms.

"Time enough for you, Da," she said. "It's his mother he needs now."

Since then, when he walked at night, Mickey had felt the cord growing taut with every step he took. David was home, lying on his side in his crib, mouth slightly open, sleeping and breathing a small damp spot onto the bear he held tightly with one arm.

"Should we close up early?" Helen asked, but her voice seemed to come to Mickey from miles away.

He shook himself slightly and faced her. She was examining him too carefully and he felt naked in front of her. He straightened and shook his head.

"Of course not. It's not even three and we both have work to do." Helen stood still, her kind face suddenly dented with hurt in a mysterious way Mickey could not define. He hadn't meant to be rough. But now it was done, and he had to stay the course he'd chosen. He walked swiftly past her to his workbench, where he rifled through the box of repairs until he found a necklace made of the thinnest gold chain he had ever seen and tangled in dozens of knots. He picked up a needle, greased its tip, lowered his monocle, and began working. The necklace suited him perfectly. It would take him hours to untangle the knot of chain, and the next time he raised his head darkness would be falling, a gray film that pressed against the windows and matched the bitter cold outside.

That night, Mickey slept only two hours before awakening suddenly to the feeling that something soft had wrapped itself around his throat. The house was stiff and eerily still, as if it were sheathed in ice under a black, starless sky. He picked up his watch from the table at his side and brought it so close to his face, his nose touched the cool metal. It was nearly one o'clock. Time for Bo's first circuit, he thought. Though of course Bo was back home in Detroit now, forty years old but still strong, wearing civilian clothes and lifting furniture. Or dead, lying in a shallow grave under a scrim of dirt and snow in Korea.

Mickey rose and put on his robe and glasses. A pair of heavy wool socks hung over the wooden form that held his sport coat and he picked them up as he passed, stopping to lean against the wall and pull them on. He shuffled down the carpeted hall and opened the door to look inside the room where his son slept. David was a sound sleeper, like Ruth. He never stirred under the mound of covers. Mickey went to the crib and rubbed the boy's square little back until he felt movement— one leg fluttering like a little fin. He imagined the way his son must have kicked inside Ruth and wished for the hundredth time that he had put his hand on her to feel it for himself.

He thought of his mother, carrying four babies inside her body, and of his father who loved them as purely as Mickey loved his own son. Mickey saw an image of Ted, a cigar clamped between his teeth, leaning on a shovel as he dug a neat row around the edges of Frank's grave. Every Sunday afternoon, all the years of his young life, he and his parents and sisters had visited Frank's grave and made it as perfect as the bedroom of a long-awaited child. Mary knelt and polished the headstone with a rag. Ted trimmed the long grasses so they wouldn't cover the lettering: *Beloved Son and Brother.* Sometimes Mickey would watch from a distance—his parents crouched over the brother who once had lifted him up as high as the cupboards, as if he had become a baby again and they were tending him in his crib.

Mickey stood for a long time, patting Davy's back, soothing though there was no need. Standing there, hand connected to the warm body of his son, the tight feeling around Mickey's throat began to ease. He swayed, sleeping a little on his feet. Ten minutes later, or perhaps twenty, Mickey startled awake and his head snapped up. He pulled the blankets up over Davy's shoulders once more and left the room.

Downstairs, he looked for coffee. Ruth had made a pot after dinner and Mickey remembered seeing a thick inch near the bottom of the glass carafe. But when he flipped on the kitchen light it shone on a sink scrubbed clean, a drainer that held the pie plate and cups they'd used, and the coffeepot now empty and sparkling and dry. Mickey sighed. The floor tiles were as cold and firm as granite and his feet felt like blocks of wood.

He went into the small alcove off the kitchen where there were steps and hooks for clothes and a door leading outside. He wound a heavy scarf around his neck, the rough threads scratching uncomfortably against the whiskers that had sprouted there since nightfall. He stepped into boots but left them unbuckled, put on a coat and thick, leather gloves. He did not wear a hat. When Mickey left the house, he walked outside into air so cold he couldn't feel it. There was only a faint burning sensation on his cheeks and the tops of his feet where the boots flapped open.

The path that led to the garage was shoveled clean. The cold had been so deep for so long, there had never been a moment wet enough for ice to form. Mickey walked slowly but certainly. Once, he stopped just long enough to look up at the maze of dark wires overhead and then at the street that led east. Then a gust of faint, lethal wind took his breath away and he understood again that cold could become a cage from which there was no escape.

When he went into the garage, Mickey felt briefly relieved—the safety of a space enclosed by boards and a few degrees warmer than the outside air. He propped one of the double barn doors open an inch or two but left the other tightly closed. The car was six years old, so blue it looked black. It had the rounded hood and headlamp eyes of a hammerhead shark and its body gleamed darkly under a single bulb. He slid into the driver's seat and reached into his pocket for the keys but felt nothing except the silken lining and a seam.

"Oh, for God's sake." Mickey let his head fall against the high back of the seat and his eyes fell closed as he thought about the walk back to the house, through the frigid night, to find them. What if he had dropped them along the way? They might have fallen into a snowdrift without making a sound but sunk through a soft hole so he wouldn't be able to find them until spring. "Jesus!" Mickey rarely swore. Even alone in the car, he turned quickly, as if his mother might suddenly appear next to him. That's when he saw the keys, glinting against the muddy floor. They lay fanned out like the gate keys in a fairy tale, just to the right of his feet.

Mickey leaned over, puzzled. He would have had to jackknife his body to the left as he entered the car for the keys to fall out of his pocket and land down there. And it was strange he hadn't heard the jangling metal sound they must have made as they met the floor. Then he saw they had somehow configured so no key touched another, each pointing in a different direction like the points of a star. He shook his head and scooped them up, inserted one into the ignition. He turned it and heard nothing but a dry click and the throat-clearing noise of an engine moving in weak revolutions, too slowly to generate a spark. Mickey flipped the key back and waited several minutes for the flooded engine to drain. It seemed even colder than before but Mickey could feel himself sinking into it. Almost like a warm bath, he thought, and smiled a little to himself. His head fell forward and his chin bounced against his chest, the light, hazy sleep like a curtain he kept trying to part and enter. Some time passed before he straightened and coughed and shook his head all in one movement.

He turned the key again, pumping the accelerator pedal with a right foot he could no longer feel inside his boot, and was surprised when the engine erupted in a loud growl and started. Mickey leaned back. He would let it idle just long enough to run fluid through the internal organs of the car then get out and open up the garage. His foot hovered over the gas pedal, feeding it with his toe whenever the engine noise began to dim. He put his head back on the seat and told himself he would rest for just a moment or two. He knew he should get up and open the doors, but it was easier to lie back and imagine the sky swirling above him, dark and starlit. It was, he knew, a Korean sky. Then, for the first time, he realized it was all one sky. This was such a startling idea, he tried to raise his head so he might think it through more clearly. But it was too hard, his head too heavy, his thoughts too melted together, his arms and hand tingling pleasantly as if the stars had entered his body and were running in sparkling streams through his blood and into his gently beating heart.

27

THE END OF OUR new life began with a small white card, stuck in the frame of the storm door at the front of our house.

Jack must have pulled it out when he arrived home from work that day, expecting to find an advertisement for something—gutter cleanings or lawn care—or a note left by a friend, scribbled hastily on the back of a business card. By the time I got there, well after six o'clock, he was in the kitchen, pacing, head butted forward, as if he were pushing something heavy aside. He had a beer in his hand and there were three empties lined up on the counter. I could hear the children upstairs, fighting a little weakly, Grace whining and Matt scolding her in an exasperated, adult voice. They were both hungry, I thought. Jack had picked up Grace from after-school program but probably hadn't given them anything to eat. I opened my mouth to ask but Jack was in front of me, leaning in, shaking the card so its razorlike edge grazed my chin.

"*Look* at this," he shouted.

I did. There were letters, DHS, large, silver-typed, and inscrutable. Underneath, in much smaller print, they were defined: Department of Human Services. And there was a name: Paul Evans, a local telephone number, and a slanted, cramped note, written in miniature cursive, that said, *Please call ASAP.*

"I called," Jack shouted. "They took Edward out of school today. And questioned him. They took him." He swallowed hard then looked, for a minute, as if he would spit out whatever was left. "To their office." Jack was standing over me, his face gray and strange, his large body quivering as if he had been launched from a bow and just landed on the linoleum floor with great force. "They think I hurt him."

But it had really started the night before, during the soft, pink dusk of late April.

I was sitting at my desk staring out the back window at a dwarf apple tree that was wreathed in tiny buds. Once Grace entered school, we had converted the playroom into an office for me and I'd spent many hours focused on this particular tree. The trunk had the gnarled, bent-over look of an elderly woman and I imagined sometimes that it was wise and could, if only I knew how to ask, advise me.

I sighed and went back to my work: editing an article turned in by a young woman who covered style and travel for a prominent fashion magazine. *It is about these many reasons that you can't have too many black skirts,* she wrote. *The new Dolce is perfect to be stuffed into your purse and remaining wrinkle-free, in case of a sudden invitation and you can be sure it will look great.* I had met her twice. She was lovely and golden-haired, articulate when she spoke. One of my clients used her regularly and another was vying to get her under contract because she was cultured, and at twenty-five she had already made connections with most of the country's top designers. The fact that she couldn't construct sentences on the page seemed not to have hindered her career at all. I wished I could call her and ask her how she did it, if she had any hints for Edward.

When I looked up, the sun was on fire: gold and pink, settling slowly into a lower rim of cobalt blue. Birds swooped, their bodies dark and skeletal, prehistoric-looking against the painted sky. I sighed and looked at my watch. Eight o'clock. Only an hour until the boys' bedtime and someone had to ask the question: Is your homework done? It hung over us every night, the answer so cruel because Edward's work was never truly done, always just a guess at what the teachers wanted, what the questions really meant, how to parse the language and use it the way other people do.

Now that he was in seventh grade, at the middle school, there was

homework from five different classes but no classroom teacher to orga-
nize it all for him—just words floating in an assignment notebook,
written in his perfect handwriting. Notes like *Grid Summary* or *Genus
Identification Worksheet* with no context; sometimes he knew there
should be a handout but he couldn't find it, other times he seemed
completely lost and I wondered if he had sat in class that day with the
screens pulled down inside his head, not listening to anyone at all.

I got up from my desk and went to where he sat at the dining room
table, staring into his geography book. His eyes were open, trained in the
right direction, but opaque. I could tell when he was unseeing, *not* seeing. I looked over his shoulder and read quickly: *Three major mountain
ranges tower over Mexico. One range—the Sierra Madre Occidental—runs
north and south along western Mexico near the Pacific Ocean.* . . . Next to
the book was a worksheet. The first question asked: Which mountain
range runs longitudinally through western Mexico? Edward had written,
the Pacific. Clouded under the words, I saw the gummed, gray shadow
of erasure. My teeth ached. Whatever I said would mean slogging
through the swamp of his detachment, finding him, bringing him back
to read the words carefully, one by one, and consider them all.

"Um, Edward. I think you should read this part again. Carefully."

He looked away and began flapping the cover of the book. Closed
and open, closed and open. He'd lost his place, letting the pages flutter
and resettle, then riffling through them again. His hand, on the book,
was the same size as mine.

"Edward! Now. You have to start reading carefully and figuring out
the right answers." I put my finger next to the words he'd written, so
carefully, in calligraphic print. "This is wrong."

One night, not long before, he had finished an entire assignment
and brought it to me. It was on crustaceans—their exoskeletal bodies
and their habitats—and he had written light, hesitant-looking answers
after six of the seven questions; five of them were right. I'd felt that
white surge I always feel when such a thing happens: this is done. He's
clear, he's come out all the way, we've taught him enough and now he
will be able to live just like anyone else. I had said this to him: "You
understand now. You're reading! Everything's going to be easy from

now on." Putting it into words seemed likely, at that moment, to solidify it as truth.

Now, standing over his bent head, I cringed at my own cruelty.

I walked into the kitchen, where Jack was doing dishes, his hands working methodically over pots as he scrubbed every inch with a green woolly pad. He rinsed, then flashed the pot back and forth under the light, looking for a speck he might have missed.

"He's not doing it." I poured a cup of coffee I knew I would regret by midnight and stood, leaning against the counter, drinking it. "He's not getting it."

"Patience." Jack scrubbed once more, polishing off an invisible mark, then set the pot upside down on a dish towel that he had squared and laid by the sink. His hands were wet and foamed with soap but he wiped them on the legs of his jeans. He moved slowly, getting a frosted glass from the freezer, a bottle from the refrigerator. Pouring a beer, as thick and dark as molasses and with a German name I never could pronounce. "I'll go. You have work to do."

As Jack walked away, guilty relief washed through me. I knew I could not pick through the maze inside Edward's head tonight. Not without screaming, or stalking out onto the porch to smoke a cigarette, petulantly, chalking up my future cancer to the unfairness of having a child who had been cured, who wasn't covered with tumors but still remained in this space where I couldn't quite reach him.

I heard Jack in the other room. "Now, read it out loud, this paragraph." Then Edward's voice, mechanical, stilted, the robotic self that emerged when he was only pretending to answer but was not really even hearing his own words. I was perfectly still. There was a comma-shaped smear of spaghetti sauce on the front of the oven, but I didn't even pick up the dishcloth to wipe it away.

"Good job. Nice reading." Jack's voice was distant. Pleased. He wasn't listening, either. "So what did it say?"

There was a long silence. I waited for several seconds, but waves of itchy warmth were twitching through me like a building tide. I tell myself that I tried to be calm, tried not to overreact. And even now I have no idea why I chose that particular night to erupt. But I did.

"He's not *listening,* Jack!" I smacked my cup down on the counter, spilling drops of brown onto the clean towel, the freshly washed pot, and stalking into the dining room. "Why can't you tell? Why can't anyone else fucking *tell* when he's checked out?"

Jack stood and leaned forward, looming. He looked dark, but more weary than angry. "You aren't doing this right now. I'm taking care of his homework tonight."

"But you're not! You and all his teachers—you just don't hear it. Or you choose not to. You let him go through the motions and you tell yourself he's making progress. Because it's easier. It's easier than chasing after him and forcing him to connect."

Jack was silent, his face like granite. He was retreating, too.

"Soothing him isn't going to help." I was quieter now, facing Jack, meeting his eyes. "Neither is soothing yourself. You have to do the *work.*"

Then, behind us, there was an animal sound, humming and feral, like a swarm of insects lodged inside a growl. We both turned. Edward had stood, raised his forearm to his mouth, and clamped down on it. He came up for air, made the noise again, and bit himself a second time. A third, a fourth. Only a few seconds had passed and Jack and I were still standing, frozen, like stone statues of real parents planted on the hardwood floor.

Then I screamed, "Don't!" And at the same time, Jack lunged forward, wrapped his arms around Edward, and wrestled his elbows up behind his back. Edward was crying. I was crying. Jack was breathing heavily, raggedly, each exhalation longer than the last with dead spaces ringing in between, as if he might decide to quit taking in air altogether.

Two days later, the day after the card and the phone call to DHS and a brief conversation with Paul Evans, who said he could not discuss the "incident" over the telephone but must meet with us in person, we walked into a square room with gray carpet and a round, white conference table that was too large for only three people. I was wearing a dress, Jack a tie and suit coat; Mr. Evans was in jeans and a polo shirt and he had a beard so thin I could see small stretches of pale skin

244 / Ann Bauer

between the hairs. The easy-listening version of a Captain and Tennille song was oozing out of speakers in the ceiling.

"Okay now." Evans sat and gestured to the two chairs opposite his. There was a manila folder with Jack's name typed on its tab in front of him. "You know a report was made against you in the case of your son Edward?" He looked at us and I nodded, though he was not speaking to me. Jack's face was grim and tight. I wanted to pass him a note telling him to smile, or shrink a bit in his chair, so he didn't look so threatening.

We both knew about the report. When Jack had called the day before, he was told only that he was "under suspicion for child abuse." Nothing more.

But then Edward came home from school and explained everything: how he went to music class and just then noticed the bruises that had erupted overnight on his arm. That he was looking at them, running his fingers over to see if he could feel the new colors, when his teacher saw his yellowed and purpled skin, the bite marks, and asked what happened. How he began to explain but got only one sentence out, "My mom and dad were fighting," before she seized him—which hurt, he told us, because of the bruises—and led him out of the room and into her office. She asked which one of us had touched him and he said, "My dad grabbed me," and then she picked up the telephone and called some police-sort-of-man somewhere and told him that Edward had been hurt and, she thought, maybe bitten, by his father. The man came right away, Edward said. He was there by 10:23.

"Ten twenty-three," Edward repeated when he told us, and nodded. Then lower, in a whisper: "Ten twenty-three."

The man drove him to a building somewhere and into a room with toys and asked him questions for two hours and four minutes and it made him very tired but he didn't remember what all the questions were, only that the man wanted to know if his dad ever hit his mom or broke things or drove too fast or drank beer or whiskey and Edward said he didn't know about any of the other things but his dad had been drinking something that smelled like beer the night this happened. He'd done very well answering the questions, he reported, but since he'd had to miss lunch and recess, when the man took him back to school he told Edward's counselor, Mrs. Jackson, to let Edward skip social studies so he could eat his lunch and then Edward said he hadn't felt very good about going back to class, since he'd missed too much of the day, so the man said he could stay in the teachers' lounge and play with his yo-yo instead. While he was there, the principal came in and got them both Cokes and sat down and started asking a lot of the same questions the man had asked but it was getting late by this time and Edward didn't feel like talking anymore so he just shook his head very hard whenever the principal tried to get him to answer.

"We know about the report," I told Evans. I put my hand over Jack's, which was resting too loosely on the arm of his chair. It felt dead, nothing moving beneath the skin.

"I talked to your son for a while yesterday. Didn't scare him or anything. Seems like a good kid. But the bruises on his arms were pretty, you know, bad." Evans tilted back in his chair and stared, as if he'd just asked a question. We all waited. Then I couldn't stand it any longer.

"What Edward should have told you—" I began.

Evans held up a small, pink hand. "Edward told me how he got the bruises." But again, he waited. And smiled, as if he were delivering great news. "He told me he bit himself. In great detail, in fact." He laughed. "He must have told me every word you guys said that night . . . what you had for dinner, what time everything happened. He's kind of funny that way, isn't he?"

Now there was something curling under my palm. Jack's hand with fingers stretching and crouching, like an animal awakening after a long sleep. "Then. There's no problem." My husband's voice was low and pocked with breaks. I tried to recall if I'd heard him speak today, before this moment. "Right?"

"Weeeellllll . . ." Evans opened the folder and stared into it. "Not exactly. The report was made. So I have to ask you some questions now. Just our routine. We have to fill out all the forms, you know, make the state happy. Also." He pulled out a pen. "There were a few things that came out during the interview that troubled me. For instance, how much do you drink?"

Evans's voice remained mild, but suddenly Jack was alert, wary, his entire long body tight and coiled in the chair. "Excuse me?"

"Per day. Would you say one drink? Two? Five?" I was listening to his voice—rising crisply at the end of his questions with certainty that his mission was right, his need to know everything entirely justified. I heard echoes in my head and wondered how often I sounded exactly like this. Superior, judgmental. Could Jack close his eyes and wonder which of us was speaking?

But his eyes were open now. Wide open. "Why do you need to know this?"

Evans checked his watch and sighed. "Sir, if we can just get through this."

There was a long pause. "Three, on average." Jack's hand had sprung alive now, all tendons and strain. I removed mine from his, as if it were the conduit to an electric shock. "Some days less."

Evans looked down, eyes moving across the page as if he were scanning the list of questions, deciding which ones were most important, which ones might be triggers, clues in our case. "Have you ever had a problem with alcohol?"

I glanced sideways, too fast. Jack didn't even look at me; he was alone with Evans now. "Yes."

"When was that?"

"About twenty years ago. I was twenty-two. Everyone I knew had a problem with alcohol."

"So what'd you do about it?"

"I quit drinking so much."

"Why's that?"

I imagined myself getting up, moving around the table, and pushing Evans over on his hiked-up, tilted chair. But Jack was perfectly still, only his mouth moving. "I got arrested. DUI. I realized I was getting out of control."

"Ever been out of control since?"

"In what way?" I heard a weak note in Jack's voice. No one else could have detected it. But I knew Jack well enough to guess he'd begun to feel confused and wrong. He was forgetting he did nothing to Edward, that if anyone was responsible for what happened, it was me.

Evans's chair creaked; he looked like a surly teenager, tipped back on his chair, with inadequate facial hair and a sneer. I hated him as deeply as I had ever hated anyone. "Ever, say, hit someone? Break things because you were angry? Act out in a sexually aggressive way?"

"No."

Evans's check marks were getting broader, more dramatic, every time. Pen sweeping over paper with a long, soft scratch. "Ever had fantasies about doing any of those things, or planned it but just not gone all the way through?"

Jack was silent for a moment. When the word finally came out, it was small and absolutely toneless. "No."

Evans turns to me. "All this sound right to you?"

But I was lost by that time, watching pictures flash through my head: Jack coming home from work each night the year after Grace was born. Changing into sweat clothes, eating his dinner with a fork standing in front of the sink, then leading Edward downstairs to do brain gym. The two of them crawling back and forth on the gym mat, where Jack had pasted words and pictures, reading aloud as they humped along; performing the odd cross-patterned jumping jacks with arms bent at the elbows, V-shaped over their chests, to slap the opposite shoulders; going inside the darkened closet with a flashing light to do eye exercises; running in place together as they chanted with their hands tented into triangles, fingertips pressed to the center points on their foreheads.

Other images came, too. Swimming, because it was a vestibular activity and floating on water was supposed to help children learn to trust. I saw Jack standing in the pool for twenty, thirty minutes at a time, his hand certain as stone, an inch under Edward's back. And the big rocker where Jack would sit, holding Edward forcibly on his lap, singing the only songs he knew, *"Drivin' that train, high on cocaine, Casey Jones you better watch your speed."* Until eventually, Edward would relax against him and begin to hum along.

Evans was staring at me now, waiting. "Yes," I said. "That sounds right."

"Okay." Evans flipped the page with a conductor's flourish. He righted his chair and sat square at the table, as if everything else had been preliminary, now he meant business. "Here's the thing." He paused. I could have sworn I saw him start to smile. "I asked Edward if he was mad at you. You know, if you did anything that made him feel uncomfortable or upset. And he said not lately, but he told me about something that happened when he was, uh, younger. You made him drink . . . he called it 'tea.'" His tone, the stress he placed on the last word, made it sound even worse than the truth. Toilet cleaner. Angel dust. Hemlock. "He said he didn't like it and didn't want to drink it but you made him."

"But you don't understand," I said, before I had any idea how I was going to answer. "This makes it all sound wrong. If it's anyone's fault, it's mine. I'm the one who . . ."

Now Jack was alert. He raised his hand again, closed it over mine, and squeezed. Hard. Turned sideways, the diamond on my wedding ring bit into the little finger of my left hand.

I opened my mouth again to explain about the sleepless nights and the death in Edward's eyes but realized, as I looked at the pen hovering in Evans's hand, that Jack was right. Any excuse would hurt us. Hurt him. Maybe even hurt Edward. I closed my mouth and swallowed.

"Here's the thing . . ." Paul Evans looked down and flipped through his sheaf of papers. He looked uncertain for a moment, which almost made me like him. "We obtained Edward's medical records from that time, and there was a lot to go through. That's why"—he raised his head and made eye contact with Jack, who was as still as any living human being I'd ever seen—"I couldn't talk to you yesterday. I was trying to catch up on it all. And there's a note here from a Dr. . . ."

Evans was paging through again, endlessly it seemed, wetting his fingers and pushing papers by their corners, and the room was tilting, my ears ringing. I suddenly, desperately, needed a glass of water. "Aha! Newberg. Barry Newberg."

"You can't!" I tried to remember the language I'd heard on TV. "Medical records are confidential and you can't obtain them without a court order."

But Evans was shaking his head. "Except in cases of suspected child abuse."

Jack's hand kept tightening around mine. I could feel my fingers purpling.

"So we found this notation where you actually told the doc"—did he laugh at this point?—"that your husband was giving your son marijuana. And it seems he was a cop at the time?"

Evans raised his eyebrows in disbelief, as if this were all an elaborately amusing farce. "So we went over to the local precinct and talked to an officer . . ."

"Simmons." The name came out of Jack's mouth like the creak of a rusty hinge.

But Evans was shaking his head. "Nooooo. It was, um, Torkelson."

I turned to Jack and mouthed, *Danny?* And he nodded.

"Your partner at the time, right?" Evans smiled when Jack nodded. Then spoke almost as if he were confiding in us. "We find that's where you get the best information in these cases."

"These cases?" I asked.

"Oh." Evans waved his hand in the air as if dismissing a proposition I'd laid out before him. "Tons of corruption, abuse, child neglect cases among our men in blue. We deal with this sort of thing often enough, we know who to talk to."

There was a silence, maybe a minute long, for which I was so grateful I could have cried. "Okay, so Officer Torkelson confirmed you stole the stuff from an evidence locker there, said it was hushed up when you were let go, part of the deal." He narrowed his eyes at Jack. "Less embarrassment for everyone, right?"

Jack didn't respond. I finally yanked my hand out of his and wiggled the fingers until they burned with recirculating blood but was sorry I had when I saw Evans staring at me.

"So?" I asked, sounding like an insolent teenager. "What does this mean?"

"This *means*"—Evans leaned back and his chair let out a nearly human whine; I wanted to scream at him to stop moving—"we're charging your husband with felony drug possession, theft, and distribution of a controlled substance to a minor."

I was afraid to look at Jack but when I did he seemed too calm, his head suddenly appearing enormous and leonine, somehow hairier than it had been when we walked through the door. He was thinking about something, looking down at his hands that seemed to be working a sum, finger by finger. "I'm bonded, for my job," he said quietly. "In a bank."

"Not for much longer." Evans squinted at Jack and there may have been a flicker of something like sympathy in his eyes. "You may have time to put in your notice and quit before the revocation goes through. With some trials I'd say you have a chance to beat it but here, we've got the child, the cop, the doctor. It's not going to happen."

The room was spinning. So gray and still and square, suddenly it seemed like a tomb.

"Now." Evans turned to me. "We're not going to take the child away. As far as we can determine, from what Newberg says, it was all some sort of crazy deal where your husband was trying to medicate the kid so he could sleep. So it's still illegal." He let out a bark of a laugh. "I mean, clearly, this is not what normal people do. But according to the school you've been a good mom, always there for conferences and such, and it's tough dealing with a kid who has problems, of course." He was wheedling, trying to get me on his side. "As of today, you're primary guardian. Think of it like sole custody, if you were divorced. All three kids, not just Edward, and we're going to require your husband to go for treatment and counseling and then . . ."

He kept talking. I'm sure he did. Thinking back, I see us in the room, spinning on an axis formed by the table, the way children do on a merry-go-round, their faces appearing only once per revolution and even then as a streak of skin and eyes and hair that bleeds into the background.

Then Evans gave me something to sign and I did it and I felt the space between Jack and me expanding. We stood and I turned but I no longer even recognized my husband. He was wearing a brown jacket that didn't fit. It was too short, the hem circling the tops of his thighs, making him look as if he'd been cut exactly in half.

"You can go to the police station and turn yourself in now, or wait at home and they'll come talk to you in a few days." Evans said this part lazily and his voice seemed to come from the end of a long tunnel.

"Either way, shouldn't be too bad. No one is going for a long jail sentence here, just a way to keep you from doing anything like this in the future."

"Oh," Jack said, as if he were only vaguely interested. His eyes, behind the thick lenses of his glasses, were glazed with something that looked like plastic film and his face appeared both younger and older and more like Edward's than I had ever seen before.

We moved toward the door in a loose herd and actually shook hands with Paul Evans before leaving his office. Saying good-bye, taking the card he placed in my hands in case I had any questions, we walked out into the parking lot and felt the hard spring sunshine on our heads. I looked at Jack and he was staring down at the blacktop, shoulders loose, arms hanging too low, as if he had left the frame of himself behind.

28

DURING THE SUMMER between seventh and eighth grades, Edward grew to tower over me. Suddenly, this boy I used to listen for all night and carry because he was too tired to walk began to sleep twelve hours at a time, eat six meals a day. He gained four inches between June and September, another two before Christmas. It was like watching a science experiment. Sometimes when I walked into a room where he was standing, I would discreetly measure myself against his body to track his progress. For a long time, he thought it was I who was shrinking. He didn't notice, until I pointed it out, that he was taller when he compared himself with other people as well.

He never bit himself again after that night when he was thirteen. In fact, he never hurt himself in any way. The state ordered me to take him to a psychiatrist, who prescribed a "cocktail" of Ritalin and two antidepressants, which I filled in case they checked, then dumped down the toilet the moment we got home. I kept all the children very close that following year. Other than interviews and occasional dinners with my parents, I barely left the house. I constructed an elaborate set of rituals for the four of us: movie night on Friday, homemade pizzas on Saturday. Homework was done during a set time each night—all of us together, their heads bent over books and math pages while I edited articles. And once again, Edward improved.

It didn't happen all at once, the way Jack left. And that unfairness rankles me to this day: I had to endure the firestorm of drunkenness and injustice that swallowed up my husband and destroyed our marriage in an instant, while Edward's progress occurred infuriatingly slowly, over many years.

I never knew whether Jack blamed me, or himself, or Danny, or God. I tried to ask him, the evening of the day we were interviewed by Paul Evans. But he either wouldn't tell me, or he couldn't. He'd been drinking straight through since noon, not quietly, the way he always had before, but with a vengeance. Around nine o'clock, I stood blocking the refrigerator, preparing to ask him a question, but he put his hands on my shoulders and moved me, gently but firmly, to one side. When I made as if to step back in place, he shot a look at me so full of hate, I knew it would be dangerous to do anything more. I got into bed alone that night and listened to him pace, slamming things. Toward morning, I heard him begin to mutter.

He never quite sobered, but he had lucid moments and in one of them he told me that he had to leave. He looked sorry, but determined. And as if he knew me only slightly.

"We'll get you a good lawyer," I said. "Really, when the whole story comes out, it might be okay."

He shook his head, like a horse does. Strong tendons moving in his neck, no opening for me to suggest anything else. "You take care of the kids," he said curtly. "I can't do this anymore."

The police called at six-thirty the following morning to say they would be arriving to take Jack into custody by noon. "Shift change," Jack moaned from where he sat hunched over on the couch, looking as though he might vomit, or die. "They're just getting the day's business in order." I waited for Jack to go into the bathroom, then called my father at his office. All the years of my life, he had arrived there at seven o'clock so he could spend a quiet half hour with *The Wall Street Journal*. He sounded irritated at first, then tight. He told me to hold on. I heard the door close, though he probably was alone on the executive floor. Then I began telling my story and got about halfway through.

"Christ! How could you be so stupid? Two college-educated adults and you act like . . ."

I waited and held my breath so I wouldn't cry. I was thirty-four years old, but I could have been twelve. "Okay." When his voice came again, it was gentler. He'd reset, wiped his broad forehead, ordered his thoughts. "I'll be there in fifteen minutes. *I'll* talk to your husband. Make sure he's there, understand? I don't want to make this trip for nothing."

I agreed, though I knew by that time I had no control. If I announced Abe was coming, Jack certainly would leave. If I didn't, I was taking a chance. The only sure thing I knew was to keep him drinking. When he came out of the bathroom, I handed him a cup of coffee spiked with at least a half cup of dark rum.

In the past, liquor had made Jack soft. But now, it was like kerosene on a fire. By the time my father arrived, Jack was packing his car with things he deemed essential: a sewing machine, a case full of wrenches, six bags of Goldfish crackers. I was watching out the window. As my father switched off his Cadillac's engine, Jack was trying to force a bicycle into the trunk of his car, scratching the paint over and over with the hand brakes as he pushed it down.

As large a man as my father is, he was dwarfed by my husband. He stood in front of him, looking up, talking. I saw Jack sneer. Then my father reached out and touched his arm.

They sat in our dining room until past ten, talking in low tones. I gave the children their breakfast and got them off to school. I heard my father insist he would pay for a good attorney, Jack should trust him, sit tight, do nothing for now.

"You have lousy judgment," Abe said. He leaned back in his chair and I heard the joints creak. It was time for Jack to take apart and reglue all our old wooden furniture; he did this every spring, after each season of dry furnace heat. I wondered what would happen if he were gone and imagined our chairs and tables and desks lying in splintered pieces on the floor. "You've always had lousy judgment. But you're the best father I've ever known." He leaned back, shrugged out of his suit jacket, and put it on the chair next to him; it was the size of a small quilt. "Good fathers don't abandon their children. You"—he squinted at Jack—"don't abandon your children."

I was hopeful. But when I looked in, I saw the emptiness in Jack's eyes and knew he wasn't really listening. I wasn't surprised at all when he agreed with everything my father said, thanked him, walked him to the front door, watched him drive away, then turned and told me, sadly, that it was time, he was leaving. And then he did.

I waited until the following day to tell my parents Jack was gone. I'd been through this before and I knew how to schedule the days with meals and television shows, remain level and cheerful around the children, straighten the house an extra inch in order to make up for the imbalance. I called after the children were in bed, our second night alone, and when my father answered, I told him immediately. No preamble.

I was on the front step, smoking a cigarette I didn't particularly want because the smell of its burning matched my mood and the wet, foggy spring night. After I said it, I inhaled deeply and held the smoke. Waiting.

"He was a great father, a good man," Abe finally said. "Don't you ever let your children forget that."

But they did forget, all except Edward, who seemed to retain everything in a mosaic pattern in his head: the butterfly that landed on his hand once when we visited the Badlands, a restaurant with a scythe on the wall, the Grateful Dead song Jack taught him when he was two. For Matt and Grace, Jack became simply an absence. By the time he'd been gone a year, they were startled when anyone mentioned him.

"You have hands just like your father's," my mother told Matt one night when we sat around their table.

"Who?" he said, before he realized. Then he looked down, embarrassed and silent.

My mother looked more hurt than surprised, but she covered the moment well: getting up to refill the serving platter with slices of roasted turkey, passing it around the table. But as she sat, she said very softly, "He had such beautiful hands."

My parents grieved Jack like a lost son. And this brought us together in ways we never had been before. That night as we washed the pans and silver—my mother wearing blue vinyl kitchen gloves, her hands deep in soapy water; me waiting with a stiff, white dish towel to dry— she told me about the months following Mickey's death.

"Ruth pulled away from us." My mother stared out the window, scouring the contours of a roaster by touch alone. "I don't know if she blamed us in a way, or was afraid that we blamed her . . ."

She paused. Even her hands stopped.

"What happened to her?" I asked. "Where is Davy now?"

"I don't know." She resumed everything at once—speaking and scrubbing simultaneously. "That winter, she moved back in with her parents, went back to work for her father. As far as I know, her mother stayed home with Davy."

"Grandma and Grandpa never saw him?"

My mother shook her head. "A few times. They went over and brought him things. But it was strained, I think: Ruth's mother watching over them as if they were strangers."

She handed me the roasting pan, water running off it in thin, lighted strands. For a moment, I saw Jack standing at the sink in the glow of our nighttime kitchen.

"Of course," my mother continued more briskly, "your father and I were just moving back here from New York, looking at houses, thinking about starting a family of our own. I don't think I realized at the time that my parents were almost as heartbroken over Davy as they were over Mickey. I suppose I didn't understand, back then, that you can lose someone who's still alive."

She turned to me and for once, it was I who looked away, shifting my eyes down to the pan that I kept rubbing, over and over, though it was long since dry.

"The last time we saw him, he was maybe seven years old. Then Ruth's mother died, her father went into a nursing home, and Ruth moved with Davy to Omaha, where her brother lived. There were no laws back then, no grandparents' rights. So when they disappeared"—my mother raised her gloved hands, the gesture of surrender—"that was just the end of it."

When I thought of Mary and Ted having to relinquish their grand-child, Ruth's actions seemed cruel. But there was a part of me that understood. After Jack left, I sometimes imagined that the children and I were on an island, connected only to one another. And despite how I came to rely on them, I felt strangely distanced from my parents, no longer afraid of what they would think or say. In a life without Jack's perspective, I found no one else's opinion really mattered.

Once, after a conference on public policy, I went home with a state demographer I'd interviewed about his report on the rising immigrant population. He lived in a sleek, modern-looking one-bedroom apartment overlooking the river in east St. Paul. Our sex was hurried and though he was decent and thoughtful, I felt nothing at all. Afterward, I sat wrapped in a blanket, watching the water move under willow branches and a waxing moon, and wondered if, perhaps, it was I who had changed rather than Jack. My body rather than his hands.

29

I SAW MARIEL for the first time in seven years at the funeral of her father. My mother read the notice in the newspaper one summer morning and called to make sure I knew. She offered to go with me, but I declined, asking her to stay with the children instead.

Mariel was, impossibly, even thinner than before. A small, dark crow of a woman whose black hair was threaded through with silver. Her mouth had a hard set and when she took my hands, hers felt so cold I recoiled a little.

"I'm sorry about your father," I said.

She shrugged. I suddenly realized she was a rich woman now. All that hidden money funneled down into a single heir.

Mariel had never returned my calls and then, in the weeks immediately after Jack left, when she left a message saying she'd heard, she was worried about me but not surprised, I didn't return hers.

"You remember Scott?" she asked, turning slightly.

And there he was: not the bully I remembered, but a softer version. He was middle-aged now; his face had filled out and become a little jowly. He wore glasses that shone in the afternoon light. When Scott put his hand on my arm and leaned in to kiss my cheek, he smelled clean, like limes and soap. "Good to see you. It was nice of you to come."

Then he drifted away and Mariel and I stood with a distance between us that seemed to grow though neither of us moved. "So, I hear you're doing well. Publishing in some big-name magazines." She smiled, smugly, I thought, and I almost walked away. Then I looked again and saw that it was only the sharp lines of her face that made her appear to be mocking me.

"I am doing well," I said lightly. "The work is good."

"How are the children?"

I winced, thinking about our last conversation. "They're fine. Really quite good, actually. Grace and Matt seem happy and Edward is . . . well, he's okay."

"I'm glad." She looked away. "But about Jack, you know. I'm really sorry." There was a flash as she raised her hand to push back a section of her hair and that's when I saw the diamond.

"You're married? You and Scott?" The most amazing thing, I thought, was that my mother had missed that announcement.

"A little over a year now. We went on a cruise to Alaska and there was a chapel on the ship." She splayed her slim fingers in a so-you-see gesture. "It was spur of the moment, but I'm glad we did it."

"Things are going well?" I asked, waiting breathlessly. Somehow this seemed linked to what had happened between Jack and me, my own ability to judge men.

"Yeah." Even with no flesh on it, her face softened. And I knew this much was true: they were together. And I was alone.

I was relieved when fall came and the children went back to school. Their routine helped us establish a natural rhythm: a family of four that separated at the beginning of each day and came back together afterward to spend quiet evenings watching TV, eating popcorn, reading in lamplight. Matt and Grace both had been placed in advanced programs at school, as well as special groups for children from "nontraditional" families. So far, Edward had been keeping up in all his classes, though exactly how he did it was a mystery to me.

"Did you get your homework done?" I asked one clear, cool morning in October.

Edward was sitting at the table, staring out the window, his eyes mirroring the blue of the sky outside. He pondered. "I don't know," he said. "Maybe."

I sighed and brought him the little white teapot in which his morning cup of Darjeeling was steeping. He poured the tea carefully and measured in exactly one-half teaspoon of honey, stirring slowly. I reached into the refrigerator and handed Grace a carton of yogurt and a spoon. A flicker of memory crossed Edward's face.

"I need lunch money," he said. "My account is a negative number."

I pulled my checkbook out of my purse, wondering where all his money had gone; Edward rarely ordered a hot lunch, unless it was pizza. I flipped through the register and saw that I had given him a $20 check just the week before. "Sweetheart?" All three children looked up. "Have you been buying lunches for other people?"

Edward wrinkled his forehead and took a sip of tea. "I'm not sure," he said. He added one more drip of honey and stirred again, watching bits of dust glitter in the steamy air above his cup. "I might have. That would be a nice thing to do."

Matt and Grace laughed. Edward's face went blank for a minute, but then he looked at them and he laughed, too.

"Okay." Feeling muddled, I tried a different approach. "How much do you need? How far overdrawn are you?"

"Overdrawn?" His head was down, eyebrows furrowed. After so many years of trying to recapture all the words he'd missed, Edward had grown to hate it when I used one he didn't know.

"How big is the negative number?"

"Two point nine five."

"Two dollars and ninety-five cents?"

He nodded.

I comforted myself with the fact that clearly he wasn't buying lunches for the whole class; I probably wouldn't have to go to the school to straighten this out. I wrote another $20 check and handed it to Edward. He folded it neatly in half, corners matching up perfectly, and slipped it into the small front pocket of his backpack. But for just a minute, when he pulled the pocket open, I saw a square of paper inside.

"Wait!" I dove for the backpack. Edward flattened it shut and hugged it to his body. We struggled for a few seconds over a strap. He was far stronger, but still gentle. Eventually, he let me pull the backpack away from him; I reached in and pulled out two identical checks dated nine days apart.

"Edward! You never turned in your lunch money." I picked up the old check and held it out, facing him, but he looked away, eyes sliding back to the window.

"So?"

"Well, that's why you're overdrawn. You didn't give the school your money."

"I only ordered hot lunch once," he said stiffly. "It was September fourteenth. And Alex wanted chocolate milk once, on September twenty-third, so I got him some. That *was* nice of me."

"But you have to pay first if you want lunches or milk," said Matt. I gulped back what I'd been about to say and took a bite of cereal instead. I leaned against the counter, holding my bowl, and listened to Matt explaining for the third time how money works. To Edward insisting, again and again, that it was only one lunch. And a carton of milk, for his friend. Which *was* nice of him.

Finally, Matt sighed like an old woman and asked for the check, saying he would take it to the cafeteria himself. I mouthed the words: *thank you.*

I put my bowl in the sink, cleared the children's dishes, and began on Grace's hair. Matt had pulled out his homework—the empty sheet of math problems he told me he had finished the night before—and was firing questions at Edward.

"What's a hundred and eighty divided by thirteen?" Matt's head was bent over the sheet.

"Thirteen, remainder eleven," Edward said through a slurp of tea.

"Five hundred divided by forty-one?"

"Twelve, remainder eight." His voice was rising and falling, a half note off its usual mechanical tone. He seemed to be watching Matt's hand move. Suddenly, Edward stood and leaned over his brother; he pointed at a pencil mark on the page. "No, I said eight; you wrote six."

I stopped braiding and walked over to the boys. Matt was erasing, as if this happened every day: he had made a mistake. His older brother noticed . . . and spoke. In one instant, I had the shifting, satisfied feeling you get when tumblers move very smoothly in a lock.

I squeezed Edward's shoulder. He reached up and tapped my hand awkwardly with the flat back of his. "What's four thousand two hundred and sixty-six divided by thirty-seven?" I asked.

"One hundred fifteen, remainder eleven."

I had no idea if this was the correct answer. But I said, "Good. Good for you."

EPILOGUE

THE OFFER CAME in May of 2003, more than two years after Jack left, just as Edward was finishing ninth grade. An editor in Rhode Island who had worked with me long distance called to say he needed someone on staff, right away. The country was in recession and his publication—a sharply sarcastic literary and political quarterly with a libertarian bent—had quadrupled its circulation. He couldn't offer much in the way of salary, and nothing in terms of moving expenses, but he would give me a managing editor title, excellent health insurance, and stock options in a growing company. Even my father had to admit that the opportunity was too good to turn down.

I needed a full-time job. Without Jack's income and benefits, I had slipped back into the parsimony of our early years. I shopped carefully and put off buying things for the house until the old items were so worn or broken they had to be replaced. When Matt fractured his wrist during a soccer match at school, I'd paid bills for the emergency room visit and orthopedist's office over a ten-month period. I'd been fretting over money for the majority of the past fifteen years and I was ready to be done.

But it was more than that. I'd never quite managed to knit our family back together after the loss of Jack. I loved our children with a fierceness worthy of two parents, and other than the time I spent working, I was rarely anywhere but with them. During the day, when they went to school and Scout meetings and violin lessons, they seemed happy. But as night stole in, particularly in the fall, I felt a sense of sadness in our house—as if the space Jack had occupied were still there, open and dark and empty. We'd be baking cookies or watching a movie and suddenly there would be a moment of grief or fear so deep I felt as if I'd tumbled into cold water. Several times, I looked around the room and read the same feeling on the boys' faces, confusion and the beginning of tears in Grace's eyes.

It was the house, I decided. And this city where Jack and I had made all our plans. "You're mourning the future you expected to have," a psychologist once told me. "You need to create a new one, without your husband." But I didn't know how. When the call came from Providence it seemed to be a sign: this was our new future. I would be able to reconstruct our family in this completely new and unfamiliar place.

But it had to happen fast; the editor wanted me there within a month. I worried about how Edward would make the transition and spent most of my hours on the phone with high schools out East, transferring records and setting up his schedule. Property values in Minneapolis had climbed and I knew I would need the money, so I sold our beloved house and rented one, over the telephone, in a tiny bay-side bedroom community just outside Providence. My real estate agent came to me on a scorching afternoon, triumphantly waving a full-price offer, and I signed the paper, accepting it, then spent the next seven hours wandering through my house touching things—the walls and molding, those loose glass doorknobs that sometimes caught the light and sent out prisms of color.

It wasn't until the next day when I called a local moving company that I panicked.

"You want to leave in two weeks?" the man asked me, as if I'd said I wanted to hire a camel caravan to do the job. "There's no way. We're booked out till October."

It was the same all over town. No one knew what people did in these circumstances. "If it was a company moving you, ya might be able to edge in," one mover told me. "Most won't admit this, but we save blocks of time for the big corporate clients."

With nine days to go before we had to be out of the house, I logged onto my computer, desperate, and typed in *moving companies*. Miraculously, fifty-seven links popped up. I clicked on the first and filled out an online form listing my possessions, typed in my date of departure, and held my breath as the system ticked for thirty seconds or so. Then, my confirmation appeared in bold letters on the screen.

I was already on my way to Providence, driving the van through Pennsylvania, banks of low mountains covered with trees, windows open, Will Smith pattering out his good-boy rap on the stereo when my cell phone rang and someone from the moving company who identified himself only as "D" said brightly, as if it were a joke, "There's been a problem with your shipment. It's going to be delayed. Significantly delayed. And if you ever want to take delivery, it's going to cost you a lot more than we thought."

I took the children to the beach our fourth day in Rhode Island. I'd done everything I could, using the last of my cash to buy air beds and a small microwave at Kmart. We'd gone to the library, applied for cards, and checked out stacks of books. But the house, an empty little bungalow so unlike the high-ceilinged one we left back home, felt lonely and cold despite the sunshine and summer heat blowing in off the bay.

I sat on a blanket on the sand, gripping my knees, squinting, trying to keep track of which bobbing heads belonged to me. Over and over, I watched Matt standing ready, waiting for a wave, only to launch himself stomach-first onto its crest and ride it out toward the horizon. Edward stood taller than most of the other swimmers. He was my landmark— water dripping from his long curls, shoulders slightly hunched, one hand scooping down into the ocean and rising, allowing the drops to fall in a shower that twisted and glittered on its way down. But I noticed he kept looking at Grace, too, checking to see that she was near him, reaching out to touch her head between every handful of the Atlantic. She understood his rhythm and tipped toward him at the appropriate times.

They emerged from the water shiny as seals and hungry. I took them to a clam shack along the beach where we sat on tall stools around a square table. I let them order sodas that arrived in enormous glasses, unnatural colors, orange and cherry brown, fizzing merrily, straws sticking out with their paper wrappers still covering the ends.

But when we went home, the house was dark and it echoed. The children sobered immediately. They brushed their teeth and lay down on their uncovered air beds and we listened to the growl of trucks making late-night and then early-morning deliveries to the Dunkin' Donuts down the street.

The next morning, I bought a small television with a built-in VCR even though I had to charge it to a credit card.

"Can you return it if our stuff comes?" Matt asked anxiously. "You must be running out of money."

"It wasn't much," I lied. "And wouldn't you like to be able to watch a movie?"

I saw the struggle in his face. "Yeah, I guess." He lifted his shirt to scratch and I was startled to see a few dark hairs curling across his belly.

That afternoon, I called the police in several states, the FBI, the Federal Highway Commission, the state patrol, the Department of Transportation, the Better Business Bureau, and the American Movers Association. Each conversation was exactly like the one before.

"You say you hired these people over the Internet? And then you just handed over your keys and left town?"

I would sigh. "Yes."

"Well, who came to look at your things and give you the estimate?"

"No one. I did it all, um, online." Not unlike buying books, I wanted to shout; Amazon works this way. "There was a pdf file, a form I filled out that was supposed to calculate how much furniture I had to move."

"Okay, so what's happening now?" the voice on the other end of the line would ask. "Where's your stuff?"

"I have no idea. First, they told me it was in storage in Ohio. Then they said Arkansas."

A long pause.

"So how do you know they won't deliver, eventually? Maybe you're just going to have to be patient."

How to explain? It was the tone, the canned words of the person who called who would begin politely in an accent that was sometimes Middle Eastern and then something like Chinese, then moved in a rushing wave of words that grew stronger and harsher and more obscene. His name kept changing, though it seemed to be the same man and he swore he had given me only the one (Mike, Joe, Zakir) he was using that day. Once, he convinced me that I was remembering incorrectly. I began to apologize, then heard him say, "Fuck you, lady, we got your stuff and the price is nine thousand dollars today," and stopped.

"They say they will. But the price keeps going up and I just don't think . . ." For years, I had made my living using language. I put words in order to form coherent meaning. Yet I couldn't find the ones I needed to tell all the nuances of this particular story.

"So pay them. Later, you can take them to court, hash it all out there." It always came down to this, except with the woman from the highway commission. She had known plenty of other people in my situation and was curt but sympathetic. "Don't you send them a dime," she warned me. "That never works. They'll take it and then you'll be out your goods plus the money. It's how the scam works."

Finally, when it seemed I'd exhausted every other option, I dug through the file I'd brought with me in the car: closing papers from the house sale, bank statements I'd not had time to reconcile, the two letters Jack had sent me—one from a jail in Louisiana, the other from rehab. The divorce decree I'd had drafted but never signed, a yellow arrow tab still pointing to a blank line. Just when I'd nearly given up, I found what I was looking for toward the bottom of the pile: ten digits written on an overdue slip from the library.

I took my cell phone into the bathroom and locked the door. The children were watching MTV, sitting in a clump around the little television; I hoped the voices of J. Lo and Eminem would drown me out.

I dialed and breathed out as I raised the phone to my ear. I'd begun crumpling the paper, anticipating the jeering automaton that would say, "The number you have reached has been disconnected," when Jack answered and startled me. His voice was creaky, as if he'd just awakened from a long nap.

"You're there." My heart continued its rapid hoofbeats. Odd, because talking to him again felt in most ways familiar, inevitable, like shifting a car into gear.

"Clearly."

I told him the story in shorthand. It all made sense now that he was on the other end of the line, interrupting only to say "Yes" and "How much?" and "Bastards." He asked none of the questions I'd heard before. When I finished, he had only one. "Which airport is closest to you?"

I didn't recognize him at first. The man who appeared in the terminal was gaunt, dark, and hollow-looking, his body curved like a *C*. His hair was long, gathered into a loose ponytail that hung down his back. His beard was long now, too, and mostly gray. I glanced up as he exited the gangway, but my eyes drifted over him, looking behind him for someone I knew. Seconds later, he was standing silently in front of me, gazing straight down.

"You're still beautiful." He didn't touch me.

"You still have distorted perceptions of reality." I looked straight up into his face, wondering if I looked different to him, too. If after two years apart, I seemed smaller or older or like a person who only reminded him of someone he used to know. I recognized the old marine duffel he hoisted onto his shoulder. "Follow me," I said and led him through the airport, out into the damp night and my minivan in the parking lot.

"How are the kids?" He had waited until I was merging into traffic to speak. Dazzled by the streetlights that crackled sharp and white, and the speeding cars that left their ghost shapes behind, I hesitated.

"Okay." I sped up and moved into the left lane. "Scared, I guess. And . . . They're angry." The tires smacked the road, over and over, with the slap of wet washcloths.

He nodded. "They should be angry."

It was so reasonable. And just like that, the old familiar burn of marriage started in my gut. "It's so easy for you, isn't it?" I gripped the steering wheel, my elbows poking out like chicken wings. "Well, you should know, angry kids are really hard to raise. *Alone.*" I hit the last word hard.

"I'm sure you're doing a good job." His voice was dreamy, unfocused.

"Yeah, well, what choice do I have?"

I looked over and saw that he was really back now: the husband with hard, hateful eyes. "Jesus. I don't believe you're doing this," he said. "It's not fair. I just ditched my entire life to come here and help you."

"Your entire life?" A truck with a ten-foot-long mermaid painted on it rushed past us and milliseconds later, there was a gush of air. I lost my hold on the wheel for a minute and we shimmied loosely. "And what, exactly, does that consist of," I hissed, easing off the gas, regaining control. "Your life?"

"Not much." He spoke softly and stared at his hands, at the worn wedding ring he still wore. Dull gold the color of a dying fire.

During the time he'd been gone, I'd heard from Jack occasionally. There was no pattern but often he would call just as I had decided he was probably dead. The last time was in winter. He'd called at 2 A.M. from somewhere in northwestern Canada. His words came out slow and slurred, as if they were sticky and he was having trouble shaking them loose. He said he lived in a place with spiders the size of his palms and had worked for a few weeks as a dispatcher for the local volunteer fire department.

He told me he still loved me. I could hear wind rushing in the background. I asked him if he was driving. He said yes but he was pulling over right there because suddenly, talking to me, he realized he was drunk and never should have gotten behind the wheel.

Then he disappeared, nothing but emptiness in my ear. I lay in bed for hours, still holding the phone and staring at the blank ceiling where my mind projected an image: his car, whatever he drove now, skidding on the ice, spinning like a ballet dancer on one wheel against the backdrop of skeletal trees and snow.

I'd copied his new phone number on the slip marking my place in the book on my bedside table. Around 4 A.M., I turned on the light and stared at the line of digits. But I didn't call him back.

I worried the children would be confused by their father's sudden appearance. And they were.

For a long time, I'd believed Jack would die wherever he'd gone, so I'd made a habit of telling the children they probably would never see him again. Then, he appeared in this strange place, so thin and quiet he was like a totally different version of their former father.

Grace was young enough she might have forgotten the way Jack used to be. She told everyone we met at the grocery store or the library that her daddy had been "let out" of Alberta so he could come back to us. When I tried to correct her, Jack shook his head and put a finger to his lips and said later that she was probably on to something.

But just a few days after Jack came to Rhode Island, Matt asked if I ever thought maybe Dad had another wife and children somewhere else. I laughed and told him he'd read too many true-crime stories but after he left the room, still looking uncertain, I began to wonder myself. The idea lasted only a few minutes, though. Deep down I knew the last thing Jack would choose was being tied to more people.

I drove back to the beach one brilliant afternoon, because I had a theory that sunlight might magically heal my husband the way ultra-violet machines are used to cure jaundice. When Jack slumped into a dead-looking ashen sleep on his beach towel, Edward walked around him, examining him from a number of angles, as if Jack were a painting framed against the Atlantic, then turned and spoke to me, holding my eyes with his. "I do still love him, you know." Edward swiveled and squinted toward the water, coughed, and nodded twice. "Even though."

The first week after Jack arrived, I never slept more than a few hours at a time. Every night I awoke to the sound of his snoring. He lay in his clothes on the bare floor in the living room, head resting on his duffel bag, refusing even a blanket. The noise of his breathing wafted down the short hallway between us and echoed through the empty house, like a ragged engine on a faraway street. In all the time we had slept together, I never remembered minding his snoring; back then I would lie next to him, letting my body vibrate with the rhythm until it lulled me to sleep. Now, it made me feel hollow: the *snort-pause-snort.* And then the silence, breath held, during which I heard only my own heartbeat.

Every day was the same for a week or so. I made phone calls to the

police and the transportation authorities each morning, checking on
their progress. There was none. Then we drove to the beach and the
library; we went out for coffee and ordered it "regular," the way they did
out East, with heavy cream and spoons full of sugar. My house had an
outdoor grill, so we had hamburgers or steaks or fresh fish for dinner.
And slowly, Jack's color came back. It was like watching a baby grow:
his cheeks filled out and his body seemed to unfold a bit. He was still
skinny but no longer looked like the ghost of a person we once knew.

It was a Wednesday in August when Jack disappeared for several hours
one afternoon and came back driving a large U-Haul truck with a cab
and a swinging boxcar in back. "It's time," was all he told me. The children said nothing as he and I changed into old, paint-spattered cutoffs
and tank tops, tied bandannas around our heads, and laced up our hik-
ing boots. We did everything but apply jungle paint to each other, but
by that time I suppose they were used to their parents behaving like no
one else's.

I ordered two large pizzas and Jack got our emergency blanket out
of the car and spread it on the living room floor. I had rented three
movies and stacked them on the floor in front of the TV. Just past eight
o'clock I opened the front door and Jack and I stepped out into a night
so wet and warm it seemed to lick my skin. The moon, fuzzy in the
mist, was oversize and orange.

"Make sure your sister brushes her teeth," I called over my shoulder before closing the door. Three pale faces floated in the window,
watching us go. I waved and motioned with flapping fingers. *Go eat, or
watch TV.*

Two of them backed up and disappeared into the murk of the
house; only Edward, in charge for the night, remained. Above us, he
loomed nearly as tall as Jack. And I thought about the day we'd come
back from the airport, how father and son had stood feet apart, facing
each other, eyes blinking rapidly as if they were communicating in a
language I didn't understand.

"Do you think they'll be okay?" I asked now, looking back. There were no lights on in the house and Edward was wearing dark clothes, so only his eyes were visible, shining like blue stones in the murky dusk.

Jack looked up at the window and stopped for a moment. Then he turned abruptly and moved on. "They'll be fine," he said.

Already, my feet were sweating. We got into the enormous truck that wallowed in my muddy driveway. Then Jack was driving and we were rattling over a wooden bridge and across the bay, windows open because there was no air-conditioning in the cab, entering a wavering light where sky and water bled together in a soft charcoal gray. The waxing moon moved with us, a dented peach bobbing in and out of the dark, rippled waves below.

He lit a cigarette and drove with his right hand on the wheel, smoking hand propped half in, half out. Whenever there was a choice of direction to be made, he turned smoothly, still one-handed. Obviously, he had driven this route before.

Twenty minutes later he stopped in an industrial park just off the highway. Behind an electrified fence lay a village of cement buildings, unmarked and windowless.

"This is it?" I said as he switched off the engine. "You're sure? How did you find it?"

He reached under the seat and slid out an ax and a set of bolt cutters that looked like a tweezers magnified until they were the length of my arm. "I made some calls."

"Calls." I unbuckled my seat belt. "To whom?"

Jack tilted his head to one shoulder and looked puzzled, reminding me of our boys when they were two or three. "Drug dealers mostly. It didn't take too long to find out your movers are Israeli mob. Small-time. This is what they do—this same scam over and over." He lifted his hips off the seat to strap on a leather tool belt, looked at me and grinned. "It helps to know all the right people."

A memory flashed in my mind: Jack, young and soft and dark-haired, bent over a crib, singing "Sugar Magnolia" like a lullaby. "And how do you know them?"

"Rehab," he said, opening the door and stretching one leg out of the truck until it touched the cement. "Two months. Court-ordered, after a little incident in Winnipeg. Think of treatment as an international trade show for the underworld. Turns out you meet some amazing and influential people in the drunk tank."

The ground looked a long way down when I opened my door; I had to jump from the cab, and the concrete was hard against my feet. Mist curled in ribbons through openings in the fence, meeting and congealing into a low cloud of fog.

We passed a dome that churned and shucked and made conveyor belt sounds—the source of all the steam. A few yards past, we found a gate that had been left unlatched and two inches ajar. It was three-quarter-size, no more than five feet tall, with a metal bar on top.

Jack turned to face me. "Won't be easy," he said gravely, looking wide-eyed and excited and, for just a fraction of a second, like the man I once married.

The first thing we did was pace off the alley, like people following the instructions on a treasure map. Jack had the locker number, 1368, written on his hand in green ink. We found it at the end of a row that branched off the alleyway. Hardly convenient. But better, Jack said, than a locker on the main artery because it was hidden.

Then he pulled out the bolt cutters, and this is what I remember most vividly. This tall, skinny, gray-bearded man—like Moses in Wal-Mart clothes—fitting the lobster claw of a bolt cutter around the curved top of the padlock, planting his feet, squeezing. Muscles standing out in plaits under his skin. There was a loud snap and the lock flew, arcing overhead, glinting in the hazy moonlight, hitting the dirt with a solid smack that echoed in my chest. And for the first time in years, my blood washed through me in a warm rush.

I had done nothing, but I was breathing hard. Jack's arms shone with sweat in the moonlight. But when I bent to pick up the padlock he barked at me, "Don't!"

I straightened. "Why not?"

He threw the bolt cutters down, wiped his forehead with one arm, bent and grabbed the lock himself. He slipped it into his pocket. "You're not touching anything. Nothing I haven't handed you. Do you understand me? You're not breaking any laws."

"What about you?"

There was a pause, thirty seconds during which crickets played and the dark deepened by a degree or two. Then Jack turned to face me, eyes hard. "What about me?" He was almost sneering. "It's not like I have anything left to lose."

By midnight that conversation seemed like a memory that might or might not have been real, as did the children we left behind. I'd been walking the same dirt road for ten thousand years, hauling things, piece by piece, down the long alleyway, through the narrow gate in the fence, being careful not to touch the live wires, and loading them into the van. Bruises covered my thighs, lavender clots with faint edges of green. We'd found all the things I thought I'd lost forever—the antique buffet my parents gave us one Christmas, a Van Gogh print in a wood-cut frame, boxes of china plates we received for our wedding. But now, they all seemed like weapons designed to mark my skin as I carried them. Every time I took a step, my feet rippled with pain. And I had never in my life been so dirty. There was a layer of dark sweat and dust gummed to my cheeks, hands, and arms, slick and tight to my body as a wet suit.

"We'll just throw these clothes away when we're done," Jack had said when he first raised the corrugated door and we saw how filthy everything was. I nodded, not knowing that very soon I'd be fantasizing about peeling off my skin and throwing it away, too.

But even now, when I met up with him on the path, I saw how much he liked it. Jack wore the grime like a warrior: face painted, eyes and teeth shining through. He was wheeling a cart stacked with boxes but reached out to steady me when I stumbled as we crossed. His hand felt steady and cool.

"You don't even look tired," I said.

He set the brake on his handcart and lit a cigarette, eyes glittering in the flare of the match. Inhaling deeply, he shrugged. Smoke wafted from his mouth as he spoke. "It's a beautiful night. And I think I've finally found something I'm really good at. I could be a pirate." Then he cocked one eyebrow at me and blew a smoke ring shaped like an egg that floated and wavered and broke apart in the air. "Except real pirates travel by ship, not U-Haul."

I sighed. I knew I should keep moving but I stood instead, crossing my arms over my body and reaching up to rub my own shoulders where they ached. Jack flicked his half-smoked cigarette onto the ground and reached out with both hands. I let him work my neck and my back, the way he used to. Standing there in the wet, hot air I leaned into him and went slack, and in that moment it felt like he had been with me all along. He knew where to touch, exactly what route the pain in my neck traveled. I didn't have to say a word.

"It'll be over soon," he whispered and another image flashed in my head. A white room with a television on the wall, picture but no sound. It was a hospital. Jack had said the same thing to me, over and over, each time I was in labor. He was lying then, too.

Later, as I was walking back from the locker, a box of linens knocking against my knees, I heard my cell phone ring. I dropped the box and ran toward the truck but by the time I got there, the sound had stopped. Even the crickets had gone silent. It was that crevice of time between night and day when the earth seemed to lie perfectly still.

I opened the door to the cab and picked up my phone. There was no call-back number on the screen. I stood, debating. I could have imagined it. Or the children could be in trouble. I pictured them getting spooked by the stillness of the strange, empty little house, stuffing their clothes into pillowcases, tying these to the ends of sticks, Tom Sawyer–style, setting off in the dark to find us.

I looked toward the alley. The box I'd dropped was lying on its side in the dust. In the distance, our old antique pie safe had suddenly come to life. The wheels of the cart, invisible behind the broad molding at the bottom of the stack of cupboard doors and drawers, squealed under its weight. I tossed the cell phone back onto the seat and reached into the cooler for a bottle of water. It was the best thing I had ever tasted, sweet and lemony.

I could still hear the wheels. Then, in the periphery of my vision, police lights began to flash.

They were ice blue and my first thought was that I missed the bright cherry-red ones. Then a squad car rolled up next to me with no siren, moving over the speed bumps stealthily, like a cat. I watched the officer get out of his car, adjust his belt, and walk toward me. Too tired to panic, I smiled instead.

"A little late to be moving, don't you think?" He was forty-five or so, blond, thick around the middle, and clean-shaven.

I sat, for what seemed a long time as he approached, thinking about the phone call I'd have to make from the police station. *Dad, you have to come out here right away. Jack and I have been arrested. The kids are all alone in an empty house on the bay.* I wondered if they would allow me to call long-distance, or if they'd make me reverse the charges.

I opened my mouth to say something then heard the disembodied voice of my husband. "I'm afraid that's my fault."

He was coming around the back of the truck, having covered the distance from the gate in half the time it should have taken him, but wasn't even breathing hard. He nodded at the officer, as if they knew each other from way back, and slid the cart out from under the pie safe, which teetered for a moment, then settled into balance. "It was the only time I had off work."

They watched each other. The cop was probably older by a couple years. But his face was soft and cared for, while Jack's was an ancient-looking ruin of edges and lines and planes of dark stone.

"I know how it is." The policeman shifted from one foot to the other, patting his belt. "Even so. I'm going to have to check some ID."

I turned and took a step toward the truck. But again, the man who left me and our children, who had been gone for twenty-six months' worth of middle-of-the-night fevers and Christmas concerts, materialized at my side, like someone who could time-warp over short distances. He slipped his hand around my arm, caught me in the act of reaching for the door handle, and worked his way down so his fingers laced into mine. We stood on the hot cement holding hands, the pie safe erect beside us like a totem, swaying slightly in a warm burst of wind.

"She didn't bring hers. But I have mine." He reached into his pocket with his free hand and gave the officer a card. "But we're running behind. Gotta have the truck back by morning. You mind if we keep going?"

The cop shrugged, then turned back to his car, which was still running, blue lights revolving, a stream of voices and static coming from the radio inside. As I walked down the alleyway, I heard him reading off a name that wasn't Jack's and a license number, using animal names where there were letters in the code. *Rabbit-Panther-4-6-9.*

When we returned, arms loaded, he was leaning against the driver's door and everything was eerily quiet. Both the squad car's engine and its squawking radio were off. The stars had sputtered out. Gray light swelled on the horizon and even the ugly warehouse across the road was illuminated in the pearly glow. The children might be waking up already, I thought, and wondering where we'd gone, if we were ever coming home.

Jack and I were walking together now, side by side. Only a few things were left in the locker that lay a hundred yards behind us. I knew the police would seize them and everything that was in the truck, take it all, and I was glad. Anything to be done lifting and walking. To be able to take a shower, even in jail. The cardboard box I carried was light but felty with thick, wet dust. I put it down and prepared to be handcuffed.

"Hey," the officer called roughly. And Jack stepped forward. There was a beat of silence. Then: "Want me to help you get this in?" The cop tipped his head in the direction of the pie safe that we had left on the path, poking up into the lightening night sky.

I stood, frozen. But Jack grinned and said, "I'd appreciate it. It's a heavy son of a bitch."

Finally, I found my voice. "Thanks. I'd be afraid I might drop it." At that moment, I wasn't sure I could trust myself to pick up an apple. "And it's important to me. It was Jack's." I caught my breath, remembering in that instant that he had been carrying an ID with a different name. "Uh, my husband's . . . mother's." Even I could hear how my own voice had become like a rush of water. Endless. "I never met her, she died before we met, but I've always loved this. . . ."

No one said anything for a minute. Then the officer shucked off his belt and took off his hat and handed them both to me, and he and Jack communicated in that choreographed way men sometimes do, moving instead of talking, the policeman tipping the end of the cupboard down, turning and backing up the ramp of the truck, Jack crouching, bearing the weight, steering from behind. I waited in a puddle of street-light. From inside, there was a clunk, a grunt, two sighs. Then the wash of low voices, like a song I could faintly hear though I couldn't understand the words. They were inside for a long time, through at least two or three shades of morning.

When they came out, the officer took his belt and his hat and put them on and then he nodded at me and waved one smallish hand. He was wearing a thick gold wedding band that gleamed like liquid. "Have a nice morning now," he said before he drove away, without even his headlights on.

After we hauled the few remaining items from the locker and put them in the truck, rolled up the ramp, closed the rear door and latched it, Jack and I hoisted ourselves up into the cab. He had handed me the keys and nodded toward the left, so I was in the driver's seat this time, easing the truck out of the parking lot and onto the highway. Clear, pale sunlight had washed over the night sky. The water in the bay sparkled, white on blue, as we crossed.

Beside me, Jack let his head fall back against the seat. He reached out to take my hand. And I waited to feel something—anger or healing or the heat and electricity of the padlock's flying through the air. But instead, all I felt was his hand, rough and warm in mine, like a part of my own body I'd forgotten was missing.

"I want to be a family again." He was staring out the window at the blur of trees and buildings that grew thicker as we neared Providence. "I want our kids to have a father." He took a long breath. "And I still love you."

I kept driving, eyes on the road ahead, on the movement of yellow dashes as they raced toward us and were sucked under the front wheels of the truck. Behind me, the weight of everything I owned swayed from side to side.

"I'm sure you do . . . want to." I spoke deliberately. With every minute that passed the sun brightened and as it did, I could feel myself hardening. After the past two years, I imagined I was like a superhero—able to form a shell that was invisible, impenetrable. But rock hard. At least that's what I kept telling myself.

"I want that, too." I choked and swallowed. Then continued. "But how would it work? Did you ever sort things out with the police in Minneapolis? Are you free to come back to this country and start over?" My voice was pleading. "I mean, will they let you? And can you? Can you forget about everything that's happened . . . just go back to working a regular job and mowing the lawn on Saturdays and making small talk with the neighbors and showing up for school conferences?"

He was silent and I wondered if he'd fallen asleep. I began to blink. I was tempted to pray. But just as I was about to say something—to God or to Jack himself, I don't really know which—I heard him answer.

"No." His eyes were closed when I turned toward him, his voice low and old. "I don't believe I can."

We never spoke about it again.

Jack and I slept for a few hours after we returned to the house. Then the children helped us haul in all the furniture. Exhausted and sore, all five of us went to bed that night long before dark. It is one of the only times I ever remember falling asleep despite a clear, insistent light pouring through my windows. The next morning I awoke to exactly the same sky—summer's dawn nearly identical to evening—and Jack was already gone. There was a person-size space among the clutter on the living room floor—the place where Jack's duffel had been, where he stretched out at night. I went into the dining room, where he'd set up the table and chairs, hastily, the afternoon before. There was a note lying on the table's worn surface. *I love you. See you some time. J.* My French press sat at the top of the page, full of hot coffee.

I rooted through a half-emptied box and found a mug that looked clean. Pouring, leaning in, eyes closed to smell the steam, I was, for just a moment, back in our kitchen in Minneapolis. Jack was upstairs, Matt in front of *Sesame Street,* Grace in her crib, and Edward locked inside his mind.

There was a soft noise behind me and I turned to see Edward, grown now, shuffling through a wad of packing paper. These days, it was odd for him to be up so early. He ambled toward me looking dreamy, curly hair standing out around his head in a lion's mane, yawning.

"Your dad is gone," I said and took a sip of coffee.

Edward's face didn't change. He continued to come closer and when he was a few inches from me, he raised his hand and set the back of it against my cheek.

"I knew that might be true," he answered.

We stood like that for a few seconds, and then he let his hand drop away.

ACKNOWLEDGMENTS

To Rupert Heath and Sarah McGrath, for their wise counsel, masterful editing, and unflagging support. And to Samantha Martin, for her willingness to ask the tough questions.

To Patricia Foster and Susan Lohafar, for teaching me how to tell a story.

To Steve Rosse, for his thorough critiques and endless enthusiasm.

To Irwin and Rita Boris, for providing space, child care, countless meals, and an irrational faith in my abilities.

To Raymond Flood, for sharing his memories of the Korean War.

To the editors at *Atlantic Unbound, Brevity, Salon, Fourth Genre, The Sun,* and *River Teeth,* for publishing the early stories and essays that fueled this book.

To the members of Buffalo Springfield and the Grateful Dead, for making the music that inspired my characters to sing.

And to Chris Columbus and Robin Williams, for creating in *Mrs. Doubtfire* a film that taught both Edward and his real-life counterpart about the bonds of love between parent and child.

A WILD RIDE UP THE CUPBOARDS

1. Bauer shows us two families, past and present, dealing with kids who don't fit the norm. Discuss how these two families cope, comparing their parenting styles and attitudes. How are Mickey and Edward alike? How are they different? What are the similarities and differences between Rachel and Jack's marriage and that of Mary and Ted?

2. The degrees to which these two families confront their respective sons' unusual behaviors are very different. How much is this a function of the personalities of their parents, and how much do you think is a function of the times? How were attitudes toward disabilities different in the 1940s, '50s, and '60s?

3. What benefit does the reader get from reading the stories of Mickey and Edward side by side? Does the reading of one influence your interpretation of or reaction to the other?

4. Edward's story is told in the first person, from Rachel's perspective. Mickey's story is told in the third person, from Mickey's perspective. Why do you think the author decided to narrate the stories differently? Does it influence the way that you read them?

5. How much of a role do you think religion played in the strengths or weaknesses of the Donnelly family? In what ways?

6. What does Rachel learn about her son through her exploration of her family's history? Do you think it is helpful to her? Does she learn anything about herself?

7. Do you think Rachel is a bad mother for wanting so badly to alter her child's behavior and abilities? Is she trying to "change" him or "help" him? Is there a difference? Does intervening to the degree she does mean that she loves him less or more?

8. Rachel thinks of the "real" Edward as the little boy she got to know as a baby—the one who made eye contact with her and smiled at his parents—not the older child she sees now who is withdrawn from the world. Which do you think is the "real" Edward, or is there even such a thing? Do you think Edward is happier when he is engaged with the world, or when he is inside himself?

9. Are Rachel and Jack right to intervene in Edward's health as they do when they decide to try giving him drugs? Do they go too far? Who is to say what is "too far" in such a situation? Should it be up to the family or the state?

10. One of the issues that Rachel and Jack face with Edward is whether they can keep him in public school classes with mainstream kids. Do you think he is better off in regular classes or in a private environment?

11. Do you think the schools in your area ought to mix kids with learning disabilities into regular classes? Why or why not? Are there ways that the mainstream students can learn or benefit from the presence of their disabled peers, or is it too much of a strain on the teacher?

12. What do you think of the special school that Edward eventually attends? Even though Rachel and Jack make little money, they don't qualify for financial aid. Is it right that a school like this would cater mostly to inner-city and low-income families?

13. Do you think the state is right to accuse Jack of child abuse? Is he a danger to his children?

14. Jack's response to the state's accusations is to escape the situation and leave his family, whereas Rachel wants to negotiate with the police. Why are their responses to the situation so different? And what do you think of the way Rachel ultimately handles Jack's decision to go?

15. In the course of the novel, we watch Rachel and Jack's relationship evolve and crumble. Do you think their marriage would have survived had they not had problems with Edward? Would they have been happy? How has Edward changed each of them over the years?

16. The novel shows an intensely close relationship between Edward and his younger brother. As Matthew gets older, what are some of the ways he helps Edward, both at home and at school? Do you think Edward also helps Matthew? Do you think Matthew suffers for having Edward as an older brother? Are there ways that he benefits?

17. What role does James play in the novel, and why do you think the author made his character a gay man in the 1950s? What challenges does he share with Mickey and Edward?

18. Mary manages to sustain her marriage, though she loses both of her sons. Rachel ultimately lets go of Jack in order to hold on to her kids. Which one is right? For a woman, who should come first—her husband or her child?